Ghama

Afterlife Story

by

Richard Riverin

ISBN: 1-4033-4938-X (e)
ISBN: 1-4033-4939-8 (sc)
ISBN: 1-4033-4940-1 (dj)

Printed in the United States of America
Bloomington, Indiana

This book is printed on acid-free paper.

1stBooks – rev. 03/21/05

Contents

Prologue

Most people believe in the presence of God. After all, the more we know about the complexity of the universe and the more we realize that it just couldn't have happened without God's help; therefore the conclusion that God does exist.

But then what does He look like? Was He created too? No, for sure, God is God, He always was and He will always be.

That means no beginning!

If we agree to that then we must also conclude that He has always created, modified, and enhance the universe. Otherwise he would have sit forever doing nothing and after an infinity of zillions of years doing nothing He would suddenly change and start to create... That is so farfetched that it would take an imbecile to believe it. It would be more probable that He would have found a way of killing Himself! Who could stand an eternity of idleness?

Let's say He waited 100 years after His beginning then the universe would be an infinity of time less 100 years, since God had no beginning. That means the Universe too has been there forever, it had no beginning; it was always there, just as God was always there.

But then, could the Universe as we know it be the same as it was a zillion zillions years ago?

That would mean that God has done nothing for a zillion zillions years? No for sure, that couldn't be.

The universe has to be changing, evolving; and it may be changing as per God's will.

Billions, zillions of stars, billions, zillions of galaxies made out of billions of stars are moving, as new matter is being created.

These stars like our sun have planets gravitating around them and for some of the stars; there are planets gravitating at just the right distance to sustain life.

Protozoa, algae, fishes, plants and eventually mammals will evolve on these planets leading to sentient species.

Some of these species intelligent as they may be will never think about the possible presence of God, will never even develop sentiments like love and compassion. Most of them will never wonder about the possibility of life on other worlds and will never have the curiosity to try to get there.

Mankind might be a rare species; we might have such rare potential that great beings might be trying to help us in our evolution.

Can you imagine a species of intelligent ants capable of dreaming, of loving, capable of hate and compassion? Praying for an afterlife in Heaven?

Over an infinity of time, in an infinite universe, is it impossible that we would be the only ones? The only species ever to be capable of these emotions?

For sure, there has been great civilizations before us and some of them were utterly destroyed; at least in their initial form, corporeal form.

Some of the stars are exploding in supernova giving birth to a destructive wind of super energy that reaches at light speed the neighboring stars systems scouring all life from their life sustaining planets over a distance of hundreds, thousands of light years; millions of planets burned to cinder and some of them inhabited by sentient and hoping species and it is possible that some of those species having reached a high level of evolution, having built great civilizations were destroyed in a flash of irradiation.

That is only a theory but a highly probable one for we have already discovered the super novas.

Does it mean that God is evil? That He doesn't care for those species?

It is impossible to guess for God is probably not like us and we are probably not created to His image. We are

the result of an evolution that took place on Earth
under certain climatic conditions.

Would there be other species, sentient species like
Mankind?

It is an inevitable conclusion that there have always
been civilizations that have evolved all over the
infinite universe. Even if there would be only one life
sustaining planet for a million stars, one that would
give birth to a sentient species over a period of a
billion years of evolution, we come to the conclusion
that a million of different sentient species are either
living now or have been living and evolving inside each
galaxy and there are an infinite number of galaxies!
Some must have evolve under similar conditions and
resemble us quite closely.

God has probably seen a great number of civilizations,
maybe an infinity of them blooming to a high degree of
evolution and wisdom before they were destroyed or
before they found a way to achieve immortality.

Each civilization might be like a grain of sand in an
infinite beach but the tiny distances between those
grains of sand is so enormous compared to the size of
our planet that we are likely to believe that we live
alone in our galaxy.

We humans are so tiny that we are totally invisible to a
far away observer, for whom our stars are the atoms from
which are made the matter of his world.

And yet, powerful beings, God Himself perhaps are
helping us in our evolution.

Each one of us wonders and hopes for the presence of
God, we wish for His approval and we dream of a great
afterlife in return for our good actions.

Can you imagine that God listens to the prayers of
billions of individuals from zillions of species all
across the infinite universe? That He listens to the
prayers of even those individuals from species that have

not reached maturity yet and are bound to self destroy in a short term?

I have very good reasons to believe so. Somehow we are probably all important for God's grand plan.

We might be pieces of a grand chess game, potential soldiers in a war between our kindly God and a devilish one. There might be more than one God or one God and one Demon of equal power; possibly a species of compassionate Gods and a species of evil ones are fighting each other over the universe; the first one working on establishing order and peace over a beautiful universe, the other one trying to transform it into chaos.

That theory is close to Hinduism.

Many years ago, I drowned and experienced a separation from my body. I could see and hear the people rushing to my help, trying to find my body and save me. The very fat lifeguard was running like a gazelle underneath and I found it very funny to see him dive overboard with such spring in his legs.

I felt so wonderfully good, I couldn't care less if they found me or not. As I was beatifically enjoying myself floating over the beach, I saw that the big fat lifeguard had found my body and was now bringing it to the lifeguard cabin where he intended to work me back to life.

At one point, I got sucked through the cabin's roof, right back into my body and I was now coughing and feeling miserable again.

After that wonderful experience, things started to happen; things that you don't want to talk about for fear of being ridiculed or even worst losing your friends.

I can tell you though that I have been in contact with spirits over the years and some of them of an inhuman kind, some kind and some evil. A few times I saw miracles happen.

I asked myself what I would have done if the lifeguard had not rescued me.

I might have ceased to exist after a short moment; the atoms of my soul might have started to disperse, my soul losing its coherence as it became subjected to certain forces.

But my will to live, my satisfaction of what I was, my curiosity, my thirst for knowledge, my compassion and interest in other people might have strengthened my soul coherent bond and I might have happily started to wander everywhere, looking at the plants and the animals and I know that in such case, I would have soon become mostly interested in people. I was so utterly happy and feeling so marvelous that I wasn't submitted to impatience or any kind of negative emotions.

I would have listened to people's prayers and sometimes I might have found a way to help.

After a while, I would have tried to find other spirits like me, kind ones with whom I would not have minded to share thoughts and souvenirs and maybe I would have left with them for a visit of the universe.

I would have visited other worlds, inhabited ones, have a look at their cities, and listen to these sentient beings' thoughts and possibly their prayers.

After a long time, millions of years later perhaps, I would have returned to my home world and possibly found it empty of life.

It is probable that in such case, I would have then tried to find another inhabited world, one with a species worthy of my interest, a species that would have the potential of evolving into a great civilization and I would have tried to help them creating opportunities, special occurrences for some key individuals.

That might be what billions of spirits are doing right now, all across the universe. Some of the most powerful spirits might have become God's supervisors, archangels, each with special duties and some of them able to do wonders, great miracles. These super beings are probably able to speak with God. They are probably able to tell

God, which one of those species would have the potential of becoming helpful in turn if they got the chance to evolve to maturity. And possibly, God would chose an individual unit of that species, give it a spark of His Godliness and the mission to help his species in its evolution.

His brothers and sisters would call him Atlas, Buddha, Confucius, Jesus, and Leonardo De Vinci perhaps; he would be known under many identities and described as the Son of God.

People would build religions after Him, religions that would comfort people and give them hope and courage even though some people would use them wrongly to achieve personal power and wealth.

The truth is unknown but all hope is possible. We are not left alone this I know, and those who deserve an afterlife and wish for it might well get it.

What about Heaven, can we get an afterlife in a wonderful world where we would be all awoken in young and delightful bodies?

After all an eternity of wandering around as ghosts might not be what most people are hoping for. I felt so wonderfully good while I was floating over the beach that I would not have wanted anything else.

Maybe later though; as I got accustomed to my delight, I would have wanted to be with my children, my parents and my closest friends. Maybe I would have been happier in a healthy and immortal body on a strange yet delightful world where I could meet everyone I had known before.

And eventually I might have started to wish for a new purpose, one in which I could be useful to God's grand plan.

That world, gigantic and beaming with life of all kind, where all trees would bear nourishing and delectable fruits, where there would be no insects nor viruses, no sickness but yet the exciting possibility of being killed by a predator. That world in which we humans could roam fearlessly in enhanced bodies, that world exist for I have described it in details to God or one of his angels as I wrote this story. I named it Ghama-2 and it is located at a distance of 90 light years from Earth.

Yes writers write and perhaps, sometimes, God creates the worlds they have written about.

In this story, a species of immaterial beings called The Guardians, universal voyagers, came into contact with some of our descendants on Ghama-2. They visited that world and discovered an abandoned city. The city was built by a species that had achieved its highest possible evolution. They had left the city a billion years before and the city contained universal enhancing devices that could transform anyone into a Godlike being.

Many species had heard of it and are already on that planet searching for it. The first species to find it would become so powerful that they would become the masters of our galaxy. Many of those species are worthless and evil.

The Guardians found the two human cities on Ghama-2 and they observed our descendants, reading their thoughts and sharing their emotions and they realized that mankind possesses a rare quality, compassion! They decided that we should be the ones, the all-powerful ones that will take control of this galaxy they call the Milky Way. They tried to speak with the humans on Ghama-2, to tell them about the city and its location but were unable to communicate with them.

Strangely enough for the Guardians, these humans had not a shred of telepathic power.

So the Guardians used the timeline to find their world of origin, Earth. Once they reached Earth, they looked everywhere to find at least one person to whom they could speak but there was not even one of them. They traveled to the past and finally found one person, 700 years in the back time, a person which blood had been altered by repeated immersion in pulsating magnetic field. That person could hear them; the Guardians had finally found a way to help mankind.

10

I am that person and now my mission is to write a book, a novel relating the fictive adventures of a group of heroes, leaving Earth for Ghama-2 to find that city and enhance themselves with the devices left by that ultimate civilization into Godlike beings. The Guardians will influence certain people to come to my art gallery and discover my book. Shall they read it; they will have done their first step in becoming some of the chosen for the coming odyssey.

I am writing that book for the purpose of recruiting some people, possibly you! Will you join your efforts to mine and participate to the most exciting odyssey in all human history?

Please read that story and forgive me for my mistakes and unusual ways of expressing myself, I am writing it in a beautiful but foreign language which I have recently learned for I am of French origin. Welcome to Ghama-2!

Glossary

Bill: Bill Rate is a genius; he is also highly cultured, likable and charming. He owns a software business and is one of the richest men on Earth.

Father O'Leary: Duplicate of the initial Father O'Leary, mid-age Catholic Abbott and preacher. He is extremely courageous and possesses incredible oratory acumen. The reverend father is a man with a magnetic personality whose company is highly appreciated by everyone.

Garry: One of Joan's twins. Garry grew up with his sister Nancy. He shared her friends even into adulthood. Garry knew what women want and could seduce almost anyone. He likes to talk for hours with his friends. He is very kind and funny and appreciated by everyone.

George: George W. Wood is 69 and President of the USA. George is a man of great resources and a born leader; he was very athletic, handsome, highly cultured and likable.

Joan: Elderly woman working at Naples library. She is highly educated, very beautiful and very athletic. Her courage has no limit. She had a previous life and was once known as Joan of Arc, the Maid of Orleans.

John: Elderly gentleman, retired Navy officer and secret agent. John is a born leader. He was also the best close combat fighter in the navy. His sixth sense warning him of incoming danger was an important factor in the success of his missions. John is a very kind and serious man and he looked like Sean Connery.

Krishna: Krishna is 59 and former Middleweight boxing champion of the world. He is also a preacher promoting a new global religion based on Hinduism, Christianity and Islam. Krishna is extremely talented in sports and is a black belt in Judo and karate. He was the undefeated ultimate fighting champion for a number of years and also an Olympic fencing gold medalist.

Les Semeurs: A species that evolved on Ghama-2 and reached its ultimate level of evolution. They got bored, stop breeding and went into extinction. Ten thousands of them chose to go into deep sleep awaiting the members of a younger species with whom they would share their ulterior life. They stored their souls in the enhancing devices that were left for those who would be brave enough and resourceful enough to find them.

Nancy: One of Joan's twins. Nancy is a very determined young woman. She has a hot temper, but she forgives very quickly. She is as beautiful as her mother and also very brave. Like her brother Garry, she is quite a seducer.

Nicole: Nicole Teaseman is 46 and once the sexiest Hollywood star. She isn't very brave and this just adds to her charm. She is kind and likable, very beautiful and athletic.

Richard: Elderly gentleman, artist-painter and science fiction writer. He possesses an exceptional intuition of coming events. He is the first human able to communicate with the Guardians. He is also the only one who fought victoriously a demon and succeeded to imprison it in his brain. He is a tight lip joker and a storyteller. He is very interested in others and likes to know everything about them.

Tom: Mid-age CIA agent, strong like an ox and quick like a panther, he looked like Arnold Swatzerneger. Even though Tom is not a big talker, his presence is highly appreciated and most comforting. Like John he is a very well trained fighter.

Chapter One - Richard - First contact

I have been dreaming almost every night for the last two weeks and each morning as I woke up, I remembered glimpses of those dreams. I tried to focus on them but just could not retain anything. I had that feeling that those dreams were unusual, important perhaps for my future.

My mother had had those strange forewarning dreams, a special talent surely and she could read her dreams; she was very good at it and I wondered if I had not inherited it suddenly now at the age of 62.

Probably not for I would have had them before but then why do I have that gut feeling that these dreams are of great importance?

There has to be a way of remembering them, maybe I should tell myself before going to sleep tonight that I will remember everything about my next dreams. Self-suggestion, self-hypnotism, that's the solution. Tonight, I will repeat it in my mind, all the time, until I get asleep, "Tomorrow morning I will remember my dreams".

I did it last night and this morning I remember those strange landscapes, that multicolored sky with six visible moons and those fruit trees. There were people and tall birds, taller than the people and walking with them. There was a sense of great wisdom and dignity in the way those birds walked and mingled with the humans. The people looked very happy and relaxed, some of them had live teddy bears on their shoulders. Some were playing while others were picking fruits from the lowest branches.

There was such a feeling of peace and serenity that I wanted to become one of them. But then I saw a black cloud floating menacingly over their heads like a somber presage of great dangers to come.

Suddenly I was flying away from them and now I had stopped over a group of aliens, bipeds with a rat face and pointed ears. Their body was covered with brown and gray fur and their hands and feet were clawed.

They looked fierce, ferocious and evil. There were now thousands of them and they were listening to a demon.

"Get to that city and you will become so powerful that you will be able to enslave and torture every sentient being in this galaxy." The demon said.

"Kill everyone that come in your way." The demon added.

Suddenly I was transported over a city of people mingling with the tall birds and the teddy bears, the city was beautiful; white houses with red roofs, trees and flowers, parks and small lakes and half a dozen golf courses. The city had been erected between the seacoast on south side, a river branching on two sides and the jungle along the last side.

There was a marina and all kind of sailboats.

I could sense that these innocent people were completely unaware of the terrible menace from those wicked aliens and demons.

Somebody had to help them, to warn them. Moreover, there should be an expedition and the people had to find the city described by the demon before anyone else.

Then I was transported thousands of miles away to a jungle of very tall trees and I saw a camouflaged city sitting on its canopy.

The people had carved their homes inside the trees and the branches were as wide as roads. There were safety nets on the side of those branches and the people seemed to be calm and very happy. There were gardens, flowers and fruits everywhere. There were birds, all kind of birds flying around and singing or calling each other. Little furry animals were scurrying everywhere.

Somehow I knew that the people from these two towns were the descendants of the survivors of a spaceship crash landing. They had called their two cities, New Alexandria and Jungletown.

Then I woke up and remembered everything, crystal clear.

15

What a strange dream!

The following days, I dreamed again and each morning I was remembering them clearly. My dreams had become more than ordinary dreams, they had become part of my life and I felt that I was living in two worlds.

Now I can sense the presence of very powerful spirits as I dream of far away lands on another world and I guess they are using those dreams to communicate with me.

Maybe I am becoming insane.

Last night, I woke up suddenly in fright. Could it be...oh no, I thought, I am not going to start hallucinating at my age, I told myself. These are dreams, nothing else! But then how come I am so afraid to close my eyes and sleep the rest of the night?

I forced myself to look back and remember what it was.

There had been a ghost, many ghosts speaking to me at the same time, and I could feel their alien-ness, there was the sensing of enormous power, knowledge and extreme intelligence. I felt like a tiny insect spoken to by giants. They had shown me stars rushing into a black hole and I was a tiny speck amongst a cloud of meteorites, I was falling towards that black hole at tremendous speed from unimaginable height.

That was a dream; a nightmare and I won't have the same nightmare twice, I told myself.

So I called for relaxation; it came and I slept again. But the dream came back and they were there waiting for me. The spirits had not thought that one could be afraid of movement or vertical distance and they comforted me. They showed me more scenes of those nice people from another world.

At daytime, I was afraid that I was loosing my mind and I was trying to forget the dreams but I just could not forget anything. Moreover, my contacts with the spirits were not frightening anymore, in fact I felt comforted by them and I am becoming anxious to get asleep at night. I want to see more of that other world, its exquisite landscapes, its fauna and the smiling people picking fruits from the multicolored trees...

One night, I woke up right in the middle of my dream, loosing contact with the benevolent spirits, the Guardians, they called themselves. I jumped in one desperate attempt to get away with my thought thread from the hard core in my brain.

It had been happening for years. When I dream, my thoughts are like a thread flowing along the neural ways but there is one of those ways that ends into a cul-de-sac. If my thought thread pushes forward once it gets to that dead end, something terrible will happen, I know it, I would probably die or worst...

Is there something worst than dying? Yes, there is something there, infinitely scary, lurking but unable to escape. For that hard core is its prison.

I could not sleep the rest of the night, so I got up, put some clothes on and went outside. My condo is on the shore of an alligator infested lake and there is a trail snaking its way on the lakeshore up to Marco Island Airport right into the everglades.

It was in the middle of the night, there would be no one outside at this hour and there were the alligators, the Florida panthers and the black bears to be wary about. I released the safety catch of my long knife sheath and went on the trail.

I have flirted with danger all my life, unafraid of losing it for I knew after that drowning experience that I wouldn't really die, only my corporeal envelope would be gone if I lose my life and I would feel wonderful again.

When I lived up north, in Canada, I used to go skiing across the plains and the forested hills, alone, and knowing that if I broke an ankle, I would not survive the night in such cold weather. I was going for long rides where nobody would go, almost certain that I would come back home safely. Stupid optimism perhaps or the intuition that someone was watching over me, protecting me, I don't know, but I was feeling elated by the risk and yet confident of the outcome for I was in a real

17

good shape and my years of practicing judo and yoga had given me a rare sense of balance.

I am now almost 60 years old and every time I look at the sky on those starry nights, I feel an unbearable attraction to go there and visit the worlds gravitating around those stars.

Those spirits, The Guardians, they are showing me scenes of another world and they said they want to help mankind get to that old city first... wouldn't it be great if they could somehow transport me there to lead an expedition?

Tonight, I will question them.

I walked for an hour, came back to the condo, had a snack and went back to bed where I laid awake and daydreaming of exciting adventures on that strange world.

The following night, I was dreaming and in contact with the Guardians. They said they saw very clearly what happened just before I woke up the night before. They asked me if I wanted to be relieved from the presence of what was lurking in my brain hard core. They could do it, they said, but there was a risk. For they believed there was a demon inside there, kept imprisoned there, by an unknown force. They had never seen that yet, for the demons are powerful adversaries and immortals.

They would guide it out, they said, and push it into an alternate universe, so far that it would never find its way back.

The demons, fortunately, are not very intelligent. They are cunning and think highly of themselves rejoicing in their power over weaker individuals and enjoying the pain and the despair they can cause to others. The danger for me was that it might be able to destroy my brain on its way out. But the chances of that happening were very slim for they would be there protecting me, acting as a barrier.

I could also chose to live the rest of my life, knowing that at any time, the hard core in my brain might weaken and liberate the demon who would then torture me and have its fun with me, its helpless and desperate victim. The demon could also take my soul and bring it to Hell...

I remembered how it happened, the demon had been haunting me ever since I had drown and been rescued. I had lived an out of body experience, which had made me a focal point. If there was a forest of ten thousand trees and the lightning hit one, it will be the tree I am hiding under and yet I would somehow survive it. All kind of things was happening to me, amongst them the haunting.

The first time it came for me, I was picking wood and coal in the shed for the night. My mother had forced me to go to the shed against my will and to my shame; I had slashed her with harsh words.

I knew that something would happen, that's why I had rebelled so hard. I always had an intuition of coming events but my mother wouldn't back out, I had to go, period, and end of discussion.

I went inside the shed without bothering to turn on the light for I told myself I was not going to cave in to my fear. Beside that, I just remembered upon second thoughts, the light bulb was burned out.

I had rolled the two feet log against the shed door to make sure it would not close on me. I went to the coal stack and picked up the shovel and filled my pail. Then I walked to the wood cord and loaded my arms with the firewood.

I was taking my time to prove to myself how brave I was.

I turned around and picked up the pail of coal and I sensed or saw a movement of some sort of life inside the darkness of the shed. I saw a shape of utter darkness!

My hair tried to levitate out of my head as I jerked back in terror. The door slammed shut! I was stiff and tense with fright and unable to move.

The shed was pitch black with the door shut and there were no windows. I sensed a movement and I could still see the shape of darkness for it was something else than darkness, it was the utter negation of life, its pitch blackness silhouetted I don't know how against the total darkness of the shed. There was a coldness coming from it and I could see some movement, there was a continuous movement inside the entity, it was like the flowing current of dark masses.

It looked at me; I sensed it, as though I could see its malevolent gaze. Then it moved towards me; I felt I was going to be engulfed in that negation of life and suddenly I cried in terror, the most desperate cry you could hear in a lifetime.

For I knew that what was coming would be worst than death, infinitely worse, for the beast was coming for my soul. It would take my soul and would bring it to hell where I would suffer forever. Forever would I be plunged in utter despair with no way out.

Anger flooded inside, I felt the spreading of an unknown force as I revolted against that horrifying fate. No, I thought, all mental claws out, I will not surrender. God, you won't abandon me, please! Suddenly I felt I could move and I don't know why I did it but instead of backing up, I plunge into the blackness, rushing for the door, which I hit at full speed, hands first. The door burst out and I ran shouting inside the house.

The day after, my mother took me to the church to ask for help for she didn't want me to be haunted again. The priest, Father Poisson was his name, did some prayers, sprayed holy water on me and told me to get lost, to go back to hell. He was looking angrily at me as he was showing me his crucifix. The whole ceremony was exorcism, that's what he called it. Nothing happened, and we came back home. I saw the demon again the following year and many times more over the next few years.

The last time, the demon came for me was at the Benedictine Monastery on the shore of Lake Humphrey Magog.

I was going there for a few days every year so that I could forget about the materialistic world and plunge myself into prayers and meditation.

It was the law of silence there and the walls and ceilings were very thick, we could hear nothing at all once in our cell with the door closed.

I was going to the 5 religious offices per day to listen to the monks' beautiful chorals and I was spending the rest of the day walking the miles of trails through the forest surrounding the monastery.

At lunch and dinner, a monk would recite on flat tone voice philosophical and religious verses. Since they had made humility vow, they could not show that they were good at reciting verses thus the flat tone.

One night, as I was lying down and reading in my bed, in that small and blank monastery cell, I saw a black cloud coming through the ceiling. It was coming from the cell occupied by a Rosicrucian. I had met the guy, the Rosicrucian, outside of the monastery as I walked the trail and we had talked about his organization.

"We are a secret group," he told me, "working against the spread of demonic influence on Earth. We are not part of any recognized church. We are led by a spirit, an angel and we work for periods of sixty years with a 40 years laps in between."

"Why is that?" I asked.

"We don't want to get known or to become too powerful and then feared by political leaders, dictators and religious leaders. Sixty years seemed to be the maximum. There is also the fact that for the last few centuries, Earth was visited regularly, every fifty years or so by members of a very wicked alien species called Gargoyles.

A few spaceships of them land in secret places. Soon after a lot of people disappear. We are food to them. They have such terrible weapons that they can destroy our planet if they wish so.

The only way we can fight them is through astral trips. We can disembody ourselves; leave our body and travel, fly as ghosts all around Earth until we find one of their ships. Then we enter it and manipulate its

21

computers through telekinesis, start its ignition and fly it into the sun. We must do that for each of their ships. When we are done with the ships, we have to chase the gargoyles one by one until we kill them all."

"Is it easy to do those astral trips?" I asked.

"Not easy at all." He replied. "You have to do mental and physical work out, meditation, spiritual enhancement; you have to learn how to draw energy from your surroundings. There are initiations for each level of emancipation. I am here to proceed to the fifth degree initiation and that will involve an out of body astral trip, my very first one. The danger is that it could attract an evil spirit and if one come; there is no guarantee that I could survive such an encounter."

I remembered that conversation as I watched the black cloud coming through the ceiling. It looked at me! How did I know that it was looking at me? I don't know but I knew it and suddenly it rushed towards me at an incredible speed. I could not escape so I got very angry and all mental claws out; I brace myself for the onslaught. It was on me, inside of me, I felt its nauseating presence and it was like I was being step over by an elephant. I tried to inflict pain to the dark mass, the evil spirit, mentally, for the spirit was immaterial.

It did not work so I started to push while I was calling for God's help. I push and compressed the dark mass and kept on pushing at it from all sides and it shrank! I felt it shrinking and I went on pressing until it had become smaller than the tip of a needle and now it was imprisoned in a node of mental energy, there, in my brain; there was a hard core in my brain, a black hole imprisoned by a bubble of mental energy and I could never let my thought thread flow into that bubble.

The Guardians seemed to be highly interested in my story. Once I finish it, they were silent. Then I told them to go ahead and do whatever had to be done and get it over with.

I was terrified as I felt my thought thread moving to the forbidden area towards the hard core and had a tremendous feeling of panic as it penetrated it.

22

I saw or sensed the exultation of the demon as the prison wall was destroyed but before it had time to exact vengeance, it was taken away, swiftly, by the Guardians and I could hear its enraged howling as it disappeared into another dimension.

In a moment only, The Guardians were back and I decided to ask the questions that had been bubbling in my mind for a number of days.

Why did you come in contact with me? I asked them. Do you want me to go to that world, to mount an expedition to the abandoned city? Why did you not just pick some people from one of these two human cities and carry them to the abandoned city?

They told that they tried that and a very strange force of unimaginable power prevented them to do it.

"Our action is limited there" they said, "and we believe that the only thing we can do to help is to snatch your soul and the ones of some other well chosen people from your world, transport you there, give you a new body with some improvements..., and wake you up close to one of the human settlements."

"You can you do all of that? Are you some kind of God?" I ask.

"We are not what you call God," the Guardians said, "we never met such an entity even though we have traveled across the universe for millenniums. The concept though is fascinating and we think that it does exist. It might be dwelling on that world or maybe a spark of it is there for we never experienced before the presence of such a powerful force as the one that prevented us to help mankind over there.

But we can create material things, from the atoms in the air; we can recreate you body and put your soul back into it. We can travel in time so for us it would take no time at all to take you and some others there."

"Well, now that it is all possible, I am not sure I am ready to die right away." I answered.

23

"You don't have to die right away," the Guardians said, "beside you are the only one with whom we can communicate and you will need help, companions, for that mission. We think that you should talk about it to a lot of people and recruit a number of them."

"Easier to say than to do for if I talk about it openly, I will be taken to a mental hospital and kept there until I tell the doctors that it was an hoax." I replied. "What I can do is write a book about a group of people going to that world in a mission that will decide the fate of mankind.

I will display the book in my art gallery.

Some people will ask me what the book is about and I will tell them it is about a group of people in a mission on another world. I will also tell them that I wrote it to recruit the true heroes of a coming odyssey.

I will write in the book that if they want to be amongst the recruits, they will have to buy one of my paintings; one of a number of paintings that will show scenes of that other world.

I will then proceed to make those paintings and once I have enough of them, I will sell them in an auction. I will invite all the people that bought the book to that auction and the ones who will risk a sizable investment to buy one of the paintings would be the ones you will take to that world. And I want to be one of them.

I believe that the only ones that will spend a large sum of money are the ones that have the ability to listen to their intuitions, the ones that might be influenced by God to do it and these are the ones that I want as companions."

"That is a good idea, we will look around for the best individuals" replied the Guardians, "and try to influence them in coming to your gallery."

"Very good and thanks for your help," I said, "I am so excited by the prospect of having that afterlife on another world, thank you, thank you, thank you, I love you."

The book will be used to attract the potential candidates for the mission and the deal would be sealed by the act of actually spending an important sum of money to purchase one of the paintings.

We want believers; people able to take decisions, even to the point of reducing the digits showing their buying capacity. For what is the point of having a printout showing great buying capacity if you are afraid to use it...?

There might be too much to write for only one book and if it is so then I would continue the story in a second book. I should not delay though. There is a feeling of urgency, I sensed it, they did not explain why because telling me about the immediate future may change it and then there would not be any spaceship later on going to Ghama-2. So, as soon as the story had gone far enough, I will print a limited edition of a few hundred books and display them right away in the gallery.

Some people will read the book, I think, and some of them will believe the story and buy one of the paintings before it is too late, before the partial destruction of the United States by terrorists happen, perhaps.

These buyers will be transported at the moment of their death to Ghama-2 and we will be awoken altogether, wow, I feel so excited that I wouldn't mind so much to die right away. I mean as soon as I have written the books, made those paintings and recruit enough of my future companions to have a chance to make it through all the dangers that will be awaiting us.

Who knows, maybe the book will be modified in the far future and the new version brought back to our present time by the Guardians.

From now on, anything can happen, sometimes fiction becomes reality; a writer may have visions of coming events and sometimes the fiction readers make the fiction become reality.

I read once that all the worlds and the personages created by the writers exist in another universe, from Robin Hood to Cyrano de Bergerac to Superman...

I am calling that world Ghama-2, I guess it is a good name for that world.

For once, I feel important. I would have like to be tall and beautiful, strong like an ox with great athletic abilities but I am just the average guy. I tried to get the best of the body and mind I was given though. I went to university and succeeded to get a Bachelor degree in chemistry developing my mind to its maximum potential. I practiced Judo for years and all sorts of other sports, racquetball, badminton, golf, skiing. I was born the average guy but I am proud of what I did and learn. What I am the most proud of is my compassion and my ability to see the child in a grown up person. I usually find something to love in most people, I am also a true believer in God and I felt his presence all along, right to the point where I am now.

Who knows where our souls are taken to, even the guardians don't know; but in my case, I know where I am going, I am going to Ghama-2 to save mankind and perhaps to meet face to face with God.

That night was over and even though I did not sleep much, I felt very energetic as I sat in front of my computer to start writing the book. The only problem was that I had just recently learned to communicate in English and now I had to write and this at an age where we are often searching for our words.

I had to empty my mind and let my subconscious do part of the work as I started to write it. The book would not be a literary marvel but hopefully, it will be good enough to attract the potential heroes of the coming odyssey.

It took me many months but finally, the first two books of the trilogy were printed and I had them in display in the gallery.

John Foster was the first to be compelled by my book. He came one day to the gallery, saw the book and bought it. John was a most amazing man. Six feet five, former Ireland track and field champion and still in top shape at 84 years old. He showed a very calm and cultured behavior and he impressed me a lot.

I will start the story with the events that preceded John's visit to the gallery. These events played a most important role in his decision to lead the mission to Ghama-2.

Chapter Two - John in mission to Pakistan

It was 10:15 AM, Monday March 12th. John opened the door and walked rapidly inside the Naples Municipal Library. He went immediately to the counter and looked at a very beautiful woman.

"Hi Joan, I am so pleased to see you today after such a long absence."

"John...I didn't see you for months, what happened? I was so worried about you!"

John Foster was a handsome elderly man in his late seventies, holding himself straight and giving the appearance of a vigorous athletic person. He was a retired navy officer, tall, slim waist and a full head of white hair and Joan Davies had no doubt that he was made of the stuff of a true hero. She did not have to look at his medals to believe that; just a look at his piercing blue eyes was enough. He had a calm and understanding expression and when he looked at her she felt that there was nothing a person could hide to this man.

This troubled her since she could hardly hide the effects his presence had on her.

"Three months ago, when I came back home from the library, a man was waiting for me in front of my condo. He was sent by the Florida CIA headquarters to fetch me. I had to go with him immediately, extreme urgency... I would have called you if I could but it was not possible. I worked for the secret services for the last twenty years prior to my retirement. I worked most of that time in Iran, Pakistan and the Middle East and I speak their languages without discernible accent. They needed me to go to Pakistan to retrieve two nuclear bombs suitcases from the hands of a terrorist group.

I came back one week ago from that mission. As soon as I got here I came to see you but you were absent for the rest of the week. Finally we meet again and I am very happy to see you."

"So am I." said Joan. "I loved my coffee breaks with

you...you said you were retired from the navy..."

"That I was, and I never thought they would call me again but they needed my experience, my contacts and my ability to speak the language. There was also the fact that nobody is suspicious of an old man. They thought that I could really help and the mission was important, it could save the life of millions of people."

John did not mention his other talents. He was a black belt in Karate and Judo and had achieved incredible performances in all combat sports. He was a dangerous man for the enemies of his country, even at his age.

At 18 years old, a Bully had attacked John. He had been forced into a fistfight, which he had lost shamefully. Since then, he had disciplined himself to one or two hours of training every day. He had taken the decision to become stronger than most other men, stronger or faster. He had also developed over the years an acute intuition of imminent danger. He could feel it coming. He always knew in advance when something bad was about to happen and had so far escaped it.

Men, John thought, can change their destiny continuously. If I feel that something bad is going to happen, I can either do nothing about it and let my destiny shorten my life or I can change my destiny by immediate action.

At the age of 21, he started to read on psychology and motivation and became very interested in people. A few years later, he was able to read one's emotions through his unconscious body language and that ability had been most useful.

"So, what did you do over there? Joan asked. I am sorry; I should not have asked that question; but tell me, did you succeed with your mission? Was it worth it?"

"Yes, it was a success, but I prefer not to talk about it, there are other matters though about which I would very much like to talk with you..."

"John, let us go to the coffee parlor." said Joan. "We will be more comfortable there and we will talk at length. We have much to talk about and my colleague here at the library can manage for a while without me, it is not busy today."

"Wonderful". said John.

They walked to their usual coffee parlor. It was nice and sunny outside, Joan was euphoric and John felt great. They walked slowly enjoying their companion's presence.

John Foster used to come twice a week to the library. He usually came early afternoon and stayed for a few hours looking through a number of books waiting for Joan's coffee break.

They talked about different matters and they always found something interesting to talk about. John would often ask Joan what she thought about a subject of actuality. There seems that there never was idle talk between them but healthy interesting exchanges that transformed Joan's half an hour coffee break into a short period of intense intellectual pleasure for both of them. It had been going on for six months. Every week John would meet her at the library. He had taken the habit to go twice a week, every Monday and Wednesday.

One day, John came back from the library and as he got home, he saw a car occupying his allotted parking place. There was someone in the car and John had the intuition that this person was waiting for him. It could become unpleasant, for John had many enemies.
First, I should block that car, he thought, and he stopped his car right behind the stranger vehicle. The man came out at once and walked quickly toward John's car. John unlatched his door in case he would need to propel it in the face of the potential foe. He released his safety belt and grabbed his special umbrella made out of armored plastic plates strong enough to deviate a bullet and with a stainless steel tip that could be used as a bayonet. John was an old man but in a short burst of energy he could still put down an enemy whatever his size.

The man stopped at a safe distance from John's door and took from an inside pocket, slowly and using only two fingers, his CIA badge which he showed to John.

"What are the name and the phone number of your immediate superior officer?" John asked in a clipped voice.

The stranger gave him the information and John picked up his cellular and called the CIA headquarters. At all time he kept his eyes riveted on the stranger. The CIA officer who answered his call didn't seem surprised and told him that they had sent one of their agents to meet with him. John thanked him and closed the connection. Then he went out of the car and shook hands with the man.

"Now, what can I do for you?" said John smiling. "For a while I was worried expecting the worst."

The man had been worrying too and his relief was evidenced by the disappearance of two tiny wrinkles between his eyes and a slight lowering of his shoulders. John read much more about the stranger in one or two seconds of acute observation of his body language and came to the conclusion that he was facing an honest man.

"Your help is needed at once," the stranger said, "it is a matter of life and death for millions of American people. I was ordered to take you right away to the CIA headquarter."

John couldn't agree less with that turn of event; he had done more than his share for his country. In fact, his life had been a long courtship with death and soon now they would embrace; he didn't have long to live and he knew it.

I deserved my retirement, he thought, *and there is that dear Joan for whom I feel unexpectedly strong emotions. I am in love with her. It took me seventy-eight years to find the right woman and now I may very well loose what is left of my life if I take that mission.*

He did not like it, and beside he was too old now. Also, if he finally came back from there, God only knows when, Joan might not be working at the library anymore.

"Let me explain Mr. Foster," said the CIA agent, "we know you are retired but there is nobody else that can talk the language and walk there without attracting suspicion and accomplish this mission successfully. We found out that a terrorist cell operating at the frontier of Pakistan and Afghanistan have recently acquired two nuclear bombs... five megatons nuclear suitcase bombs.

The terrorists contacted Iranian officials; they want to sell their bombs. We tapped their conversation. We found out that an Iranian envoy is being sent to meet with them in three days. He will be carrying a suitcase with twenty million dollars in it. We have plans to kidnap the envoy and replace him by one of our men. You would be that man and take the envoy's identity. You speak the language, you have been in mission there quite a few times, you would know what to do or say, they will not suspect you.

If you accept that mission, you will try to get inside the terrorist hideout and make sure the bombs are there. Once you are sure, you would send a signal to your team by pressing on an implant that would be inserted under your armpit. As soon as the signal is received, your team will burst in to help you get the bombs and eliminate those fanatics.
There should be no mercy; we heard them talk in length about using those bombs to destroy some of our cities. They were jubilating. "With Allah's help" they said, "we will kill millions of Americans..."
We have a jet waiting for you and we have already selected a group of our best men to assist you in this mission."

John had never before refused what he considered his moral obligations and he was too old to change, he didn't like it but he did not hesitate.

"All right," John said, "let's go."

The mission was top secret and John could not call Joan to tell her that he was leaving for Pakistan.

"Anything else than the truth is not possible with Joan" John thought, "and then what can I say?"

John decided not to call her.

John and the CIA agent left for the CIA headquarter. Three hours later, they were there; they showed their identity cards to the guard, went inside and walked directly to a conference room.

Five men were sitting at the long table; amongst them, George W Wood, the president of the United States.

John knew him very well having been at a time his personal bodyguard. He had saved his life once in Texas…

"Hi John, old friend." said the president. "I am sorry to have called you from your retirement but I had to, there is too much at stake, millions of lives, our country partially destroyed, our economy gone…I had to call for your help."

"I understand Mr. President, I will do my best."

John was briefed on the mission then taken to a medical room for the implant. The surgery didn't last long; they cut the skin, inserted the signal device and sew him up.

Then the CIA agent took him to a military jet at the Jacksonville International airport. He went to his seat and sat with much relief. It had been a long and tiring day. He had that surgery, and the small implant fixed inside the skin of his armpit was hurting a little bit.

He could sleep much of the trip but he doubted it. He was afraid that something would go wrong, he had the intuition that this mission would not be an easy one. John went into meditation, he had a lot to think about for he might just be about to loose his life.
How many terrorists will I have to kill? He asked himself.
John thought about his life. He had participated in the Vietnam War and the Panama's attack. He had done secret missions in the Middle East a number of times. He had killed for his country and felt very bad each time for he had great respect for life.

I have fought for freedom in my country and in other parts of the world, I have killed people and they were not all bad people but people that were doing their duty for their own country. Some of them were parents and their death must have devastated their family.

John felt remorse for the suffering of those innocent children that had lost their fathers in his hands and he didn't like that mission one it.

Maybe I will be captured and tortured... I have less resistance to pain, as I am growing older--But I have a duty, there is no way out and I will just do my best to prevent the use of those bombs. If I fail, I will go to heaven, maybe...if there is one. But come to think of it, what will I do there? I am not very good at praying, I am a man of action and I like to do things or watch sports at TV.

What John really liked was to go in the forest and walk a trail in the wilderness. He would sit by a stream and listen to the murmur of the wind through the foliage, the laughing and gurgling of the stream on its way to nowhere, the creaking of the trees rubbing each other Companionably; the chirping and twittering of the birds. He would watch the squirrels running after each other or hiding nuts in places they will surely forget.

John liked to day dream that he could fly through the trees, fast, and drive out some of the wild life that he had not seen in a long time; bears, wolves, otters, deers, maybe even a mountain lion or a wolverine and share their thoughts, participate to their hunt.

But this side of John was well hidden; he wouldn't let anyone know that he was secretly a daydreamer.

My greatest joy is to meet with Joan and feel the turbulence of my emotions. Will we be together in heaven one day? And if there is heaven, will it be a place of devotion? A beautiful and fleecy whiteness where I will adore and congratulate God? But after a few hours of devotion and adoration and praising, what will I do? Is it such a blessing then to have an afterlife? Would it not become unbearable after a while? Perhaps God will

34

give me a feeling of great happiness, an everlasting
happy feeling, but then I will still know that
this happiness is artificial, that I became a useless
just-feel-happy adoring machine.

Moreover, if I am not the same man after my death, if I
have been changed into a happy adoration machine then I
have truly died. It will not be me as I am now with my
memories of good times and hardships, I will be another
creature. No, and come to think of it, God doesn't need
any worship. To think that He does is belittling the
Almighty. So either we die and we are done with and good
riddance r we are sent to another world as we are,
unchanged, with our memories, our built-over-the-years
qualities and abilities to meet with new challenges. If
the latter is true, will I be able to take Joan along
with me? Is there an anteroom in the afterlife in which
we can wait for the loved one to depart from the world
of the livings and join the dead?
God, please, I don't want to be changed into a
worshipping entity! I prefer everything to end at my
death! But in such case tell me, why am I risking the
rest of my life and the possibility of unendurable
Torture, if I am caught alive? Is it to help my country?
To prevent millions of people to die just a bit sooner
than they would anyway? What am I doing, going into this
mission? Have I turned nuts? Maybe Alzheimer has paid me
a visit, coming unexpectedly and without an invitation.
No, John, stop that, you know why you are doing it, you
have a reason to do it, a very important reason. If you
don't do it and millions of people dies and millions
more people suffer from the loss of their family
members; you will feel dirty inside for backing up on
what you consider a moral duty. You will feel shameful
and will lose your pride. That's important enough...
that's the only thing that really counts... my sense of
honor, my decency, my self-esteem. I like to
think that I am a man; a real one, a hero. It might be
immature and useless to think that way, possibly, but I
would not be happy without the conviction that I am a
great guy and I will not fail my country people.

John's meditation induced sleepiness and he was now
sleeping very deeply.

He was in a cloudy place; there were rows of people,
millions of rows, billions of people, all looking

towards a great light. There was Joan a few rows away, he wanted to join her but he could not move. John looked further to her right and there she was, his mother, a little further still was his brother, he had protected him and loved him so much until death took him away.

He tried to call them but again, could not utter a sound. He could not talk to anyone of them.

A hooded tall being was coming towards him now and it looked like Death. The hooded man stopped in front of a very ugly man. John recognized him; that was Yasser Arafat; not a doubt about it.

But what is he doing here in heaven? After all everybody knows that he was the leader of a gang of self-bombers and innocents' slayers.

Arafat saw the hooded being coming and tried to squeeze into his chair and turn invisible. The hooded being stopped in front of Arafat and gave him a tremendous slap in the face.

"What are you doing here, you miserable vermin?" said Death. "You are a slippery one aren't you? That must have been another mistake. Ever since God gave that Saint Joseph the job at the admission office, we have had those mistakes. You vermin go to hell!"

Arafat disappeared in smoke but just before he was turned into smoke, John saw the terror in his eyes. The hooded being resumed his walk between the rows and soon was out of sight.

Suddenly there was a booming voice.

"You don't adore me well enough; I will throw you to hell!" said God.

John knew that he was the one being addressed by the almighty and he was scared even stiffer and more toothless than he had already been these last few years.

"Please Sir God, I call to your pity," said John. "Please forgive me Sir; please don't throw me to hell; I will adore you better, I promise."

Suddenly he woke up, transpiring.

My goodness, John thought, that could not be, it is just a dream. God in his infinite wisdom surely has a better plan for my afterlife, if I deserve one, that is to say. Otherwise why would He give me an afterlife at all? Maybe I should tell God what I would like as an afterlife.

"What I would really like as an afterlife dear God, is to travel from world to world and discover the secrets of creation. To visit the galaxy and stop from time to time on one of the inhabited worlds and share the thoughts and emotions of the sentient beings there; and maybe help some of them in achieving their goals.

I would like to embark on a million years trip with my dear friends, with Joan, with my brother, my mother and father, my uncles.
I would like to be able to communicate with them at all time, to love them, have fun with them, and make physical love to Joan...
Hey that would be heaven for me, to fly with them at incomprehensible speed. Wow! Now, if you listen to my thoughts dear God; that is what I want. I will do everything to deserve it."

The jet landed. John was taken to the American Consulate and immediately brought to the colonel in charge of the secret service operations. There were three men with him.

"Hi John," said the colonel, "let me introduce you to your team. Tom, Walt and Martin will be your colleagues for that mission."

The men were very friendly, respectful.

"It is a pity that we had to call you for that mission, John." said Tom. "We have been informed of your courageous navy career. We learned all we could about you and here you are, the hero of a dozen missions. You look in great shape, I am sure you will be very helpful but it is a sad thing that we are forced to ask a 78 years old man to risk his life again."

"It is all right," said John, "I thought a lot about it during the flight. I came to the conclusion that my life had been an unfair deal and this as far back as the first time my mom told me that I was going to die, that everybody die, sooner or later, that we are born to die. I believe I was two years old at that time. I got at that moment my very first nervous breakdown...Could you imagine that? Two years old and already a broken man..."

John kept a serious face. Everyone was looking at him, wondering if he had just lost it. Then looking at their long faces, John smiled and all of them started to laugh. Tom hugged him, and everyone clapped hands with him.

It was clear that they were worrying about the coming events and that small joke convinced everyone that John was the right man to have with them. That man is a cool one, they thought.

"Ok, "said the colonel, "let's go on with the briefing. The Iranian envoy arrived today at the Iranian embassy with a suitcase chained to his wrist. It must contain the money for the transaction. We have relaying teams watching the embassy and the terrorist hideout 24 hrs a day. We tapped their communications and we found out that the envoy is going to meet with the terrorists tomorrow morning. We have two unidentified cars to chase after the envoy's car and proceed with the interception. We will wait until it gets in the poor sector of the city. Then one of the cars will pass the Iranian's one and stop in front of it. You will be in the second car and will block its rear. You will kill the bodyguards and kidnap the envoy and questioned him. Then you kill him too. We will scramble all the communications in that sector and nobody will be able to report what is happening or call for help.

John, you will take his place. We have prepared a special suitcase for you. It will contain the money but will also contain a gas capsule with a mechanism to release a very powerful odor when you activate your implant signal.

We have done much research in the development of odoriferous gas as armament. This gas was recently developed. The odor is extremely offensive, unbearable.

The first second, they will be under shock, they will think that somebody had just been very impolite; then they will try to move away from the odor, they will vomit, you will take advantage of the confusion to kill them. At the same moment your team will burst in to help you. You will not smell anything; you will all be given the antidote.

So, the first thing you do is to make sure that the bombs are there, then you activate your implant, you kill them and fetch the bombs. Is that simple enough?"

"A piece of cake!" answered John ironically.

"Now get to bed all of you, try to sleep a few hrs, the kidnapping should take place tomorrow morning at 9:00 AM."

Too simple, John thought, as he was shown to his bedroom. *It won't work...*

John woke up at 6:00 AM, did 45 minutes of work out, took a shower and went downstairs to meet with his colleagues at the cafeteria.

They talked a little, made some jokes to relieve the tension, checked their armament and went to the car.

At 9:00 AM, they were parked on the street watching the Iranian embassy. The envoy's car came out and moved towards the old city. They followed until it moved into the poor sector. Tom called the driver of the second car and gave him the signal to move ahead and released its load of nails. They did it and all the tires of the Iranian envoy's car went flat.

They must have realized what was happening for they pressed ahead but the way was blocked. They hit the car blocking their way but with the flat tires their car didn't have enough traction to push its way through. Walt had moved his car right behind the Iranian envoys car and trapped it in between.

Tom opened the door and ran to the front of the envoy's car and inserted an odoriferous gas capsule in the grid. In 2 seconds, the Iranians opened the door and surged out with submachine guns firing.

John shot and kill one of them, three more went under
the bullets of Tom and Walt. John ran to the envoy who
had just come out of the car and knocked him down with a
punch at the solar plexus and a quick short swing to his
neck with the side of his hand. Tom picked the envoy's
body and swung it on his shoulders then ran to the
American car and dropped it inside.

The envoy was injected with truth serum and woke up with
a little capsule of ammonia opened under his nose. John
questioned him. He told them that he was going to meet
with one of the terrorist at a gas station a few miles
away. Once there, he would identify himself and give his
password. The terrorist would then return to his car and
the Iranians would follow the terrorist to his hideout
where they would exchange the money for the bombs.

So far so good, thought John, *at least we kidnapped the
envoy without any casualty and I don't even feel tired.
In fact, I feel just great, full of energy. I will
probably be tired once it is all over but not
before. This new gas armament is really cool.*

Tom was sitting beside the envoy; he grabbed his head
and broke his neck. He had his orders; no witness must
be left alive. They drove to the gas station in the
unidentifiable American car. The tires had been
unaffected by the nails since they had been previously
filled with latex.

Once they got to the gas station, John went out and
walked like an old and feeble man. He had a long beard
stuck real well with crazy glue. For the next day or
two, the skin would come apart before somebody could
pull it out. *I looked venerable*, he thought, *a holy man,
a holy Muslim.*

A man walked to him and said: "Allah be with you, are
you the Iranian envoy?"

"Allah be with you too. Hell to America." said John for
that was the password.

"Where is the money?" said the terrorist.

"In the car and well protected by my three guards. The
suitcase is linked to a belt loaded with explosive and

any attempt to get the money will result in its destruction."

"I was ordered to take you and the money to our temple. You will come with me and your guards will wait here for your return. Once we get to my headquarters, we will count the money and if it is all there, I will take you back here with the bombs."

"There will be no such nonsense," said John, "We were ordered to follow you to your place in our car and once there we are to exchange the money for the bombs. My guards will protect me at all time. Our heads will fall if we disobey."

The terrorist was hesitant, John looked at him in the eyes but he averted John's gaze. He smelled unclean and bad waves were coming
out of him.

This man is rotten to the bones, thought John; *he would kill his own mother without hesitation if it brought him good money.*

"Since that seems to be Allah's wish, follow me then." said the terrorist.

They followed him for 10 minutes and entered into the northern part of the poor sector. *A dangerous place to take a walk,* thought John, *you would be knifed in the back for a pair of shoes here.*

Finally they stopped in front of small temple. John went out of the car and waited.

"Take the money with you and follow me inside." Said the terrorist. "Your guards will stay in the car."

John went back to his car and shook hand with his companions.

"Good luck my friends." Said John.

They wished him the best and Tom clapped him on the shoulder.

"It is an honor for me to share that mission with you John." Said Tom. "I did not tell you yet but you saved my father's life; Bob Hardings, you remember? I am his son. He told me you are his hero, the bravest man he ever met in his life and the most dangerous fighter in close combat."

God that was a long time ago, John thought, *during the Vietnam War. Our platoon had been ambushed and Bob and I were the only survivors.*

Bob had been shot in the leg and John had stopped the bleeding and carried him on his back until they reached the pick up location, miles away. John had used his special gift, that feeling of imminent danger to move around the enemies and following his intuition they had finally made it.

"Thank you Tom for your kind words." said John. "I remember your father and I liked him like a brother. I heard that he passed away. Please accept my condolences. I will not fail you here."

John took the suitcase and chained it to his wrist. He put on a thick belt, loaded with plastic explosive and went out of the car. He followed the terrorist inside the temple.

Putting on that belt, John thought, *is like giving away the few good years left to me. If we can't get away with the bombs, I will have to detonate it and there is enough explosive to destroy the whole building along with the nuclear bombs. My chances to get away with my life and the nukes are not very good. Farewell Joan, I wish we had met a few years earlier.*

Three guards were waiting inside and they were pointing their AK 47 at his chest.

"I will disarm you," said the terrorist, "and then you will follow me in the office."

"There will be no such thing," said John, "if your men shoot me, I have enough explosive in my belt to destroy the building. I will not surrender my arms. My suitcase is chained to my wrist and connected to my belt. Any

attempt to take it from me will result in your immediate
death. My men are waiting outside; they have by now
brought the car right against the temple. The car is
also loaded with explosive."

"What, what..."said the terrorist, "it was understood
and agreed that you will come disarmed..."

"You thought," said John, "that we would be stupid
enough to come here with twenty million dollars, without
any guarantee that you have the bombs or that we will
have a fair deal? Allah informed our holy leader that
you intended to take the money and kill his envoy. In
his great wisdom, he sent me, a dying man, and I assure
you that I will not hesitate to detonate my belt if I
think that there is foul play here."

"Also," said John, "One of my man is a nuclear engineer.
He must come with me to check if the bombs are in good
order. Once you have shown me the bombs, I will give you
my suitcase; you will count the money while we check the
bombs. Then, we will get back to the car with the
bombs."

John turned around and made a hand sign to Tom to come
with him. When he turned back he saw that the terrorist
was giving instructions to one of the guards who left at
once for the office. The terrorist looked at him
angrily.

"Follow Me.", he said.

They went to the office. There were many men inside.
John counted them; there were the three guards still
pointing their submachine gun, covering Tom and himself,
the terrorist and two leaders. There were two big
suitcases on a long desk.

These must be the nukes, thought John.

"These are the bombs," said one of them, "now hand me
your suitcase and make sure to disconnect it from your
belt."

The man that spoke was surely the leader, John told
himself, *he is used to give orders*.

The leader looked down at John with the composure of a man of great dignity.

Another one of those damned holy man, thought John, ready to kill millions of people and his own mother and sisters if need be. Well, I am going to kill that one first... As soon as I disconnect the belt, they will start shooting. They want the money and keep the bombs. I read it in their faces. They never had any intention to surrender the bombs.

John activated the gas capsule in the bottom compartment of his suitcase. The leader looked at him with a very offended expression; he had never been farted on that bad. Every man backed up, it was the right time. Everyone except Tom and John were under shock of the unbearable odor. John pulled his gun, shot the leader in the heart and threw himself under the desk. He rolled over and shot another man in the legs. The man fell and John shot him in the head. Two more men fell on the floor under Tom's bullets and he was rolling himself under the desk shooting the last two guards in the legs. They both rolled away from the desk and shot the falling guards in the head.

That man is fast, thought John, and quick minded too, I never had a chance to warn him of my intentions, what a partner!

They were all dead; Tom grabbed the two very heavy bombs and lifted them from the desk.

Tom is incredibly strong, thought John as he picked his own suitcase and one of the AK47.

There is no point in leaving twenty million dollars to those fanatics, he thought.

They came out of the temple and ran towards the car. There was a crowd of people outside, encircling it; some of them were armed. John put his suitcase on the ground and started to shoot in the crowd, he killed some of the armed men first. The crowd parted and Tom ran to the car, the door opened, he threw the bombs in and turned to grab John's suitcase as John was rushing in.

John fell; he had been hit and had lost consciousness. Tom could not rescue him, they had received orders, the bombs were too important. He had already taken the money suitcase from John's hand, he closed the door and the car left at full speed.

John woke up in a cell. The bullet had only grazed his head leaving a sizable lump. He was aching and terribly hungry and thirsty. He had been kicked everywhere by the angry crowd.

So, I am still alive, thought John, *but they took my clothes, my shoes, everything except my underwear. I am chained too; by one ankle...God my ribs hurt, some of them must be fractured. They kicked me, bruised me good. I suppose they thought I deserved all of it; I must have killed twenty-five of them today. They will probably have their fun with me. Torture followed by execution! That's what is awaiting me. I must be strong, there is a way of ignoring pain, I was better at it when I was younger, now it just doesn't seem to work so well anymore.*

Anyhow, I can't do anything about it, fretting and despairing will not improve my situation so I will forget about my misery and dream about a comfortable shelter in the forest, just beside a gurgling creek. Joan is with me, we are roasting two hares over a campfire and we have plenty of water to drink--.

John woke up from his dream at the sound of a key turning in the lock, the door opened and two men walked in. One of them carried a plate of stew and a bottle of water. They looked at him.

"You were unconscious for days now," said the oldest of the guard, "we had to force you to drink some water, we did not want to loose you before we could rightfully execute you. But before that, we need you to answer a few questions. If you answer truthfully, we will give you the food and the water. First, who are you? Second, why did you shoot our people at the temple?"

"My name is John Foster. I am a retired US navy officer. I came here to take two nuclear bombs from a terrorist cell before they were delivered to an Iranian envoy.

Those bombs would have been used to kill millions of
innocent people. Please contact our consulate; they
will surely confirm my story. "

"We won't do that for now," said the guard, "we will
keep you here for a while. You may be useful. We can
possibly trade you for some of our imprisoned brothers
or get a sizable ransom from your government. The
Iranians would also pay a good price to get their
hands on you."

They gave him the food and left. John spent endless
hours in that cell. It smelled bad; he could relieve
himself by sitting or standing over a hole in the floor.
There was a narrow bed with one sheet, no window.

A man was coming twice a day with a food plate and
stayed until he finished the food, going back with the
empty plate. It was always the same man. John still had
his implant and from time to time, he would press
on it to send a signal. Just in case, he thought.

One day John asked the guard if he was a member of a
terrorist cell.
"I am a member of an Afghan tribe that had fled
Kandahar." He answered.
"What is your name?" asked John.
"Khamir."
"Do you stay in that building all day long, Khamir?"
"Yes"
"What do you do of your time?"
"Nothing."
"Are you alone all day long?"
"Yes."
"Would you like to play card with me? We can bet. I will
pay you later on all the money you will win. That is if
I can."

"I should not talk with an infidel and it would be
sinful to play with an American."

"But, I speak your language, I know the Koran, I am a
just a feeble old man dying in that cell."

A few days later, Khamir came in the cell with an old pack of cards. They played card everyday afterward and started to talk at length.

John told Khamir that not only had he read the Koran book, he had memorized it. He had also read the Christian Bible.
"You know Khamir," said John, "I am not much of a believer in people that call themselves prophet and start their own religion. I believe in God and in the existence of guarding angels, spirits that sometimes watch over us and even help us.

Over the past millenniums, there have been a few exceptional men who built around themselves an army of followers after they declared to have been in contact with God. Amongst the followers were some people who could write about what their leader said or did. Their books were kept for a long time and rewritten by others. For centuries now, these books, the Bible and the Koran, were extensively used to convert people and influence them. Do you know who wrote the Koran?"
"No."
"Let me tell you what I know about it." Said John, set upon turning the guard into a potential ally. "The Koran is a book composed of writings about the revelations made to Muhammad by Allah. Muhammad lived in the seven century. One day he told his friends that he had spent some time in the desert and he had receive revelations from Allah. He told them that he had been chosen by God to be his prophet.

Well some people didn't like it and they threw him out of Mecca. He left in an exile called the Hegira to Medina where he established his own religion. That was in the year 622 C.E. Later on, eight years later apparently, he led an army to conquer Mecca in the name of Islam. His army won the battle and that set the stage for a unification of the Arab world.

But he died 2 years later. Somebody wrote a booklet of those revelations. The book was called the Koran and it required from the ones-who-submit (the Muslim) to believe that there was only one God and Muhammad was his prophet. It also required from the Muslims to make five prayers a day and to give alms to the house of worship called a Mosque. They should also give to the poor, make fast during daylight hours for the whole month of Ramadan and make one lifetime pilgrimage to Mecca. Soon after Muhammad's death, a major disagreement amongst his followers split them in two groups, the Shiite and the Sunni.

I don't know who wrote the Koran and I don't know who wrote the Bible. The two religions are similar except that for the Christians Jesus is one with God and at the same time the Son of God. According to the bible, he was born from a virgin woman called Mary. Who knows if Mary was a virgin, women don't talk to people about what they are doing behind close doors. Beside, I am quite sure that she did not say she was a virgin since it was commendable for a wife to make love with her husband. It would have ridiculed and belittle Joseph. It is probable that the writer decided to embellish the story somewhat and added that on his own. But again I might be wrong and the whole story might be true. Anyhow, it is not important. For God could have implanted a part of himself in that baby any time he wished and Mary wouldn't be less holy had she made Joseph happy.

Unknown people have written parts of the Bible and other religious books, as the pages became unreadable.

Religious books are excellent tools used by preachers to pass on their messages but some of the writings are questionable. For example, I found some contradictions when I read the bible. In one place it is said that God is infinitely forgiving and would not carry grudges; He would forgive one's sins if one ask Him before one's death happen. But if you are unlucky and die too quickly, then the Almighty will burn you in hellish fire for a long time, more than a few hours of unimaginable torture, in fact for many days and more, for years, centuries, even much more than centuries, forever. Yes forever!

So if you are Hitler or Bin Laden or anyone of the maddest and most sadistic leaders in the history of mankind you can still go to heaven if you ask God to forgive you before you die. That doesn't sound right to me.

You may be a good person, generous and humble and have a

moment of weakness and commit one of the capital sins. For example, you make love to another person than your spouse and then get kicked by a car without having time to ask to be forgiven. Well though luck, you are going to Hell man, oh yes, it is written, there is no way out, you will be tortured forever in Hell.

That sounds foolish but it is exactly what preachers have been telling people for centuries.

Now, Muslim preachers are telling their followers that if they kill a lot of infidels, Americans and Jews and whoever else are at the wrong place at the wrong time, doing it in a suicide bombing, you are going straight to Heaven. Does that sound right?"

"I don't know; I will have to think it over." said Khamir.

"The problem," said John, "is that many followers don't question the preachers. This is the truth they say. It is written they say. And a lot of people believe anything that is written.
After all, some will think, the preachers have consecrated their life to the word of God. They are holy men! It is a known fact. Everybody respect them.
Well, let me tell you Khamir that many preachers will not go straight to heaven. Some will possibly go to that hellish place they are scaring us about if there is such a place. But I don't believe it, for I don't believe in God's wrath over sins. For undeserving people, there is most probably no punishment except that when they die, there is no afterlife, good riddance, that's all.

So when a preacher says with a strong affirmative voice that Jesus said this or Muhammad said that and it is written, just remember that the guy is using the book's writings to carry his message and influence his listeners. If his message is a message of love, tolerance and compassion, then it is for the best and we should not worry about the source of the message. But if the message is questionable, then it should be rejected."

"I often wondered how come Muhammad let the filthy Jews won the wars against our brothers." said Khamir. "Might it be that he wasn't God's prophet?"

"We will never know who really were: Abraham, Jesus, and Muhammad and those that came even before them, Confucius and Buddha." said John. "Those exceptional men may have been guarding angels; Guardians that gave us some help in our evolution.

Who knows! God might have guided them or put a tiny spark of his godly being in them. But it is comforting to think that there is a chance the Almighty is watching us and wish us to evolve to a higher level. It is comforting to think that he is choosing some people to help and guide us. That may be so and perhaps the Almighty is doing the same for the multitude of sentient species living on billions of inhabited worlds in this infinite universe.

The Jews are no more filthy or evil than your Arab brothers and we are all brothers on Earth, we breathe the same air and drink the same water and we all have dreams and emotions."

"That's not what is being taught to us at the Mosques." said Khamir. "Do you think we shouldn't go at the Mosque?"

"I believe," said John, "that some people need a place where they can assemble once a week and show themselves to their neighbors dressed in their best clothing. They can say hello to each other and speak a few kind words, congratulate each other for their most recent achievements. This way they feel that they belong to a community in which the members share mutual beliefs and goals.

To pray God, to sing together and to listen to the deep thoughts of one of the members of the community, one of the sons of that community, who has now become the preacher, is most comforting to those people.

This is why churches and Mosques have been built and preachers have been preaching. This once a week communal meeting at the church is a good way for some people to overcome their loneliness.
And when there are marriages or when the community looses one of its members, they all go to churches and give or receive kind words. Religions and churches are

wonderful; it is a great comfort to believe that when we are going to church on Sundays, we are preparing for ourselves a nice place in heaven and our life is worth something. Most people believe that by going to church, they are doing their best for the evolution of mankind.

The day people stop going to churches will be a very sad day for many of them. Religion is important and very useful as long as it is not used to control other people and achieve personal power."

"If I understood correctly the whole of your message," said Khamir, "I come to the conclusion that you don't believe in religion but you think it has a beneficial influence on mankind. I believe in Allah and would like to go to heaven and I need to follow the writings of a true religion. Would you to tell me then which religion you find the most credible."

"I like the two religions, Christianity and Islam, but there is another one, a much older one called Hinduism. That religion was born here in Pakistan, which was part of India at that time, for it dates back to prehistory. It has no binding rules; a Hindu can believe in one or more Gods or none at all. The core of their beliefs is about reincarnation and Karma. The writings say that all living things, people, plants and animals live in a continuous cycle that goes on forever. The next life you get is determined by your merits in the preceding one. I heard about some people who remembered their previous life and a survey tends to confirm that belief. I came to believe in the presence on Earth of reincarnated people. But only a few since our present time billions of people could not have all had previous lives, there were not enough people before.

I pondered about it and came to think that most people's souls dissipate into nothingness soon after being released from the body. Only a few souls have enough compassion power and knowledge or maturity to stay whole and resist the forces of chaos. To survive death, one must reach a high level of personal achievement."

Khamir and John had many such discussions over the following days.

"Tell me," said Khamir, "what should one do to reach a high level of personal achievement."

"We start our life on the first level." said John. "We have basic needs, instincts. We try to survive, get water and food and clothing for us and for our family. Then we want security and we try to make sure that we will have food tomorrow and the following days and years. That is the first level.

Once that is taken care of, we try to get other people respect and admiration. We want to show everyone and ourselves that we are more intelligent or resourceful than most and we work hard to develop our abilities and make a personal success in a suitable career. That is the second level.
But that is not quite enough yet to survive death. After we have got people's respect and admiration, we try to get their friendship and love and we realize that it is difficult to get it once we have proven our superiority. So, we try to become the best possible persons for our own personal satisfaction, hoping that friendship and love will follow. We learn as much as we can because it is pleasant to know things. We work out because we feel good when we are in great shape. We become interested in people and listen to them because that is the most interesting thing on Earth. Yes, other people! We help others because we feel good inside when we do it.

We try to be humble because we realize that for whatever we do or have done, we are not important, we will be forgotten quickly after we are gone; beside, being important becomes a real burden. We get pleasure in small things like having a pleasant chat with another person or daydreaming for an hour in a beautiful and quiet place. That is third level.

If we die after we have reached that third level, we may be awarded a different kind of afterlife than a reincarnation on Earth or a quick soul evaporation; a more exciting afterlife."

"Your words carry a great wisdom, John." said Khamir. "I never thought about these things. I am told what to do and I do it for I want to go to heaven. I do my best to

52

follow the right path. I never questioned my leader's words before."

Khamir left that day with much to think about. Afterwards, his behavior changed, he wanted to reach the third level and go to heaven or at least get an afterlife. He started to ask a lot of questions and slowly began to look at John as a father.

Soon after, he was telling John of his every day's events. More weeks went on and John was making sure to be on the loosing side in their daily cards' games. He now owed Khamir the equivalent of thousands of American dollars and reaffirmed regularly his intentions of paying him later on, when he will get free.

John was day dreaming one morning when he heard gunshots. Somebody was running to his cell door. A key turned in the lock, the door opened and there he was, Tom, with a set of keys in one hand and a gun in the other. He unlocked and took off the chain from John's ankle and helped him up.

"Take that gun dear friend and follow me," said Tom, "it is great to see you alive."

"Oh my dear Tom, I am so glad that you came back for me, thank you Tom."

They ran a long corridor and found three doors at the end. Tom opened the one in front and went out. John was just about to follow him when one of the side doors opened; he quickly stepped sideways and pivoting, faced a guard who was already leveling his gun on him. John shot him and froze. For at the very instant he was shooting the guard, the back door had opened and a gun had been pressed on his back. He turned slowly around, raising his hands; it was Khamir...

"You will have to knock me down, so that nobody will think I let you escape." said Khamir. "Farewell John."

"God bless you Khamir, good luck to you too."

John hugged him then hit him hard between the eyes. He would have black eyes for a few days but no broken nose. He would not loose one tooth or suffer a bone fracture.

John followed Tom outside up to a waiting car, and they rushed away.

John sat comfortably on the cushioned seat; it had been a long time with nothing else than a rough mattress on a cement floor and a square wooden chair.

"Tell me Tom," said John, "How in heaven did you find me?"

"We thought you were kept prisoner somewhere around here since the terrorists never showed your body. We had a few agents trying to find you over the last few months. Then, last week, we caught a phone call conversation between the terrorist cell leader and the Iranian embassy. The terrorist asked for a ransom of $1 million to deliver you alive in their hands. When I found out about it, I asked the CIA headquarters to send me here. I came back yesterday and caught your signal as I was driving in this area yesterday afternoon. The signal was very weak; the battery must have weakened up over the months for I doubt that the signal could be caught further than a few hundred feet."

"This is just too much of a coincidence," said John thoughtfully," I sent the signal twice a day to spare the battery, one time in the morning and one time in the afternoon. This is only 2 seconds in a whole day, and you were there just at the right time, passing in front of that house, within a hundred feet of it and just before they were about to hand me over to the Iranians…"

"I was lucky, isn't it?" answered Tom joyfully.

"I am not so sure about the luck of it." commented John. "It looks more to me that this chain of events was somehow willed by God or some kind of guardian angels."

"These are odd thoughts coming from one of our most notorious country hit man." replied Tom seriously. "But I too, often wondered about some unbelievable coincidences in the past."

"I come to think that my life, the short span of life that is left to me, might still serve a greater purpose and I wonder in which way I might still be useful. I don't have much left Tom; I was diagnosed with a brain tumor six months ago. The doctor told me it was impossible to remove it."

"I am sorry to hear that John," said Tom, "how much time do you still have?"

"One year more or less." replied John. "There is a woman with whom I wish to spend much of that time but I don't know if I should. She seems to like me a lot and I am in love with her but…"

They landed at Miami International Airport the day after. John thanked Tom, hugged him and they shook hands warmly.

"So, my dear Tom, you came back for me," said John with much emotion. "You saved me. I wish you the very best in your life and if you come to Naples, I have a room for you. I will be your friend forever."

"I will call you, John."

Tom left with water in his eyes. He had lost his father but he had paid his debt.

The day after his return, John went to the library but was told that Joan was away for one week. So he went to visit Naples downtown, the Fifth Avenue south, and stop by an art gallery called La Belle Image. They had an exceptional selection of interesting artworks, high quality paintings. Many of these had been executed with impulsive pallet strokes leaving a rich looking and very thick texture. The colors were soothing and they depicted scenes of another world.

John walked inside and started to look at the paintings. An elderly man came to him and addressed him in a thick French accent. John told him he had been in Paris quite a few times.

"Paris is a beautiful City," said the French salesman, "the only problem is that there are too many French people living there."

John found that very funny and kind of liked the salesman.

"In Fact," the salesman said, "I grew up in France but I am Italian, my name is Robert Pisano, please to meet with you."

John and Robert shook hands warmly and started to chat and joke about France and the French people. John was having a good time. He asked Robert about the paintings illustrating scenes from another world.

"The artist is in the back painting right now." said Robert. "He also wrote a book, here it is, "Ghama-2, An Afterlife Story" and its sequel "Land Of Magic". The scenes are from this world; the artist, my boss in fact said he is seeing them in his dreams."

John looked at the book, opened it, read the first chapter and got caught.

"I will buy the book for now." John said.

After paying for it, he went in the back to meet with the author and saw a man completely absorbed in the making of a painting. The artist seemed to be in a trance and ignored or didn't notice John's presence. He was doing the sky, sliding colors over colors from left to right, adjusting the texture left by the passage of the knife to enhance the beauty of the already rich looking sky. The moment came when the artist was satisfied and he turned around to face John.

"I apply the paint in very thick texture at the bottom where the subject in my painting is closer but the sky, except at the top, must be absent of any texture if I want to achieve the illusion of great distance." He said.

He didn't say hello, he just spoke to me as if we were old friends, John thought, *as if we had been talking for hours and this subject just happened in the conversation.*

It was now evident to John that I knew of his presence in my back. I had volunteered an information when none were asked and this indicated to him that I wanted to convey my appreciation for the man I had guess he was. He felt that in one fraction of a second, as our eyes met, he had been evaluated and approved as a person; for he was sure that I would have just said hello with a salesman's smile otherwise.

John liked quick thinking but even more he liked to be approved by a quick thinker. *There is nothing wrong in being a slow wit*, John thought, *after all it is not one's fault, but I prefer the company of the others*.

"I just bought your book after reading the first chapter and now that I have met with you, I know that I will enjoy the rest as well." said John.

"That book was written for you," I said, "you are one of the chosen and I am very glad that you bought it. Your next move will be to buy one of the paintings."

"I am not in the market of buying art but I will be back I guess." replied John.

He left me to my work after shaking hands and went back home. Once there, John took a shower, prepared himself a drink, two ounces of London Dry Gin in a full glass of lime soda and plenty of ice cubes, and sat down in his most comfortable chair. He had a sip and started the reading of it. He read it for two hours and stopped for there was much to think about and his eyes were getting dry. Beside, he liked it that way, taking his time to digest a few chapters before resuming the reading.

John felt tired, closed his eyes, fell asleep, and got caught in a very strange dream. He was seeing scenes of that world, Ghama-2, and some beings were talking to him.

"You have been chosen, your descendants need you, your race needs you..."

John woke up remembering the dream. He then went to the kitchen to make some coffee and to warm up a frozen dinner. The lunch was eaten quickly for John was now completely caught by the story. He drank the last of his coffee and went back to the kitchen to pour some more of the delicious coffee in his cup then went back to his sofa and resumed his reading.

On and off, reading then sleeping and dreaming, he went trough the books. Two days later he had read it all, the two books one after the other and was left shaken by it. He had not slept a full night just quick naps to restore his vision and his energy and understood now that this was much more than simple fiction, these books had really been written for him and some few other chosen. John knew that the dreams were no dreams, he had been in contact with spirits, they had talked to him, convinced him that they wanted him to be part of an incredible odyssey, an afterlife odyssey...

He decided then to go back to the art gallery to meet with the book's author.

I was very pleased to meet with John for the second time.

"So you are back." I said. "The story is fiction but who knows, sometimes between fiction and reality lies a very thin line and it could be crossed over... I hoped you will buy one of the paintings depicting life on Ghama-2. If you do so, you will be awarded a second life at the end of the present one. There are a few strange facts, unexplainable..."

"I know," said John, "that you are trying to convince me that there is more to the story than fiction. You are careful as you do it, you don't want to reach a point where I might start thinking of you as either a lunatic or a con man."

"I assure you John that I am neither one nor the other." I replied sincerely.

"I believe you Richard for not only did I read your books but I, also, have been in contact with the Guardians."

"Wow! I thought I was the only one with whom they could communicate." I said.

"You were the first one but not the only one anymore." replied John. "You see, the Guardians have scanned your body and found that your blood had an unusually high level of iron and your cells had a very high level of magnetism. They can now induce biological changes in the people they wish to communicate with."

"The Guardians told you all of that?" I said with surprise. "You must have had long conversations with them."

I was a tad jealous as I realized that John had surely gone much deeper than me with the Guardians.

"I wanted to learn as much as I could from them." said John. "You see I am a cautious man and I didn't know what could be their ulterior motive. They want me to lead the human expedition on Ghama-2. They said that I have the necessary military skill, combat experience, and psychology and they discovered that I possess a sixth sense that warns me of danger. Apparently they can rebuild us as we are now with our inherent abilities and add a few improvements of their own."

"What kind of improvements?" I asked.

"They just said that we will be more functional and less vulnerable; otherwise we will keep our personality but we will be young men again." replied John.

"That will be great to be young again, isn't it John?"

"Fantastic!" He replied.

"But now that they can communicate with anyone they wish to, they can just go back to Ghama-2 and talk to the people there, get an expedition force from locals… they don't need us anymore." I said worriedly.

"I ask them about that." replied John. "They said they thought about our belief in God and angels and came to the conclusion that these entities exist; they believe that they might have been led themselves by superior beings to you and me. So they think we are important for the success of such mission. They will only contact some of the people who have read your books; they will try to influence the ones with the greatest potential in going further and acquire one of your paintings. They said that if those angels exist, they should be the ones to influence the right people to come to your gallery. The Guardians will help a little bit in providing dreams to those who have already been influence by the angels to buy your books."

"This way," I said, "everyone of the potential candidates will still have freedom of will and only those who listen to their intuitions and are ready to spend an important sum of money in acquiring one of my paintings will be awarded an afterlife on Ghama-2. That is very close to my plan, the one I proposed to the Guardians."

"I know that you are doing well and you don't need the money Richard but it would be easy for most people in attributing a financial motive to your plan. The people that will go further will be the luckiest ones or the most intuitive."

"Talking about luck," I replied, "I intend to mail my books to a few of the most resourceful and luckiest people on Earth. These people would otherwise never hear about Ghama-2."

"Who do you have in mind?" asked John.

"I don't know why exactly but a few names came to my mind: Bill Rates, Donald Rumps, Nicole Teaseman, Queen Elisabeth the Fifth, Krishna the former middle weight champion, George W. Woods, our president."

"I know George very well since I have once been his bodyguard." said John. "I saved his life once and I am just back from Pakistan where I was sent to fetch 2 nuclear bombs, suitcase size. If he doesn't come to your auction, keep one of your paintings for him. He would be a great man for this odyssey."

We talked a long time about it....

Chapter Three - Joan the librarian

John was with the beautiful Joan at the coffee shop. He looked at her suddenly realizing that he had been lost for a while.

"You were caught in some kind of meditation," said Joan. "I didn't want to interrupt."

"Sorry Joan, as I grow older, I sometimes loose the thread of time, I get lost in my thoughts. Last week I bought a book, a most extraordinary book that is. I want to talk it over with you. If what I learned in that book is true, our very life may be transformed."

"We are quite old already," said Joan. "It is difficult to believe that after all we experienced, our very life would be transformed by the reading of a book. It is not that I doubt you, John, on the contrary, for you are exciting my curiosity."

Joan was very happy; John always had something new to talk about. She had been worried and afraid that something had happen to him. She remembered the first time they had met, their first coffee break together, her feelings afterwards, and her intuition that she had finally, at the age of 68, met the man of her dream.

At the beginning, Joan was hoping he would invite her for dinner and she would have a chance to know him better. But he never did and Joan wondered why. Was he married? She thought, he had a ring but no, he told her that he was a widow and was living alone. She never asked him why he would not try to go further with her.

They were not old physically. Both of them were in fact in great shape for their age; in better shape than a lot of youngsters but she felt that it was not proper for her to press him or to ask him why he would not invite her to dinner.

Joan had lost her husband 10 years before and had never met a man since for whom she would give away her freedom. She was working as a host and a guide at the library four days a week, 10 to 6 and used much of her spare time in reading.

Joan was a very unusual woman. She was living alone on Mainsail Drive in Naples, Florida. She lived in a first floor condo erected 25 feet from the shore of an alligator and crocodile infested lake. She loved her lake; a few hundred dwellings on one side and nothing on the other side apart from the mangroves and the areas of long grass, saw grass, where the birds walk in search of small fishes and insects right beside the sleeping alligators and crocodiles.

She would usually start her days with 10 minutes exercise followed by 15 minutes jogging on her balcony and then she would jump in her canoe and paddle along the far shore. She would even venture into the long grass areas knowing that at any time one of the big crocodiles could attack her for invading its territory and that would be the end. She was exhilarated by the presence of danger; she thought that her life would loose much of its interest if it would not be something that she might loose at any time. She likes paddling her canoe close to the long grass, making as little noise as possible but the birds usually flew away croaking a warning to the crocodiles. Some would slip soundlessly into deeper water but others would awake at the last moment and jump in the water in a tremendous splash. Sometimes they would emerge close to the canoe and look angrily at her. She would then look calmly at them and keep moving with the paddle in between her canoe and the closest one, showing no fear. She thought that if a predator can feel the fear emanating from a person, it would consider it as a prey or as a weak animal invading its territory and would attack it.

So far, her theory had proven true and after 2 years of her daily routine, they would probably go on tolerating her presence. After her 2 hrs of early exercises and a refreshing cold shower she felt fresh, full of energy for the day, and proud to look like a young woman at 68. Joan took great care of being dressed perfectly at all times. She would not dress expensively but she did it with taste. She would go shopping once a week to buy inexpensive little things here and there and later on combine the blouses, the pants, the skirts and other decorative accessories with taste and creativity. She looks like a lady, always impeccable and still remarkably beautiful for her age.

John looked at Joan with a new intensity
"Joan, I know you wondered why I never invited you for
dinner or made any effort to transform our friendship
into something much closer. It is not that I was not
interested, on the contrary, I will tell you why now."
John took her hand, look at her and said: "Joan, I love
you since the very first time I met you. That first
time, I felt your emotional response; I knew it was the
same for you. We had just been struck.

We had met our perfect match. I thought with much
sadness that it was unfortunately too late for us; I
love you and I know that you love me too..."

"Oh John I love you too, why do you say it is too late?"

"I thought it was too late but now, after reading that
book…I believe we may have a chance. I believe there is
a destiny but we can modify it by our very actions. We
were destined to meet each other but too late to enjoy
it. I don't have very long to live. I got a brain
tumor, I am dying."

"Oh no," said Joan stricken.

"Please Joan, don't be so sad, something great happened
last week and I believe that we have a chance to live a
long life together but on another a world; a most
fascinating gigantic world; a world where all the plants
were genetically enhanced a very long time ago. All the
trees are bearing nourishing fruits; a world without
viruses, bacteria, and insects; a world without sickness
but on which you may be killed for there are predators
there, and other sentient species, some of them very
dangerous."

"John, you are really stirring my curiosity, I can't
wait to hear more about it but not here, what you are
telling me is too important to do it here in a coffee
parlor. Would you come to my place, let's say 8:00 PM
tonight? I live close to Marco Island, it's the first
time I invite a man there but we have much to talk
about. I will cook a plate of vegetables, zucchini,
tomatoes, and onions with a good thickness of cheese
over it. I have a few bottles of Pinot noir and I
will have a home made dessert..."

"That's wonderful, it will be great, give me your address and I will be there."

Joan gave him the address, hugged him and kissed him on the cheek. He held her tight for a moment, told her how happy he was to have an evening with her and let her go.

She left for the library with moist eyes. She was troubled, filled with emotions.
John paid the addition and left the restaurant to return to his condo. Once he got there, he decided to walk in the park and think the matters over.

The guardians John thought *are a very old specie.*

He remembered clearly his contact with them. It was dream like but so real that he didn't have a doubt about the reality of this contact. They spoke to him and he learned that they were there before the previous universe collapsed. They had protected themselves into a sphere of warp time energy; they were inside that bubble at the time the universe collapsed into the ultimate black hole. Then, there was a terrific explosion, and all the matter that had been swallowed came back out as hot gas.
The gas molecules started to attract each other and form particles, which started to coalesce into bigger masses. As the masses increased in size, the forces of attraction between the particles increased. There came a point when nuclear reaction started and the masses transformed themselves into suns. Matter was ejected through terrific explosions and became planets.
The guardians saw the planets being formed, they saw life coming out on them and they observed the evolution of that life into plants, mammals and ultimately sentient species.
The guardians are traveling across the universe; they visit the galaxies and when they discover worlds inhabited by sentient species, they stop for a while to observe their doings. They very seldom interfere. They share the thoughts and emotions of individuals of a specie and after a while they resume their infinite voyage. They can travel into the past and come back at their actual time but they can't go into the future. These guardians are neither evil nor kind, as we would think in respect to ourselves.

They travel and guard the universe against the influence
of the demons that also survived the last big bang and
help vicious species to dominate, enslave and destroy
other sentient beings. One billion years ago, the Jinx
eliminated all sentient life in our galaxy and then
destroyed themselves with internal wars. Only a few
survived on the planet Ghama-2 but they degenerated and
lost all their knowledge and technology.
An advance civilization, Les Semeurs had already left
that world before these terrible times leaving their
cities protected by bubbles of space-time energy that
would remain active for billions of years. They also
left a mechanism to prevent any ship to fly over the
planet.

Any spaceship flying inside the atmosphere would crash
on the surface. All but one of the cities left by Les
Semeurs had stood well protected inside their bubbles
over the billion of years since they left. That city was
accessible. The space-time bubble of energy protecting
it somehow became inactive.

The first specie to find it and access the knowledge
spools left into their libraries would become as
powerful as "Les Semeurs "once were. They would become
super-beings.
Two hundred years from now, an American spaceship will
land on this planet. In fact, they will be crashed on it
by the automatic mechanism. The spaceship will be lost.
There will be no possible ways to communicate with Earth
but there will be survivors. A low technology
civilization will flourish over a few centuries and the
humans will start doing trade with some of the friendly
species living on that huge world.
500 years after the crash, the guardians passed by that
world and observed it. They saw the lost city and they
wanted to help the humans to discover it and become the
next great race. For that to happen, humans needed help.
The guardians traveled in the past and followed the
humans backward and came to earth. There was much
interference; a high level of radiation prevented
telepathic contact. So they came further back, before
the nuclear bombs started to explode everywhere. They
came to our time and finally made contact with an
individual whose cells magnetic energy was unusually
high which facilitated telepathic communication… They
contacted that human, the artist and author, in his

dreams and showed him scenes of Ghama-2. They induced him to start painting those scenes and write a book on that world and illustrate it with paintings depicting those scenes.

They want to take back with them some Earth people. The chosen ones must be men of action, with unusual qualities or powers. They must also be people who can accept the unbelievable; trusting their intuition and instinct. They must have unusual mind power and compassion. They should be able to modify their destiny by direct action and that first action would be to buy one of the paintings depicting life there.

Joan left the library at six and went home. She likes the work at the library, meeting with people. Many of them become close friends, even confidants. Back home, she sometimes watches television but she is too active to sit for hours in front of the TV. She likes to read and she is always trying to find something to do. She would prefer a more adventurous life.

Joan Brunet grew up in Germantown, Maryland. A village located twenty-five miles from Washington, DC. Maryland is certainly one of the most beautiful states in America; with hills everywhere; lakes, and the seacoast near by. She loved it there. When she finished her high school, she looked for the best university at the lowest cost. She discovered McGill University. That University was as good if not even better than Harvard or Georgetown at one fifth of the cost. It was located in Montreal, province of Quebec, Canada.

Joan went to Montreal and fell in love with the city and its people. There was always so much to do over there, so many activities, and its downtown streets were always crowded with people.
French people just can't stay in their home or their backyards; they walk outside, in front of their houses and talk with the neighbors.
In Montreal's old port, the streets are paved; there are hundreds of shops of all kind. Some of the streets are closed at weekends to allow the artists, the musicians, the acrobats or the comedians to give their shows in their allotted portions of the streets and collect some money from the passerby's.

Joan lived in Montreal the best years of her life. She graduated from McGill with a bachelor degree in Biochemistry and was immediately hired by an important pharmaceutical manufacturer where she worked for twenty years.

In her early forties, Joan decided that it was about time to get married and have some children.

She met David Mathers and thought he was husband material. She married him one year later. David was good company at that time, he was athletic, handsome, very intelligent and the only child of a millionaire businessman.

Joan's parents were most favorable to the wedding. They had been after her for years trying to get her married before it would be too late to have children. She was not in love but she thought that love would develop with time. She became pregnant almost immediately after the wedding and gave birth to adorable Nancy. One year later, Joan gave birth to Garry. With two young children and a husband making good money, she decided to quit her job, abandon her career, and consecrate her life into raising these children the best possible way.

Twenty years went by like a flash. David became very involved in his father newspaper business making acquisitions and working 16 hrs a day. David's father retired from the business and moved to Florida to play golf and enjoy living. A heart attack took him away one year later. David was very affected by his father's death; he became a different man and started to drink heavily. He was not at home very often, and most of the time he was nervous and hot tempered. When the business flopped, he was a broken man. He got employment here and there, loosing his jobs one after the other. Finally, like his father, a heart attack took him from his misery.

Joan's relationship with David had been a sad one. Love never bloomed up with time as she had hoped for. There had been no romanticism, the great love she was aching for, the sharing, never happened.

But now there was this man, John Foster, he was the one she had been waiting for. With him she would not loose her freedom, but live wonderful moments. She wanted to care for him, to cherish him until the end.

Chapter Four - The Seduction

John arrived in time at her condo. When the bell rang, it was exactly 8.00 PM. That was part of his military training, always be there on time. For business appointment he would arrive twenty minutes in advance with a book in his hands. He would sit comfortably and read his book until it was time for the meeting. For an invitation at someone's home, he would never ring the bell before time. It was not proper, he thought, it would possibly force a person to receive him before being ready or before the house had been tidied up.

Joan opened the door smiling and said "John, I somehow knew that you would be here at 8:00 sharp. I don't know many things about you yet but I can guess some of your character's traits."
"I have no doubt about you ability to read people," said John.
"Would you like a drink before the meal?" asked Joan.
"A dry martini or a cold beer." replied John. "What will you have yourself?"
"A dry martini is a good idea, I will have one too. Have a look around while I prepare the drinks or just sit down; I will be back in a moment."

Joan went to prepare the drinks while he walked around the living room, looking over every thing. There was a rust sofa and two easy chairs, a sculpted green and black granite table, a beige marble tiled floor. The walls were the color of the floor but a shade paler. There was a large size original oil painting over the sofa, showing three women sitting in a field with two houses and a church in the background. The style was creative and the colors were soothing.

There were shelves loaded with books, an old TV set, and a stereo.

Comfortable ambiance, John thought.

A picture of Joan's family caught his attention. There was Joan with her husband and her two children at the age of ten and twelve years old.

Her husband was handsome, John thought, *solidly built; he had the look of a businessman. A good man he seemed to be, but not striking; probably not an exceptional person. The girl seemed to have a tempestuous personality and the boy looked easygoing, very calm. The children have something of their mother, courage, and self-confidence...*
John never had children; he took a closer look at the picture. *They are real good-looking,* he thought, *I would like them. Will I ever meet them?*

John knew he did not have long to live now, he had the intuition and so far his intuitions had never failed him. He went to look at the books disposed elegantly on the shelves. A moment later, Joan came back with the drinks. He took his glass.

"Joan, lets make a toss to our future," John said, "I have reasons to believe that great adventures are awaiting us."
"To our future..."

Joan sat in one of the easy chairs and John on the sofa.

"Joan, let us come back to that book Ghama-2," said John. "The author is a local artist who owns an art gallery on Fifth Avenue South where the book is already in display. He illustrated the book with some of his own paintings depicting life on that world.

Friday night is the official launching of the book at the gallery, there will be a cocktail with hors d'oeuvres, a pianist will be performing and they will proceed to auction the paintings illustrating scenes on Ghama-2.
I am highly interested in buying one of those paintings. I know that it may sound foolish but I believe the artist's claims that the owners of those paintings will be transported to that world at the moment of their death. They will wake up in the body of a young adult. A body compatible with their aura and the way I understand this is that this new body will perform as good as the best you ever got with your present one and that would include the special powers or abilities that you have developed here on Earth. We will remember our past life and will be able to use our experience to help some of our descendants, already living there, to

find a very old city built by a civilization that left
the world a billion years ago.

I want to be one of the chosen and I want you to come
with me. We will contact our descendants already living
there and recruit a small army of volunteers to help us
in our efforts to find the lost city and get inside.
When I read the book, I fell asleep after a few chapters
and I dreamed. My dreams were very strange; they were
not dreams really, I was in contact with the guardians.
They said that the first species to enter the lost city
would become a race of super-beings. There are some
mechanisms that could enhance the brainpowers many
thousand times. The enhanced people will be able to
manipulate the matter of their own bodies and the
surrounding matter. They will be able to transform
themselves at will, to fly, to travel from world to
world at the speed of thought. They will become the
masters of the galaxy.

Some of the species on that world have found out about
the city and are trying to locate it. If one of the evil
species find it first, they will enslave all other
sentient species and kill them at will. It seems
important to the guardians to prevent that. This is why
they traveled backward to find our descendants' home
world and search for someone with whom they could
communicate. They contacted the artist and helped him to
write the book and make the paintings picturing life on
Ghama-2.

They showed me the world, the areas where the humans
live and some other species live. They showed me the
lost city too and it is a marvel. They can't transport
us in its vicinity; something prevents them to use their
powers on that world. There are a few places where
they can create a new body for us. Some of those are at
the proximity of a human settlement. We will be awoken
in one of these places.

They will snatch our souls at the moment of our death
and carry them back there and transfer it into a new
body. The guardians can manipulate matter and transform
it. They can transform mud into a human body. They told
me they are not godly beings and they are amazed at our
concept of God. They can do wonders those guardians but
they can't interfere more than that.

The chosen will wake up in groups of seven, in the
vicinity of one of the human cities. With our knowledge
and experience we can help our descendants whom lost all
their knowledge during the hardship of the hundred years
following the spaceship crash.
Since they will pick our souls as they travel back to
the future, there could be years between our deaths, it
doesn't matter; we will all wake up at the same time, at
the present time of the guardians, which is seven
hundred years from now. I told them that I want you, my
dear Joan, in my team. I also want my friend Tom who
recently saved me from a jail in Pakistan.

You can share the ownership of your painting with your
son and daughter, as I will do with Tom. Their souls
will also be picked up and they will wake up with us and
be part of our team. I expressed my wish that the artist
also joined with us. He will be the sixth member.
The last member will be a priest.

The Guardians said that they are fascinated by our
concept of religion and they believe that it may be a
very important success factor to have a priest with us.
They found one with exceptional powers and contacted him
and he will be at the auction.

Once we wake up on that world we will be on our own. The
Guardians will not be able to contact us anymore or to
interfere. We will have to protect ourselves at all
time, against predators and Aliens and even again some
of our descendants.

Joan, I would like you to come with me tomorrow to meet
with the artist. We will talk about it; and Friday night
my dear Joan, we will make a great step towards our
future life together; we will go to the auction and buy
one of the paintings."

There was a long period of silence following the entire
story. Joan was assimilating all the implications.

"John, that story is just incredible. I am demolished
inside at the thought of that brain tumor that is about
to take you away now that we have found each other.
Tonight, you will sleep with me. We will enjoy our
companionship and won't get separated from now on. And
you know what? I believe your wonderful story. I am

71

elated at the thought of the coming events. What a wonderful opportunity. You are sure it is not a dream?"

"No, Joan, it isn't, it is real. We now have a chance to live a life of adventures together."

"Incredible when you think about it, those guardians might even be watching us right now. They are probably listening to our conversation and sharing our very thoughts."

"Joan, it is true... When you come to think of it, many religions mention the presence of guarding angels that could share our thoughts and sometimes help us..."

"So these angels are in fact a species of invisible beings able to travel across time and space and doted with powers to accomplish what we consider miracles...."

"Yes," said John, "and think about Les Semeurs who contrary to the Guardians, were material beings. They achieved, through their evolution and sciences, mental powers similar to the guardians. Incredible, isn't it?

They roamed the galaxy for millions of years and disappeared one billion years ago. They left some principle, powers, mechanisms that are still functioning today... so powerful mechanisms that they prevent the guardians to interfere on their world one billion years after they left it. Mechanisms so powerful that they can still prevent spaceships to fly over the world one billion years after they left...

That lost city contains all of their accumulated knowledge. They left ways of accessing it. They were hoping that one day it would help another race to evolve to its maximum potential. It would allow its finders to become one of the most powerful species in the universe, a race of supermen and quasi immortals."

"And those aliens," said Joan, "hostile and lethal to all other sentient beings must be prevented to get there. We have to find a way to be the first and close the city to the undesirable. What a fascinating dream, can you imagine us flying together in the shapes of eagles under strange skies or swimming in the shape of sharks in the oceans of far away worlds?"

"Yes," said John, "it is a marvelous dream but we will have to prepare ourselves for that trip. It will be the most important mission ever, throughout all mankind history."

"What do you have in mind, John?"

"I think we should call Tom and your children and ask them to come over here and talk it over before we wake up there. I intend to invite the last two members too, the artist and the priest. We should spend some time together, the whole group. We should get to know each other; learn the inherent abilities of each one.

We should train to fight as a group against predators, enemies, and monsters that may outnumber us. We must develop trust and friendship. I am an expert in war, in combat. I intend to train you all or should I say, show you how to train yourself. I would like to teach you some tricks in Karate and Judo.

Everyone should start practicing with swords; knives throwing, close combat fighting, with knives or open hand. We should practice with bows and be able to hit a moving target.

I asked the guardians about armament and they said that the mechanisms left by Les Semeurs prevent the use of technological arms. Nothing superior to archery can be used there. So I asked them to give us each a sword, a knife, a bow and arrows, good clothes, good booths and some hiking equipment.

They said they would do that. At least, we will be able to defend ourselves against aliens or predators even against our fellow descendants if need be. That priest shall be trained too; I will try to convince him. Everyone must become an asset. Some of us must learn everything they can about computer programming. I believe that once we get inside that city, there will be technological wonders, equipment, and computers.

They must have left devices they considered easy to access but they were so far ahead in their evolution that we should learn as much as we can if we want to have a chance to use those devices. "

73

"You are right," said Joan. "Are you hungry? It is all ready."

"Oh yes I am hungry; I should have not gone so deeply into the subject tying to cover it all in one shot, I get very excited talking about this mission."

"I understand how you feel about it, I am in a turmoil inside myself. You made me fall in love with you coming to the library and give me company in my coffee breaks. Then you disappear for three months and when you come back, you tell me that you are in love with me and you never invited me to dinner because you are dying.

Then you tell me, no problem dear, we have a second life waiting for us and we will remember all about this one. And now we are already making plans as if we are just about to die... Tell me; how is it that this artist and you were the ones contacted? It is not that I doubt you; but do you have an explanation?"

"I talked about it with the artist. He told me that twenty years ago, he opened a biotherapy clinic in Montreal. He had a bachelor degree in chemistry and had always tried to keep himself up to date by reading monthly-published books like "Sciences et Vie" a French scientific magazine.

He read about the use of pulsating magnetic fields to cure a great number of diseases; even cancer. He opened the clinic with a doctor and put some publicity in the newspapers. The clinic filled up very quickly. Desperate people who had tried all other medicine came and got cured or got a vastly improved condition. It was an explosive success, hundreds of people were coming every day to his clinic and eighty per cent of them improved their conditions over a period of six to eight weeks with three treatments per week.

The patient was lying inside a big cylinder; the walls of the cylinder were filled with copper wires. There was a generator sending pulses of electricity and the pulsating magnetic field was generated. It was strong enough to affect all the cells of the body. He said he was using an intensity of forty gauss and a frequency of

74

thirty hertz for degenerative sicknesses and a lower frequency for the acute inflammatory conditions.

One day, the doctor did not come but representatives of the college of physicians came with the police and seized all the equipment and he found himself with a lawsuit for illegal medicine.

He had to close the clinic permanently but he kept one of the machines and kept giving himself treatments every week for the last twenty years. He said that he couldn't keep credit cards on himself; they got demagnetized too quickly. He thinks that all the cells of his body have increased their electrical charges over the years. His blood test shows an exceptional iron content and he believes that he might be one of very few people on earth with such a magnetic condition. That has possibly helped the telepathic communication with the Guardians.

Last year, I broke my right leg. It was such a bad bone fracture that they had to insert a metal pin to join the bone and they gave me a small magnetic pulsating field generator to be attached at all time to my leg until full bone regeneration. Well I felt such improvement in my every day energy level that I bought it and kept using it.

That would be it. This is why we were both contacted in our dreamy state when it is easier for the Guardians to contact us. So, both the artist and I have a very high level of iron in our blood and a very high magnetic charge in all our cells."

"Incredible," said Joan. "I did not know about that therapy, the pharmaceutical industries must have prevented that technology to spread. It would have reduced their sales dramatically. And the physicians must have felt threatened too; less sick people, less money for them..."

They went to the kitchen and Joan opened the oven to pull out a big pan of baked zucchini, onions, tomatoes covered with a thick layer of melted cheddar cheese. It smelled delicious. There was a stick of bread fresh of the day, French bread, and a few bottles of wine.

John helped her carry the plates to the dinning table.
He opened a bottle of wine and filled up the cups. Joan
came to him and kissed him on the mouth, warmly,
tenderly and the kiss became more passionate. They
hugged each other and John could not hide the effect she
had on him.

He felt shy about it, a little ashamed of not having
been able to control it. He tried to part from Joan hug
but she kept her embrace and said:
"after eating, we will go to my bedroom, keep some of
your energy for that moment dear."

He kissed her again and said "don't worry my sexy
seducer, I am not dead yet."

They chat a little, laugh at nothing and enjoyed their
meal. They would break pieces of the French bread and
dip it in the warm vegetable juice and eat the chunk of
zucchini making sure they have in the same spoon some of
the onions and tomatoes, pulling the cheese with it. It
was the combination of the various tastes that was
making it a delight.

They ate a lot but didn't feel filled. They swallowed
gulps of the delicious wine between each bite and when
they finished Joan said: "I have in the refrigerator one
of the best dessert you can find in Naples. It is called
baba-o-rum. It is like a small cake loaded with rum and
covered with whipped cream and real maple sugar lumps. A
delight, but you know what, I can see that you are
showing your manhood dearest, it must have been a long
time...come with me, I will take care of it and we will
have our dessert later on."

She came up to him, he stood up with no shyness this
time, they hugged and kissed and they walked to the
bedroom. They undressed and she turned on the music.
John sat on the bed and she came to him aware of her
nudity and its effect on him.

She was just as beautiful with her small and firm
breast, her flat and firm belly and her beautiful legs
as any young woman. Her age only showed up from the neck
up and that did not look too bad either. John started to
caress her slowly, extending the length of his fingers,
adding something to them that could go deeper, his aura.

He massaged her delicately but his fingers were reaching inside. He willed the transfer of comfort from his fingers. Joan felt comfort and delicious pleasure everywhere he massaged her. He started to stimulate her in two or three sensitive points at the same time.

She tried to pull him to her but he resisted a little longer until he could feel that she was just about to have her orgasm and then he went inside and started to make love to her. Slowly, concentrating in sending her pleasure waves and trying to control his own very intense pleasure. He didn't want to come too quickly so he would stop sometimes and kiss her and think tender thoughts trying to forget his sexual needs.

But now it was really too intense and he went on faster but not too fast, enjoying as much as he could before he abandoned himself to the most intense pleasure and finally let go into a wonderful apotheoses. She felt him coming and her own pleasure intensified, she let go too and felt the most intense orgasm she ever had in her life.

"John, I never felt so much pleasure. You are a wonderful lover. From now on I keep you here. We will make love every day. Sometimes when we will be sitting together, I will caress you and excite you to the point where your manhood will almost explode out.
And then I will take you to bed. What do you think? Is it a good idea? Will you stay with me from now on?"

"Yes Joan, we don't have much time left to ourselves. I will stay with you. What about that dessert, I feel ravenous. Making love do that to me. It is not that I have been making love often. In fact since my wife died three years ago, I never had a mistress. At my age we don't have much sexual needs and to make love to a person just for the fun of it without a real emotional bounding did not appeal to me. When I was a young man though, I wanted to take to bed any beautiful woman I could lay my hands on. At that time, I was not concerned about emotional or even intellectual affinity."

"Did you love your wife? How long were you married?"
"I married her eighteen years ago. I was sixty years old, retired and lonely and I needed company. I did not

want to finish my life alone. She was a good person,
fifty-five years old, cultured and beautiful.

We traveled a lot together. We would go to the beach
sometimes. She was catholic, very religious and was
devoting herself to many charitable causes, working
without salary. She was a very kind and honest person. I
respected her for her qualities and felt great
tenderness and friendship for her. I loved her
as much as you can love another human being whom you
respect and approve every which way.

We went on with our life together; we companionably
participated to many events and felt the comfort of each
other's presence. When she died, I felt despair. My
loneliness came back with more intensity than ever. It
was not the passionate love described in books. Maybe
we were too old for that. That was before I met with you
and realized that age has nothing to do with love
intensity. I loved my wife but did not feel what I feel
for you. You are the person I hoped to meet one day and
I intend to love you, to protect you and cherish you for
the rest of my life. "

Joan felt his sincerity and promised herself to give him
her own protection and unconditional affection for as
long as she lives.

"Shall we go for the dessert?" Asked Joan.

They enjoyed the baba-o-rums and were now drinking their
second cup of coffee.

"I am going to call my children," said Joan, "and ask
them to come over and spend some time with us. They are
living in Montreal, sharing my house. Garry has the
basement for himself. He likes to invite friends over. I
have never seen a guy with so many friends.
They talk and talk and listen to rap and other modern
music, drinking beer and this so late at night that
Nancy will often find a whole lot of them in the
morning.

They are lying around, sleeping on the sofas or on
cushions placed on the floor. Garry usually sleeps all

78

his mornings. He is presently studying to become a
waiter in a fine restaurant. He wants to work on
a cruise ship with two of his friends for two years,
make some good money and then invest it all with them to
open their own restaurant together. His courses start in
the middle of the afternoon and ends at eight p.m. Nancy
is studying at Concordia University in Medicine.
She has a boyfriend but there is nothing serious between
them. He sleeps there too. He owns a small grocery and
supplies the food. Garry gets along well with him.

They have their spring break coming in one week and to
my knowledge they have not plan anything yet. It is now
10:00 P.M.; they are probably there right now. "

Joan picked up her cellular from the kitchen counter and
went to the living room where she sat comfortably on her
favorite sofa, the one that had enough space for two.

*She is obviously very excited at what she is going to
tell her daughter*, John thought, *I might as well bring
her a glass of wine. It will be a clear message that I
want her to take her time and enjoy it fully.*

John brought her a glass of wine and sat on the sofa
right beside her, bringing his head to the proximity of
the cellular so that he could hear the conversation.

"Hello Nancy," said Joan." How are you doing?"

"Very good mother and you?"

"Very good too; I have a boyfriend...He is with me right
now."

"What?" cried Nancy, "Oh my God, are you telling me that
you are in love mom?"

"Yes my darling, I am in love, romantically in love,
just like in a fairy tale and with a very special man."

"Wow, cool, I was so sad that you had to live such a
lonely life in Florida. It is such a dead place there.
How does he look like?"

"You know," said Joan, "that I could not stand the cold
anymore and I felt that I was loosing too many days of

whatever is left in my life. A day inside because of the rain or the cold is such a waste. Here it is sunny almost all the time. I like canoeing on my lake and I like the work at the library.

I thought a lot about it last year before taking the decision to move to Florida. You had both reach the age when you want to live in your own apartment but you had no money so I left you the house. I miss you though; I miss you a lot. But to come back to my new boyfriend, he looks great. He is seventy-eight..."

"Seventy-eight, my God! You look like a woman in her fifties; why did you choose such an old f...man?"

"Well, I understand what you might be thinking, but that man is in better shape than most youngsters." "Where did you meet him?" asked Nancy.

"He started to come to the library and each time he came we talked together. After a few days, he was timing his visits so that we could be together at my coffee brakes. This has been going on for a few months and then he didn't come for three months and I was wondering what had happened to him. I was very worried and heart broken for I had already fallen in love with him. But He is back now from Pakistan where he had been sent on a mission by the CIA. He is a true hero, a retired secret agent and maybe more… he didn't tell me everything yet.

Last week John went to downtown Naples to an art gallery where he met with the artist whom had painted scenes of another world. There were books for sale, one was titled "Ghama-2, An Afterlife story" and the other book was its sequel, "Land of Magic". The artist told John that he had written those books to recruit a number of chosen for the greatest odyssey of all time. John bought the books and as he read them, he fell asleep a number of times and each time he was contacted by the Guardians who explained to him that if he wished to, he could be one of the people to whom they will give an afterlife on Ghama-2. He could be one of the heroes of that coming odyssey.

John wants me to go with him there and I am just about to embark into the greatest of adventures. We are chosen for a mission on another world, can you believe it? And

80

we would like you and Garry to come over next week. It is very important. John thinks that he only has a short time left. He is dying of a brain tumor... Would you come with Garry on next direct flight to Miami? You can use my credit card to buy the tickets."

"Mom, have you lost your mind? That story is just unbelievable; this guy must have done something to you…there got to be some money scam somewhere; do you have to buy something to be one of the chosen?"

"Yes, dearest, I have to buy a painting depicting a scene of Ghama-2. There will be an auction next week…"

"I knew it!" exploded Nancy." These two guys, John and the artist are going to get away with everything you have in your bank account. How could you have not seen the machination, that's a scam, can't you see it mom?"

"Nancy darling, don't worry, I have not lost my mind; sometimes the most unbelievable is true. I won't spend any money before you meet with John and the artist. But I need the two of you to come over to Naples right away."

"All right mom, we will go."

"We will be waiting for you at the airport. It is only an hour and a half from Naples if we take the 75, which is called here the alligator alley."

"Mother," said Nancy worriedly." Are you sick? What you say doesn't make sense. Maybe you should call a doctor, it sounds like you have lost it."

"Don't worry my little sweetheart, I am sane but I need you here. Please!"

"OK, we will go, I will call you tomorrow to let you know when we will get to Miami."

"Bye Nancy, I love you."

"Bye mother, I love you too."

"She was worried," said Joan. "I am sure they will come as soon as they can."

81

"I understand her," answered John. "That story is so unbelievable; she may even be thinking that you are the one with a brain tumor which is affecting your sanity. Are you tired? Would you like to go to bed? It is 10:30 PM..."

"Oh no, I would never be able to sleep, I am too excited about everything."

"Then," said John. "Give me your favorite brush; you will sit on a cushion, on the floor here between my legs and I will give you a head massage. It will relax both of us and we will be able to sleep. Otherwise we will be in bad shape tomorrow and we have plenty of things to do. I would like to do some canoeing with you, very early, when the fog is rising from the lake. I intend to wake you up at 6:00AM. I will prepare the breakfast and then we will do some work-up, the canoeing, and after a shower, we go downtown to meet with the artist at the opening of his store."

"A head massage John, I never got that from another man before. It will be welcome, I need to be pampered a little, and there is still a little girl in me."

"Yes, I saw the little girl in you and loved her." said John just before kissing her on the mouth.

John started to brush her hair with the movements of a hairdresser doing a hair cut. Then he brushed them slower for a long time and finally started to scratch her head with his nails delicately extending his aura into he skin cells and sending waves of comfort and tenderness. He touched her head with his own and went on with the scratching while he was mixing his aura with hers, sending powerful waves of love and tenderness. Finally, he put himself in a half-asleep state and sent his sleepy waves into her aura.

Joan felt such comfort that she fell asleep. John took her in his arms, lifting her effortlessly and carried her to her bed. He pulled the sheets to her chin, took off his clothes and lied down beside her, over the sheets, bare. He then increased his metabolism as he had often practiced in Yoga so that he would feel comfortable without anything covering his body and was out himself in no time.

Next morning they had a short breakfast of toasted tomato sandwiches with lettuce and pumpernickel bread. A cup of strong coffee, and they were on the balcony doing elongation and exercises. They went for the canoe ride. The air was fresh and cold, there was a dense fog and all the alligators and crocodiles were there on the lake.

"They love the fog," said Joan. "If a big one comes for us, we will have to race away and after a while it will stop its chase."

Wonderful, thought John, *what a way to start a day.*

"I am not worried about it," said John, "I brought my long knife and if we can't escape, the saurian will have the last surprise of its long life."

They came back an hour and a half later, had their showers and drove downtown. They met with me at 10:00 AM.

Chapter Five - The auction

"Hi Richard," said John. "I would like you to meet Joan
Davies. She will come to the auction tomorrow night and
buy one of your paintings."
"Hi Joan, I am so pleased to meet with you. You look
great, maybe I misunderstood but I thought John told me
you were sixty-eight years old, you don't look older
than 55 at the most."

"Well, now you know. I usually don't tell my age. Thanks
for the compliment. So... you are the one, the first
human being ever contacted by the guardians. It is an
honor to meet with you."

"No personal merits there, it just happened that I have
an unusual iron level in my blood and a high electrical
charge on my cells and that was the key that made it
possible for the guardians to establish contact with me.
My only merit is that I did not reject them too
violently when I felt their presence in my mind.

I tried to convince myself that it was just a dream but
after a while I welcomed them and asked them who they
were and what they wanted. I could have kept my mind
close or turned hysterical but I don't get scared easily
by the unknown."
"I believe," said Joan, "that there are many others with
whom they could have established contact. I am sure that
they selected you for a reason and now that I see you, I
perceive that you are a man with exceptional qualities.
But I also feel that you are fighting a sickness. Are we
going to loose you too?"

"Well, I will try to finish the third book of the saga
but yes I am fighting a stomach sickness and I am
loosing the fight. My stomach is covered with nodules. I
may last another year at the most."

"Let's talk of our immediate future," said John. "I had
a long contact with the guardians two nights ago. They
showed me the approximate location of the lost city.
They told me that they intend to transport on Ghama-2
three groups of people. Each group will comprise seven
members who will awaken together. Each group will be
transported to a different location but in the vicinity
of one of the human's settlements.

84

I asked them if I could choose the members of my group and they agreed. I choose Joan with whom I am deeply in love. I also took the decision to add to my team Tom who recently saved my life in Pakistan. There will be Joan's children Nancy and Garry and the Guardians chose a priest; father O'Leary as the sixth member of my group. They said there is something about him that puzzles them, we will meet with him at the auction, I am quite curious about him. That makes six and I would very much like to have you with us as our seventh and last member."

"That's great, I accept with pleasure. My wife left me a few years ago to live closer to my daughter. I call her sometimes to chat about everything. I tried to talk to her about Ghama-2 but she didn't want to ear about it; she said she has no interest for adventure and beside she doesn't believe the story. I don't have any friend, I am alone except for my daughter and I want to go, I will not miss my chance for an adventurous afterlife."
"Great," said John. "Let us meet, the whole group at Joan's condo next Wednesday. We will make plans to fully prepare ourselves for the mission. Let's say 10:00 AM. Will you be there?"
"Count on me, I will be there." I said enthusiastically.

"I wish to take my time here John," said Joan, "I have a genuine interest for art and to look at each of the paintings will be a great pleasure for me."

"Sure let's do it sweetheart." replied John.

Half an hour later, Joan tried to buy the books to no avail. She got them free. They left me to my duties and went on for a walk on the beach. They went down the Fifth Avenue south, which is downtown Naples, then turned left on Third Street up to Broad Avenue and then right to the beach and to the main tourist attraction, the pier.

Palm trees and ferns on one side border Naples beach. The multi-million dollars houses are almost unnoticeable. There are no boats, just one of the most beautiful beach there is. There is the pier, very long and wide, with fishermen here and there and the pelicans

swimming lazily underneath, waiting to steal the
fishermen's catches or for the thrown back fishes.
The sea covers a desert of fine sand; there are no
urchins or anything to cut into your feet. You can walk
deep into it and swim safely late mornings and early
afternoons but one should keep away from it at evenings
and early mornings for the sharks are more aggressive at
those times and may be just waiting for you.

John and Joan removed their shoes and walked on the wet
sand, they went on the pier to watch the children
catching fish and their joyful interactions with their
happy parents. The fathers would show them how to put on
bait or how to take the hooks from the fish mouths. Most
of the time, the children would throw their catch back
to the sea or to the pelicans swimming by the pier.

John bought two sandwiches and sodas and they sat
comfortably under the shade. After a while, they went
back to the condo.

That night they went for dinner at the Ritz-Carlton on
Vanderbilt Beach at Pelican Bay. There were musicians
and a dancing floor. They ordered a bottle of red wine
and an entrée of mussels marinated in white wine and
garlic. Then they had a three-pound steamed lobster
served on white rice.

"Let's dance," said Joan. "It has been a long time since
I did it and it may be our last chance at it."

They danced for one hour and hug each other dearly
during the slow dances, and then they came back to the
table, ordered coffee and a chocolate dessert called
"Profiteroles au chocolat". Four balls of ice cream
covered by chocolate and served on a mint chocolate
sauce with a garniture of raspberries and blackberries.
It was divine.

They came back home at midnight. Joan got another of
these exquisite head massages; they made love and slept
contentedly.

It was Friday night, the auction night and a large room
had been rented at the Marriott hotel on Marco Island

for this occasion. I had mailed hundreds of invitations to my clients and to a number of well-chosen potential candidates for the mission. Some of them were celebrities and I had invited them in the hope of getting some very lucky members for that expedition to Ghama-2.

The auction had been schedules for 8:00PM and I was a bit anxious to see if many would show up. In my artist career I had many shows and some of them had been real success and others real flop. I had come to believe that people are not willing to do much on nights following superior solar activity. All over the planet, people seemed to be in the same mood, probably due to an increased bombardment of neutrinos.

But now, it was 7:00Pm and with still one hour to go before the auction the room was almost filled with all kind of people.

I had my name clipped to my coat and was welcoming everyone that came in. Robert Pisano, my sales associate was there too to help and I had hired for the occasion a "maitre-de-ceremonie", supplied by the hotel.

Joan and John walked in and I immediately went to them to shake hands.

"I am so pleased to see the two of you." I said, as I shook hand with the beautiful Joan. I could not repress my feeling for her. It was love at first sight. She looked at me right in the eyes and I knew that she had just found out my intense feeling for her. I left her hand regretfully but quickly enough to hide what had just happened to John.

"It's a pleasure to see you John." I said hoping that he hadn't noticed anything but that extraordinary man had not miss anything.

"It is a pleasure for me too," said John, "I hope there won't be any problem between us."

"I know what you mean and I will always respect you John." I replied. "I will be your ally and your friend."

He knew that I was sincere and a man of honor, it was easy for him to read me.

"It seems to me that your auction will be a great success." said Joan warmly, changing the subject adroitly.

Oh boy, that woman is real bright and just wonderful, I thought, *My God would I love to kiss her. Now come Richard, you better control your thoughts and emotions, you don't want to lose John's friendship, don't you? Stupid!*

"It looks like that," I replied, "we have some real celebrities here and a very interesting man, one that outshine anyone here. I can almost see an aureole over his head, a real saint I tell you."

"That is probably Father O'Leary," said John, "the Guardians have found him and told me they wanted him to be part of our expedition."

"I didn't send him any invitation." I said. "How in Heaven did he find out about the auction?"

"The Guardians have communicated with him while he was asleep," said John, "they told him about the auction and the need for a preacher in this expedition."

"Well, let me introduce you to the reverend father," I said as I led them to the father who was looking at the paintings displayed at the end of the room.

"Father O'Leary," I said as we came beside him, "let me introduce you to two persons I consider very important for the coming odyssey. John Foster and Joan Brunet."

"Hello John, Joan, it is a pleasure to meet you. Richard told me about Ghama-2, the importance of this mission for mankind and his joy of having recruited the two of you. Richard told me that you are a retired secret agent John, a warfare and combat expert and yet, I see in you a compassionate, respectful and highly cultured man. No surprise that the Guardians have contacted you. And you my child, Joan, you are an interesting person. I believe I met you before; you were different at that time. There are some souvenirs that I have difficulties to recall, souvenirs it seemed to me, from past lives. I read about many religions, some of which like Hinduism talk about reincarnations. I am not sure about it but it is possible. God might decide to bring some of us back in this world if it suits his grand plan. Anyhow, I understand why Richard is so proud of having you here tonight."

"Richard seemed to forget that we still have to buy one of his paintings to become part of the expedition." said Joan. "And with all the people here tonight, I am not sure I have enough money to win a bid on any of the paintings."

"That's true, even for me." said John. "The Guardians believe that a superior entity has led them here and they will not interfere to make us win a bid. They believe that the ones who will acquire the paintings are probably the ones that entity, God perhaps, wants for the expedition."

"Oh boy, I didn't think about that." I said. I kept one painting for the President of the United States and I mailed one to my daughter. It never came to my mind that I might lose the two of you for that expedition."

"Let's not forget that if it is God wish to have the four of us there, we will end up with one of the paintings." said the reverend father. "Miracles happen sometimes."

The catholic priest was an imposing man, 6'3", and 245 lbs of heavy muscles. He looked more like a retired football player than a man who had consecrated his life to the word of God. He had a deep and soft voice, very kind eyes and it seems that everything he said had more than one meaning.

What an interesting man, thought Joan, *I would talk with him for hours on end and would never be less than totally fascinated.*

The father questioned us about Ghama-2 and our conversations with the Guardians. John told him about his conversations with these immaterial beings that called themselves the Guardians and the abandoned city

they had showed him. He told the reverend about the
aliens, the predators and the demons that will be
awaiting us, that will try to kill us as we move towards
the city.

"So," said Father O'Leary. "It will be a dangerous
mission and our chances to get to the city and even get
inside are slim at best. I have been in Somalia for the
last three years preaching the word of God to terrorists
and killers and against all odds I am still alive and
here tonight. There is no point to worry about the
difficulties of that mission; we will do our best.
I never talked myself with the guardians, but I felt
compelled to come here last week and buy the book. God
has strange ways to influence things to go one way or
the other without taking away from us our ultimate
freedom. These guardians might not be aware of it but
they may very well be acting under the influence of God.

They suspect its presence and are hoping that He will be
the one that will ultimately choose the members for that
mission. I would have loved to communicate with the
guardians. They probably know the answers to so many
questions. I felt almost dragged here a few weeks ago
when I bought the book. I pondered about it and prayed
and felt that the story was true. I had the intuition
that God wanted me to participate to that great
mission."

"If we all get one of the paintings, we will meet there
on Ghama-2," said John. "You will be part of my
group Father O'Leary. Seven of us will wake up there, at
the same location and at the same time even though there
might be years in between our last moments on Earth. The
guardians told me it is the first time they came in
contact with a specie like mankind with the concept of
God and religions. It might have been quite a shock to
them."

"Yes, "I added," they are fascinated by the concept,
they don't know for sure of God's existence and they
never felt his presence but they were puzzled at the
complexity of the universe and were really hit by our
concept. Now, they think that the universe might have
been designed, created by an entity that was there, that
has always been there, always working on the making of
it, redesigning it like a tapestry."

90

"The guardians existed before the last big bang," said John, "they have been there for so long they don't remember their beginning. They believe they are immortals but they are not sure. Maybe the demons could destroy one of them but they are in great number, living together, each one adding his own powers to the multitude. So far, they were able to resist the assault of the demons and even counteract their influence here and there during their travel across the infinite universe.

They said there is on Ghama-2 a principle or a power stronger than them all of them together. It is protecting the planet against visitors and prevents anything to fly from one point to another at a speed greater than 100 miles per hour. Moreover, that principle prevents them to play a more active roll in helping the humans. It will let them transport a few humans on the surface but they feel that they are forbidden to do anything more. They are very puzzled by that. They think that if there is a Godly being in the universe, a Presence that created it, there is a chance that He or part of He is right there on Ghama-2. "

"Fascinating," said Father O'Leary. "I am very happy to meet three of the people with whom I will share the coming odyssey."

The auction is starting; there are about one hundred persons in the gallery and only a dozen paintings showing scenes of Ghama-2 are available.

"I will start the auction now," Said the auctioneer, "and as we told you in our invitations, there are some rules. The last bidder for each of the paintings will have to come to this desk and proceed in front of me to a bank wire transfer to the artist bank account. Once the transfer is done, you will imprint your thumb in the back of the painting and sign your name beside it. Once this procedure is done we will move on to auction the next painting."

"Joan," said John, "you might not have to disburse a large sum of money if you bid on the least interesting piece and I believe they will keep the most beautiful for the end. Let's play safe. If you agree, Reverend

Father, we will not bid against Joan on the first piece.
She will be able to get it at a lower price. Then it
will be your turn and I will not bid against you. "
"My dear John, I have already chosen my painting," said
Father O'Leary. "I want that piece over there.
It has a religious meaning. You can see a cross, an urn
half filled with red wine and over it the white circle
represents the body of Christ. The poppies' field in the
background is symbolic and represents the gathering that
came out from the seeds of the preachers' words. I
really want that one. "

"So be it," said John. "We will not bid against you on
this one. "
The first piece auctioned represented a couple of humans
clothed like the ancient Romans traveling in a boat
through an old city. Looking at it, we could have
thought it was Venice but the landscape was different.
The young man was carrying a sword on his back and his
lady had a long knife at her belt. The colors were
beautiful and I had done it with heavy pallet knife
strokes. Many people were trying to buy it and so
did Joan following John's advice. The bidding price went
on from $1,000.00 and now reached $100,000.00. John
looked worriedly at Joan but she went on bidding;
$200,000.00; $300,000.00. Three hundred and
fifty thousand once, twice, awarded to Joan Brunet for
$350,000.00.
"My God," said John as Joan came back from the
auctioneer desk, "I didn't know you had that kind of
money. "

"I just spent most of the money I had accumulated over
the years and I had promised Nancy not to spend any
money before she arrives here and meet you and Richard.
But the money would have been useless since I am
covering my expenses with what I get from the library. I
didn't really need it except as a security. I would have
left it to Nancy and Garry but the painting I just
bought is for them too. It will belong to all three of
us. "

"Did you notice the two guys who were bidding against
you Joan? They don't look like the kind of guys the
Guardians would have chosen as potential candidates. I
sensed evil waves coming from them. "

"I am surprised, I said, "that they bided so high; they don't look like the kind of people that would let their money go easily. I don't see how they could possibly help our descendants in that mission."
"I noticed them too," said Jan, "they are rotten sun of a ditch, excuse my language reverend father but I believe that's the only place they would shine."

I could tell that Joan had some character and didn't like to have been forced to buy the painting at such a high price by these two scumbags. I decided that I would reimburse her after the auction.

The next painting to be auctioned was showing three ladies in an alien garden looking at the ocean. It was a night scene very appealing to a sailor like John. Many people wanted it including the two snobbish scumbags.

Again the bids went on and on. John was trying to buy that one and was getting more and more annoyed as the biding went on and on. Finally he got the last bid at $600,000.00. He had just spent about all he had in bank.
"I thought for a while that I wouldn't get one tonight." said John, taking a deep breath and releasing it loud enough for Joan to hear it.

The third one was the religious theme. Joan, John and I were feeling sorry for the Abbott for we knew that he would not be able to buy one of the paintings at the price they were going already. But surprisingly, the father looked confident, he was even smiling.

The auctioneer started the bids at $10,000.00 and nobody made a bid for it. I gave the auctioneer a sign to go down. I somehow knew that Father O'Leary should have that one but didn't have the money for it.
"Who is going to offer $8,000.00 for that fine painting?" said the auctioneer. "Nobody? Let's say $5,000.00."

Father O'Leary raised his hand.

"Five thousand once, twice, awarded to you Reverend Father for only $5,000.00, congratulations."

At that moment, the two snobbish men raised their hands and one cried "$20,000.00, I will pay $20,000.00 for it." The other one shouted "$50,000.00" and suddenly everyone were raising their hands.
Everybody now stood up shouting that the auctioneer had gone too fast, complaining that they didn't have time to raise their hands. Some were offering large sum of money to the father for his painting but he refused with a sympathetic smile. The reverend father proceeded to his wire transfer and came back to sit beside me.

"Come now ladies and gentlemen," said the auctioneer, "it is too late for this one, let's proceed with the next one."
"But I could not raise my hands," cried the snobbish man, "I tried but they wouldn't move."
"We still have a few more paintings so you will have your chance." said the auctioneer.

John, Joan and I were looking at the priest; we knew that we had just witnessed something extraordinary. The priest had his eyes closed now and was seemingly praying, thanking God probably for his help.
"That is all I had, "whispered Father O'Leary to Joan, "I guess I will be joining you on Ghama-2."
"That's a miracle!" I said under deep emotions.
"Something is going on here; I am starting to feel like we are pieces of a much larger game."

The auction went on. The auctioneer was now offering a scene of horse-riders on a wet beach galloping under a stormy sky. A beautiful woman got the last bid for one million two hundred thousand dollars.

"I recognize her," said Joan, "she is a cinema star and I believe her name is Nicole Teaseman, a famous actor."

"I mailed her the books with an invitation," I replied, "but I wasn't thinking she would be coming. I guess the guys of the second or third group will be very happy to share the adventure with her."

"For a man who is dying of a stomach cancer," said Joan looking at me straight in the eyes, "you seemed to have kept all of your manhood."

"I have to admit that I fantasized often about her but that was before I met you." I replied unable to hide the attraction I had for Joan.

Joan didn't comment and I appreciated it for there was no point in telling me that she was already in love with John, a wonderful man who outshines me by a parsec.

The next painting was showing two women on a castle balcony staring at the mysterious sea of Ghama-2. It was a night scene and we could see on the left another castle sitting on a hill with the USA flag.

A tall man who seemed very sure of himself bought that painting. He looked like a king and was smiling contentedly.

"That one is the king of the casinos, "said Joan, "he is Donald Rump a very rich man."

"My goodness, the luckiest people of the world have not failed to come." I said. "I invited him as well as Bill Rates and Nicole Teaseman and they all came. These people must have an excellent gut feeling for rare opportunities; they are now getting a rich afterlife after having got all the richness they could on earth."

The next painting represented a princess sitting under a tent on the beach. She was looking at the sea.

The two snobbish men and many of the other people in the gallery tried to buy it but again, the bidding went very high and finally a well-known lady got it.

"That lady," said John "is none other than Elisabeth the Fifth, Queen of the United Islands."
She was sitting only one row behind us and she was radiant. We had turned on our seats to look at her and she apparently knew who we were for she winked at Joan.

"I guess I will meet with you one day." She said with a royal smile.

One of the lucky buyers was also easy to recognize. It was Krishna, former undefeated welter weight boxing champion of the world, undefeated and five times champion of Ultimate Fighting, undefeated karate champion of the world and he was walking with the agility and controlled power of a panther as he came back from the auctioneer desk with his painting in his hands.

I looked at John's face and I saw real admiration in the way he was looking at the ultimate fighter.

"I watched all his fights." said John. This man will be an incredible asset for his group on Ghama-2."

"I know John," I replied, "I watched them too and this is why I mailed him an invitation along with the books."

Then there was a landscape executed in a novel way.

These access key paintings should not fall into bad hands, I thought, *too many strangers have bought one already, and these two evil men should not get one. I will tell the auctioneer that I am keeping the rest of the paintings except for that last one. I will sell the others later on to decent and worthy people.*

I went to the auctioneer and told him that except for that landscape, I wanted to keep the rest of the paintings.

"The next one will be the last one," said the auctioneer. "The artist just decided to keep the others."

Many of the people present showed their disapprobation. Some had come from far away to buy one of the paintings. The most indignant were the two snobbish evil men. It looked like they wanted to buy one at all cost now and apparently regretted not to have gone further in their bids.

"These two men are getting desperate." said John. "You took the right decision, in cutting short the auction."

"Yes I was getting afraid that some of the people buying those paintings were not the ones that should represent mankind on Ghama-2 and I would be surprised if these evil men get the last one." I said.

96

"Why is that Richard?" asked the lovely Joan.

"If you look in the back dearest," I replied, "there is a man who has remained silent all through the auction. This is Bill Rates, the billionaire, the genius and I believe he will take the last painting."

"Attention, Ladies and Gentlemen," said the auctioneer, "we have that one left but it is the most beautiful and the biggest in size. Let us start the auction at $1 million."
The two snobbish men looked at each other and suddenly one said to the other, "Let's buy it together."
The other nasty looking fellow agreed and raised his hand.
John looked at the quiet man that had not yet participated to the auction, Bill Rates. He had seen that man before at TV and He didn't look special in any way except that the young man had built an empire in the computer software. He was considered one of the richest men in the world.

The bids went on and on and had now reached the incredible sum of $40 million dollars and that last bid belong to one of the two evil men. Bill Rates raised his hand and said, "$100 Millions!"
Everyone became silent; nobody was able to bid more than that.
"One hundred millions once, twice, awarded!" said very quickly the auctioneer.
All the buyers congratulated each other under the jealous gaze of the less fortunate ones. The two snobbish men left empty handed. They were furious and worried. They seemed to fear incoming punishment for their failure to buy one of the paintings.

"You talk to me about them Richard and then the Guardians told me that they do exist and there are some of them on Earth and I now believe that these two men were sent by Demons." said John. "They would have been traitors to our race. I have the intuition of great dangers awaiting us. We may have to fight against more dangerous opponents than the alien species and the predators roaming the world of Ghama-2."

"But we may have just experienced a miracle," said Joan. "Not one painting went for less than $350,000.00 with

97

the exception of the one our reverend father bought for $5,000.00. Incredible isn't it? Everyone looked to be in a trance, unable to move...Maybe our Father O'Leary is a kind of magician or else.... He may have been helped and if it is so, we might be helped in turn so I am not worried about this mission; we will not fail."

John asked every one of the lucky buyers if they would come to a very special meeting the following Wednesday at 10:00 AM at Joan's condo. Everyone was willing to come and John told them to be ready for a trip that might last 2 weeks, possibly more. He would not say any more on it.

"It is a surprise," John said smiling. "But it is very important."

John had contacted a man just before the auction, a man whose life he had saved while he was working for the CIA. He had jumped on the gunman shielding his protégée with his own body, risking his life to protect George W. Wood, the governor. That man was now president of the USA. John had told him the story, he had told him all about the auction and Ghama-2 and George had believed him and invited all the chosen, the lucky buyers of the access-key paintings to Camp David for extensive training.

The next few days, John and Joan went canoeing and fishing in the backwaters, between the ten thousand islands just south of Marco Island. They set down a cooler in the center of the canoe and John fixed a tiny motor to the square back of the 18 feet canoe. They sat down and John turned the motor on; twenty minutes later as they got far enough between the islands, he shut it down. They picked their oars and paddled noiselessly until they found a good spot. John anchored the canoe, and they secured the oars on its side to give themselves maximum maneuvering space. They had bought live baits, small fish and large shrimps.

Joan liked to use the fish bait. She was casting it, making it bounce on the water towards the mangroves then reeling it back to the canoe. John just hooked on a shrimp making sure he was not piercing its heart and threw his line a few feet from the canoe. In two hours, she caught a three-pound Bass, two Red Snappers, one pound each and a five pounds mullet. She caught some catfishes, which she threw back in the water.

"They are good to eat but a little too slimy for my taste." She said.

John used the shrimps and caught a few snooks and many catfishes. He kept the biggest snook and returned his other catches to their element. Small snooks have too many bones and not enough meat but the snook is considered the best catch in Florida. A big manatee surfaced close to the canoe and looked kindly at them. "It must be weighting many hundred pounds." Said John very interested.
They stop fishing to observe it. It came very close to the canoe and Joan patted its head. After a while it left.
They filleted the fish right there and threw the remains in the water; they wrapped the meat in plastic and placed it in the cooler covering it with ice. A few hours had passed already and they had enough fish so they returned to the condo to prepare their feast. Fried fish, French-fries and two bottles of excellent white wine.

Joan's children arrived at Miami International airport Sunday late morning. Joan hugged them and kissed them on the cheeks.
"I am so pleased to see you," said Joan. "Let me introduce you to the man that has brightened my last few days."
Nancy and Garry shook hands with John and were surprised by his iron grip. John did not squeeze their hands very hard, just firmly. That was enough though for anyone to understand that he was still a man of exceptional strength and fitness.
They took Alligator Alley to cross Florida and stop at midway for a snack. They stopped again about fifteen miles from Naples to have a look at the biggest alligators you could find in Florida. Hundreds of them were lying side by side on the bank of a narrow arm of unmoving water.

"How they can find enough to eat for all of them is beyond me." said John.

"Can you imagine driving on that road before they fixed fences on both sides?" said Joan. "People must have been blocked sometimes and probably reached Naples with a few teeth marks on the bumpers."

That night, they had Szechwan food; spicy orange beef, spicy shrimps vegetable, white rice, won ton soup and egg rolls. Joan had warmed up some sake and they had a good time. John told them the whole story about Ghama-2, the book, and his contacts with the guardians, the incoming mission and his intention to have them join his team.
Joan showed them her new painting. Our painting she said, since I spent almost all the money I had kept for your inheritance.
Nancy and Garry believed John. They felt his sincerity and even though the story was preposterous, they had the intuition that it was true; all of it...
They were in awe, excited but certainly not ready to leave their life the day after to go there.

"It's great," said Nancy, "that we don't have to die all at the same time. I don't think I would abandon my life here before I even have a chance to do some of the things I had plan for my future. But now we have it all, our life on earth and then an afterlife on Ghama-2. That's cool."

"It's cool," said John, "but there are some important changes coming to your life. I hope you will accept what you will be proposed next week..." And John wouldn't tell what. Nancy and Garry were very interested to know everything about John and they questioned him for hours on end. He had to tell them about his past missions, his experience, his philosophy and what he thought was the purpose of life.

"I once read about a man, the last man alive for humanity had been destroyed." said John. "He was traveling from world to world, asking the inhabitants what they thought was the purpose of life and if they knew about God. He was answered foolish things and even got imprisoned for asking on one of the worlds. He finally reached the world whose inhabitants were the oldest in the Universe. Giant cockroaches peopled it and he went to meet with the king of the cockroaches and asked it the question.

"Is there a God," asked the man, "does He care about us, is there heaven or a purpose to life?"

"There is indeed a God," the cockroaches' king told him, "and I had lunch with Him quite a few times. That was a very long time ago for cockroaches are immortals. God kept forgetting and loosing the tread of our conversation. He always had his mind somewhere else. But there is no heaven, I asked Him and he also told me sternly that there was no purpose to life. What the heck would it have a purpose for? Tell me, He said. You just mess around that's it. That is what He said."

"Well that is just a story," added John, "and I am not going to let the cockroaches of a disillusioned writer influence my beliefs. But it came to my mind that if we want to have an afterlife in heaven, we might have to build it ourselves; we may have to build heaven ourselves and find a way to take the people souls there."

"And how will we do that?" asked Nancy.

"This, I don't know." replied John. "But if we succeed with our mission, we will be able to transform ourselves into Godlike beings and who knows, we might then be able to do it."

Nancy and Garry loved John's presence for he was quite a storyteller but more than that, he was so intensely present, so magnetic. It was evident that they really liked him and it was mutual.
The next two days passed very quickly, everyone was living the best time of their lives. John realized that Garry was lacking the necessary self-confidence that would allow him to face difficult challenges. Garry would naturally aim for the less difficult ones. He did not have great ambitions and he was not interested in becoming rich or famous. He knew how to enjoy himself though and there was no one better than him to make friends. He was enthusiastic, laughing heartily at little things and praising everyone for their achievements or their talents. Never would he be boasting about himself. He was keeping in excellent shape; he was not tall, 5'8", very thin, 140 lbs. but solidly built for his size.

Nancy is very different, John thought, *she is very ambitious, and competitive. She wants to handle all kind of challenges; she has a hot temper not yet under full control. She likes sports and very few people would be able to follow her on roller blades on a hilly terrain. She is an excellent jogger too. She even did some boxing. She is intelligent, interested in people, she makes friend easily and she is so much fun to be with that she keeps them even if she gets sometimes impatient with them. She wants to become a doctor and a psychologist and help people.*

Her boyfriend killed himself with an overdose suffering from manic-depression and one of her friends, a girl with whom she shared an apartment for a while almost did the same suffering from the very same sickness. That little Nancy has been hurt, too much for her young age.

John liked her a lot. He liked them both a lot and thought it will be great to have these two in his team.

What they need, John thought, *is to go through the hardships and the humiliations of a boot camp; a few years in the military would forge them...*

It was Wednesday morning and I was the first one to get to Joan's condo. I shook hands with Joan and John and then Joan introduced me to Garry and Nancy. A few minutes later, the reverend father knocked at the door.

Once he had shaken hands with everyone I told John and Joan that I had ask the reverend father myself to come earlier for I had to have a private discussion them before the rest of the chosen arrive.

"I became last Friday a very rich man," I said, "and my friends I just don't need the money. I wouldn't know how to use so much money for I am just an artist and I am happy with what I already have. So, I have decided to reimburse you the money you spent at the auction. But then I believe that each one of us should be able to afford any luxury we may need or wish for the rest of our lives on earth.

In each of these envelopes, John and Joan, you will find $5 million dollars and for you reverend Father is an envelope with $70 million dollars; you might use it to build a church and an hospital in Somalia when you return there. I also have an envelope for your friend Tom, John, with the same amount."

"Thank you Richard." said John and Joan simultaneously. "Thank you my son." said the reverend father.

There was no need for them to tell me anything else and I would not have liked it either.

"You look quite surprised Nancy and Garry," I said, "you have probably thought that I was a con artist that had taken advantage of your mother but you see, she is too good at reading people. I doubt anyone could hide his intentions to her and the same is true for John."

There was a knock at the door; Joan went to open it and a tall man with the look of Arnold Swartzenneger walked in.

"My name is Tom, I am John's friend and I came here to meet him."

"Hello Tom," said John joyously, "let me introduce you to my friends."

We were now sitting altogether in the living room, all the seven of our group; Nancy and Garry had brought a chair from the dinning room and seemed to find that reunion most enjoyable.

"So you are the brave guy that went back to Pakistan to rescue my sweetheart." said Joan gratefully.

"John once saved my father's life, I had to do it." answered Tom seriously.

There wasn't an ounce of pride in his reply and I could tell by the exchanges we had with him already that Tom was not trying to get the admiration of anyone. He was calm, sure of himself, sincere and warm to everyone. He really impressed me and I was sure it was the same for everyone else.

A little later the other people arrived, Bill Rates, Donald Rumps, Krishna, and Nicole Teaseman.

John thanked them all for coming.

"Most of you," said John, "were never contacted by the guardians and yet, you read the Ghama-2 books and bought one of the paintings at a very high cost. It shows to me that either God or the Guardians subtly influenced each one of you and it also shows that you are capable of listening to your gut feelings, your intuition.

One more thing you are all very lucky people and now luck has played on your side again and you will be awarded an afterlife on this very exciting world Ghama-2. Maybe luck is an ability, a kind of sixth sense genetically transmitted from lucky parents; who knows, the universe is so mysterious.

Last night, I communicated with the Guardians and asked them if they could produce a map with the emplacement of the two humans' cities on Ghama-2, Jungle Town and New Alexandria and the emplacement of the abandoned city. They showed it to me."

Suddenly, there was a fog in the living room and an intense light formed in the center of the fog; it lasted for a few seconds only, maybe less and then as quickly as it had formed, it was gone and floating over the table was a map of a section of Ghama-2.

We were caught by surprise, none of us expected it; it was evident by the way we looked at each other.

"So," said John, "here is the map they showed me. Some of us here, Tom, Nancy and Garry came to my invitation; and even if they didn't buy a painting, they are co-owners of one. Every one of us is going to Ghama-2.

There will be at least three groups of seven people who will wake up there; that's what the Guardians told me and it means that you Richard, has some more paintings to do.

The three groups will not be awoken at the same place but the members of each group will be awoken in proximity of each other and at the same time.

One group, I was told, will wake up at proximity of New Alexandria which is located on the seacoast of a large island and one group near Jungle Town which is located a few thousand miles away on the same continent. The lost city is on the other side of that large sea.

Our two groups may never meet. We are eleven people here; Queen Elisabeth could not come. There were 14 paintings at the auction, access key paintings that will open the world of Ghama-2 to their owners; twelve of them were bought and Richard has decided to give one to his daughter Helen. She doesn't believe the story but will become never the less part of one of the teams. That means that one more person plus Queen Elisabeth will join with you later.

The president of the United States invites all of us to come to Camp David, which is where we are going now. I didn't want to tell anyone before because I have reasons to believe that we are being watched and may even be attacked before we have time to prepare ourselves for the mission.

The president of United States is awaiting us, so let's go. We can walk to the private airport located five minutes away from here, at the end of the street. I will answer your questions on our way."

"Not that fast, now;" said Donald Rump who had been watching the map like all of us, the map that was still floating in the air, "I don't want to offend you in any way but I certainly want to take a closer look at that map. Can you hand it to me please?"

John understood Donald Rump reaction; he had forgotten that he was here with presidents of very large corporations, decision makers and for those people, the sudden apparition of a map from nowhere, from the very atoms of air, was a shocking event.

He handed the map to Donald who squeezed it between his fingers and rub the lines with his thumb.

"It doesn't have the feel of paper," said Donald to Bill Rates that had just moved closer.

"Let me have it for a moment," said Bill in an engaging way.

Donald handed him the map.

"You know John," said Donald, "I didn't believe the story. Richard mailed me the books assuring me that there was more to it than just fiction and he added the invitation to the auction.

I read the books and liked the story and thought that if some people are going to get an exciting afterlife I should be amongst them. So just in case, I decided to come to the auction. It is just one and a half hour car driving from my Palm Beach mansion and I had planned to be in Palm Beach at that time. So I came and got excited by the auction and decided to buy one after I saw our reverend father getting one for $5,000.00. That looked miraculous even though I didn't believe in miracles.

And now, that map appeared from nowhere and it is the first thing ever seen on Earth that is not affected by gravity.

I am amazed and suddenly I must admit that I wonder if the whole thing isn't the truth after all."

"Nothing else than the truth, Donald." answered John seriously. "I have really talked with the Guardians. There are with us right now, listening to our conversations."

"What do you think about all that Reverend Father?" asked Donald. "The presence of those aliens, the Guardians, is it not turning the scriptures into a fallacy? I thought that Christianity has been about the creation of man in seven days… and by the way, reverend you are the only one here that doesn't seem under shock with the sudden appearance of that map."

"My son, I have seen miracles happen before." answered the reverend Father with an engaging smile. "Those Guardians have probably evolved from a more humble beginning like all living things in the creation. They came from God's universal creation and the theory of evolution is not against the teachings of Jesus.

Nothing is simple; everything is complex, like a multifaceted tapestry; the tapestry of the universe. What is happening today is wondrous, amazing, marvelous and exciting. I am not sure that it is a miracle though; it may be the product of extremely advanced technology or highly developed mental powers. What our own technology can do today would have look miraculous two thousands years ago, isn't it?

I have seen ghosts, spirits and Demons as I traveled across Africa; I have seen what Black magic could do to the unfortunate victims of sorcerers so I am not under shock with what happened today.

Moreover, I have prayed and asked God for guidance and I believe that those spirits, the Guardians, have only good intentions in regards to us. They wanted me to come along for they believe that I can somehow have a good influence on you and the other members of our group. I may also be able to protect you against Demons.

There is also the saying that very rich people are not supposed to get easily to Heaven and Ghama-2 might very well become that place we are all hoping for. Is it not said that it will be more difficult for a very rich person to get to heaven than for a camel to pass through the eye of a needle? So my dear Donald, you may need to talk to me in private before you leave this world."

"I am sure he has a lot of sins to repent for." said Nicole Teaseman tease fully.

"And what about you? Charming woman! How many men have sinned because of you?" replied Donald lustfully.

We started to make fun of each other under the approval look of the reverend.

Bill flexed the map paper, folded a corner of it and pressed it firmly between his fingers and when he released the corner, the paper regained his previous appearance without a trace of having been folded.

"If you don't mind John, I would like to cut just a tiny piece of it for further analysis. Would you have a pair of scissors Joan?"

"Sure; just a moment Bill." replied Joan agreeably.

"Can I hold it please?" asked Nicole in her most charming way.

Bill handed her the map and after a moment it was Tom's turn to ask for it.

We all held it in our hands, flexing it, pulling at it slightly, and rubbing our fingers on the ink lines.

I thought that it was made of plastic but I wasn't sure.

"Here are the scissors." said Joan as she handed them to Bill.

Bill took back the map in one hand and tried to cut a tiny piece of it to no avail. The paper seemed to slip in between the scissors blades.

"Would you have a razor blade, Joan? And maybe something to put under the map, a piece of wood would do."

Joan brought him a blade and the wooden square she used for cutting the vegetables and Bill put the map on the wood and tried to cut a piece of it with the razor blade but after repeated trials, the map paper showed not even a trace of abrasion; it resisted to all his efforts.

"Let me try!" said Donald who could hardly believe it.

"Let me see if the ink can be washed out with water or solvent." said Bill once Donald had given up.

We tried everything but the ink resisted just as well as the paper to all kind of abuses.

I thought we should try to burn it but was afraid to damage this very precious artifact. Donald didn't have such worries as he pulled out a lighter from his pocket but the paper was totally unaffected by the flame.

"All right," said Bill Rates, "I am convinced that I didn't spend all that money for nothing. That paper isn't made of any known substance thus I have to conclude that the Guardians exist and they are with us right now. The next conclusion is that we are going to get that afterlife on Ghama-2."

"I believe it too." said Donald. "But now that I am convinced that I will one day wake up on that world with six other partners to face all kind of predators and aliens, I feel that there is an unfair situation here."

"What do you mean Donald?" asked John with the air of a man that had already guessed what was coming up.

"Richard told me that you and your friend Tom are the best close combat fighters the CIA ever had and then there is Father O'Leary that look just as strong as an ox plus Richard who seemed to know how to defend himself… and what do I have to help me? The charming but defenseless Nicole Teaseman, plus Queen Elisabeth the Fifth, and Richard's daughter; there is also Bill who is quite the opposite of a James Bond… highly unfair situation isn't it? Maybe the Guardians should rearrange the two teams."

"Not as unfair as you think Donald," I replied, before John could say a word.

"What do you think Tom?" asked Donald. "You have been very quiet, unperturbed by the apparition of the map and you remained silent. I can use a man like you and if you join my team, you will have the charming company of Nicole."

"I prefer to stay with the first group." answered Tom.

"If you let me explain Donald," I said, "there will be an extraordinary fighter in your group, possibly even better than John and Tom."

At that moment, there was a knock at the door. Joan went to open the door and here he was, walking inside with the agility and grace of a feline, Krishna.

"Hi Krishna," said John, "I was hoping to see you for our meeting and I am very glad you came."

109

"Hi everyone, sorry that I am late but there was an incident; some people tried to kill me as I left the Hotel to come here. Three gunmen were waiting for me."

"Did they follow you here?" asked John.

"No, and we don't have to worry about them anymore."

"Krishna," I am glad to see you," I said, "I was just telling Donald who complained about the unfair distribution of fighting experts in the two teams that he will beneficiate with the contribution of possibly the best fighter in the world and that is you my friend.

Donald, this man, Krishna, will be an incredible asset to your team; moreover Bill's ingenuity might prove even more valuable. You will have a genius in your group and even if he doesn't look formidable now, he might be even bigger and stronger than you in the new body the Guardians will give him."

"I don't think there will be any weakling," added John, "the Guardians have already told me that they will give some improvements to our new bodies and if they can make an indestructible map from the air you can imagine what they can do to improve us."

Bill brought the map to Krishna.

"There was flash of light and that map appeared just over the table a few minutes ago." said Bill. "We tried to cut it and burn a corner and it resisted to flame and blades, we can not even scratch it."

"It is a map of Ghama-2." added John.

John told him about our conversation prior to his arrival.

"I would like to have that map, do you mind?" Ask Bill looking at John.

"I would like to have it too." said Donald instantly.

"Can I have it?" asked Nicole sweetly. "I would frame it and put it in my living room beside my painting."

"Well, I see that everyone here want it; I am not the one to decide for the map appeared in Joan's condo and thus she should be the one to decide who will have it."

"Thank you dearest for handing me the hot potato." answered Joan with a smile. "I think the map should belong to the United States government; we should bring it with us to the president of the States at Camp David; he will decide what to do with it."

"That's fair enough." said Donald. "All right let's go.

Donald was taking the leadership, he was used to be the one to boss everyone around; it was not malicious, and it was done without even a thought about it. I looked at Bill Rates and John for these two were also natural leaders but I saw in their expression that neither had felt offended; after all Donald was the one who had delayed our departure and it was normal that he was the one to say let's go.

John explained on the way that every one should and will be trained to the art of war. Some of the best strategists, psychologists, intelligence experts, and combat teachers were already there waiting for us.

"We will be there for three months. Each room will have computers and everything you need to keep your business going and you will be able to use the private jets for some of your appointments. It will be a change to your routine, a period of your life away from the usual stress and I am sure that you will enjoy that experience.
Then everyone will go back to his own life but it will be important to learn how things are made. We should become jacks-of-all-trades, able to build with our own hands almost anything from clothes to sailboat. We shall learn medicine, even how to make surgery. The government will help us. We will be given special training in military hospitals. We shall become expert swordsmen and archers, knives and axes throwers. "

John looked at Nancy and Garry, and said, "If you agree to it, I wish to send you, my new young friends to a boot camp at the end of our three months training at Camp David."

They looked at him with a non-committal expression. It seemed to me that everything was suddenly rushing too fast for them; they had their own routine in Montreal, their friends, their own projects and now the world around them seems to be in turmoil, everything was changing. They were embarking on a train with no known destination, a train going so fast that they may very well be unable to jump out.

I saw their expression and came closer. I took them by the arms and told them:
"You look worried and I guess that you are thinking about your present studies. You don't want to fail your courses and you are wondering if it is OK to leave everything behind and follow us at Camp David. Then there is the boot camp...Let me tell you one thing, we usually go to school because we want to find a job, make some good money and enjoy life. We also want to be proud of ourselves, right?"

They were silent and I went on:
"If you come with us, you will study all kind of things, very useful things. Not many young persons your age would have the chance to learn that kind of things. In the military, you can go to University and become doctors or physical trainers or whatever interests you. And beside that, you don't need to worry anymore about money; I got an envelope for you.

I gave them the envelope and they stop to look inside.

Everybody else stop too.

"Five million dollars! I can't believe it." shouted Nancy.
"Five million dollars" Repeated Garry not believing his eyes.
"And I have an envelope for you too Tom." said John, as he remitted him his five million dollars envelope.

I looked at Tom's face as he pulled his check from the envelope.

"Will it bounce?" Asked Tom looking at me straight in the eyes for the check had my signature.

112

"No Tom, it won't." I said.

"Thank you Richard, I believe it is about time for a change of career, that money will change my life."

"I don't need the money," I said, "and I made a lot of it thanks to you Bill. I thought that we should all enjoy whatever is left of our lives and I have a feeling that it will not last very long."

Nancy looked at me for a moment.

"That's not a prank? Is it? You are giving us real money, five million dollars?" She said.

"Why not," I answered, "I don't need much for myself and I don't even know how to spend the interest of the money I just made. Besides, between the books and my paintings, I make enough money for my needs. Like John I am dying, I got stomach cancer. With God's help, I might be able to complete the third book of the Ghama-2 saga before I watch the flowers growing by the roots. So you are rich, both of you and young. You don't need to worry about anything, just enjoy yourselves, right? Cool?"

"Cool, cool," they shouted. Everyone was looking at them. Everyone was smiling; they could all remember what it was to be young and everyone kind of shared their happy and joyous moment.

I started to sing a French ballad; a traveler's song and everybody were singing my verses after me as we proceeded towards our destination. We were happy, singing and laughing all the way to the private airport.

"Ils ont des chapeaux ronds, vive la Bretagne Ils ont des chapeaux ronds, vivent les Bretons ton, ton, ton, soin, soin, soin, soin."

Then once we got there by the private jet, before embarking, I shouted: Hip hip hip, yay, hip hip hip, hurrah! And everyone shouted after me.

Well, it is not every day that you are embarking on a trip that will carry you to another world with the mission to save mankind and to win immortality. So we were all feeling elation, and we were all very grateful to those guardians that were watching us right now.

I was thanking them all the time and I am sure that my companions were doing the same.

There were double rows of seats on each side of the small jet. John sat with Joan. They talked for a while about the recent events.
"You know John," said Joan. "I have thought about the new members who will constitute the second group of chosen. They are very interesting people. There is that quiet genius, Bill Rates. He never tried to be recognized, he doesn't try to attract other's interest, and he looks so calm. I like him a lot. And what about this one hundred millions he gave for the last painting; that was spectacular, awesome."

"Yes," answered John. "This man is somebody and may very well be the one that will succeed to activate one of the mechanisms, the enhancing and knowledge transfer mechanisms left in the abandoned city. He might be the most important man for that mission. Who knows?"

"Possibly," said Joan, "but other factors could be as important as computer knowledge or human genius. For example, Les Semeurs may have left principles or powers that might be activated only in the presence of a combination of a species member's qualities; or maybe by telepathy or by telekinesis or even great empathy. There might be activated fences that will not let anyone pass without a certain intellectual level or soul quality level.

Maybe someone must have a body or a brain that could be enhanced to an extremely high level to be let through. Or maybe we will need God's help; who knows if Father O'Leary might not be the key person amongst us."

"Wonderful Joan," said John. "You don't lack imagination. But first of all we have to find that city. Even if the Guardians give us a map, we won't be able to use it and we will be on hostile ground. We will have to fight our way up to that city and again we still have to find it…just to find it will necessitate a lot of intuition.

114

"The Guardians might give us the ability to feel the direction to the city, John." said Joan. "Otherwise all of this would be useless."

"You are right," said John, "they told me they will rebuild us with some improvement; that ability to feel its emplacement might be one of those improvements."

"You told me that you often got away from tight situations using a kind of sixth sense, John," said Joan, "if the Guardians give your new body some improvements over the present one, they will probably be careful in not taking away that special ability."

"I certainly hope so," replied John, "that sixth sense of feeling impending danger would perhaps save our lives as well as our ability to fight as a group and to maintain a team spirit.

We will need the help of the local people already there on Ghama-2, our descendants. Someone amongst us has got to be a natural leader able to raise an army of followers. Maybe a master politician or a master preacher could do it. I know I am not one of those and I don't see anyone amongst us that can do it except that very strange Father O'Leary."

"But there is still one more member to be added to the second team, one not yet amongst us who will buy the remaining painting. Maybe he will be the one with that kind of ability," said Joan.

I was listening to John and Joan conversation having taken a seat right behind them and I had a surprise for them. I had one of my paintings delivered to the airplane before our meeting at Joan's condo. I had put it into a large leather case and I intended to offer it to the president of the United States.
This man would be able to raise an army of followers after all he had been reelected against all odds. He had the television chains, the newspapers and even the CIA all working against him and an opponent that used the most negative campaign to destroy his image and yet, he had won his reelection. That man I admired, he was no ninny, no puppet; he had his principles and he had done

115

his very best for his country, he would be a great asset
to the second team and a good companion for my daughter.

We arrived at Camp David in middle afternoon. It was
such a beautiful place, a place where a president could
find the peace of mind and the rest necessary to go on.
The ambiance would naturally lead to agreements and good
sentiments. The whole world had been improved by the
decisions taken here by powerful leaders and they all
loved it.

A majordomo directed us to our assigned rooms. Once I
got to mine, I asked the majordomo if he would take care
of my painting suitcase left into the airplane. I asked
him to bring it into the room where we were to meet the
president and hide it behind the open door.

Some of us had a nap after a good shower and others just
went out for a walk. We were expected at 6:00 PM at the
dinning room.

I had a shower and then went out immediately to walk one
of the trails winding its way into the nearby forest. I
walked for an hour and came upon a lake. There were
spruces and weeping willows and a few inviting large
rocks where one could sit and relax looking at the lake
and wondering on the mystery of life and that's exactly
what I did for the next hour. Then I regretfully left
that wonderful area and returned to the president
mansion.

They were there already, in the dinning room, all of
them along with the trainers and teachers. I had come
back just in time and felt relieve for I had forgotten
the passage of time sitting by the lake. It was 6:00
sharp as the President walked in.

John went to shake hand with the president and then
introduced each one of us, the fortunate chosen, and we
all shook hand with him before he went to sit at the end
of the table. Everyone sat in turn.

"I know you must be wondering why I am so interested in
the Ghama-2 story." said the president. "Well I have
reasons to believe the truth of it. I read the book and
I sensed a ring of truth to the story, intuition perhaps

116

but more than that, I felt a presence very close to me, telling me that I should do something about it. I wouldn't tell that to anyone else but you all bought the paintings; that means that you believe in supernatural, paranormal phenomenon."

"Mister President." started Donald.

"Please call me George," interrupted the president, "and that holds for everyone here."

"George," said Donald, "I am not a supernatural believer; I mean I was not before that map appeared from nowhere as we met at Joan's condo. Joan would you hand him the map."

Joan brought him the map and the president looked at it a little puzzled.

"The map is weightless, see! Moreover, the paper is indestructible; we tried to cut it and to burn it." Commented Bill Rates soberly.

"It represents the emplacement of the two human colonies and the lost city on Ghama-2." said John.

"I decided to give you the map," said Joan, "I believe it should belong to the United States government."

"Thank you." said the president. "So you won't laugh at me if I tell you that I have a strong intuition that I don't have much time left. I believe I am about to be killed. I made too many enemies. The Arab terrorists and the fanatic Muslim leaders of Iran and Iraq are plotting schemes for my assassination. I thought I should do whatever I can to help you; in fact, now that I see a tangible proof of the Guardians existence, I would give a lot to be one of the chosen myself."

"When you say a lot, would you give a million dollars?" I asked. "What's the value of an exciting afterlife for you?"

"It would be invaluable." George answered.

117

"Pardon me for the interruption," I said, "but it is possible for you to be part of the coming odyssey. I brought something with me, my last painting, the majordomo placed it behind that door."

I stood up and went to fetch it.

"Let me show you that painting George." I said as I pulled it out of the leather case.

The painting represented an orchard, and it had been done with very heavy strokes of my largest pallet-knife. The colors and the heavy texture add to the unique style to make it one of the most beautiful paintings I have ever made.

"Would you give a million dollars for it?" I asked. "This is your access key to Ghama-2."

I had a hard time keeping a straight face. For my eyes had cross John and Joan's faces, smiling in appreciation for the move. They guessed that I had it planned.

"Now mister President;" I said, "look at it; we can see behind the orchard two women and a boy gazing at the far horizon; a river cuts the grassland. The colors are soothing; there is immensity, that painting is yours if you are willing to spend a lot of money for it."

"How much?" asked the president. "I don't know; whatever you want. One million dollars even more if you wish..."

"We got a deal then," I said. "Please sign this invoice."

I picked it from my back pocket; it already had the name of the buyer, George W Wood, and the description of the painting. I took my pen and put down the numbers quickly; I wrote $500,000.00.

I am that gracious sometimes for who would not give a good discount to the president. I presented him the invoice for immediate signing.

Who knows, I thought, *we may be bombed right now and we need a natural leader with us.*

He signed it and asked me if I could wait after dinner
for the check.
"No problem," I said, "as long as I get it before the
day's end."

Does he think I will wait a month, I joked to myself
silently, *I should even feel a touch of irritation*.

I always made silent jokes for I would probably be the
only to laugh at them. The same for the songs, I sing
them inside my head and I always remember a good one.

I am done with people complaining about my singing; I
became a silent singer and joker, partying with myself,
living in a happy inside world.

"We just got our master politician," said John softly to
Joan's ear.

"Thank you mister President and welcome amongst the
chosen," I said.

"That is just wonderful," said Nicole Teaseman, "I feel
very comforted by your presence in our group, George."

"Thank you Nicole," said George, "I will do everything I
can to get you safely to the lost city."

"Now Donald," said the reverend father with his biggest
smile, "you should feel better now about the fairness of
the composition of our two teams; not only did you get
Krishna to help you in close combat but you have now the
most physical country leader in the world on your side.
Your group will be made of four men and three women, one
of the men is a genius, another one is the best close
combat fighter of possibly all times, another one is a
natural leader that can raise an army of followers if
need be, and you Donald, possibly the most cunning
weasel of the present time. Then you have the three
women; an irresistible beauty, a true queen and
Richard's daughter whom I believe to be quite an
extraordinary person."

"Thank you father O'Leary," said Donald, "I believe we
will make a great team and welcome in George."

I looked at Donald's face trying to find out his real feelings about the addition of the president to his group. Who is going to be the true leader? I wondered; George, Donald, Krishna or Bill the quiet genius…but Donald seemed genuinely pleased with that turn of event.

"Everyone must wonder," I said, "why he or she happened to be here at that table. For sure there is an element of luck but I mailed invitations to quite a few people that I thought very well suited for the coming expedition.

The Guardians wanted a priest or a preacher in each group; they were amazed at our concept of God and religions and had started to believe already in the presence of God. They thought that a priest would possibly be able to get God's help in case of imminent destruction by overwhelming forces. They believed there should be one in each group.

We got a Christian preacher here, Father O'Leary who will be in John's group. I thought I should select one of different belief for your group, mister president. One that may raise an army of followers and I chose one; he is an African American hell Raiser, a big mouth, and a joker; some of you have already guessed since he is sitting with us at this table; let's have a word from the undefeated, the one and only, Krishna, the best welterweight boxer of all time and the undefeated ultimate fighting champion."

Krishna stood up.

"Thank you Richard." He said. "It will be an honor for me to teach a few things to that group of sinners. If anyone needs a private conversation with me, I will be pleased to help."

Krishna sat down under our applause.

Everyone was laughing and saying "oh no, not you Krishna "but in fact we were all happy about it.

"Mister President," I added, "he will be in your group, you will have to ear his boastings all day long. He will probably try to convert everyone to his religious

120

beliefs and in case you don't know, he started a new religion and called it the Global Religion. I sent him the book and offered him to come to the auction. After reading the book he came and bought one of the paintings."

"I have to tell you my friends," said Krishna, "that I won't be with you for long. I was diagnosed with liver cancer just as I was about to achieve total control of my body through yoga and meditation. That's the irony of life or maybe God didn't want me to become overly proud of myself. Anyhow, my diet is down to no fat food and yet I have a hard time to digest the simplest meals.

So, I will teach you what I can about close combat and team fighting and the use of a latent sixth sense that I call ultimate awareness. I may be able to do it for two or three weeks at the most. John and Tom are possibly just as good as I am in fighting so they will be able to help me with the training and take over once I become too weak. The three of us will help the rest of you in learning as quickly as possible the art of killing and disabling enemies in close combat."

"I am sorry to hear about your sickness," said the president, "and this is why we should start the training tomorrow morning. In the afternoon, the warfare experts will train you on the art of army combat, the best strategies and so on."

We all gave a word of comfort to Krishna and soon everyone was talking at the same time. This first reunion was a very happy moment for us. The reverend father soon became the pole of attraction, he had such brilliant comments and questions that everyone started to question him. They wanted to know how it was in Africa and how he had managed to survive trying to Christianize the bloodthirsty Islamic fanatics in Somalia and Sudan. The reverend never tried to uplift himself or boast about his courage and fights and he had all kind of anecdotes to tell, amusing ones or ones that would lead the questioners to ponder about the mysterious ways of God.

The training started the day after; physical and combat training in the mornings and teachings in the afternoons. There were snacks in between and joyous dinners at night.

I could hardly walk or even bend myself that first night and it was the same for Joan and John. We were not young anymore; late sixties for me, early seventies for Joan and middle eighties for John and we all went to bed early.

The next morning, it was tough to hold a sword even if the sword was made of very light aluminum alloy. We had ample protection; moreover, the sword tip was squared and there was no cutting edge. John was teaching me the basic of swordplay while Tom was teaching Joan.

Krishna was busy teaching open hand combats to the rest of the teams.

There were so many tricks but the most important as John was telling me was to sense your opponent next move and be ready to pounce or parry.

"Empty your mind Richard," John was telling me, "you must not think, you have already told your body to react instantly and I have taught you what to do. Let go all tension, you are full of energy, happy, confident and relaxed but in maximum alertness."

John moved and I counter moved and it went on and on for an hour at the end of which I could not hold the sword anymore.

"I quit for today John," I said, "I just can't move anymore; I am too tired."

"You are learning quickly Richard and I am very pleased with your progress; in a few weeks you will become quite good at it." John said seriously.

And that felt sweet, suddenly, I was very proud of myself.

Over the following weeks, we came to know each other pretty well and every one of the chosen revealed oneself as a most likable and interesting individual. Tom was a very quiet man and would rarely open to the others but he was good audience for people like Donald, Nicole and the reverend father who were the most talkative.

John was the second most interesting person of the group after father O'Leary. Everyone was quite different, some like Bill and Joan would prefer the background to the stage but would be extraordinary interesting when forced to give their opinion.

Garry and Nancy, Joan's children, were having a good time for they were laughing at silly little events all the time. They were young without the slightest worries in the world and they had a lot of fun. Garry was teasing everyone, pulling pranks on the president or the reverend father just as often as with everybody else and this in total disregard for their importance.

They were learning fast and everyone liked them.

One day John asked the reverend father why he was not interested to practice sword fight.

"I got my quarterstaff, son," replied the reverend father, "and that has served me well over the years. With my staff I can push back someone without hurting him and if that is not enough, well I can show you what we can do with it."

"Why don't you reverend?" replied John. "I am most interested in all kind of weapons and it would be instructive to see what you can do against a good and young swordsman. Would you fight Tom?"

"Certainly if it can help the teams." replied the reverend father.

Tom was right there and he had heard the conversation.

"All right reverend, let's put on our helmet and our protecting gears, I wouldn't want to hurt you." said Tom amicably.

"I don't want to hurt you either my dear Tom." answered the reverend, kindly.

They put on the protective gears and faced each other.

"Are you ready father?" asked Tom.

"Yes my son, as ready as one can be."

Tom tried a Pointe to the father belly; he hit straight forward at full speed making sure he would stop his movement just as the square tip of his sword would touch the reverend father but he never came close; the father parried easily with his quarterstaff without even moving his body. Tom then tried to hit the father on his helmet but again the stroke was easily deflected. The father then backed up one step and holding his quarterstaff with both hands tried to sweep Tom legs from the ground.

It had been done very fast, faster than anyone could expect from a big man like the father. Tom tried to parry with his sword as he realized that he wouldn't have the time to jump but there was no way he could deflect it, the sword was too light in weight and he could not hold it strongly enough to deflect the terrific blow from the long and solid oak stick. The staff hit the sword and went on to Tom legs. Tom jumped to prevent having his bones crushed by the blow but the reverend was already stopping his stroke. The stick never the less swept Tom who drop the sword, felled on his hands ready to jump at the reverend. At that moment, He felt the light touch of the baton on his helmet and he knew that he had lost the fight. The reverend father could have crushed his skull easily had he wanted to.

"That impressed me a lot, reverend father." said John with admiration. "I have heard before that a good swordsman would lose a fight against a good fighter armed only with a stick; and now you have proven it. Beside that, I never thought you could be so quick, congratulation, I am very glad to have you in my team."

"You impressed me too." said Tom with awe in his voice. "You are terrific."

The days passed and Krishna became very ill. The doctor came to tell us one night as we were having dinner altogether that Krishna was dying and wanted to talk to us. We left our plates and walked quickly to his room.

"It is true, right? The whole story about Ghama-2 Richard?" asked Krishna in a whisper.

124

"Yes Krishna," I replied, "it is true. In a moment, as you let go, your soul will be snatched by the Guardians and you will wake up in a young and vigorous body."

"So long then my friends," said Krishna, "see you in heaven."

Krishna died as soon as he finished his sentence. I could feel a movement of air rushing over the bed and it was over as quickly as it has come.

A few days later, as John was teaching the guys open hand combat, I decided to take a walk.

"Where are you going Richard?" asked Joan.

"I am too tired to do anything else than having a walk and I know of a beautiful place where I can sit by a lakeshore and relax. Would you like to come?"

"Sure, let's go." replied Joan happily.

We walked in silence through the woods and were rewarded by the sighting of a few deers and hares and a flock of partridges. Each time one of us would detect one, one would indicate silently to the other what he or she had just spotted. I felt certain complicity between the two of us and warmed up even more to her presence on my side. We reached my favorite spot on the lakeshore and sat on the big rocks gazing at the far shore of the beautiful lake.

"So what do you think Richard?" asked Joan as she caught me deep into reverie.

"I was thinking about you Joan." I replied. "In my late sixties I can look backward to a long span of life in which I met a lot of people and yet no woman has ever impressed me as much as you did. You are a truly remarkable person Joan."

Joan knew that I was not making a pass at her and I would have not have done it for a few reasons among which was my sense of loyalty to John and also the knowledge that I was in no way as remarkable as John was. This guy was a true hero, tall, handsome, and cultured with an imposing personality and a leadership quality that rivals with the president.

"Thank you Richard," said Joan, "I find you myself most interesting. I am in love with John but I am attracted to you. I noticed that you warm up every time I come close to you and I share that attraction."

"Then can I hug you and give you one kiss?" I asked not believing what I had just said.

Joan took my hand and pulled me to her and I hugged her and kiss her passionately.

"Oh my God, I will remember that moment for the rest of my life." I said, totally filled with emotion and overwhelmingly in love with her.

Oh my God, I thought, *I would make love to her just right now if it weren't for John.*

Joan was looking at me when I had those shameful thoughts and she caught all of it.

"Let's go back." Joan said as she squeezed my hand.

We watched the news at night for the world was in bad shape right now. The terrorist's organizations had grown up in strength with the open help of Iran, Syria, Palestine and North Korea and the secret help of Saudi Arabia, Pakistan, Jordan, Sudan, and Lebanon. In fact, there wasn't one Arab country that wasn't tolerating their presence.

Israel people were desperate for they had begun to think that sooner or later Iranian's nuclear bombs would annihilate them. There were treats already; Iran had signed defense treaties with Syria and Lebanon. The United States army was still trying to build up democracy in Iraq and fighting an army of insurgents and they hadn't had the resources to attack Iran and destroy the clerical leadership before they had finally built up their nuclear weapons.

Russia was in trouble with Islamic terrorists too and they were no more an enemy of the States; China though was becoming stronger every year and the Chinese were the great looming menace, the Damocles sword suspended over the democratic world.

"We are heading into disaster," said the president at one of our dinners, "and there is nothing I can do. The only way to save the world would be in destroying most of it and I can't take the decision of killing billions of innocent people."

One day, John was having an evening walk in the park with Joan when he heard a tremendous bang in his brain. He realized that he was now floating at the ceiling height of a room; he was talking with Joan, declaring his love to her and he was just a neutral observer. Then he was again seeing himself in another place, he was shooting at someone; he saw the whole scene, completely neutral, without regrets or pride. He went on seeing and reliving all other important moments of his life and they were always moments of relationship with someone.

Then he was floating over Joan at Camp David, he saw her in tears crying for help. He didn't feel any pain; he understood instinctively that the pain Joan was experiencing was a necessary part of growing up.

He loved her very much but didn't feel sadness. In fact he felt so good; he was in such happiness; that it would be impossible to describe it to another person. There was a light attracting him but before he would go there to investigate, he felt snatched by something. Some spirits were communicating to him reassuringly and suddenly he woke up far, far away.

John's death pained everyone. He was loved and cherished like a father you are proud of. Joan was devastated and Garry and Nancy suffered the loss of a father for the second time.
Many of the strong people gravitating around John cried that day. We proceeded with his funeral here at Camp David and put his ashes into ground. Father O'Leary said the last prayers:
"We pray you, Oh God, to forgive John's sins. He was a true hero to his country, a decent and kind man admired by his acquaintances and cherished by his friends. A man with whom we could sit comfortably and talk for hours on

end. We are all pained by his loss but we hope to meet
with him again on the strange world of Ghama-2.
If you allow this to happen, John will be a leader of
one of our two groups. Please God give him your guidance
and blessing, please forgive us, humans, for all the
atrocities, the violence, and the injustice that has
been our lot. Some of us are good; we can still
become a mature and kind specie and accomplish things
that You might approve of. We need your help oh God,
please don't abandon us. Amen."

"You know Joan," I said, " even though I am repeating
myself, I got to assure you that for him there will be
no time lapse, he will wake up in a moment only, with
us. For our souls will be picked up by the Guardians on
their way back to the future, to their real time on
Ghama-2. We experience the pain of his passing knowing
how lonely it will be for us without him but shortly we
will all be together again."

Once the training camp was over, Joan and I returned to
Naples to resume with our routine while Garry and Nancy
went to the boot Camp as John wished for. They thought
they owe him that much and beside it would be another
experience.

Nancy and Garry told me later on about their experience
there. Nancy didn't like the bullies in charge of the
recruits. These people were ass kickers. They loved to
smash people, to take away from them their last shred of
dignity; to make them cry, to break them and then fumble
like amateurs in rebuilding them. Well she had to go
through that and she decided that she would give them
respect; she would smile when they wanted it and cry
when they hoped for it. She knew that with her training
at Camp David, she would be amongst the best recruits
but she did not expect any acknowledgement for her
efforts and she knew she would get none.

She would carry a mental umbrella and their nastiness
would not even touch her. That is what she had decided
and she went through the whole boot camp without a
scratch to her personality and she even enjoyed it
at times.

When she came out of it, she came out with much more
control over her emotions; she came out in top shape and

with many new friends. Over all, it had been a great experience.

For Garry, the whole boot camp had been just the opposite; it had been a nightmare. He was still stuttering and was being mocked up for it and ridiculed by his superiors. He was too emotional and could not take all the injustice, the shouting, and the unfair treatments. He forgot at times that it would not last forever and often broke down in tears and despair.

Garry thought of quitting almost every single day. He just couldn't take it. But every time he thought about quitting, he remembered his promise to John and I that he would go through the whole booting camp. So he also went through and came out a better Man; much more disciplined and tolerant and with a much better control of his emotions.

At the end of it, Nancy and Garry decided to go to the same University and stay in the military for the next five to ten years. They argued together sometimes but they always shared the same friends, ever since Nancy started to bring her youngest friends at home. Garry would play with his sister and the little girls she was bringing home and later on he was still sharing her teenagers' friends.

Garry knew what women wanted and he could get into his bed almost anyone of the most beautiful girls around. He was elegantly clothed and smelled good at all time. He was a gentleman, a listener and a questioner. He loved to talk for hours on the phone, with everyone. His presence was very pleasant. He was a Don Juan who never took pride in it. In fact, he was the opposite of a boasting guy and he could keep secrets too so he was the ideal confidant for all his friends.

Every time they could get permission, they came to Naples to spend some time with their mother and they would chat about every thing and sometimes about Ghama-2.

Chapter six: The destruction of the world.

A few days after our return to Naples, I went to see Joan at the library and we spoke of our experiences at Camp David.

"There is a nice golf course right across the street from your condo," I said. "Have you ever played golf?"

"Yes I played golf for years before I got married and a few times more afterwards with David. I would need some practice though before playing again."

"Me too," I said. "I haven't played since June of last year. I had two roller-blades accidents inside of one month and each time, I fell on my left wrist. For many months I couldn't play, and then I started to write my books, there was a feeling of urgency about the writing of the first two books so I decided that I had no more time for golf. But now, we are done with the training and we don't have much to do."

"Would you like to play golf with me?" asked Joan. "Is it why you brought the subject on?"

"Yes, that's why I brought it on." I replied. "You know Joan, we can practice together for a while and then, once we get in golf shape, we would start playing two or three times a week together."

"Al right Richard, let's do it."

"May I suggest every morning for ten days? I would come to your place at 7:00 AM; we would work out for ten minutes, jog for thirty minutes and then jump in the swimming pool right in front of the golf course. We will swim for ten minutes and then move up to the driving range for half an hour of practice ending it at the chipping green."

"We could finish it off with a chipping and putting competition." suggested Joan.

"Good idea," I said, "that will be fun and I would bet that in ten days we will shoot in the eighties from the first game on."

"Great," said Joan, "let's play golf, it will be a change in a life that suddenly became quite boring."

We met almost every day from then on and became very close friends. I had never been a golf maniac and never played more than three times a week but I used to score in the seventies or low eighties for I was playing a good short game and usually drove the alleys.

I showed Joan how to practice the golf muscles in the swimming pool and how to increase her balance doing swings while standing on a rock or a piece of wood.

"In golf," I said, "you need to use all the tricks, including your brain powers. You must visualize the trajectory of your ball; you might even close your eyes thinking about how you will hit your ball and what it will do. Positive thinking makes things happen. There are no explanations for that but it works."

"I read about it," said Joan, "and I believe it too."

"I even thought," I added, "that there might be in each of us, a tiny fragment of God or a few genes that were transmitted through hundreds of generations from a common ancestor who had been in contact with God. May be that contact was enough to give our ancestor some latent powers."

"Or maybe," commented Joan playfully, "we come from ancestors who thousands of years ago had magical powers that were lost somehow but not totally."

"Yes, absolutely," I replied, "sometimes we can do what looks like miracles; like predicting a coming event, or curing a sick person, or lifting a heavy weight in a moment of panic. We can sometimes do mathematically or statistically impossible things like saying that we are going to make a hole in one on a par three and do it right after; or making a fifty feet put after telling that we are going to do that one. I know as a fact that in golf you can make things happen. It doesn't work every time but often enough to improve your score."

We started our workout and golf practice routine the following day and kept doing it for ten days. We had a lot of fun and spent hours of chatting about every possible subject.

It was quite a surprise for Joan to find out that I was also a chemist, just like her and had been working as a chemist for twelve years before switching to an artist-painter career. She was surprised to find out that I had kept up to date on general scientific know how by reading the monthly French magazine Science et Vie.

"You know Richard," Joan said one day, "I am surprised by your culture. You know a lot about history and this in addition to your scientific knowledge; but what surprises me is your interest for philosophy, psychology, and spirituality."

"This I owe to my father." I said. "He was a simple welder in life but he was reading all the time and mostly about history. He was also very interested by zoology and he had books on mammals, fish and birds even on botanic. And the sad part about it was that he had no friend interested in any of it. He would spend a couple of nights each week at the local tavern with his friends but they were there to talk about women and what happened at work. Talking against their boss or their wives was highly commendable; about who was the best fighter in town was also of great interest. There was a lot of boasting and repeating, many slaps on the shoulder and handshakes. That was their way to get the affection they could not get anymore from their wives."

"I understand," said Joan, "after all, getting back home totally drunk, a few nights each week would breach most relationships. Talking about relationship how was it between your parents?"

"Not very good, unfortunately." I replied. "My father had no idea of what women want or need, psychology was totally alien to him. They both loved each other though but their moments of tenderness had become scarce with the coming of five children."

We played our first game completing a foursome with two young businessmen. The guys were hitting the long ball and were playing a good game. One shot 89, the other 92 from the blues that is. Joan shot 86 from the reds and I

132

shot 87 from the white and needless to say that we were quite happy with our performance.

A few games later, she was shooting the low eighties and I was getting half of my games in the seventies.

Joan was good company and my taste for golf came back with a renewed intensity. We had real good time together. We made some friends, golf friends and our social life took a pleasant turn.

One night we went dinning out at one of the excellent Naples French restaurant. There were two musicians and there were three women sharing secrets animatedly. We sat on their right to catch some of those secrets, which were just about to travel at the speed of light across the town.

One of the women had a funny looking straw hat. The food was excellent, particularly the *Escargots Bougogne*. The main course was lamb chops broiled with a mix of honey and mustard and the dessert was *Creme brulé*. We had a good time and when we came back, Joan invited me inside for a drink.

"You know what," I said that night in Joan's condo. "I thought, I didn't have long to live with my stomach cancer but since we started to meet and play golf together, my health has improved and now I believe that I will be able to finish my third book that would complete the whole saga. Did you work some of your powers on me, dearest?"

"I don't know if God has listened to mine or to Father O'Leary's prayers but we have been both praying for you Richard. I cherish your company. We have met almost everyday for many months now and I don't want to loose you. I fell in love with John and I will always love him and remember the wonderful moments we had together but now I love you too...She took my hands and held them.

"Please stay alive for me." She said softly.

133

Emotions got me. I was overwhelmed and I must admit that I lost control. I cried and just couldn't stop. I was even shaking, what a shame. Loneliness had been a faithful companion, for years, and I resented its presence but it wouldn't let go and just stuck with me making my life miserable.

Loneliness likes to follow an artist and help him create beauty. For it is with its presence that most masterpieces are made.

Being an artist I knew about emotions and I usually succeeded in keeping them under control; but now, I couldn't. Joan hugged me and kissed me on the cheek and then, our mouth came into contact...

"Come with me, I will take care of you." She said as she felt my body response to her kisses.

We went to bed and made love and it was great. I slept with her that night and the following nights. We were both thinking about John sometimes and I felt uncomfortable about it and did not mention him anymore in our conversations but one night I told her what I thought about it.

"You know sweetheart, when we wake up on that other world, we should keep our relationship secret. I want you to remain John's girlfriend. He found you first and you loved him more than you love me. John is totally in love with you and for him there will be no other woman.

In my case, I know I can love another woman and there are going to be a lot of them and possibly some on the exotic side on Ghama-2. We will remain best friends but as long as John is back with us, we should not have an affair anymore."

Joan didn't answer but her eyes spoke for her. She approved my loyalty to John and she even loved me more for it but she did not commit herself. She wasn't the type of woman that would let me decide for her and beside, she knew better than me what to do in this situation.

"You said that the father was praying for me, did you hear from him recently?" I asked.

"He called me last week from Somalia, one of the most dangerous countries in the world." She said. "He opened a refuge, a school and a small hospital all at the same place. He found good use for those millions of dollars you gave him. He said he is trying to Christianize some of the tribe leaders, he is educating them and giving them medical care. He built a small church where he is doing the mass and the preaching. He asked me to give you his best wishes; he said he thinks about us and pray for us."

"God bless him," I said. "That man is an iron hand in a velvet glove. He is as strong as Tom who is probably the strongest man I ever met."

"They are both tall and very muscular." She said.

"Did you see them wrestling at Camp David? That was something to see. You know Joan, come to think of it; I will probably be the physically weakest man in our group. Even your son Garry will be stronger than me. I don't look dangerous, that works to my advantage though. I am surprisingly quick, and I played racquetball and Badminton for years. I also practiced Judo and went all the way to the blue belt. At that time I was too weak to go further than that, there was still the maroon belt before the black but these were impossible challenges. I knew all the tricks but weren't strong enough to do them.

Once at the Judo practice, I broke the shoulder of a big man who had been kicking me on the legs repeatedly. I had warned him to stop. He was one belt lower than I but much bigger and stronger. The bone came out through the skin. I took him to the hospital but afterwards, everyone was sore at me.

One of the maroon belts challenged me in a free fight at the end of the next practice. He said we would keep it friendly, no hard kick. I could hardly refuse; everyone was looking at us. I put on the gloves and faced him and the first thing he did was kicking me in the face with his foot at top speed. If he had connected, I believe I would have been killed. But like John I have a sixth sense warning me of danger probably less acute than John. Nevertheless, I knew a fraction of a second in advance what he was going to do. I moved my head and punched him with all my might on the nose and knocked him out stiff and cold. I didn't wait for another challenge and went to my locker, pick my clothes and left without a shower. I never returned.

Now I am much heavier and stronger but I would be no match for John, Tom or the Reverend Father. I would loose for sure and that means that we will be a very though lot, our little group on Ghama-2."

"Yes, but my daughter and I won't be much help against big men, predators or aliens." said Joan.

"I am not so sure of that," I said, "for with a sword or a knife in hand, there might not be much difference between men and women. We will have new bodies, possibly much better than what we have now. We will be stronger and faster and more resistant. I have the intuition that these Guardians are perfectionists and I wonder if they will not give us self-regenerating bodies like the lizards. Beside, each one of us seems to have special abilities. The guardians chose us well. You will surprise us, Joan, you and your daughter, I am sure of it. You are going to be essential to the success of our mission."

"What is you special ability, Richard?" asked Joan.

"I don't know. The only thing that comes to my mind is that somehow I get help when I really need it. I am no saint and there are no reasons why I receive that help but I can assure you that I felt the presence of a caring spirit by my side all through my life. Some miracles happened. When I was young, I was going to church every morning; I was a very pious catholic Christian. At the age of 16, I drowned in a lake.

It was a public beach and there was a very fat lifeguard; a good watcher he was though, and he saw me going under. He ran like a gazelle, dived over the board and found me. He rescued me and brought me in his arms into the lifeguard shelter where he gave me the mouth to mouth behind closed doors. He saved my life.

But I went through a very strange experience; I lived again the important moments of my life as a neutral observer.

It should have taken hours but it seems that it took less than a minute. When the observing was done with, I went out of the water and I could fly. I was floating in the air, enjoying incredible well being when I saw the fat lifeguard running and diving for me. It was funny to look at the fat man running like that. The finding of my body amazed me. I followed him while he was taking me to the shelter and suddenly I was suck through the ceiling and came back coughing.

I didn't want to live again; I was feeling so wonderfully good when I was bodiless."

"What an experience, no wonder you are so careless about your life and such a reckless daredevil." answered Joan. "Did it change you? Were you the same afterwards?"

"Maybe, I don't know for sure, it might have opened a door to another dimension or to a parallel word for I experienced two astral trips many years later.

Once, I was with my little girl Helen and I was cutting the hedges around the house with an electric cutter. I don't know if it was the vibration that did it but suddenly I heard a big clicking sound in my head and felt rushed out of my body at incredible speed. Suddenly, I was in a very strange place, kind of cloudy, immaterial and bright and there were ghosts around me, speaking to me. What they were saying was important, I sensed it but I would not listen for I was terrified that I would cut the throat of my little girl with the electric hedge cutter.

I made it back to my body in a frantic rush and kind of woke up still standing up and still cutting the hedges. There had been no time lapse; I had come back at the exact moment I had left.

That experience troubled me. I wanted to go back and meet those spirits again. They had something to tell me and I wanted to know what. In the weeks that followed, I did the bookshops and looked for a book on astral trips.

I was determined to learn how to do it willingly. I found the book I was looking for and it explained in details how to do it.

The trick was to achieve a total absence of thoughts and stay awake. One should not think that he should not think, even that is too much thinking. One should suggest himself that when the absence of thoughts is achieved, he will turn his left immaterial shoulder towards the right, turn around completely, then move backward towards the ceiling and look at oneself lying in the bed.

Turning the wrong way, from right to left would be very dangerous. For, it was written that a turn from right to left would take you to another universe where evil spirits would be awaiting you.

There is no fun without risk, I told myself with my usual foolish optimism as I lied down on my bed for my first shot at it. But I failed to do it. One need practice, I thought and I practiced nights after nights for months without ever being able to do it. One night though, I finally did it. I was not thinking as I turned around and left my body and I saw myself on the bed and horror struck me. I was dying! I had achieved dying before my time. I panicked and rushed back in my body and opened my eyes. I was alive; water was trickling from my armpits and my hands were wet and cold. I did not try again; I was too scared that it would kill me.
A year later though, I was cutting the lawn with my daughter when the same tremendously big clicking sound rang in my head, CLICK, and I was flying at tremendous speed into that other fuzzy world and they were there again, the spirits, talking to me. It was bright and I would have like to listen to their saying but I rushed back in my body afraid to cut my daughter's feet with the lawn mower."

"I heard about those people doing astral trips," said Joan, "apparently they can go anywhere, visit their friends' house and spy on them. I read that they can't go through water or mirrors though. But can you imagine the thrill of it, flying through the forest at night or going to the White House and spying on the president arguing with his wife. You might be the president of the

USA, the president wife would say, but you will pick up
your things lying around and keep the place tidy; or I
can't believe you did it with that slut...
You should have given it another try, Richard, now that
you had mastered the technique of it. The second time
would have been less dangerous."

"I tried again a few years later to no avail."

"What else can you tell me about your life?" asked Joan.

"I have been haunted." I said.

"You are going to tell me all about it, I like ghost
stories." She said childishly.

I told her how it started, how religious I had been and
even later on how I used to go every year for a few days
at the Benedictine Monastery to forget about my
materialistic goals and set back true values in my life.

"I used to go there every year to forget about the
stress of the modern world." I said. "You just walk in
and go to the reception office and tell them that you
would like to stay for a few days. They take your name
and address and closest relative's name and phone number
and they give you a room. There are no charges. You can
give them something when you leave, if you wish. The
monks are great singers and I loved the tragic religious
songs. There in the monastery, silence is law. At
the meals though, there is a monk saying deep
philosophical thoughts in a monotone voice for they make
humility vows.

There are five religious events per day at the chapel
and they sing at every one of them. In between, there
are the walks in the forest or the reading of the bible
in the library or just plain meditation.

The Benedictine Monastery was built on the shores of
Great Lake Magog. It is there, in my little cell of a
room that I won the fight against the demon that had
been haunting me for years.

One night, while I was lying down in the narrow bed of
my cell, light turned on, I saw the black smoke with red
eyes descending through the ceiling. It was looking at

me and there was such malevolence in its eyes that I was frozen, scared stiff, and unable to move.

I knew it would fly at me and try to possess me and I braced myself mentally and I raged at it with such intensity that my fright flew away. Then it rushed at me and I threw at it all the pain that I could imagine in a tremendous mental attack. I even laughed at it. I showed it that I, a human, did not fear it. God is with me, I said; get back in your hellish place. But it was already inside of me and I fought it desperately and I backed it up in a far corner of my brain. I don't know how I did it but I wrapped something around it, a kind of barrier and I felt its rage and suddenly I lost consciousness.
When I woke up, I had forgotten about it but the demon was still there inside my brain, imprisoned in a hard core where my thoughts shall never go, for it would weaken the walls of the hard core and the demon would take possession of me.

Sometimes my thought thread would go there during my sleep and I would wake up shouting but the guardians took it away and liberated me from its presence."

"Incredible," she said, "and that is not all. I can see that there are a lot more stories and strange things that happened in your life. Tell me some more; I feel like a little girl tonight, if you tell me more stories I will kiss you again..."

"No more stories for now" I said," but to answer your question when you asked me what my special ability is; I believe that I am able to resist the attack of one demon. "

"Who knows," she said, "that might be useful. What a story, let's go to bed, I am tired now, I hope I will be able to sleep after all that."

It was Christmas Eve and we were all there at the Ritz-Carlton hotel in Naples. The whole eleven of us, my daughter couldn't come and Krishna and John had already passed away. We were there, the rest of us, along with our spouses, children and special guests.

The conference room was spacious. There were long tables loaded with all kind of food. Three musicians, a singer and an entertainer were doing their best to give us a wonderful evening.

Tom, Father O'Leary and Joan were talking in a low voice.

"It might be the last opportunity to celebrate together," said Tom. "Our intelligence people just found out that the Arab terrorists have succeeded to bring one or more nuclear bombs on our territory. They also brought a new kind of virus and are just waiting for the proper time to start the attack. Millions of people will die. It is possibly the end of our prosperity. We have kept the details secret. George has just warned the Americans on TV that they have reasons to believe that an imminent terrorist attack is due to happen this year. He said that thousands of agents are searching everywhere to find the terrorists but it is too late."

"Hi everyone," said George W Wood as he came to our little group. "I believe that Tom already told you the bad news."

"It's terrible." replied Joan.

"What will you do about it?" I asked.

"The whole situation needs drastic action." replied George. "Action that I could not decide myself to take but the generals wants to destroy a number of countries that are implicated with the terrorists. If I let tem do it, all the North Africa will be vaporized under our nuclear bombs plus a number of other countries, Iran, Pakistan, North Korea, and China.

They want to proceed with massive arrest and deportation; they want all Islamic foreigners out of the country and ban religious meetings, make religions illegal.

They also want to stop all traffic between cities for a period of time, at least until we know where the virus will or already have been released.

I am getting back to Washington immediately and I suggest that you find shelter somewhere with ample reserves of food and water.

Tom, I would like you to come with me to Washington and watch my back at all time. I believe some of the generals or some high-ranking CIA officers want to assassinate me.

Good luck everyone, I might not see you again in this world, see you on Ghama-2."

"Good luck George, good luck Tom." We said as we shook their hands.

"Be prepared for the worst," said Tom before he left. "Make sure you got everything you need to survive for a few years without electricity and fuel."

They had already left the room and we didn't feel to party anymore.

"Reverend father," said Joan, "I don't think you can return to North Africa as it is about to be destroyed under our nuclear bombs and you may be of more help here in the States. Why don't you stay with us for a while, we are going to buy a house at Everglades City and shelter ourselves from the virus. We can live there our little group together."

"Please reverend father." I added.

"All right I will do that for a while. The two of you are living together now, isn't it? The reverend asked.

"Yes," said Joan, "Richard and I found much comfort in each other's company."

"But you are not married," replied the reverend father, "why don't you sanctify your relationship and get married?"

"Why not?" replied Joan looking at me seriously.

"Will you marry me Joan?" I asked as I kneeled in front of her.

142

"Yes Richard." answered Joan.

"Let's go to the nearest church where I will proceed with it immediately." said the reverend.

We left and went to the church the reverend was affiliated with; the church door was unlocked and there was nobody inside for it was late evening already.

The reverend went in the back room behind the altar and put on the some religious gears; then he came back and looked at us.

"My children, do you regret any sinful action you have done in the past?" asked the reverend.

"Yes." We both replied.

"Then your sins are absolved."

"Joan? Will you take Richard as your husband for better or worst until death part you?"

"I do."

"Richard will you take Joan as your wife…?"

"Yes I do."

Three days later, Joan and I bought a house at Everglades City, right on the river. There was a shed, a dock, a rowboat and two canoes. It was all furnished. We bought a generator and had it installed for emergencies along with a 200 gallons tank of fuel. We filled the shed with canned food and bottled water and we bought everything essential to survive for years as we moved in with Garry, Nancy and Father O'Leary.

It had taken a lot of arguments to convince the preacher to come and live with us for a little while but it seemed that he felt quite comfortable with us. He had his own room, Nancy had a room too but Garry had to sleep in the living room.

"We will build you a room in the shed which we will transform into a guesthouse." I promised.

"Then I want to build it with you," he answered, "that will be quite interesting and in the mean time I don't care about sleeping in the living room; I am always the last one to go to bed anyway."

Eight days had passed since our reunion with the rest of the chosen when we heard the dreadful news. On the first hour of January 1st 2010, two nuclear bombs exploded in New York and one in Washington. The death toll is estimated to fifteen millions people. The president and vice president were killed in the blast.

Fifteen million people of all races and religions died in the following days. The bombs had been manufactured in North Korea and sold to Iran leaders. Iran and Iraq, long time enemies, had join their terrorist's commandos to the Al Quad'a Arab fanatics and prepared the coup. China had supplied the Uranium to North Korea as well as some of the equipment necessary to their manufacture.

George W. Wood and most of the government leaders perished in Washington and the power fell into the hands of the shadow government leader, Admiral Ted Carter. He held all the powers and the destiny of America as well as the whole world destiny in his hands.

Ted Carter was very sore and didn't care too much about anything else than exacting revenge. He called the Russian leader, Mr. Putin, and asked him if Russia had anything to do with the nuclear attack and the Russian answered with a firm denial.

"We knew that something was going on but didn't know the details." told Mr. Putin.

"The world will survive if Russia stays put." said Ted Carter. "For I intend to exact proper retribution for everyone sharing responsibility. If you launch anything at us, we will destroy your country no matter the consequences. At this very moment, we are launching missiles but we won't attack Russia and your satellite countries unless you force my hand.

We are going to destroy the Middle East, North Korea and China's capital. I will talk to you later." Ted Carter closed the line.

The decision had been taken secretly after weeks of discussion with the other leaders of the shadow government. They had come to the conclusion that there was no other way. If the Arab terrorists destroy Washington, which is most likely to happen, the whole Arab population shall be destroyed. They were all enemies, the whole population had been brainwashed to hate and kill Americans. Anything else than total annihilation would bring revenge and additional terrorist attacks.

A few hours later, the Arab people were dancing with joy in the streets at the news of the terrible destruction their terrorists had inflicted to the USA. Mahmoud Abbas was saying to a reporter, "It is ...it is...unbelievable". That was all he could say for he had great difficulties to hide his smirk.

The Iranian top cleric and leader Hussein spoke at the local TV telling his people that Satan's followers had been destroyed.

"Iran has nothing to do with it," he said with a faint smile, "but I will not shed water on their well-deserved destruction."

Their exultation changed into panic as the first American missiles hit Saudi Arabia. Ted Carter knew very well about their hypocrisy. He knew that the money for the terrorist organizations had come from there; not only the money but also most of the terrorists of September 11 tragedy. Ted Carter had decided they would be the first to die and their Mecca would be burned to cinder.

All the countries of the Middle East were destroyed inside of one hour. Israel had not been hit and Israelites had been warned to leave their country by any which way before the radioactive winds hit them. Many left aboard airplanes or boats but for the greater part, Israel population did not escape. They made their farewell and prepared themselves and then the killer wind destroyed them all.

Soon after the Arab countries, Iran and Pakistan were
hit in turn. Pakistan could not be trusted, Ted carter
had decided, it was the same as Saudi Arabia, a
friendly government on the surface allowing the
terrorists to prepare themselves on their territory,
possibly financing them or supplying them with the
nuclear bombs. Then it was North Korea's turn to be
burnt into cinders and an hour later Peking was hit and
totally destroyed.

Ted Carter called the Chinese and Indian leader to
deliver an ultimatum.

"You will start dismantling and destroying your nuclear
arsenal now and I mean in the next 24 hours or face
complete destruction. We have developed and put into
orbit, satellites with sensors capable of detecting your
nuclear missiles and nuclear power plants. You will
destroy your nuclear arsenal over ground and we will
watch.
In thirty days we will start bombing your undestroyed
nuclear sites. We will watch you carefully and any
hostile activity will result in your annihilation." said
Ted Carter.

China and India leaders knew that this time there would
be no backing up from the Americans, they had no choice,
they hastily accepted and proceeded to destroy their
nuclear arsenal inside the thirty days limit.

Thus those two countries were allowed to survive the
American might. Russia and its allies kept quiet and the
world survived Armageddon.

In the following weeks, millions of USA residents of
Arabic origin were rounded up and deported to Africa.
Fuel was rationed everywhere in the world since no more
oil could be imported for the Middle East was reduced to
cinders. The terrorists responsible for New York and
Washington destruction had not been captured yet and
were actively searched. They had an enormous quantity of
the most dangerous virus ever made by men.

They didn't know what to do; their leaders had been
killed, their countries had been destroyed, the Arab
nations did not exist anymore, and Allah had not
protected them.

They had been told that one day the Arabs would conquer the world but that would never happen now and they were wondering if their Islamic leaders had not misled them. Would they go to heaven if they sacrifice themselves? They were in doubts now but they had no more countries to go back to and they could avenge their brothers.

If they release the virus though, the whole world population might be destroyed inside of a few years, even their brothers who had been deported to Africa. Brainwashed and stupid as they were, raised in violence, they chose to destroy the world and release the virus.

The nuclear explosions had changed the weather and when the terrorists released their virus, the USA was hit by a number of very powerful hurricanes. The virus was carried across the seas and people started to die all over the world.

In one year, the plague killed one hundred million Americans and 80 % of the world population. In some countries the whole population perished. China and India were devastated; the high population density had favored the rapid spread of the virus.

United States, Canada and Mexico surviving leaders unified their countries. America called back their ships and airplanes from their bases abroad. New America closed its frontiers including an area of one thousand miles of seawater all along its coasts. Admiral Ted Carter was assassinated two years after the USA retaliation.

We watched the nightmare at the local TV channels and we Survived, our little group survived at Everglades City, living mostly through fishing for two years.

There was no TV channels working on anymore but we were able to catch the news at the radio.

The Everglades City grocery stayed open, offering mainly produce, fish and fresh meat. They were getting it from the local farmers and fishermen. The reverend worked at the church located two miles from our house on the main street and he organized a choral with Nancy's help. The small church attracted everybody in town for the Sunday mass with the choral and the sermon and stories of the reverend father. Joan and I just loved it and would not have missed it for any possible reason.

At night, we were playing Boggle or card games and the reverend was sometimes simulating great anger at Garry his usual card partner when Nancy and I were winning. Garry liked the reverend like a father and Nancy seemed to be completely taken by him. She was in love with the reverend but tried to show it as tender friendship.

In daytime, we were often going fishing between the ten thousand islands a place that had become known as a refuge where many pirates and escaped convicts had once hidden. We were catching sea trout, bass, red snapper, sharks, catfish but we usually threw the last back in the water. It is not bad but the meat smells a little.

The virus was gone now, it had either died or the survivors were resistant. New America reorganized and there were hundred of thousands of empty farms and millions of empty houses with no known living owners or heirs.

People were invited to participate to local counties lotteries to acquire those farms and empty houses. The unclaimed estates would become governmental properties and it was the same for the billions of dollars of unclaimed bank accounts. The government had plenty of money and no debts anymore for the New America government leaders had stop all traffic and exchange with the outside world. There was no more stock market and no more civil lawsuits for these had been abolished. Arbiters elected for one year settled all conflicts. Good sense and fairness prevailed over the multitude of laws that had afflicted America and there weren't much need for attorneys anymore.

Everybody that couldn't work could ask for social welfare and got plenty of it and for this reason, there was no more poverty. In fact, most people wanted to work and getting a job and work was considered a privilege.

There would be no more construction for years to come everybody could own a house, a mortgage free house. They were there for the takers. The needs were different now

148

since there was plenty of everything. The country needed to develop new technology, a novel defense system to protect America. People would have to reorient their careers or just take over an abandoned farm and become farmers.

The leaders decided that they didn't need the rest of the world; there was enough in America to cover anything one may need and beside everybody that had survive the plague outside of America hated the Americans whom they consider as bloodthirsty war-mongers.

"So what do you want to do Richard?" asked Joan.

"I believe we should take on farming." I replied. "I love the countryside and the company of animals and farming would be healthy and pleasant. I am done with fishing."

"All right then," said Joan, "do you have a place in mind?"

"Yes, I would like to live in South West Virginia. It is so beautiful over there with the mountains and all those lakes and plenty of forests."

"What about you, Nancy and Garry?" She asked.

"I want to go to Silicon Valley and work in one of the research centers." answered Nancy.

"I will go with Nancy." said Garry.

"And you Reverend Father?" She asked.

"I am going to travel across America and then possibly in Europe." He answered. "I need to move, I have been fidgeting these last two years."

The day after, Father O'Leary took one of the abandoned trucks and left wishing us the best. We also left the same day with Garry and Nancy for South West Virginia.

"We will help you to start with the farm and then we will go to Silicon Valley." Nancy had decided.

We took over one of the abandoned farm and started to plant seeds for all kind of cereals and vegetables. There were a few horses, pigs, cows, chicken, geese that were living in liberty all over the farm land, most came to watch us and we started to feed them; a few weeks later they were back to the barn and they seemed to be happy to have us to take care of them. We also adopted a couple of stray dogs and cats.

It was fun and we just loved it. Months later, we look with much pride at our wheat and cornfields ready to be harvested and our long rows of vegetable.

We had books on how to operate the tractors and mowers but we were very pleased to get some help from the neighbors.

Once our harvest was over with, it was time for Garry and Nancy to move to Silicon Valley where they had already got a job in a space research center. They had applied through the Internet and got it after a telephone interview.

There were many changes to our new society; incarcerated people had been wiped out by the plague and the prisons were empty.

Laws were changed and became more severe. Criminals could not use them to evade justice anymore; murder and rape convicts were executed on same day as they were sentenced. The use of truth detector was mandatory before a suspect would go to court so very few mistakes were made if any. Stealing was obsolete as a crime since everyone had everything they wanted. So the prisons had remained almost empty with the exception of those that had been convicted for violence and these usually had a short sentence.

Government spending was oriented towards research and development of new technology; miniature spaceships were built and different kind of engines tested. Faster than light became the goal. Engines using nuclear fusion were developed along with new energy field generators. When used at full capacity, these generators created an unbreakable energy barrier protecting the spaceships from radiation, debris and meteorites.

There had been a rumor that the prototype of those energy field generators had been found already made in one of the most protected research centers. Somebody had put it there along with instructions telling how to use it and to build it. That person, human or alien, had entered the facilities without being detected.

"I wondered if the Guardians had anything to do with it or if it could be one of our groups that came back from Ghama-2 after having been enhanced into a Godlike being, who knows?" I said.

"Whoever did it," replied Joan, "has just given us a tool to build an impenetrable defense system."

Life went on for us, we missed the presence of Joan's children but to compensate a little, we had made friends with the neighbors and we visited each other regularly. Our farm lied at the foot of the Appalachian Mountains and in addition to the farmlands; we had acres of forest and a dozen lakes.

We loved to ride our horses through the mountains and to camp somewhere, somewhere beautiful and at night we built campfire and sometimes roast a partridge or a hare over it. We were also spending a lot of time looking at the stars in total darkness and wonder what would our lives on one of those worlds orbiting around them.

"I wonder my dearest," I said on one of those nights, "how it will be over there. We will be awoken altogether, the seven chosen of our group and there will be four men apart from your son Garry and only two women…"

"I know what you mean Richard," answered Joan, "and we will all be young again and probably loaded with hormones in those new and energetic bodies…"

"And I can imagine that if the Guardians make you as beautiful as you were in your twenties," I added, "there will be some jealousy and hard feelings towards whoever gets your favor. You will become a wonderful but poisoned gift to the lucky one; and speaking of the lucky one, will you go back to John, or will you stay with me?"

"Richard, I know how much you love me, and I love you too, just as much but differently from the love I had for John. We have live through many things together; we have build over those years a bound that will never be broken. Moreover, the reverend father has blessed our union. So I am not going to dump you and return to John.

But John will love me just as much as you do, possibly even more. Then there is Tom and the reverend father and these two will be just as young, vigorous and loaded with hormones as you and I will be.

In different worlds, different customs, different rules. it would be unfair for me to be one man's woman. I hope you are not jealous for I believe that the best thing for all of us is to make myself available to all of you."

"I am not jealous Joan," I replied, "and this way, I am not losing you. I am sharing you with my best friends. That's a much better solution for me than to give you back to John. But tell me sweetheart, do you think you will be able to seduce the reverend father?"

"The Vatican rules will not apply off world." She replied. "And I noticed the way he looked at me sometimes at Everglades City. I don't think he will be able to resist."

"All right, then what about your little Nancy?" I said lustfully.

"I know what you have in mind; you are already to cheat on me honey."

"Well, I was thinking that since you are going to do it with all the men, I might as well try to my charm on her."

"Nancy will be just as hot and available as I will be; I know my little girl." replied Joan. "She was already in love with the reverend father at Everglades City and she will think the same way as I do; she won't be as you said a poison gift to the reverend. So you will probably have her too."

152

Time went on and we now had two dozen cows, as many pigs, a dozen lambs, a bunch of chickens, three horses and litters of cats and dogs.

The rooster was waking us up at 5:30AM and we were up in a moment and under the shower. We usually had a solid breakfast of ham and eggs with two toasted slices of homemade bread, a glass of milk and a big cup of coffee. Then Joan was milking the cows as I was feeding all of the animals. Then I usually collected the eggs and headed back to the house with them. If there were no urgent chores to do, we were usually going for a horse ride.

We loved our horses and it was a real pleasure to ride them for a few hours. We went fishing and picnicking somewhere almost every day. We never got bored; growing wheat and corn, all kind of vegetables and taking care of the animals was a lot of work. Nevertheless, there was some spare time and I started to write the third book of the Ghama-2 saga.

One day, the phone rang and Joan answered it. She was speechless for a moment then said.

"Please give us one week, it might take us all that time to get there and we want to be there for the funerals."

"What happened Joan?" I asked worriedly.

"Garry and Nancy were accidentally killed at the Silicon Valley research center." She said with heartbreaking sadness. "They were working on the development of nuclear fusion engines…"

I took Joan in my arms and hugged her.

"They were 26 and 27 years old and still living together these two." Joan said. "They grew up together and they died together. We have to go; they will wait for us for their funerals."

I took the bike and rushed to our closest neighbor.

"Hi Harry, Hi Nicole," I said as I got there. There were rocking on the front balcony as I use to do with Joan.

"Hi Richard." They said. "How is it going?"

"Not well," I answered sadly, "we just got a phone call from Silicon Valley; there was an accident; Garry and Nancy died an hour ago.

Joan and I are going to drive there and assist to the funerals. You know that it is not safe to travel through the country with all those bands of bandits that are setting ambuscades these days. We don't know if we will ever be back here. Would you mind taking care of the farm during our absence? We can leave the barn doors open and give their liberty back to our animals but they will miss our presence. Beside, if we don't come back some will starve this winter."

"No problem," said Harry, "with ten children to help us, we can easily take care of both farms."

"If we are not back in one month, the farm is yours." I replied. "Thank you and God bless you." I said as I jumped back on the bike.

"Give our condolences to Joan, God bless the two of you, good luck Richard." They said.

I rushed back to the farm where Joan was busy preparing the provision for the long trek.

I put oil in the truck and added some coolant to the radiator. Then I started to load it with everything we needed for the trip, tent, coolers pack with food, guns, fishing rods, axe, hammer and tools. The country was almost deserted of population and the roads were mostly empty of circulation and we could get stranded in the middle of nowhere. We were finally ready and we left for a trip that might be weeks long.

We traveled for many days and had been able to refuel in a number of almost deserted villages. We slept the first night in a deserted house and I woke up in the middle of the night with the feeling that we were watched. The invisible watchers were not friendly; I could sense a menace in the air. I woke up Joan.

"Joan, are you asleep?" I asked softly.

"No, I can't sleep," she answered, "there is an evil presence in this house."

"Let's get out of here." I said. "We will drive for an hour or two and sleep in the truck."

After that, we were setting camp beside the truck every night.

We were half way to Silicon Valley when I lost control of the truck. I must have hit a pothole or something; maybe I was not paying attention. I was still under shock, I don't know why but I lost control and the truck went over the cliff of a ravine. A few seconds later, the truck was immobilized after a few turnovers. I looked at Joan; she was bleeding but she was still alive. I realized that I could not move my legs.

"I am sorry Joan," I said, "It is my entire fault; I didn't pay attention. You are bleeding; can you move or do something to stop the bleeding?"

"No, I can't move, my neck is broken." She answered sadly.

"I can't move my legs; I can't help you and I am getting weak, internal bleeding maybe." I said.

We knew it was the end for us. There would be no help. Only a few people would travel these days.

"We can hold hands." I said.

I took her hand in mine and it was getting cold and lifeless.

"These were wonderful years at the farm; did you enjoy them as much as I did?" I asked tenderly.

"Yes, I did Richard," she whispered, "good bye my darling, see you on Ghama-2, I hope."

I sensed her soul leaving her body.

"Good bye Joan." I said with despair.

My old companion, the loneliness was back at my side. It was going to give me company, faithful to the end. I didn't feel the pain anymore. I left my body and looked at it and was suddenly snatched away. I was in the bright cloudy world and the spirits were talking to me, they were saying something about Father O'Leary but before I could hear some more, I was taken far, far away.

As we were taken to the far future, New America built thousands of those newly discovered energy generators and set a chain of them all along its borders. All of it was done secretly and one day, they were activated, all at the same time and this created a protective bubble of impenetrable energy covering all of North America.

The country was now totally closed to the rest of the world and would escape potential retaliation. It would remain closed for the next centuries.

People from all over the world were wondering what happened. Russia, the French-British New Republic and China sent surveillance satellites but none could get any picture from under the bubble. There was no radio transmission; nothing at all would come through it.

World business had to be redeveloped without the expertise of the Americans and the French-British New Republic took over and became the most powerful country of the world. Nuclear arms were banned and destroyed. Islam was also banned in most countries and their religious leaders imprisoned or killed.

In the years 2200 to 2250 the first manned spaceships left New America for a survey of discovered planets showing presence of oxygen and water. They flew at a fraction less than light speed towards Proxima Centauri, 4.28 light years away, Bernard Star, 5.8 light-years distant and Ghama in the Eridani constellation, 89 light-years from Earth. A gigantic planet had been discovered circling that star. Strangely enough, its gravity seemed to be the same as Earth.

Over the following centuries, New America colonized many planets inside of a 50 light years radius. First contact with Aliens occurred in the year 2556. Mankind had been discovered and would now have to fight for survival. New America spread the news of their first encounter with hostile alien species and for the first time in centuries opened its frontiers to foreign countries' ambassadors.

Earth nations and New America unified to form a world government. People could travel across the world again but each person had to carry a wrist bracelet that served as a communication device, a tracing device, a computer and a microphone. It could also detect violent brain waves and inject automatically a drop of a very powerful soporific and call the police. Justice was swift and fair for lie detectors and truth serums had been perfected and were used for all suspects.

Undetected crime was no more possible. More of those energy generators were built and a bubble of impenetrable energy was successfully set around the whole planet. Earth was now protected from alien invasion but was it too late? There were rumors that a species of vampire had already secretly landed and people were found dead and bloodless.

The guardians had answered my questions about the future of mankind for I either saw those events happen or the informations and images were communicated to me as they took me to the far future and to Ghama-2 where American spaceship had finally landed after a hundred years voyage. Its crew had been awoken from hibernation as the ship neared the huge planet but when the ship came close, a strange force had force the ship to crash at low speed on its surface. Most of the crew had survived the soft crash and eventually built two cities, Jungletown and New Alexandria. The Guardians finally told me that I was to be awoken with the rest of John's group near New Alexandria and wished me good luck.

Chapter seven: The awakening

John woke up suddenly and looked around him. He was lying in soft golden grass, dry but silky in texture. On his left was a wall of purple stone striated with laces of gold. He looked up, the wall was hundreds of feet tall; it was not a wall, it was an immense tree for he could see branches, way up, hundreds of feet up, coming from the tree trunk wall and then dividing and subdividing into a multitude of smaller branches and at the tip of each of the smallest ones were little sparkling colored spheres.

Those spheres are so far away that they look small but they got to be huge, thought John.

The colors were constantly changing. Even the colors of the stony wall were changing. The gold laces were now turning into green and the purple surface into violet. He stood up and looked around. The rock-strewn wall was the bole of a gigantic tree and it was as hard as diamond to John touch.

It is warm to the touch, John thought, *there must be some chemical reactions taking place; the energy contained in this tree must be enormous.*

There were other trees, hundred of meters apart, and this as far as he could see. Each tree was of a different color and the colors were changing everywhere, all the time.

The trees must be a thousand feet tall, John thought, *and the lowest of the branches are at least 200 feet over my head.*

He looked at the grass again, kneeled down for a much closer look. There were no insects. The air was fresh and there was a symphony of fragrances, an effluence of odors, playing with his olfactory sense. The sensation was most pleasuring.

My God, John thought, *this must be a new sense, one of those improvements the Guardians told me about; it is*

*like I could read the odors, differentiate all of them.
The odors come from the trees; each tree has a distinct
odor and the odor change as the trees change in colors.*

*I am waking up on another world, a very different world
and it is awesome.*

He looked at his body. He was strong and muscular and
the skin was firm with a healthy appearance.

I am young again! Thought John.

He jumped a few times and then walked a few minutes.

*Well, very well; that body seems highly functional but
where are the others, and where is my outfit?*

John looked around and saw something a few yards away.
He went to investigate and there it was; the promised
outfit.

There was a beautifully carved sword in a silver
scabbard and a knife in its leather case; a bow with a
quiver of arrows and the clothes; the pants, the shirt,
a cape, the boots, and a large feathered hat.

*My God, the Guardians must have watched the TV or maybe
they went to a cinema; surely they got their idea from
the movie "The three Musketeers ".*

*Blue pants, golden shirt, blue and gold cape and blue
and red hat with a golden feather. Wait till Joan see
that!*

John put the clothes on then looked at the straps and
holsters. The scabbard could be fixed on his back beside
the quiver of arrows with the handle protruding over his
shoulder.

This way, thought John, *I can get the sword just as fast
as if it hangs on my side and it will not hinder my
movements. I can even run without having to hold it in
place. I will fix the knife case to my belt*. Now where
will I put the backpack? *It will have to put the strap
around my neck and let it hang on my left side. I have
to get familiar with the straps.*

159

The knife case leather seems to be made of alligator hide and the boots seemed to be made of a shiny plastic like material. John flexed it, plied it and tried to craze it but the plastic was unaffected and regained its initial appearance as soon as he released it. The surface underneath was ridged with thousands of little extrusions and when he pressed his hand on that surface, it stuck quite firmly.

John put them on and walked with them and they didn't stick to the grass. On an inspiration, John went to the tree wall and pressed his boot against the shiny and rock hard surface and it held on the surface just like if it was glued to it. John could easily unstuck it if he moved his foot sideways, peeling it from left to right or right to left, but there was no way he could pull the boot out of the wall if he pulled downward.

That is too good to be true, John thought; *let's see if there are some gloves to go with the boots in the backpack.*

John found the gloves, put them on and climbed a dozen feet up the rocky wall of the immense tree. After a few trials, he could easily move up and down and sideways on the shiny and diamond hard surface. He could hold himself with only one hand once he pressed his glove firmly on the wall; he could even hold himself on the wall with one foot.

It is just like being a lizard or a spider, John thought, *I can climb up and down effortlessly. I must be much stronger and resistant than in my prime time on Earth.*

John came down the tree wall and looked at his clothes. They were very soft, light and comfortable. He pulled the sword quickly out of the scabbard and made a few swings. It was very light in weight and easy to handle; the heft of it was reassuring.

This sword is made for me, he thought.

John was delighted. He was young again, he felt full of
energy and confident that the Guardians had given him
what it takes to succeed with his mission. And now he
had to find Joan.

Joan woke up at the foot of a gigantic tree. Like John
she was amazed at the silkiness of the grass and the
colorful and color changing tree bole. She felt
wonderful and young with an acute sense for detecting
the slightest odors. She looked at her body.

Just perfect, she thought, *I wish I could see my face.*

She looked around and found her clothes and equipment.
There was a bag, which could be carried on her back or
her side. She looked inside and found amongst other
things, the greatest of treasure, a mirror! She held it
in her hands for a while before looking at it.

What kind of a face did they give me, she asked herself.

Finally, she looked at the mirror and there she was;
another person!

A new face, she thought, *but I can live with it and what
a body they gave me. Wait till Richard sees me! Oh my
God what am I thinking; John is here too, my old hero.
He will like me too, I am sure. Both of them will find
me beautiful, I can't wait to hug them both and show
them what I look like.*

She felt a most delicious sexual need at the thought of
them.

*If their bodies give them the same kind of sexual
pressure*, she thought, *they will get a hard on as soon
as they see me so young and beautiful. I can't deprive
one of them of my charm treasures. I will have to
do something about that situation. In another world, we
can make new rules of behavior. I wonder if John is
jealous? Richard isn't, that I am sure. And now my
children are alive again and the Reverend Father O'Leary
too and Tom. What will they look like? I wonder if I
will be able to recognize anyone of them at first sight.*

She put on the clothes and pulled the beautifully carved
sword from its scabbard and made a few swings with it.

That sword is so light in weight and the handle seems to fit so perfectly in my hands... Joan had a feeling of déjà vu. She could almost remember a time in her life or possibly a previous life when she used to hold a sword like this one.

My God, I am truly fit for that mission, she thought, I feel so strong; it's wonderful. Thank you Guardians, thank you for that body and for everything.

Joan inventoried the backpack and found a most interesting pair of gloves and a first aid quit.

She put the clothes on and found her way with the straps.

The sword and the quiver will go on my back, she thought, *and the backpack will hang on my side.*

Everything is surprisingly lightweight and I can jump and run without holding on the sword. All right, let's go find the others.

Joan left to find the other members of her team, walking energetically, relaxed and with all of her new senses in alert.

It was more or less the same for the others and me. We woke up alone, realized we were on another world, and marveled at it. We discovered our new acute sense of smell. We all tried a few jumps, walk a little and found our clothes, arms and hiking equipment.

We all found easily our way with the straps and got on our way to find the others. The outfit was amazing, beautiful and light in weight.

The only exception was Garry. He had a suspicious mind and was easy to take offense. For him, the stuttering had started at the age of thirteen and went on and on, for years. Joan told him it would stop when he got older. Classmates would sometimes mock him and that hurt. The most maddening was that sometimes he could speak for five minutes without any problem even for

162

hours without much of it and when it was important to speak straight he was unable to.

He had come to the conclusion that he had been treated unfairly.

So when he woke up, his first thought was that somehow the Guardians had not played fair with him. He looked suspiciously at his body and thought that it was rather small. He felt good though but boyish.

He found a sword and a knife, a bow and a pack of arrows, a backpack and the funny clothes. He set himself up and started to look for the others.

He saw a young girl, probably 12 years old but she was too far away to be sure.

"Hello," Garry said, "as he went to her. He realized as he came closer that something was way wrong. The girl was very young, no more than twelve for sure but she was taller than him by quite a few inches.

"My name is Garry, "he said. "I am looking for my sister Nancy and other people too. Have you seen them?"

The girl started to laugh; she even fell on the ground giggling helplessly and she couldn't stop. It was maddening.

"What's wrong with you?" asked Garry belligerently.

"Hello Garry, my little cute Garry. You are so cute with your little bow. You look like a cherub. Don't you recognize me? I am your sister Nancy in my new body."

"I knew it," he said, "I knew something was wrong with my body. How old do I look to you?"

"Nine, maybe ten."

"I don't get it. Why me? That is so unfair. We were supposed to wake up in young adult bodies. That's what we were told."

"Yes; but we died in that explosion and we were awarded a second life. Don't you think that we are privileged? There is nothing less fair than the gift of life."

"Well, you are right but if there is something wrong to happen it usually happens to me. So, now I have to grow up again. The women here will treat me as a little boy. They will kiss me on the cheek; that is all I can hope for."

"Maybe there are little girls, nine or ten years old that will kiss you on the mouth."

"Yah, Yah, they will be flat like an iron board though and too young to chat with." said Garry as he started to giggle too.

In fact, everything is so funny, He thought, *it's great to feel so boyish again.*

They went together to find the others and after a while, decided to shout. Others answered them back and a few minutes later they met with a young woman and four young men and did not recognize any of us.

The young woman ran at then and swoop Garry in her arms and then holding him in one arm, hugged Nancy with the other.

"I am so happy to see you again. I was going to your funerals with Richard when we died in a car accident. I was so sad. And now I got you back and at the age I loved you most. You are real cute."

"Mother," said Nancy. "Don't start on that cute thing. You see, that eleven or twelve years old look is not what I was hoping for and Garry, look at him, it's true that he has that little cute cherub look but we both think we have been unfairly treated. We had just become adults and now we look like kids again."

"It's OK," said Joan, "I am sure you will grow up. The Guardians are a very old specie. They might have thought you would be more useful that way; but now, let's see who is who behind those young men's smiling faces. Let's guess who our team leader is."

Joan and her children looked at the four young men. One was bigger and looked strong like a bull but with the kindest eyes.

"That one is either Father O'Leary or Tom, I would say he is the first." said Garry in a joyful tone.

"I am," said the preacher." And as always the truth is coming from the mouth of the very young."

Everyone was laughing. The three others were about the same height and physical strength but one of them was moving with the grace of a feline.

"You are John," said Joan.

She went to him and kissed him on the lips. They hugged for a long time then she moved back from the embrace and looked right into the eyes of the two remaining poker faces. She felt something coming from one of the two, a powerful tenderness scent if that could be described as that. She kissed me on the lips, a kiss that lasted for a while under the surprised eyes of John who stood stiff and unmoving.

"Thanks for holding my hand." She said tenderly.

She moved backward and gave a handshake and a kiss on the lips of the last one and said "It is good to see you again Tom."

On earth, Tom looked and acted like Arnold Schwarzenneger in his action movies while John had the classy, cultural and serious look of Sean Connery in his late movies.

Now they had a young and very different face but their personalities hadn't change.

Joan took my hand and pulled me to John.

"John," said Joan. "You certainly don't look like the old man with whom I fell in love. We have known each other and love each other for a number of months before you died. Soon after, Richard and I started to play golf. We met many times a week and eventually, Richard moved in with me and we spent eight years together.

Richard told me that he wanted to give me up to you once we get to Ghama-2 since you were my first love. He asked me to keep our relationship secret for he didn't want to hurt your feelings and lose your friendship; he also said that he had the greatest admiration for you.

But John, I can't accept that offer; I can't let Richard decide for me. I loved both of you but Richard lived with me as a companion and then as my husband for eight years. Father O'Leary blessed our union.

I believe John that you are the kind of man for whom any woman would fall for and I did fall for you, and I loved you and I remember our moments of sharing with great emotion but I am not your wife. If I was anyone's wife it would be Richard.

There are no rules of ethics, dignity or decency that could apply to our situation. We are waking up on another world and the rules should be different.

If we succeed with our mission, we will become immortals. Think about it; nobody can live forever with the same person and beside, nobody should belong to anyone.

We have young bodies again and we will feel very horny most of the time. I already feel a sexual urge just looking at you or at any one of the men here and I am the only woman in our group. It would not be a good thing if only one of the men here has me. So, I declare myself a free woman. I believe that I have the right to kiss and make love to anyone of you.

Jealousy would be childish; we have a mission to accomplish and anyone might be killed at anytime."

John was astonished; there had been no time lapse. He was with Joan one hour ago, walking in the park at Camp David and Joan and him were lovers. There would be no other between them. And now, Joan was different; she had live eight years with Richard. John felt a pang of jealousy and anger.

How could he? John thought. *We were friends; that was treacherous! Or was it? Joan must have been devastated by my death and she had nobody else. Richard was there and he entertained her with golf. And she couldn't know for sure that the story was true about Ghama-2. She had the right to be happy and live with another man.*

John looked at both of us and smiled.

"You are right Joan. You are not my property." said John. "But I love you just as much as one moment ago, when I passed away."

Joan kissed him on the mouth, passionately.

"Thank you John," she said, "I knew that you would understand and I just found out as I kissed you that I love you just as much as before."

John then turned towards me, looked at me right in the eyes, right into my soul and found nothing else than tenderness, comprehension and esteem for him. He shook hands with me to my greatest relief and everyone was happy.

"I may look only eleven," said Nancy. "But I am almost thirty years old and I am not a minor. I am fair game for the horny ones and I expect to be laid by some of you gentlemen. I hope that each one of you will eventually show me his manhood. I feel horny like never before."

The men were red in the face and fidgeting but Joan was unperturbed. Nobody answered.

"All right, let's change the subject," said John. "We must try to find the nearest human city. Does anyone have an inkling of its emplacement?"

"I have the feeling that it is in this direction," I said.

Nobody else had any kind of intuition about it.

"All right, let's go for it then." said John.

167

We walked for a length of time in an unchanging landscape; there was those gigantic trees well spaced apart and the silky golden grass but nothing else; no other life, no birds, no insects, not even the whispering of the wind, total silence and the symphony of fragrances.

"Those trees, "said Joan, "are in constant color transformation but the crystal looking spheres at the tip of the tiny branches are just sparkling. There are neither dead branches nor dead trees anywhere. I have a hunch that these trees have been there for millions of years. Maybe they were growing at the time of that oldest civilization that modified the plant life of this world. This would be one billion years ago.

The trees might be immortals. There are no animals or birds here; they must fear them. The trees may be able to defend their selves and they may be the power or the principle that protects this world against intruders and crashed the spaceships. "

"Yes, "answered John, "they are loading themselves with solar energy all day long and when you touch them, they are warm. Most probably that energy is accumulated somewhere and is discharged at night.

This area might not be a safe place for any living being and we better get out of it before dark. "

We walked a fast pace for hours and finally emerged from the gigantic tree forest. The grass was different now, coarser and green.

There were bushes now and some of them in full bloom; some with berries of various shapes and colors. Wild grassland flowers grew in the grass and all kind of trees, sparsely distributed, were offering the most amazing fruits to the passersby. Some of the fruits were lying on the ground and a variety of birds and little furry animals were filling themselves on them.

Their joyous chatters were most welcome after those hours of dead silence. Some of them were chasing each other just for the fun of it and all those little animals and birds seemed to have a great time.

168

We were overwhelmed with an incredible variety of fragrances. A big creature was picking a fruit from a tree a few yards away. It was as big as a horse and look like the centaurs of the Mythology. It had an incredibly muscled man's torso attached to a horse body. His arms and hands were twice the size of ours and its face wasn't human; it looked like a cat. The whole body was covered with a short and dense fur except on the palm of its hands and the fur was colorful and very beautiful.

It turned its head and gazed at us.

"What a beautiful animal!" said Joan.

"Thanks." It said. "You look good too but I wonder how you can stand on only two legs without falling. You are most amazing creatures. I see that you carry swords and bows; are you some lost warriors from another world?"

I looked at the face of my companions and they were as baffled as I was. Everyone heard the centaur talking in perfect English, with classy and cultured intonations.

The centaur had talked like an English gentleman; or did he? Its mouth hadn't move.

"Would you like to taste one of those fruits?" It said. "I can pick some from the highest branches where we find the most delicious ones."

"Please do," said Joan, "we accept gratefully. Do you have a name? Mine is Joan."

The centaur picked fruits for everyone and came slowly towards us. When it was close enough, he bended his body and extended its large hands holding the fruits.

"Genamel, that's my name." It said as we picked the fruits. "I have lived a long time and never saw the like of you. Everyone wants to know where you come from."

"Its mouth didn't move," I said, "what we are getting is telepathic communication."

"We come from another world," said Joan, "and we just woke up in the gigantic tree forest."

"The old ones are better left to themselves." It said. "You would not have survived the night had you stayed there. And to answer your coming questions, we too came from another world, many centuries ago.

Our spaceship crashed on this plateau, where we survived. The plateau is vast enough for us but it is impossible to escape from it. It is so high that on a cloudy day we can't see the ground and the clouds never reach the height of the plateau moreover, the forest of old ones encircle it, leaving us the central surface."

"How big is that plateau?" asked John.

"To cross it takes two weeks of gallop." answered Genamel. "And to cross the forest of old ones that encircle it takes half a day."

"I don't think that we can run as fast as the centaurs can gallop for half a day." commented John. "That means that to cross it to the edge of the plateau will be a close call for us."

"And when we get to the edge and take a look downward," I said, "we might decide that it is impossible to climb it down. And then it will be too late to come back across the forest before nighttime."

"Don't worry about that Richard," replied John, "the Guardians thought about it and gave us what we need to do it."

"Who are those Guardians you are talking about?" asked Genamel. "And how did you come here? We didn't see any spaceship landing on the plateau and we centaurs are everywhere, we would have notice it."

At that moment, I decided to have a bite at the mauve and blue fruit.

"Wow! It is so, so delicious." I uttered out. "It tastes like a mix of fresh raspberry and blueberries in ice cream."

Everyone had a bite in turn and exclaimed themselves at the fantastic savor.

The Centaur waited patiently for us to eat our fruit.

"The Guardians are a species of ghosts, immaterial beings with great power. They snatched our essence, our soul as we died on our planet hundreds of years ago and brought it here. They created those bodies and put our essence in it. They also gave us the clothes and weapons."

"Very strange, we never heard of them before even though our spaceships have traveled extensively across the galaxy for centuries." said Genamel.

"We are here on a mission." John added. "A very important mission that might affect the freedom of the species inhabiting the galaxy. We have to get to the edge of the plateau and climb it down."

"But how will we climb it down?" I asked worriedly. "I have always been afraid of heights; I might be so scared when I will look downward that I might freeze, unable to move."

"It won't be dangerous." replied John. "Let me show you."

John took off one of his boots.

"You see," said John, "I can't bend it backward, nor frontward, only sideways. Now look at the sole surface, it is ridged. If you press your hand firmly on it, it gets stuck and the only way to unglue it is to open your hand sideways. I tried to climb one of the gigantic trees with my boots on and I could do it just like a lizard. Moreover, we have a pair of gloves in the backpack and they function the same way as the boots. You can hold your whole weight with one gloved hand only if you need to."

The Centaur seemed very interested by our boots, gloves and swords.

"I will leave now," said Genamel in a most gracious

171

way, "but we will meet again once you get to the other side of the plateau and before you cross the forest of old ones. I wish you hind luck until then." And it left galloping joyously.

"I found another variety of fruit." cried Nancy as she looked at her gold and purple fruit. It was the size of a grapefruit and it smelled real good.

"Wait," said John. "Let me check that one first. Some of those fruits might be poison for us."

John smelled his fruit calling for his intuition of coming danger.

"What do you think?" asked Nancy. "It smells good to me, can I have a bite now?"

"I have no bad feeling about it." said John as he was opening the fruit with the knife. He put a drop of juice on his tongue and closed his eyes trying to concentrate on the slightest of his body signals. Nothing seemed wrong with it, so he took a small bite and smiled.

"Wow! That one is just as delicious as the one the Centaur gave us." He said.

"Where did you find it?" asked Joan.

"Right there, they grow on that gold leafed tree." She answered proudly.

We went to pick one and tasted it and it was exquisite. We all ate more than one and I felt energy spreading inside.

"These fruits are highly nourishing Joan." I said.

"They taste like extra firm strawberry cheesecake." Joan answered. "They have a fruity flavor with a solid protein or fat content."

We felt real good. We had walk for hours and the fruits had given us back our energy. Some of us sat down while others lied down in the grass. There was no biting insects here, no crawling things; just plain good smelling grass. The wind was whispering something trough the leaves, *you will be happy here*, it seemed to be telling me and as I tried to catch the wind secret murmuring, I heard the birds' chirping, the small furry things' chattering and the nearby creek chuckling. It was just wonderful.

"Look at the sky John." said Joan dreamily. "It is different from our Earth sky and yet those strange colors are soothing."

"Beautiful." John answered. "And I can't stop looking at those moons; all six of them have an atmosphere and their colors are slightly different from each other. I wonder if these moons aren't as big as Earth."

"Maybe they are inhabited." said Joan.

"And the people living on them," said John, "might be wondering about our new world. They might try to imagine what kind of species is roaming this giant planet."

"We have already met one of those species, and we spoke with it." said Joan.

"Can you imagine my friends," I said looking at Joan and John, "how marvelous it is to be here on a new world?"

"With a group of friends," commented joyfully the reverend father."

"With women to love and guys to wrestle with…" added Nancy tease fully.

"What incredible adventures are awaiting us?" said Garry all excited.

"I never felt that good; that clean inside." said Tom. "I even wonder if that new body could be empty of viruses and bacteria."

"That's a good observation." answered Joan. "There are no insects crawling in the grass and I believe that the Guardians are too smart to recreate the intestinal flora of germs and bacteria."

"They probably found it repulsive and decided to improve our digestive system with no need for the parasites." said Nancy.

"Or they knew that this world does not allow microscopic life on its surface," said Garry, "and they had to do some changes in our system." commented Garry.

I started to daydream looking at the sky and thinking about the wonders this new world was going to reveal to us and fell asleep. When I woke up, the sun was still high and I would have bet it had been at least 12 hours since my awakening. *Daytime is probably longer on this World*, I thought.

Garry came back running, he had ventured a little further to investigate some of the plant life.

"Hey guys," he shouted, "there is a creek and a pond with a sandy beach close by. Maybe we can bathe there."

"Yes, I would like that a lot." said Joan.

"All right, let's go my friends." said John.

We stood up and followed Garry to the pond. The water was crystal clear. We looked everywhere for any kind of dangerous inhabitants.

There were small fishes but nothing else and the water smelled good. Nobody wanted to be the first to take off his clothes.

"Well Garry," said Joan with a smile, "won't you take your clothes off and get in? After all it is your pond, you found it."

"No way," said Garry, "you go first."

"It had to happen sooner or later," said Joan, "we are all horny like hell and we want to bathe. So we are going to have it all. I will undress, slowly, sexily, fill your eyes with it, men. Then you do the same and we jump in the water. Then we make love. I will take you all, except Garry of course."

"I will have you too." said Nancy in a young but husky voice.

Joan undressed slowly and we, John, Tom and I came closer, and touched her breast and thighs and we started to kiss her everywhere. She escaped and ran to the water and we, in turn, undressed quickly.

We were laughing in the water, kissing Joan, caressing her.

I sucked one of her nipples as I put my hand between her tights. In the same time, John was kissing her on the mouth and Tom was licking her other nipple.

Nancy went to Father O'Leary and pressed herself in his arms, kissing him with her pretty little mouth. She touched him and he had a tremendous erection.

"Take me to the grass," Nancy said.

The reverend father took her in his arms and kissed her in turn. Then he brought her into his arms and laid her in the grass and started to caress her with his mouth and after a while, she guided him in.

He went delicately, afraid to hurt her. He inserted himself only halfway in and started to make love to the young woman who was emitting girlish sounds of pleasure.

It was the first time for the Father. He had never made love before and now he was doing what would be on Earth the gravest of sins. His pleasure was increased tenfold by the thought of it. It was forbidden to kiss a girl on the mouth and he did it and kissed her slowly, savoring it, as he was taking her. He had the most tremendous pleasure as he let himself go to the full sin.
She cried of pleasure as she felt him come and had the most exquisite orgasm herself.

In the mean time, Joan was making love with Tom. I was waiting eagerly for my turn and John was lying in the grass, spent and relaxed. The father and Nancy watched Tom come to heaven and pulled himself out regretfully to let me have my turn at the beautiful Joan.

She had died in the car crash just hours ago, leaving me with my old friend the loneliness and there were many kisses to be given and received and I covered her mouth with mine and we made love eagerly, passionately.

Now, everyone felt better, and we were not shy anymore. Nancy was in John's arms kissing him on the mouth and after a while they made love. Each man had his chance at enjoying little Nancy's charms and father O'Leary took his turn with Joan.

We walked, bathed, ate fruits and made love for hours.

"Now we are a close group of very satisfied people," said Joan. "Some of you might think that making love so often today could have hurt me. You looked a little worried John, don't be. I feel great and I had multiple orgasms. You know you can become addicted to sex and I am just the one to become addicted. I don't know if the Guardians did something with my body to make me like that but if it is ok with you, we should have that kind of sexual orgy everyday."

"It is the same for me," said Nancy in her girlish voice. "You can have me any time. I feel horny all the time."

We couldn't agree more.

Garry had left the group when the orgy started. He didn't feel any sexual urge in his nine years old body and beside he would not have made love with his sister and mother.

That's why they gave me a ten years old body, thought Garry. *The Guardians didn't want me to have sexual urges and no one to make love to. Beside, being small might be helpful if we ever need someone to get through a narrow space. The important is that I feel great, like never before.*

So Garry went to patrol around and stand guard against possible predators. Now he understood that after all it wasn't so unfair to be the only one in a nine years old body with only two women that he wouldn't touch.

He had grown up with girls, sharing his sisters' girlfriends. He understood them. At the age of sixteen when he started to feel something else than friendship for them, he knew what they wanted. He could get them easily and started to enjoy fully their presence. They were all after him.

Everything was so different around here. There was that forest of great trees about one mile away on his left, and the strangest vegetation all around. There was such a diversity in the trees' shape and foliage on this world; such a variety of fruits and flowers, that one would wander for ever in his search for new essence or scent.

Garry picked something that looked like an orange and took a bite. This time, it tasted like a real fruit but not like an orange, it tasted like a mix of pineapple and cantaloupe. It was really delicious. The leaves of that tree looked like green tulips, they were about 12 inches long and all of them were oriented upwards on a solid little red stump. The bark of the tree was blue, leathery and very soft. Garry pulled a little piece of it and cut it off. It looked like leather.

We can make shoes with it or a belt, Garry thought.

It was very resilient and after cutting a narrow band he tried to tear it apart to no avail.

This leathery bark can be used to make an excellent rope if a few narrow bands were spliced together, Garry told himself. *Maybe I could make a javelin, using the bark to fix my knife at the end of a stick. This way, I could possible defend myself against a big predator.*

So Garry spent an hour finding the right stick, then carving the end of it to receive the knife handle. He then spliced some bands of the leathery bark. He found some very sticky resin exuding from the bark of a needle tree and used it to glue the narrow strips, which he twisted around the end of the stick and the knife handle already placed into carved end. The glue dried very quickly and the final result was excellent.

Garry practiced for a while at throwing his new javelin. The knife blade didn't break even when he missed and threw it on a rock.

I don't throw it hard enough, thought Garry, *I am too small and feeble, and I don't have enough power. What if I can help myself with a gadget, something to help me throw it with more, much more power?*

Garry thought for a while about a makeshift gadget that would add velocity to his throws. He found some bamboo like trees and cut a length of twenty-four inches. Using some more bands of the leathery bark, he fixed in the middle of the javelin shaft and perpendicular to it, the two feet long bamboo. The tube was sticking out and was fixed in a way that it could easily bend backward. He then inserted a three feet stick in the bamboo tube and tried to throw the javelin again.

He had added a total of five feet to his arm length and the javelin went much faster and farther. He then improved the grip of his throwing stick with glued bands of leather and tried again. After a few throws, he was beginning to hit his target with enough velocity to kill or maim a predator for when thrown at a tree, the javelin was hard to pull out.

Garry practiced for an hour and got very accurate. *They gave me an excellent body*, he thought, *for I improved my skill really quick and I don't get tired at throwing the javelin.*

Garry was very proud of his makeshift javelin thrower and quite anxious to show it to his friends.

Let's go back to the beach, he thought, *they are surely done with the orgy now.*

He came back to the pond with a new spirit and quite proud of himself.

The orgy was over and we were all relaxing when Joan came to think about Garry. She looked everywhere and he wasn't there. Joan went further, looking everywhere for Garry when she heard something and turned around to face a beast; a wolf like beast, snaring at her.

She had left her sword and knife behind at the pond. The beast charged her so fast that she knew she wouldn't escape.

That's where I loose my life again, thought Joan, *right here, on my very first day on Ghama-2; too bad that I will never know the outcome of our mission. Sorry John, sorry Richard, I failed you miserably. How stupid, how dumb it had been to venture in a strange land, unarmed, after all the warnings and the preparation that John had imposed on us all.*

She couldn't move, scared stiff and cold; her terror gaining on her shame as the beast got closer. Suddenly, a javelin hit the predator in the chest and it dropped kicking in agony at Joan's feet.

Joan looked behind at her savior and was surprised to see the little Garry standing proudly behind her.

"That was a lucky hit," said Garry. "I made that javelin and thrower gadget while you were in orgy mode and I had plenty of time to practice before coming back but I can't believe I threw it right in the beast chest and pierced its heart."

"Garry, my dear little Garry, you just saved my life." exclaimed Joan. She hugged him and kissed him a dozen times more on the cheeks. When she finally released him, Garry went to the wolf and pulled his javelin out then cut the claws, which he put in his backpack.

Joan and Garry came back holding hands. We were dressed and very, very worried. Joan told us her story and we were all over Garry.

He was our little hero.

"Thank you for saving her life Garry, I will never forget it." I said.

John did the same thing followed by the other men.

"Thank you Garry," said Nancy, "you are the weakest man here and yet you are the one that saved her from that giant wolf like beast. You are my hero, little brother."

"And you are very clever," said the reverend father, "and resourceful for you found a way to compensate for your weakness."

"What happened today should serve us a good lesson." Said John, "I tried to make you realize that this mission will be a dangerous one for the Guardians had warned me about it. All kind of predators is roaming the surface of this world and we have to protect ourselves at all time. Joan should not have left the campground unarmed but I feel responsible for what happened today. I should have been aware of Garry and Joan leaving the safety of our little group.

I believe I failed you as your leader. I was too taken by the sexual frenzy to notice Garry's departure and then I fell asleep. Maybe somebody else should lead the group from now on."

"I don't think so," I replied immediately, "for if you failed to notice their leaving, we failed too."

"We have not yet taken the habit of functioning as a team." said Tom. "No one should venture alone even if it is to go to the bathroom. There should be a companion at all time watching your back."

"There is one point that I wish to underline." said the Reverend Father. "I believe that we have been led to that close call. How are the chances that Garry who had gone quite a distance away would be right behind Joan as the beast charged her? And how are the chances that his makeshift javelin would hit the beast right in the heart as it jumped on Joan? Even with one hour of practice, the beast was in movement, it was rushing at Joan."

"I believe I see where you are heading." Reverend father said John. "But even if this time we received God's help, we should not believe that He will be there to protect ourselves again. We got to help ourselves first otherwise we will not even be worthy of His help.

And from now on, nobody should walk alone and unarmed on this land right?"

"Yes sweetheart, I have learned my lesson." said Joan warmly as she took John in her arms for a hug.

We looked at his javelin and the throwing gadget.

"Very clever!" said John. "We should all make one javelin for ourselves fixing a cutting stone instead of our knife at the end of the stick. We have to keep the knives for close combat.

The knives can also be helpful in our descent from the plateau. If the plateau is many miles high, we might have to spend a night or two on the cliff. We will need them, the blades are unbreakable and we can insert it in a small cavity and hold ourselves in a net made out of this leathery bark rope. We should splice bands of it and make the longest ropes we can carry in our backpack.

Garry led us to those pine trees where we spent the next few hours splicing ropes. Now the sun was coming down and we decided to find ourselves a shelter.

"Who knows what wicked things our way may come." I said jokingly, thinking about a movie title.

There was nothing to serve as a shelter so we cut branches, made pointed sticks with them and planted them in the ground with their tips pointing outward like so many lances; that was Nancy's idea. Then we just lied down. One would stand guard for a while then would wake up his replacement. That's what John had proposed and he had offered to stand first guard.

The firework started as darkness fell on us. The crystal spheres at the tip of the gigantic tree branches were emitting energy. The whole gigantic-tree-forest came afire with tremendous sparks and thunders everywhere.

The centaur was right," said John, "we would not have survived the night had we stayed there."

Many hours later, the firework finally stop and we fell asleep except for John who said he still had first watch. After a while he woke up Tom and lied down beside Joan. We heard cries and roars all night long.

The night was filled with moving shadows but we were left alone.

Father O'Leary replaced Tom and later on woke me up. I took my turn at the watching and worrying for the last few hours of darkness. Joan and the children were spared and they well deserved it. We woke up at sunrise and I was hungry.

"Three or four eggs sunny side up with a dozen slices of crisp bacon and a full plate of hash brown and I will be ready to go," I said.

"Now come on, Richard, don't start on that." Said Reverend Father O'Leary, whom I had guessed, had a weakness for good solid food.

"Let's sample some of the fruits around," said Joan, "maybe we will find some that would be a suitable eggs and bacon substitute for our breakfast."

Nancy found one kind that tasted like ham and did nicely with the ones offered by the centaur, which tasted like extra firm strawberry cheesecake.

We filled ourselves, went back to the pond for a cold bathe and we were on our way; moving in the direction I believe was the city of New Alexandria. We were now carrying a javelin in addition to our sword, knife and bow.

John believe that we could face an attack by a family of wild dogs or even lions but there was the risk of loosing one or more members of our group should such an encounter happen. So we went on carefully and John was at my side leading the group. We would rely on his sixth sense of incoming danger to walk around the predators.

Tom and Joan were right behind followed by Nancy, Garry and the Reverend Father was guarding our rear. He was the only one without a javelin. He had a quarterstaff though and had proven at Camp David that he knew how to use it.

"I always carried one on my pilgrimages," he said joyfully.

I could see that John had great respect for him, he felt comfortable with the father guarding the back of our little group. We had seen him doing some practice swings before we left and we knew that the reverend father was a true warrior of God.

A few hours after we left the pond, we went into a field of very tall grass, it grew up to our shoulders and the tips were loaded with cereal grains. The grass looks like a kind of wheat.

Garry was too short to see anything and Father O'Leary set him up on his shoulders and was now walking right behind us. Tom had taken his place guarding our rear.

The fruit trees were everywhere but sparsely planted through the wheat field. We walked two or three hours with John opening a trail with energetic swings with his sword, sometimes we switch place and it was my turn to open the way and finally, we came out of the cereal field into a vast plain.

Far away on our left raised forested hills and in front and to our right, was mostly grassland. There were rectangle made out of differently colored grass, pounds, small forest, small fruit trees growing in bunch and larger ones standing alone in a most beautiful arrangement.

"The landscape looked like a well-tended park." Said Nancy.

"It is absolutely beautiful," I added in awe for to my artist eyes, it seemed that the cloud formation and the colors in the sky were matching the colorful and elegant landscape.

"What a fascinating world." said Joan, happily.

Here and there, we could see some elegant bouncing grazers.

"They look like some kind of gazelles." said Garry.

The birds were singing their heart out and some of

them were flying just about us. Joan extended her hand and a beautiful blue and gold bird came to perch on her wrist looking at her without fear.

We stopped amazed at the scene and Joan started to caress its head. It sang something in delight and more of the birds came to perch on our shoulders and we extended our wrists too and they jumped on them waiting for our caresses.

"They are so cute." said Nancy.

"That's the kind of world I was hoping for." said John. "It is so much better than rows of adoring people."

John told us about his dream during his flight to Pakistan.

"I could see my mother and Joan," said John, "and my brother but I could not move; I could not talk to them and they didn't even see me. There were thousands upon thousands of rows of people adoring God or what look like God. They were there in adoration forever; what a nightmare."

"My son, don't worry about it," said the Reverend Father, "God wouldn't do that; He doesn't need our adoration. In fact, we are here to open the way to the multitude for this beautiful world will be our heaven shall we succeed."

The birds seemed to listen to our conversation as we petted them.

"We have to go now." said Joan to her bird.

We started to walk and the birds flew away singing happily.

We let them go for we were hungry and beside all pleasure must end if we want to have them again.

We went to a bunch of short fruit trees and picked some of their fruits and had a little picnic.

After a while we left and walked for hours before we met another cereal field.

John offered to take Garry on his shoulders before
entering it.

"I will carry you for a while." said John looking at
Garry.

"That I will do, if you don't mind John." said the
Reverend father. "God is taking much of the weight out
of my shoulders and we need you and Tom unimpaired
to protect us. You will be the fighters and I will go on
being the carrier for I am used to carry the word of God
everywhere I go and now I am carrying a carrier of
truth, a child, and a hero."

"Hey come on now," said Garry in an amused way," I may
look like a child but I am a grown up even though I feel
like playing and pulling your hair sometimes.

I don't know if it is my hormones; I remember being a
man on Earth but I feel real boyish now."

"Why don't you enjoy being a boy again," said Joan.
"Just let go, forget you are a man. We would like to
treat you like a child, hug you and play with you. It is
instinctive I guess."

"Beside," I said, "we are very grateful for your
mother's rescue and we don't know how to express it. We
don't want to offend you Garry; we respect you and
consider you our equal in all ways but please don't take
offense if we kiss you on your chubby little cheeks
or throw you in the air and catch you back for sometimes
you are irresistible."

At that, I grabbed Garry and threw him in the air,
caught him back, kissed him on both cheeks and set him
back on the ground laughing.

After that, Garry was talking and joking all the time.
The quiet and suspicious young man changed at that
moment to an open hearted and most amusing kid.

We resumed our trek through the long grass enjoying the
birds' songs and our new acute ability of
differentiating odors...

185

"Look," I said in a low voice as I stopped the group.

There were hundreds of large moving masses in the grass. We saw one of them. It looked like a blue hippopotamus with two short round horns over a pair of green cat eyes. It was covered with a soft looking fur.

"They are almost as big as an elephant." said Nancy softly.

One of the beasts noticed our presence. Either he heard Nancy's comment, smelled our presence, or simply read our thoughts like the Centaur; I don't know, but it turned its head, looked at us with interest and came galloping in our direction.

"I don't feel any impending danger," said John quickly. "Please be ready but don't show any aggressiveness."

The large animal stopped a few feet from us. Nancy walked to it before anyone could stop her and petted its muzzle. The animal emitted a strong purring sound of pleasure. At that moment, the whole herd seemed to notice us, and they came running toward us from everywhere to finally stop a few feet from us; we were surrounded!

The beasts looked at us with genuine interest; they did not show any sign of aggressiveness.

Joan walked to the nearest one and started to caress its muzzle and it too emitted a strong purring sound of pleasure.

At that I too walked closer to one of them and patted it talking softly and it purred.

John, Tom and the Reverend Father with Garry on his shoulder waited patiently but ready to come to our rescue if need be.

My beast had a very soft fur and like Joan and Nancy, I always liked the presence of animals; so it was quite pleasant for me to sense the beast pleasure as I was caressing its muzzle. Nevertheless, I felt a little wary and wondered if like the bears they could be omnivorous.

What if one of them decides to taste Nancy or Joan or have a bite at my hand?

They were friendly now but that could change at any moment.

"If a pack of lions or whatever kind of carnivores charge them from behind, they will crush us as they stampede away." said John fidgeting.

We had to move on and I was wondering how we could do it for there was no space between the beasts; they were packed solid all around us.

After a while, I asked my beast if it could move aside and let me pass looking at it straight in the eyes and trying to convey my message with sheer power of mind.

That's how stupid I can be; how in Heaven could the beast understand me? And yet I thought it might work. That's the thing about overoptimistic people and I have always been one of them, they always think that somehow they will manage and get out of trouble.

"Please, gentle one, would you move aside and let me pass? We have to go on now; we are on a mission and we can't delay any further." I said placidly.

And it somehow understood what I said and moved aside pushing another one away. The crowd opened up and we walked slowly through the herd.

"Well, well," said Joan, "we are going to give you a surname Richard; talker to animals."

"To shorten it a bit," said the Reverend Father joyfully, "we can use an old Hebrew translation: Yahwehameh, meaning One who talk through Yahweh."

"Come on now, both of you, who needs a surname and beside it was just straight foolishness on my part to assume that I could talk my way through the herd." I replied.

"Telepathy might work more often than not here my friends." said the Reverend. "After all, this is possibly Heaven where anything is possible."

187

"It is heaven to me." said Garry." I love this place.

"I have never felt so alive and so good." added Joan. "What a wonderful world where birds and beasts come to us for a little caress."

"I am very happy too Joan," said John, "but let's try to be more cautious next time. For a while I was a bit worried about the outcome of this encounter."

We left the herd to move on through the wheat field and we must have walked another hour or two before we came out to grassland again.

"Look over there," said John, "in that bunch of orange and purple trees."

"It looks like a grizzly bear," replied Tom, "and twice or three times the size."

"Big enough to prey on those elephant size buffalos." commented Joan.

"And it has spotted us." Tom said.

"Let's start shooting it with arrows." John said as the beast charged us.

In no more than two seconds we all had our bow in one hand and were already pulling on the string with an arrow already set.

We shot the beast as it got within fifty feet and seven arrows firmly planted themselves in the beast neck and shoulders. It seemed to slow down for a moment in surprise and then roared in anger and pain as it charged us with fury.

"Javelins now, then swords!" shouted John.

The beast was charging us with its head almost touching the ground. It gave me an idea…

There was no time to pull another arrow from my quiver, I drop my bow, pick my javelin from the ground and holding it with two hands I rushed at the beast, planted

188

my javelin firmly in its neck and used it as a pole to propel myself over the beast head. Fortunately, the javelin hit the collarbone or something real hard and I could propel myself away from the gaping mouth.

I felt a tremendous shock on my wrists and hit the ground behind the beast feet first.

The beast roared in pain, stop, and was hit immediately by John and Tom javelins in the neck.

Joan rushed at the beast and planted with all her power, her javelin in the beast chest.

Nancy and Garry released an arrow towards the beast head and one arrow got inside the right eye.

The enormous beast was mortally wounded; it crouched then lay on the grass and died.

"You were all wonderful!" I said as I came back from behind the beast.

"That's what I call team work." said John obviously very pleased with the outcome.

"I am afraid that I wasn't of much help." commented the Reverend. "I just stood guard in front of the children and I realized that I could not have done much with my quarterstaff against such a huge beast so I waited here with my sword in hand and watched the action."

"That was the right thing to do." said John with an uncontrollable smile.

John was exuberant; I had never seen him so excited. I felt the same way too, and looking to everybody else I could tell that everyone was feeling high. I was totally charged with I don't know what kind of hormones my new body was able to produce.

"I could not believe how fast you were able to move Richard." said John. "That somersault after you planted your javelin in the beast neck, using it as a pole to escape its bite and landing on your feet was quite incredible."

"Thank you John but I looked backward as I was landing on my feet behind the beast and I saw all three of you, moving at impossible speed; planting fearlessly your javelins in the beast body and I saw Nancy and Garry shooting an arrow in the beast eye; and everything, all the action, seemed accelerated."

"I have never seen people moving that fast." approved the Reverend Father.

"It got to be those improvements, the Guardians said they would do to our bodies." said Tom all excited. "Wow, that was awesome, I loved it."

"It's my arrow that found its mark." Said Garry teasingly for he knew that he had missed the beast.

"No way!" said Nancy simulating great offense." It was my arrow you little weasel."

"Calm down, you two, little darlings." said Joan.

"I believe that we are able to move faster than ever before when we are facing great danger." commented John.

"We probably have a way to produce speed hormones under great stress." added Joan.

The reverend father and I walked to the beast and looked at it silently. Tom had probably guessed what we were thinking.

"The meat might be very tasty, roasted over a campfire." said Tom.

"This comment shows that you are gifted with a great practical mind, my son." commented the reverend.

"Yes and the sun is getting close to the horizon," said John, "we might have a few hours left before dusk."

"Let's cut the filet mignon and a large chunk of his but and carry it with us on our way to our next campsite." I proposed. "I am a meat lover."

"And so am I, son" Approved the reverend father.

I pulled Joan's javelin from the beast chest and decide to have a look inside, to see if she was the one to have given the beast the mortal wound. I took my knife, cut the belly skin and looked inside. The javelin had made its way through the heart. I cut the flesh around it and pulled it out.

"You killed the beast my sweetheart." I said looking at Joan admiringly. "Here is the proof."

"Let's have a look at its other wounds," replied Joan, "I would bet I am not the only one that has given a fatal blow."

We open the neck and looked at the wounds inflicted by the three javelins and two of them had severe the jugular. We then pulled the arrow from the beast eye and realized that it had gone deep enough to pierce the animal brain.

"The beast was mortally wounded by four of us." said Joan.

"That is quite incredible; I am starting to feel that we stand a good chance of making it through to the lost city. said John.

I put the heart in my knapsack, and the other men put the thirty to forty pounds of filet mignon in theirs and we moved on, on a fast pace, looking for a suitable shelter.

"The days and nights are longer on Ghama-2," Joan told me as we walked side-by-side, "may be as much as fifty per cent longer. We had probably walked for a dozen hours, maybe more and I am getting tired."

"Are we there yet?" asked Garry teasingly.

We saw a variety of predators on our way; some of them were as big as the giant grizzly bear. But we saw them from a distance and none came too close.

"Many of the predators are sleeping," commented Tom, "they are sleeping through the daylight and they will soon be on the hunt. We got to find a shelter soon.

"That tree might do as a shelter." said John

It was a huge tree, not as big as the gigantic trees by
far but as big as the biggest trees on Earth. It had
roots coming down from the branches and there was a
large space between the curtain of descending roots and
the tree trunk. We cut one of the roots to give
passage and then block all access to our shelter with
branches we found and cut here and there.

We made a solid fence out of them. John looked
critically at the shelter and expressed his
satisfaction.

"We will bee able to sleep the night without anyone to
stand guard." He said.

We then went to pick some dead branches, cut them in
pieces and placed them over a bed of dry leaves just
outside our shelter entrance and Tom started the
campfire with the lighter gadget the guardians had put
in our knapsack.

We then had to wait until we had a solid bed of slow
burning logs before roasting the steak so it was time to
get to the nearby creek.

"Let's bathe and have some fun." said Nancy sexily.

So we went for a bathe, picked some fruits and came back
to the shelter where we talked for a while. I was under
a strong sexual urge, that new body had stronger needs
than the one I had on Earth. I was hesitant though to be
the first to ask for my sweetheart favor; fortunately,
John was not so hesitant, he took Joan in his arms, and
started our second orgy. Nancy seduced the reverend
father and Tom and I waited for our turn.

Garry just went to the farthest corner of the shelter
and fell asleep.

I had just made love to Joan when the incredibly
appealing smell of the roasted filet mignon caught me.
Garry had caught it too for he was getting up from his
far corner of the shelter.

The reverend and John had taken care of the diner after they were done with the sweeties.

I cannot describe how exquisite was the roasted meat. I never tasted anything that succulent. I believe I ate four or five pounds of meat along with five or six fruits that tasted like ripe cranberries.

Once we had finished our diner, the reverend went to the creek and got back with a few flat stones.

"If anyone got some energy left," Said the reverend, "I would need a little help to get a few more stones from the creek. We will put the flat ones over the coal with our large chunk of meat we cut from the beast plus the heart and then we will cover the meat with more stones and cover them with a good thickness of logs so that the heat from the fire will slowly cook the meat during the night.

We went to help him and had a second bathe. I also washed my knapsack in which I had carried the beast heart and the other guys did the same. After that, we closed the shelter entrance, laid down and fell asleep.

Tomorrow morning we will have another feast before leaving."

On the late afternoon of our forth day of travel, we came to another of the gigantic-trees' forest.

"Are you sure Richard we have to go through it to move towards the lost city?" asked John.

"Yes, I have a very strong intuition that we have to. The city is in this direction, it is over there; there is no doubt in my mind. Moreover, I am sure that the human settlement will be in the same direction; it is my gut feeling."

"Since we don't know how long it will take to cross the forest," said John, "we must put all chances on our side. I would start the crossing of it in the middle of the night, as soon as the firework ceases. We should try to make a fire now and prepare some torches."

At that moment we heard the sound of a galloping herd coming in our direction. We looked around for shelter and there were only the gigantic trees. We backed up to one of them and waited.

"Look," said Garry from the Father's shoulders, "it is the centaurs, hundreds of them."

They stopped a short distance from us, and one of them, probably the leader, or one of the elders, came forward and greeted us.

"Brothers in the universe," he said, "we wanted to see you before you leave for ever. You mentioned to Genamel that you are here on a mission. Would it be acceptable to you to tell us what it is about? We have been imprisoned here for centuries and we are most in need of news and revelations.

We would also like to know about the world you came from. Would you mind to delay your departure and share with us your knowledge and hopes?"

"Yes respectable leader," said John, "we will stay and share all we know."

"We can read each other mind and communicate telepathically. If one of you talks to one of us, all the centaurs will listen. But if we split our nation into seven groups, each group surrounding one of you, we will learn different things, which we will enjoy to communicate to each other for days and weeks. We will also learn much more. Would you agree?"

John agreed to it and we split. Fifty or sixty of the centaurs surrounded me; they were lying comfortably on the grass as I started to talk about Earth; I didn't have to raise my voice, they were reading my thoughts.

They questioned me about our philosophy and ethics. They were very curious about how we could express our love and tenderness or approval without telepathic communications; how respectful challenge could be expressed between males at mating time, and all sort of things related to social behavior.

I felt their pity for our loneliness. They could not understand how we could be happy without knowing for sure what other people were thinking.

They expressed their envy for our coming adventures and discoveries should we succeeded in climbing down the miles high cliff.

They projected in my mind images of their world. They had been living in peace with another specie from the beginning of their known history. The other specie was birdlike and able to fly. The centaurs envied them.

They developed a very high technology level and finally discovered the secret of anti-gravity. Now, like their birdlike allies, they could fly with the help of anti-gravity belts and they built floating cities. Some of these cities were transformed into miles long spaceships, and they started to explore the nearby worlds.

They also built smaller ships for the exploration of the nearby stars' planets. The Centaurs were peaceful and good-natured beings and I felt real kinship with them.

I was sorry for them being imprisoned on the plateau with no way out and they knew about my compassion.

Joan had been an excellent chemist.

"There is the possibility of producing lighter than air gas through chemical reactions." She said. "The gas could fill a balloon made of the leathery bark strips sewed and glued together. It would support a few centaurs maybe a dozen. When the weight would give a slightly greater downward force than the upward air pressure, the balloon would float slowly downward. The passengers would disembark one at a time and the first one would fix the balloon to a tree.

Some weight would then be added, just enough for the balloon to float slowly upward with two of the centaurs Returning to guide the balloon as it goes back up the cliff to pick some more of their brothers."

"The ones that successfully make their way down and are willing to help us, are welcome to join us in our effort to find the lost city." added John. "We will be at the human city down river where we intend to live for a while.

We hope to recruit and train a small army of volunteers there. The guardians warned us about the probability that we will have to fight our way to the lost city and our success may very well depend on our strength and number."

We told the centaurs that we now had to prepare some torches to light our way through the gigantic trees. We informed them of our intention to depart in the heart of the night, right after the firework ended.

Genamel offered the Centaurs help to prepare a few campfires for the night and we accepted with pleasure.

I wanted to know how they were going to start the fire without a lighter and I guess that everyone amongst us wanted it too for we didn't mention our little gadgets.

They got plenty of wood and then they started the fire using especially abrasive wood sticks, rubbing two of the sticks against each other in the presence of a yellowish powder that smelled like sulfur and could be found on some dry bushes.

"I will take Garry with me," said John, "for the hunting of those birds that looked like big chicken. It would be great to eat some roasted meat tonight. Maybe our new friends can help in building a shelter..."

The centaurs told us not to worry about a shelter; they would stay with us and give us the protection of their numbers. No predators will come close, they said.

John left with Garry. They walked noiselessly all their senses in alert towards the area where they had seen some of the birds. Once there, John helped Garry to get on a branch high enough for safety.
He had to throw him up so that he could grab the branch and climb on it. *At least, this way, the hunter would not become a prey himself*, John thought. Then John went to another tree and climbed it. They sat motionless for a while. Finally the chicken like birds came around.

John and Garry released an arrow and got two of the birds. John climbed down, caught the birds and threw them up to Garry who tied them up on the branch. Then John climbed back his own tree and they waited again.

Ten minutes later, a group of boars' looking carnivores came to investigate the bird's blood odor and John's next arrow pierced one of the boar's heart. The others, like the birds, ran for their life and escaped.

John and Garry came down from the trees and John sliced the boars' belly open and emptied it. He kept in his backpack the heart and liver.

Garry did the same with the chickens and together they pulled the feathers out.

John swung the boar across his right shoulder, Garry picked up the chickens and they rushed back to the camp. It wasn't easy and at some point and John had to use his sword like an ax to cut through the bushes.

They went as quickly as they could for they feared that some wicked beasts, attracted by the odor, would follow them and charge them.

They had been splashed with blood but there were no mosquitoes so Garry couldn't mind less about it; he was very pleased that John had asked him to come along and happy that his arrow had found its mark.

They reached the rest of their group, drop the fowls and the boar by the fire, got praised by their companions and quickly made their way to the nearby creek where they bathed and washed their clothes.

On their way back, they could smell the roasting meat.

"Oh my God; that smells so good," said Garry, "let's race to the camp."

They sprinted their way back and at the last moment, John tripped on something…? And Garry came first beaming with pleasure and excitement.

"I killed the biggest of the fowls." He said prideful.

"And we found some kind of potatoes," said Joan. "I covered them with stones and started the fire over it. We also got some of the wheat like grass grains and grounded it with water and the bread is cooking too."

The dinner was fabulous and the freshly baked bread too good to be true. We left our mind open to the Centaurs lying around, so that they could share our pleasure.

The crusty bread and the potatoes make such a difference, I thought, *everything is delicious and the meat is so juicy, tender and exquisite.*

"The fowl really taste like chicken," said Nancy. "I wonder how come this world has so much similitude to earth life. We are 89 light years away, the evolution was different here and the world is much older."

"The strangest thing about this world is the gravity." said Joan. "The central core of fused matter must be missing otherwise this huge world would have a greater gravity, it would crush us, and it doesn't. My conclusion is that either the center of this world is gone or more than 50% of it is missing. Who knows, there might be a world in the center where the old ones live since they left their cities a billion years ago."

"Hey that's an interesting concept," said Tom. "There may even be many layered worlds one over the other with a few miles of rock in between and a bigger world right at the center of the planet where resides the old specie."

"They may have seeded many worlds with life before they went into reclusion," said Nancy, "and Earth might be one of them. That would explain the similitude between Earth and Ghama-2's plant and animal life."

Tom was not much of a talker; he was the quiet type. He would listen with great interest when intelligent and nice people were talking to him or between themselves.

Otherwise, he would just relax. So we were somewhat surprised by his contribution to our wild imaginings.

"Let's see," I said. "Earth has a radius of five thousand miles and a surface of 4 pi times the radius square root and that gives Earth a surface of 300 million square miles. Ghama-2's estimated radius is twelve times as big as Earth; its surface has then got to be 43,200 million square miles about 150 times the surface of Earth.

Now let's look at the radius again; we said twelve thousand miles. If each layered world is five miles high and if there is three miles of rock between the worlds, we have enough space for fifteen hundred worlds with a diminishing surface as we go deeper and deeper to reach the central one.

Ghama-2' surface should be 150 times the surface of Earth and the next layered world just a bit less and so on. That means a total habitable surface equivalent to one hundred and twenty five thousand Earth's surface."

"And it might take many lifetimes to discover the first one." said Garry amusingly. "So we might as well forget about the others. Who wants to play ball? We can use one of those rubbery fruits. It will help digesting the few pounds of meat we ate, maybe even more for some of us…"

As he said that, Garry was looking at Father O'Leary who had kept silent; in his case it had been four pounds of meat at the very least.

"I got a big appetite and it fuels my prayers with renewed intensity." said the Reverend in a strong yet funny voice. "And I believe we may well need them for God to forbid our excitement as we killed that poor beast."

"I suppose, we are still human." answered Tom. "We have evolved from cave man after all, and it is not our fault if there is still a hunter deep inside."

"And the poor beast was trying to kill us," mentioned Nancy, "it was just self defense."

199

"All right, all right, I give you the absolution." said
the reverend. "Now let's play football."

We started to play ball under the interested eyes of the
Centaurs. All of us, having fun and laughing and after a
while, the playful excitement added to the satisfaction
of a wonderful meal turned the men's minds into lust for
the beautiful young girl and woman. We caught them and
kissed them.

Joan and Nancy were overcome with their own lust and
sexual needs. In a moment they were bare and we let go
for another sexual orgy.

It wasn't mating season yet for the centaurs but they
were sharing our thoughts and feelings and this brought
an immediate transformation in their system. Thousand of
centaurs had hind luck that night as they coupled with
never experienced before intensity.

The fire was rekindled with the addition of more
branches and we lied down safely surrounded by our new
friends for a few hours of rest.

The giant trees' firework had stopped. John woke us up
and we prepared ourselves for the long trek ahead. We
packed the rest of the meat into leaves and stacked it
into our backpacks.

The centaurs were up and their leader came to present
the whole Centaur nation best wishes.

"We can't walk amongst the old ones," he said, "we are
mentally pushed away and it is the same for all the
animals and birds. How you can do it is beyond us. Maybe
humans possess a mental power that is unique and
protects them against it.

Some of us are willing to risk our lives and will try
going down in a balloon. We will follow your suggestion
Joan.

There is an opening through the giant trees on the other
side of this plateau. The opening is not very large and
the forest is wider there. We do not think you should
try it there; you would not be able to get through in

between the nights and would get killed by the firework. But we believe we can run much faster than you and there is a large opening in between the cliff and the forest of old ones once we have crossed through it. So we will carry whatever we need for the balloon and built it in that clearing.

"Mixing your dung and the sulfur you use for starting a fire plus some phosphate will produce a lighter than air gas," said Joan, "you can use that gas to inflate it."

"We will do that," said Genamel, "and if we succeed, we will try to find you and join you in your great mission.

Telepathic communication is possible between us over great distances so if some of us join with you, we will be able to share your adventures and even provide a certain degree of mental protection if you are under mental attack. We thank you for sharing your thoughts and knowledge with us, we will never forget you, and if you succeed please come back and rescue us from our imprisonment."

"Good luck to all of you; we will not forget you either." said John. "I personally promise to come back for you if we succeed. Thanks for your sharing and good luck."

Chapter 8 - Down to the valley

I set afire a torch and took the lead. From time to
time, I replaced it as it burned through. We walked at a
good pace for hours and daylight came and there was yet
no end to the forest. We took a short rest and when we
got up to resume our trek, John proposed to accelerate
the pace.

"We should jog a few miles," he said, "then walk just
long enough to recuperate and resume jogging."

We did it all day long. We were in a terrific shape and
we marveled at it. But as the day went by, we started to
worry. The forest seemed to go on forever.

I was very worried for more than one reason, I was
afraid of heights. If I look down hanging on a cliff
wall I might very well let go or freeze. For me, getting
out of this forest didn't mean salvation. A quick death
by electrocution was more appealing to me than falling
from a miles high cliff. But the forest seemed endless
and if we could not exit soon, we might be spared the
choice.

It was getting dark when we finally came to the end of
the forest. There were no more trees ahead but the last
of the trees were standing right at the cliff. We could
not stay there; it would be fatal to do so; and there
was nowhere to go except down the cliff.

The canyon we were now facing was tremendous; at least a
mile deep and so wide that we could not see the other
side. There was a river, some forests and some grassland
areas, and many lakes. There were mountains down there
and they looked like small hills from our height.

On our left and far away, the river connected with the
sea and there it was, the human settlement, at the
junction of the sea.

We could not stay there, we would be electrocuted by the
gigantic trees' firework and that meant we had to start
climbing down until we could find a ledge or a cave to
pass the night.

John went very close to the abysm and looked for such a
ledge and could see one maybe one or two hundred feet
down and fifty feet on his right.

The canyon wall was rough enough to climb down if you
are a professional climber, but we were not and the
challenge was formidable. Tom and Father O'Leary joined
him and looked down but Joan, her children and I would
not come close.

"I am afraid of the heights," I said sheepishly. "That's
the only thing that really scares me. I think I am so
scared that I would let go and fall."

"We have no choice," said John. "It is that or be
electrocuted and with our boots and gloves, it will be
child play to get down."

"I believe," said Father O'Leary, "that each of us was
chosen for certain inherent or acquired abilities. I may
be able to help you. When I was a missionary in Africa,
I had to treat injured people and I performed surgeries
without anesthesia for I could hypnotize my patients.

If you allow me, I will hypnotize you and remove your
fear of heights forever. Please sit here side by side,
all of you; you too John."

We sat and faced the good Father. He started to relax us
with powerful suggestions and we were soon asleep. He
convinced us that we would never fear the heights from
now on. He ordered us to be very careful though but
calm, as we will go down. He told us to take our time
and do everything with acute awareness of our body
muscles and our surroundings. He reassured us that we
will not fall if we do so.

Then he did a short prayer and woke up everyone.

"Let's put on our gloves." said Tom.

John put his gloves on and started to climb down the
cliff.

We saw how he could unglue one foot and one hand at a
time and we started to climb down.

It became very easy with the time and we climb down for two hours before the firework from the giant trees started far over our heads. We had long passed the first ledge and were now trying to find another one large enough for all of us and suitable for a few hours of sleep. It was totally dark in between the flashes coming out of the giant tree spheres and those were the only times we could see something.

"There is the ledge we were hoping for." Said Tom. "In fact it is a cave but not very deep."

"Three of us can lie down against the wall and the other four will be sleeping just beside the abyss." Said John. That means a fatal fall if one turn on the wrong side. So we have to fix some ropes to hold us in."

John inserted his javelin in a fissure of the cliff face and tied a rope to it.

We fixed more ropes with the rest of the javelins over the ledge and looped them around Joan, Garry, Nancy and I who were the lucky ones to sleep on the very edge of the ledge. We lied down and John, Tom and the reverend looped the end of the ropes around their waist and lied down between the ledge back wall and us.

All of this had been done with quite a lot of acrobatic moves and I had been stepped over a few times.

"Good Lord John," I said, "if you push a little harder on my stomach, I will pee in my pants."

"Sorry Richard but now that you mentioned it, I believe I will have to do it too. Give me some space."

I rolled against the wall while John relieved himself then it was my turn and everybody else was doing the same thing. Finally, we were all lying down and moments later everyone was sleeping.

It had become cooler as we went down the cliff and thinking about it, I came to the conclusion that the giant trees were warming up the plateau. If it is so, it also meant that somewhere along our descent, we might hit ice and snow. These were my last thoughts as I fell asleep and they were not very comforting.

At first light, Tom and Garry climbed up over the cave to dislodge the javelins; we ate some of our smoked meat and we resumed our descent.

We climbed down much faster than the previous evening, we had become good at it, and I was often looking down without any trace of fear. The weather was getting real cold now and it was windy. There were spots of ice and our gloves or boots wouldn't stick on ice.

We came to a halt when we reached the end of dry rocky surface. Underneath was stretch, hundreds of feet long of ice-covered rock.

"Let's tie together all of our ropes and let's see if we can reach that ledge down there." proposed John.

We did that and ended up with a four to five hundred feet long rope and it was long enough to reach that ledge down there. John fixed it to his javelin and forced the tip of the javelin into a crack. He then pulled as much as he could on the rope, with his two feet well glued to the rocky surface in case it would snap or the javelin would come out of the fissure but it seemed solid enough for at least one of us at a time.

"I will hold on the rope as an additional safety, who want to go first?" asked John.

I found myself answering first and wondered when I will learn to keep my mouth shut. I supposed I didn't want Joan or one of my companions to think that I wasn't made of the hero stuff. They were all heroes to me but I was not too sure if I was as brave as they were.

I went down with no other grip than my hands to support my considerable weight. I figure I was probably weighting more than two hundred pounds with all those muscles but helping myself with my foot to take off some of the weight, I climbed down to the ledge which was about four hundred feet down below, the equivalent of a forty stories building without a sweat.

The ledge was leading to a shallow cave but spacious enough for the seven of us.

I signaled to my friend that the next one should start his descent.

Garry, Nancy, Joan, Tom and the reverend father came down and joined with me on the ledge.

John seemed to be dislodging his javelin a bit from the fissure and testing it. I knew that we needed the rope for we had not reached yet the end of the icy surface.

I quickly looped the end of the rope against a boulder and held it just in case that the javelin would not hold in and John would fall down. The reverend and Tom also took the rope. I didn't need to tell them that if John fell for three hundred feet, the rope should not be fixed on the boulder; we had to break his fall letting the rope slide against the boulder and we could do that if all of us were holding on the rope. Joan, Nancy and Garry caught the idea for they too came to hold the rope.

But the javelin held on and John reached the ledge without any difficulty.

"Thanks for holding on the rope my friends. "said John. "I was not expecting less from you. Now let's try to dislodge that javelin."

With our combined strength, we dislodged the javelin, watching its fall. At the last moment, it hit the cliff wall and bounced directly on us. In a quick movement of his quarterstaff, the father deviated its trajectory and John seized it in a lightning fast movement of his hand.

He then fixed it in a nearby crevasse and we were on our way down again. We climbed down from ledge to ledge using that technique and found a cave many hundred feet downward. The cave was large enough for us all and we were extenuated. We had been walking and jogging for two third of a night and a full day plus and then we had done a few hours of climbing down. We slept in a narrow cave a few hours only and now another day of extreme exercises with very little food and water and we were very tired. We had spent our last reserve of energy. We lied down in the cave and fell asleep almost at once.

At first light, we ate half of the meat left in our backpack and resumed our descent. We didn't need the rope anymore and the descent was so much easier.

We climbed down for possibly six more hours and took a break sitting on a large ledge where we ate the balance of the food. We were a few hundred feet over the valley floor and looking for the presence of large predators.

Nobody was complaining but our hands and fingers were bruised and we were aching everywhere. When we started the descent, we thought we would have to climb down a few thousand feet, we never thought we were miles up from the ground. Without the rope, it would have been impossible since there were some long stretches of icy areas offering no grip at all.

"We were on a plateau," said Joan, "and this valley is in fact the world on which we will be living from now on. The flora and fauna will probably be quite different from what we have experienced on top of the plateau."

"Since we have not spotted any dinosaurs nearby," said Nancy, "let's get there. I am hungry and tired of hanging on a cliff."

"Yes," Garry approved, "let's go, I certainly need to walk for a while."

We finished our descent and now we were standing knee high in soft purple grass. There were wild flowers of all kind, and our new acute sense was overpowered by an incredible variety of scents. We were unconsciously characterizing the fragrances and in a certain way we were tasting them like you would taste a variety of spices before starting a new recipe.

There was one offensive odor that seemed to be in disharmony with the others. It was not a flower or plant life flavor, it was a slightly gagging smell and it came from our left. We looked up in that direction and heard a shout of pain and despair.

"That shout is from a human throat," said Father O'Leary. "And that terribly offensive odor must come from an alien species, an evil one. They might have captured one of our descendants. We must go to their rescue at once."

"Wait," said John, "first, let's rub our skin and clothes with some of that mud here, it will hide us and cover our body odor. We will have more chances to rescue them if we get there undetected."

We did it and moved quickly and silently in the direction of the strong alien odor. When we got real close, Garry asked us to wait for him.

"I will take a peek and come back." He said.

Since he was the smallest of the group, it made sense; there would be less risk for him to be discovered. John agreed and he left silently. He went slowly through the last few meters of grass before an opening and saw a group of aliens looking at two teenagers hands bound and tied up to a tree. They looked like brother and sister and they were scared and bruised.

There are twelve of them, not counting the ones I don't see, thought Garry.

They were bipeds, with a rat face and armed with formidable fangs and claws.

They are tall, a foot taller than John, they sure look vicious and dangerous, thought Garry.

"Grrr, I will eat that one, I am hungry." roared one of the rat faces after a bite at her arm. The bite wasn't deep enough to endanger her life but some blood was trickling down her arm. It had been more to inflict pain for she was to be kept alive.

208

"No, we must take them alive to the master leader. He wants to question them." roared the group leader.

Her blood kept on trickling down from the wound and the girl was silently weeping.

Garry went back to his friends and told them of what he had seen.

"We will split in three groups," John said. "Father and Nancy, you go left and circle them, Richard and Joan you go to the right, Tom, Garry and I will move directly to them. In three minutes, we will attack from three directions at the same time.

We will shoot an arrow at one of the bipeds and then charge at full speed and run them down with our javelins, good luck to everyone."

We parted and John waited the three minutes or so. Joan and I moved slowly towards the aliens and came out of the bushes as we heard a shout. One of the aliens had spotted one of us and roared a warning. The aliens turned to look in our direction but before they could pounce on us, John and Tom had already released an arrow and hit their targets; two of the aliens fell to the ground with arrows sticking out of their backs.

The rest of the aliens must have realized they were being attacked from both directions and froze in indecision.

Garry ran towards them, his arm fully extended backward, holding his javelin thrower, he swung and released it and his javelin came soaring and impaled an alien in the chest with such force that half of the shaft was protruding from the alien's back. That beast was the one that had bitten the girl.

He will bit no one anymore, thought Garry.

The alien roared in pain and anger and fell to the ground while the whole pack came into a frenzy action, rushing in all directions.

Father O'Leary went to Garry's rescue as one of the
aliens made a dash for the boy and split the alien's
head with a terrific blow of his quarterstaff. John and
Tom charged like berserkers. I charged too and hit one
of them in the chest with my javelin and it went through
its chest. The beast roared and went down kicking in
agony. I looked around and all the aliens
were down, some were dead already and others were
kicking in pain, unable to stand up. Tom ended their
misery cutting their heads off with a few quick blows.

Joan and Garry were already cutting the ropes holding
the teenagers to the tree. Joan took from her backpack a
little bag made of the leathery bark that we had used to
make our ropes. It contained a greasy substance that had
a soothing effect on scratches.

Joan had found it exuding from one of the fruits she had
sampled. She applied it on the bitten flesh and then
took the girl in her arms, comforting her.

"It's over, "Joan said, "they won't hurt you anymore.
Will you tell me your name?"

"My name is Sandra, daughter of Mary, daughter of Helen,
daughter of Spaceship Endeavor's astronavigator Brian
Dempsey and Bob is my brother."

"What happened here," asked John, "Are there more of
these Rat Faces? Is your settlement under attack?"

"These aliens live very far from here and we never had
problems with them until recently. Groups of them are
hunting us down. Some of us were captured and others
were killed. We are fighting them back but we have not
been able to eliminate them.

Last week, we captured some of the beasts and questioned
them. They said they were looking for Earth emissaries
who recently arrived here."

I looked at my companions and said "So far what happened
my friends differed slightly from the story I wrote. The
personages are not the same since my book on Ghama-2
was a fiction book written to attract you, the potential
chosen. But these Rat Faces attacking the humans and
looking for us was not in my book. I have the intuition

that a new factor that came into play and that factor will change everything.

The demons are here and they have influenced those Rat Faces to come here at more or less the time of our awakening to eliminate us. The demons as we all know, wish for another specie to find the abandoned city. They want the wicked one to get there first, one that will kill and torture all others over the millenniums.

They must be anticipating eagerly the watching of the desperate being tortured and destroyed.

I have been in contact with one of those demons when I was much younger. It tried to possess me but it failed. I am doubtful that they can exert a great influence here since there is that strange force that limited the action of the powerful Guardians. But if you ever have to face one, fight it back mentally."

"Make sure you maintain high moral qualities," added the Reverend Father, "this will increase the power of good in you. Ask God for His help if you ever face one, we humans can resist their attack."

"Yes we can," I confirmed, "I did it and you should be able to do it too.

The rat faces didn't know exactly where and when we would wake up on this world or we would be dead already. But from now on, forget what was written in my book. That new factor is changing everything."

John asked Sandra daughter of Mary...if she could direct us to her city.

"I am lost, I don't have a clue where to go." answered Sandra.

"Don't worry about that," I said, "I know where the city is; follow me."

I can't explain why I knew it but it was a feeling that left no doubt. Maybe I had been awarded the finder's gift, a new sense to me, similar to that six sense gifting those people whom could find water using a forked branch or a pendulum.

On our way to the city, we asked Sandra all she knew about the city and its customs.

Chapter 9 - Spaceship Endeavour, Year 2254

Bryan Dempsey was puzzled and worried. The ship computer had just emitted a warning. He had computed a safe stationary orbit for the spaceship and now according to the computer, the ship was on collision course with the planet.

Bryan considered the situation in his usual calm and optimistic way. He would do everything he could to save the crew and the ship. If all attempts failed, he would face death with serenity and will do what he could to comfort the desperate ones around him. Bryan had a magnetic personality and was liked by everyone.

Jack Duncan, ship commander and highest authority on board was standing stiffly beside Bryan looking at the computer screens. Jack was a tough and authoritarian commander. He trusted no one and had not been seen smiling since the ship left Earth.

They had been awoken from their 89 years long sleep two weeks before the ship went into orbital speed around Ghama-2. They were forty people aboard and they had been selected carefully amongst thousands of applicants. They were the fittest, the brightest, the healthiest and the most stable of all those thousands people dreaming to survey that new world and prepare the way for its colonization.

The trip had proceeded without any problem whatsoever and they all woke up in good health. The ship detectors indicated air composition almost identical to Earth, a mild climate, absence of volcanic activity, and abundance of life.

They had seen the close up of ruins and what looked like abandoned cities under semi-transparent bubbles.

Most puzzling was the gravity. The world was gigantic but its gravity was similar to earth. It might indicate a partially empty core and the theory was reinforced by the absence of volcanic activity.

"We are being drawn to the surface by unthinkable powers." said Bryan. "The ship engine is fighting it to no avail. We will crash in less than thirty minutes."

Jack Duncan ordered everyone to get aboard the two emergency shuttles and leave the ship immediately. He sent a warning message to Earth: *Ghama-2 is inhabited by powerful and hostile beings. They are using a principle, a power of some sort that is crashing our ship. That World must be banned from future exploration.*

The message was sent and Jack Duncan rushed to Shuttle 1. Bryan took the controls of Shuttle 2; he would try to keep it close to Shuttle 1 and land in the same area.

The shuttles left the ship but could not be controlled. The two shuttles were heading towards ground surface at high velocity even though they were oriented to fly in the opposite direction and the engines were firing at full capacity.

Bryan noticed that the velocity was now diminishing; *we might not crash*, he thought, *I shall be able to land it but the two shuttles have gone different ways and we will land thousand miles apart.*

Ground contact was made; there were some damage but nobody was injured.

Bryan was the first man out from the shuttle to walk on the new world. Helena, the ship medical officer, joined him. They didn't know each other before final crew selection for the expedition to Ghama-2 but they had trained and work together since and something had developed between them. They became lovers before they were placed in hibernation for the trip.

Everyone was outside now. They had landed at the juncture of a large river and the sea. There was a beautiful beach on one side and sparsely forested grassland on the other. The vegetation was beautiful, and there were fruit bearing trees everywhere. The air was fresh with an alien tang to it but rather pleasant, the temperature was in the low seventies.

It's paradise, Bryan thought, *we will be happy here and with God's help we will colonize that world. We are ten couples; we will have children, and a new civilization will bloom up with time.*

Bryan went back inside and tried to contact Shuttle 1 but no communication could be established. The computer screens were dead; there was no electricity and the fusion batteries had somehow lost all of their power.

Bryan had a hunch and decided to check it. He went to the armory locker, pulled out a laser gun and a bullet firing rifle and went back outside to shoot them in the air; nothing happened.

He gave the second officer the order to pull out the knives and axes from the armory and distributes them amongst the crew. Once everyone was armed, Bryan led his group for an investigation of their surroundings.

They sampled the fruits, tasted them and found them nourishing and very delicious.

"It is an excellent emplacement here at the junction of a river and the sea." said Bryan to the crew. "We were lucky to land here. No communication are possible with the other shuttle, we are on our own. We will survive and will colonize that world ourselves."

The crewmembers took the news rather well and some of them made jokes about the impossibility to communicate with ship commander Jack Duncan.

There will be new rules, Bryan thought, *we will built a different society with more freedom.*

"Listen to me," said Bryan in a strong voice, "there are fruits everywhere and anyone could survive by oneself. It would natural for some of us to reject any form of authority.

We must prevent the scattering of our forces and build a society where fairness and gentlemanliness will rule.

A certain form of authority is necessary; we will go nowhere in an anarchistic society but the majority must wish this authority.

We are equals here and are starting with no financial differences. If we are to form a society of people working together, we must find a motivating factor to entice everyone to do his share of the burden. The most deserving should be compensated.

We will need a leader who can keep us together. *Should I be it*? He thought as he was speaking. *Do I want to lead them*?

I am the senior officer with responsibilities and orders conferred by our superiors on Earth. But we have lost contact with Earth, forever!

Is there anyone in our group best fitted for leading? He wondered silently. The answer was negative. He had been selected second officer aboard for his leadership qualities and had been trained for that. But to lead efficiently here without being rejected he would have to proceed to an election. He would rather share friendship, companionship with the other crewmembers and let somebody else suffered from the isolation and the responsibilities conferred by a position of power. But if they elect him, he would accept the burden of leadership and rule in accordance to his moral obligations.

We will not be able to function without leadership; we must proceed with the election of a village mayor."

The people looked at each other, some said that Bryan was the best candidate and no one seemed eager to contest it; so Bryan was elected unanimously.

"I propose Helena the ship medical officer and Donald the ship biologist for the position of Village counselors." said Bryan.

Donald was the most popular crewmember aboard and his profound culture and philosophy had delighted them all. Helena was the one who would save their lives in case of injuries; everyone trusted her and respected her motherly devotion to all.

So Bryan's proposal got everyone's approval.

They conferred, the three of them over the next few days and set up the rules on which would be built their new society.

Then Bryan assembled the group again and made the following decree.

Item.

"We will all work equally on the erection of a large mansion with plenty of rooms for every couple and some more. There will be two living rooms, two dinning rooms, twenty bedrooms, one large playroom, and four bathrooms with an aqueduct system.

We will also build a food storage shed and protecting fence all around the settlement.

We will live together and this way, we will be happier and increase our chances at survival.

We don't know yet what kind of monsters might attack us and what other danger this world might have in store for us but if we work together, if we keep a great team spirit, we will build a new civilization."

Item.

"An incentive is necessary to encourage everyone to do his fair share of the work. Money would be useless since the planet belongs to everyone and there are no goods to buy yet. We have to start from scratch.

Units of due community labor hours will compensate our efforts. We will cash our units when we need help to build something for ourselves. For example, if I accumulate 300 units and I need the community's help to build myself a boat or a house, I get 300 hours of labor for free. That is equivalent to the labor of ten people working on my project for 30 hours each.

We all start in the red. It will take us about 90 days of work to complete the construction of our mansion.

Each of us should work eight hours per day, five days a week initially. One full day of work will give us one unit. We start at -48 units. At the end of the first project, some will have work more days than others, one may work 80 days for example then that one has build an asset of 32 units in the bank records.

There will be units awarded for certain feats, rewards units and some units will be deducted in case of harmful actions. The names of the ten most deserving people of the month will be written on a community board. We need to be appreciated and that is a good way. Everyone should try to get his name on the board.

Item.

Our doctor and biologist will be spared construction labor initially and consecrate all of their time to the sampling of medicinal herbs and fruits.

Item.

David, John and Sylvia are the most experienced and athletic fighters of the crew. They will consecrate their days in patrolling and surveying the immediate surroundings and report anything of special interest.

They will extend their survey to a larger perimeter everyday.

We need to know what kind of monsters or aliens might attack us at any moment.

Item.

Our laser guns or rifles are useless here and I doubt we will do much good with our axes and knives against ferocious beasts. This is why we will start the making of javelins, bows and arrows, quarterstaffs and swords immediately and once we are properly armed, Joseph the ship engineer will direct the work for the building of our strong house."

The crew was made out of exceptional people; they were the best amongst thousands of others who had applied to embark on this discovery trip and they did very well.

Over the years, they built their grand house, farms, individual homes, boats and all kind of things to enhance their quality of life.

They had plenty of time to make children and they didn't waste it. The village grew quickly. Working together for a common goal developed a wonderful community spirit, it brought the companionship and the comfort of belonging to a great family.

There was harmony and everyone did his best to be considered and loved by the others. Some of their children and grandchildren built boats, went to far lands and met with aliens. They developed friendly relationship and trade with some species and avoided hostile and wicked ones.

A friendly species looked like little teddy bears. The adults were three foot high. They had those large and irresistible eyes, a red button nose and very large ears. A soft fur, which they kept immaculately clean, covered them. They loved to be petted and they couldn't be kept away. So the traders brought some back with them.

Individuals of another species were also brought back to the city. They were birdlike bipeds, seven feet tall. They had colorful feathers and were of exquisite beauty. Their evolution had been longer than mankind; they had great maturity and wisdom. They genetically transmitted their memories to their children like many animals on Earth, but their most exceptional characteristic was that each individual carried in his mind the souls of his deceased family members; some of them being thousand years old ancestors.

They loved the company of men and they mastered their language very quickly for they were natural telepaths, able to read people's minds. They loved to talk for hours on end.

At the time of John's group awakening, the city of New Alexandria counted five hundred thousand humans, one hundred thousand teddies and twenty thousand Birdies. It spanned a surface of twenty miles along the sea and was ten miles wide. The sea, the large river and a smaller river bordered it. The fourth side was fenced all along the jungle from the sea to the small river.

The fence had been made of small and densely branched thorn trees; the thorns were poisonous and it had so far stopped all roaming predators.

The city dwellers were safe. They had farms, parks and golf courses and there were boats of all kind filling the marinas.

People practiced sports: football, baseball, tennis, badminton, judo, boxing, fencing, sailing and more.

There were arenas, theatres, and concert halls. Human civilization was blooming without technology and the people were sane and happy.

It was paradise! They called their city, New Alexandria.

Only a few adventurers would go beyond the farmlands and cross the small river. Some of those never returned and others came back with all kind of stories involving monsters and evil aliens.

No contact had ever been made with the other shuttle survivors or their descendants.

––––––––––––––––––

Jack Duncan ordered everyone to stay inside as he set foot outside shuttle 1. He carried a laser rifle as he looked around evaluating his new world.

Here I will reign over my subjects, Jack thought, *for I am the highest authority here, I represent the United States of America; this will be my kingdom. Some ones amongst the crew might not like to serve me so I better prevent any rebellion from the start. I will need bodyguards, the toughest guys in the crew, and I will give them an incentive, they will be second in command.*

Jack went back to the shuttle and ordered Bob Dawson and Peter Flinn to come outside. The two tough men were not very popular; they were troublemakers. Bob was a Karate Black belt and had been ranked in the ten best of his country. He was six foot four, two hundred and twenty pounds of packed muscles and quite handsome. He carried the facade of nice guy. He had successfully hid his aggressiveness and fooled the jury responsible for the crew selection but Jack Duncan had measured him up. He would be number one in his bodyguards' selection.

Peter Flinn was just as big as Bob. He was a respected and feared navy officer, very well trained in close combat. He had been in many fights and never lost one. Peter believed in authority and needed a leader. He would obey his commander blindly.

"Listen," said Jack. "We will build a settlement on this world and wait for Earth rescue. In the mean time I don't want any problem with the crew. Perhaps some will challenge my authority and I need someone to shut them up. I am ready to name the two of you my second in command and there will be rewards to come with the post. Will you swear to obey my commands and protect me at all time?"

Jack didn't mention his warning message to Earth before he abandoned the spaceship and the toughs, believing there would be a rescue ship coming on for them, swore their allegiance to their commander.

"Now, get inside, arm yourself and get everyone out for my first address on Ghama 2."

They rushed inside, went to the armory and armed themselves with laser guns and knives then ordered everyone out.

Jack was standing on a tree stump looking down at his crew.

"I am the indisputable leader representing Earth authority. This is an emergency situation and the codes of war are in force. To refuse one of my orders would be treason and the traitor would be executed at once."

A tremendous roar interrupted his speech; he turned around and looked at a fifteen-foot beast standing on two legs very close in appearance to the Tyrannosaurus Rex of the museums. Jack aimed his laser rifle and pressed the trigger. Nothing happened, he pressed a second time to no avail. Bob and Peter fired in turn with no better result.

They were defenseless in front of a terrifying predator and they fled to the shuttle. Jack was first aboard; he had kicked aside a couple of the women in his way and his two bodyguards were right behind.

There wasn't enough time for the seventeen other crewmembers to get aboard and Bill Colder the ship physicist shouted to everyone to pick rocks or sticks and be ready to throw them at the beast eyes.

The beast rushed at them as they back up slowly to the shuttle; it bent its neck to seize one the people. Everyone threw whatever he or she had been able to pick, even a handful of sand and the beast eyes were hit by a number of projectiles. It backed up and everyone was able to get inside. Bill was the last one aboard; he had stood guard with a broken stick in his hand, facing the beast, as his companions were getting inside. Bill closed the door behind him and locked it in place.

They could ear the beast banging on it for a long time but the door was solid enough to resist the repeated blows.

Jack Duncan didn't like it. *I lost face in front of the crew and this dirty dog, the physicist, played the hero.* Jack thought.

Jack commanded the distribution of the axes, knives and shovels and ordered everyone to be ready for a survey expedition.

Without electricity, the window cameras were not working and it was impossible to know if the beast was still there with the door close. Someone would have to open the door and take a peek outside.

"Now that the beast is gone," said Jack Duncan, "we will all go and survey the area; we need to find a suitable emplacement for our settlement. But first, you Colder, who played the hero; you will open the door and look out for the beast.

Bill Colder opened the door and saw the dinosaur at the end of the clearing, it was moving away. Bill waited for the beast to get out of sight and told the commander that they could get out safely.

The whole crew exited the shuttle for the second time.

"Take the lead Colder," ordered Jack Duncan, "and you better find us a good shelter or I will put you at the back of our line."

They walked amongst fruits' bearing trees growing sparsely across the large clearing. There was a river bordering it on one side and a jungle of very high and large trees on the other side. The miles wide clearing followed the river as far as they could see.

They saw large masses moving in the clearing, some had the appearance of dinosaurs. The river would be no shelter for they had spotted some huge crocodilians and the neck and heads of even larger beasts were coming out of the water sometimes.

"There is abundant life here," said Laura, one of the ship biologists, "and some of it very dangerous. We might be safer in the jungle."

She had already noticed the absence of insects, which was impossible according to the laws of evolution. The whole landscape seemed to have been planned by an artist. She went to a tree, picked a red fruit and cut it open. It smelled like raspberries, she took a little piece of it with her knife, placed it on the tender skin of her forearm and waited to see any trace of skin reaction.

The whole group had stop and everyone had come around her to see what she was doing. Jack Duncan was fidgeting; he had not ordered the fruit testing and did not appreciate self-initiative. He hesitated between a few possible courses of action.

After a moment, Laura removed the piece of fruit and looked for skin reddishness and found nothing. There was no irritation. She took a bite and tasted the fruit without chewing or swallowing; it had a firm texture and tasted like a blend of kiwi and raspberries. It was absolutely exquisite. She started to eat the fruit expressing great pleasure in front of all the hungry faces around her.

"Let's pick some of the fruits, "Laura said "they are delicious but don't eat them right away. Let's see if I get poisoned first. If I don't feel any adverse reaction in the next hour then everyone can devour them.

In the mean time, I suggest that we move towards the jungle where we might find shelter."

"Let's do it." Said Jack quickly, hoping that his hastiness would cover up the fact that a suggestion on a course of action had been given without his authorization.

They all pick some fruits and left in a line toward the jungle. Laura was following right behind Bill Colder.

These two fools will shield me from a predator, thought Jack who had taken position behind Laura, *and this way, I am heading the rest of them.*

They cut across the clearing towards the jungle looking worriedly around as they crossed it. They never thought it would take hours to get to the jungle for they had been fooled by the thinking that the trees here were probably the size of earth trees but now, finally, they had reached the end of the clearing and the jungle trees were hundreds of feet tall, as tall as the tallest buildings in San Francisco.

"Look at those branches overhead." said Laura excitingly to Bill Colder. "These branches are as wide as roadways interlocking themselves in a most intricate way."

"It is just amazing," replied Bill, "I can't believe my eyes; I would have never thought there could be such huge trees anywhere."

Creepers were growing downward in some kind of pattern and in some places they formed spider webs strong enough to give them access to the lowest branches. No grass was growing under the dense canopy but here and there could be found some shade lover berry bushes.

There was ample space to walk in between the trees but they were so big that they had the impression of walking in a maze of incredibly tall stonewalls. In no time they were lost and wouldn't find their way back to the ship had they wish it.

They walked over pack dirt for a few hours trying to keep the initial direction. The jungle was noisy; there were large birds or apes like cries or calls, smaller birds' chirps and twitters, and on a distance the roars of huge predators.

They sensed movements and heard furtive sounds; the jungle was brimming with mostly invisible life. They came to a wide clearing and further up, the clearing was giving way to a large lake or sea inlet.

They watched a pack of antelopes leisurely grazing, seemingly unaware of the large felines making a slow approach towards them.

Suddenly there was a vibration in the ground; something very heavy was coming up their way.

"We have to get out of here and quick." Said Jack. "What are you waiting for?"

"We can't run into the clearing with the pride of lion like predators not very far away," answered Bill, "so we will climb up to the canopy."

They ran to a spider web of creepers and climbed one hundred feet to the first of the big branches just in time to see two of the huge dinosaurs rushing below.

"We must find a shelter for the night," said Laura to Bill Caulder, the ship physicist and recent hero, standing beside her and looking at the dinosaurs.

"Yes Laura, you are right," said Bill, "and it is about time since we have only a few hours left before total darkness."

"Somehow, I am not surprised," said Laura in a low voice, "that you kept track of the remaining daylight time. You will be a very important element to our survival, Bill, a key man, but we have to do something about Jack Duncan.

He doesn't like you; he might even kill you and other members of the crew if needs be to maintain his authority over the group and build his own little kingdom here."

"What are you talking about?" said Jack Duncan menacingly. "Are you two up to something I should know? I am your commander, if you are making plans, you will make them with me."

"No, no, nothing to take offense. I was telling Bill that we have a better chance to find shelter and food in the upper branches." said Laura soothingly. "What do you think Sir? Should we climb up for a little survey and come back to report our findings."

Jack thought for a while and decided that they should not split; he would not let these two plotters go for a survey and prepare the rest of the crew for rebellion. If they go, everyone would go.

"We must stay together, all forty eight of us." replied Jack. "Bob will lead the way and you will follow right behind him."

I will name Bob Dawson my first lieutenant as soon as we get to a shelter. Thought Jack. He will be an excellent bodyguard. Then I am going to take care of those two plotters…

They climbed the creepers to the lowest branch then move from that branch to the next one up progressing in the direction of the canopy. Sometimes they would reach a large branch growing upward at a low angle and they could walk their way up for a while and they finally reached the canopy. The view was breathtaking; the canopy was a world of leaves, flowers, fruits and movements. There was all kind of rodents, apes and birds, sneaking around or flying away at their approach.

The canopy offered a profusion of fruits and nuts; they were growing everywhere. They moved on branches as wide as roads in the direction of the tallest tree and then climbed some more to reach the top. Now they could see very far away. On their right were miles of jungle and then a sea and on their left was the large clearing bordering the river. On the other side of the river was grassland giving way to another jungle. In between was the jungle canopy on which they were standing.

Jenny spotted a shelter. It was a big hole in the trunk of one of the gigantic tree. She came closer to take a look and something growled from inside. She called the commander to come and see. The occupant moved out reluctantly with much snarling; it looked like a beaver but was much bigger and his teeth were flat and sharp.

"It must have gnawed the hole," said Laura as she looked inside. "There is enough space for a dozen people here and there must be other shelters just like that one around, some of which might even be more spacious."

The entrance was a five-foot long tunnel three feet in diameter, big enough to let them crawl inside. The interior room was eight by ten foot with a six-foot high ceiling. The room walls were irregular, there were no windows so it was very dark inside when someone was crawling inside the tunnel and obscuring the room from the outside light.

There was a strong animal odor but the room was clean.

Jack selected eleven people from the crew and told them they would share that shelter with him.

"The rest of you will split in two groups." Jack said yawningly. "Bob will lead one group and Peter the other. You will search for more of these shelters. There should be more of them in the vicinity. Mark your tracks so that you will be able to come back here tomorrow morning. We will meet here at sunrise."

They found three more shelters nearby; the first two could accommodate twelve of them and the last one nine at the most. Peter didn't know what to do and was fidgeting when Laura found a smaller shelter that could accommodate only three of the crewmembers.

"I will take that one," said Laura, "with Carla. I would feel safer Bill if you could share it with us."

She was rewarded by Bill's eagerness to accept.

"All right then, I have no objection." Said Peter who decided to sleep in the last big shelter and let those three pass the night together.

Once inside, Laura looked at Bill, they locked eyes for a very short moment and when they parted their gaze, they knew they would be partners and mates on this new world. They would find comfort and strength in each other. That was the unspoken message.

That night they talked about the situation.

"I think that Jack is crazy and very dangerous. Maybe it was the loss of the spaceship that hit him or maybe he somehow hide his true self to the comity in charge of the crew selection but something has to be done now." said Laura.

"Yes, you are right," replied Bill, "perhaps we should split. We can't get along with a dictator incapable of facing a new situation. Who do you think would join with us?"

"I for one," said Carla, "and there are Fred, Jacky, Helene, Raymond, David, Esther, all of these would join with us, I am sure of it."

"That makes nine out of the forty-eight on our side," said Bill, "and I would vouch for Donna and Ed."

"And for Alice," said Laura, "and that brings the number of our supporters to twelve. We can face him tomorrow and demand a vote for leadership. Whom should we vote for?"

"For you Laura!" said Bill and Carla simultaneously.

"You are a natural leader and get along with everyone." said Bill.

Laura thought about it for a while searching for anyone that could be better at it.

"Even if I suggest somebody else," said Laura, "we would not have the opportunity to talk it over with that potential leader. And we have to do something tomorrow morning. So I accept for now the responsibilities of the leadership. Tomorrow at sunrise, we will confront Jack.

I am very well trained at close combat and in a knife fight I have excellent chances against him if it comes to that. The element of surprise would play in my favor. He would never believe that a woman would dare resist him physically. You Bill, you will have to keep his two bodyguards out of it and he chose the ones he thought were the best fighters of the crew."

"As you said, the element of surprise might help." replied Bill. "I am afraid that I might have to kill them though and I never killed anyone before. Let's do everything we can to talk our way out without a physical confrontation."

"Yes we will try." said Laura. "Let's sleep now; the shelter is comfortable and we need to be in good shape tomorrow."

The day after, they were amongst the first to walk back to Jack Ducan shelter. On their way back they got the opportunity to talk to a few of their would-be-supporters and now the whole group was standing around Jack on the twenty feet wide branch.

"Can you imagine finding a branch of that size at the canopy of five hundred feet to one thousand foot tall jungle?" Asked Laura in a powerful voice; loudly enough to be heard from everyone around her. "That world," she went on, "is incredibly different from Earth. We will never be short of surprises and bewilderment if we ever come to explore it. But before we even think of exploring it, we must settle ourselves somewhere, and build what we need to survive, to feed ourselves and to confront and eliminate or chase away the most dangerous predators.

We must get familiar with our surroundings and become comfortable in our relationship with the people with whom we will share our lives. We must decide new rules of ethics that will allow the making of a new society."

229

"I will take care of whatever rules we need, just make sure you follow my orders." said Jack Duncan roughly.

"But you are certainly not fit to set rules for all of us." replied Laura. "You had legal authority on the spaceship to force everyone to follow the rules experts from Earth had already fixed. But this is a new situation and you are already talking of killing anyone that would disobey your orders."

"Shut up you bitch or you will be the first one to be executed." Shouted Jack with spit coming out of his trembling lips.

"Now Sir, please stay calm and stop those menaces." said Carla gravely and loudly. "I propose a vote for leadership."

Jack Duncan raised his hand for a slap at Carla's face.

"Stop! Don't move or you die." said Bill in a deep and powerful tone as he grabbed Jack's wrist with one hand while holding a knife at his throat with his other hand. "If anyone moves to his defense, I kill him."

The two bodyguards were ready to pounce forward but they didn't know what to do.

Bill disarmed Jack, pulling the commander's knife out of his belt in a quick hand movement.

"We will proceed right away to the vote." said Laura.

"We have got enough of this non sense." added Laura. "We won't tolerate women beating or men killing by stupid jerks that wish to be dictators. Something has to be done now to prevent any bloodshed. Jack Ducan is a bloodthirsty would be dictator totally unfit to remain our leader. He was ready to kill me or Carla and certainly Bill who has shown so much courage against the dinosaur while the commander pushed everyone aside as he fled like a coward inside the shuttle."

"I vote for Laura as our new and best fitted leader." shouted Carla.

"And I also." said Bill. "Everyone can trust her and she has shown all the qualities of an excellent leader. Anyone that vote for Laura please raise your hands."

Thirty-eight people raised their hands. Jack Duncan was red with anger; he was shaking but he could feel the tip of Bill's knife in his neck and sense his determination to kill him and get it over with at the slightest move on his part.

"That is a majority." said Laura. "I thank all of you who just took that very important decision and the risk involved in voting for me. Now please walk to my side."

They moved rapidly to her side and the thirty-nine of them were now facing Jack, his two bodyguards, one more man Robert and five female crewmembers.

"We can't trust any of you in our back," said Laura, "so we will split. I wish you to survive. One day, our children may reunite and form a new nation, farewell."

"Wait please! Can I change my vote?" asked Robert. "I want to join with you."

"And me too!" said two of the women who had been left on Jack side.

"All right," said Laura, "come over."

On these last words, Laura turned around and left followed by Carla and Bill and the rest of the group under the fix gaze of the bewildered bullies.

The three women left behind were fidgeting, they were just about to leave Jack side and join the departing group. Jack Duncan could read their dilemma and didn't want to be left alone.

If these three women leave, Jack thought, *my bodyguards will leave too and I will be left alone.*

"Please, "Jack said, "stay with us. We will treat you well and we can protect you better than these fools.

Some of them will return and beg for mercy. They don't know that bitch as well as I do. In no time at all, a lot of them will be back. I will reward you; you will have a special status in the group. Please stay with us. If you go too, we will follow you at a distance and at first opportunity, we will kill those three traitors and the rest of the crew will come back and accept my legal leadership.

We may still do it if you stay with us but not right away. There will be a rescue ship from Earth; they have probably developed faster than light technology by now. So the rescuers might be here at any time and when they come, those traitors will be judged and executed for sedition."

Jack Duncan could be very persuasive and the three women stayed.

Laura took her group back to the shuttle. She had kept marks, she knew she could find it and she did. The shuttle content proved to be extremely useful. They built a village in the jungle tree's canopy right beside the clearing. There was a narrow branch of the river crossing the jungle underneath. They dug their houses in the trees' trunks at the canopy and fixed safety nets made out of the creepers alongside the branches they used most commonly.

Their home doors were covered with the trees' bark and unwanted visitors couldn't notice their little village. In addition they cut the smaller branches and the creepers those unwanted visitors could use to get to the village and they erected wood walls on the biggest of the branches coming their way.

They kept a look out for Jack's group, hostile aliens or predators but they never saw Jack and his companions again.

Forty-five years later, Bill and Laura were celebrating the wedding of their oldest granddaughter at the Jungletown Inn. Laura had relinquished her leadership long ago and there wasn't much of a government anyway. There was no job, no hardship, no attorneys, no lawsuits, and no policemen. There was none of the multitude of harassers and ass kickers that had transformed life on Earth into a life of fear, suspicion and often, outright misery. There were no television or telephone so people had a lot of time for communicating face to face. They would pick up the fruits and nuts in the morning and some would go down to the plow land and harvest some vegetables and grain, others would go fishing the river winding its way into and across the jungle up to the sea.

They were getting up in the morning surrounded by the living walls of the shelter-tree. With the years those walls had been rubbed to a very smooth multicolor surface, and they gave the lovely scent of fresh wood.

They could look through the windows at the playful birds, monkeys and squirrels like little furry runners and listen to their songs or disputes and inhale the fresh air. There were no plate glasses in the windows and no need for it for on this world, there were no insects, no snakes, no spiders or any undesirable visitors coming through the open windows but occasionally some of the birds or furry little friends would sneak in for the night and sought the comfort of the human company.

Except for a mild and short winter, the weather was always perfect, in the seventies and no season changes in the jungle. It usually rained early morning two or three times a week but the rain would stop at sunrise.

Jungletown people liked to sit together, in large group and the groups became livelier with the addition of children. There were storytellers and telling stories had become an art form. These would tell their fiction stories, tales concocted over nights and days for the sole purpose of lighting up their afternoon or evening sit in.

The storytellers were very popular, they would tell their stories with all the emotional play of tones of the best theatre actors.
There were musicians too and when the flutists and violinists and the drummers started, all the birds, hundreds of them would come and branch themselves all around. Some would even find a place on people's shoulders. For most songs, the birds had learned the tune and were singing along. The little chipmunk

like runners, the cluckers, the dignified beaver like gnawers and the monkeys would come too and sit amongst them.

The people had found a way of getting rid of the tyrannosaurs and the dangerous river reptiles, destroying their nests at night and inflicting on them painful injuries with poisonous arrows. They were now able to roam across the clearing. They built a riverboat and made short excursions on the river.

The wedding, Bill and Laura had come to; was to be a group wedding.

One dozen teenagers would give their vows of love and companionship to each other. They will then share the same home and beds. People had put on their fineries and many were making jokes and having fun. There was good ale and wine to lighten up everyone.

Jean, the French winemaker and ale brewer had found himself with too many friends after his first batch sharing and couldn't find a crewmember anymore to argue with. For a Frenchman, a life without arguments was intolerable.
So, he taught the basic of wine making and ale brewing to everyone but none ever came close to make it as delicious as his. So he kept doing it for everyone and enjoyed their appreciation but missed the arguing.

The teenagers had decided to go for a few months honeymoon trip on the river to explore unknown territory. They would borrow the village boat.

Laura and Bill were sitting comfortably on a higher branch and were watching the party underneath.

"Come to think of it," said Laura, "do you realize that we are now in our seventies and we still look young and strong? It may be the food we eat or our easy way of life or the constant climbing or all of it together but I believe that we will live much longer on this world.

My father once told me that the saddest thing was that when we finally reach maturity and are ready to live our adulthood, we are already too old. We should have sixty years he said to prepare ourselves for a career and then live it for fifty and finally enjoy forty years of retirement."

"You talk about your father; do you miss him, was he very close to you?" asked Bill.

"Oh yes, we were very close; we would go fishing sometimes and talk for hours in the boat. But to my shame, I have a hard time remembering his face. It became elusive. I remember his eyes; I always loved his eyes; they were like yours and that's one of the thing that caught me; that and your courage facing the tyrannosaur on our landing day."

A white dove flew towards Laura who extended her arm. It settled on the back of her hand and hopped its way up to her neck. She petted it for a while and it flew away with a piercing trill.

"I often wondered," added Laura, "if we could find dragons on this world. Perhaps there are some of them on far away lands where they live along with ogres, trolls and fairies.

There might be castles and bridges, sorcerers and what else-"

"You have been fidgeting for a long time now." said Bill. "I sensed at times your overbearing thirst for exploring this most mysterious and gigantic world. What do you think about our grandchildren honeymoon trip?"

"I would give a lot to go with them." said Laura. "There is so much to discover and it has been a little too quiet here the last decades."

"I have some news for you," said Bill. "We have just completed yesterday the making of a second boat and I went with the guys for a little happy drinking at the Inn yesterday night. We talked about following the youngsters and be ready to help if needs be.

The village population of one hundred and fifty eight can go on without us. So let's go, we will be a dozen people, a few of the crewmembers and some of the children and we will have a great time."

The day after, the two boats sailed out. There were a hundred people watching them go and wishing farewell with water in their eyes. Months later, they came back, all of them, there had been no casualties and they were bringing purring and most friendly little cat like creatures.

A few hundred years later, at the time of the Earth emissaries awakening; Jungletown population had grown up to two hundred thousand people. They lived in a joyful an anarchistic way. There were some leading families but still no unified government.

Chapter 10 - New Alexandria

We were learning all about Alexandria from Sandra, as we were moving towards the human settlement.

I was leading the group and Tom was right behind followed by John, Joan and Sandra. Further back Bob was walking with Nancy and Garry, and Father O'Leary was guarding the rear; looking everywhere at once.

Sandra and Bob had accompanied their father Johnny Rodriguez, career explorer, founder and president of the Boy & Girls Scouts of New Alexandria. They were a dozen of the scouts plus her father and her uncles Paul and Victor.

"We have crossed the river by rowboats;" Sandra said, "we were trying to find some of the rare leathery bark trees. Most of our leather comes from trade with the Teddies in exchange for flutes and other musical instruments. They are found of anything human-made or conceived but they live very far away. We thought we could find some leather near the sky wall and were hoping to bring back a good load, as much leather as we could carry."

"There are a lot of those trees on the plateau," said Joan.

"What do you mean, which plateau?"

"The one on top of what you call the sky wall." replied Joan.
"But that wall is impossible to climb; it goes higher than the clouds, miles higher maybe."

Joan told her about our awakening and subsequent adventures; she also told her how we climbed it down.

"But what happened to you?" asked John.

"We left the group for a moment and were ambushed; knock down by the rat faces and carried away for questioning.

237

We would have been tortured and killed if you had not come to our rescue. I am sure, my father and uncles are looking for us right now." said Sandra

John looked back and saw Bob looking adoringly to Nancy.

"You are too young for me," Nancy was telling him. "So stop looking at me that way."

"But you can't be more than thirteen years old and I am sixteen," answered Bob imperviously, "and a very popular pianist!"

Well that is something, Nancy told herself, I would give my charms for a musical treat. Nancy loved music more than anything.

"Maybe I will change my mind and will not be too old for you once you have played for me," Nancy said, "but don't make long plans ahead, plans that involve me. If I ever give you my charms, it will be for one night only."

John had a hard time keeping himself from bursting in laughs, that situation was most funny. Bob had stuck by Nancy since the rescue and had never stopped looking at her adoringly. How could he believe that she was thirty years old not long ago? His eyes met Joan's who was well aware of his line of thoughts. They smiled and turned their heads from the kids.

The night was coming and we had to find a suitable shelter before it turned too dark. We had reached the river and were following it down to the sea.

"There is a small island," said John, "it would do if we could swim to it. Tell me Sandra, can we swim to the island without being attacked by dangerous fishes or monsters? Would it be safe to sleep the night there on this island?"
"There are some sea monsters that swim up the river;" replied Sandra, "and many young fools disappeared in those waters. But if we can get to that island we would be safe for the night. The land here will soon be dangerous; there are the Sabertooth and they hunt at night. They are very big. Our explorers protect themselves with a big fire when they can't find a very good shelter."

"A fire would keep the predators at bay but may attract the Rat Faces." said John. "Those sabertooths; do they swim? Do you know if the Rat Faces swim?"

"Neither of them has been seen to swim. We are safe in the city because it is surrounded by water on three sides and we have fenced the last side. To come to the city, the predators would have to swim across the river and the river monsters are huge and ferocious, they kill anything that swims across."

"We only have fifty feet of water to cross," said Tom, "I would say that if we swim quickly without splashing, we have good chances to reach the Island. But who knows if there isn't one of those monsters right here, under the water surface, watching us, and ready to pounce. One or more of us may loose their life so to me, the risk is just too great."

"Yes," approved John, "it is too much of a risk; I would rather face a saber-toothed tiger at night than swimming over a sea monster."

"We can stand guard," proposed Tom, "two or three at a time, to augment our chances if one or two of those sabertooths decide to attack us."

"Then we have to start a fire right away." said Sandra.

"I can do it." said Bob. "I will show you how. There is a kind of wood we call firecatcher that burst in fire if we make a hole in a small and very dry branch, insert a sulfur tree twig in and turn it quickly with the palms of our hands.

Bob walk around and found some dry firecatcher and brittle yellow sulfur tree twigs.

"It is very easy," he said, as he proceeded to start the fire. "We have to build a few campfires, all around our sleeping place."

We looked around for dry wood, dead branches and we collected a huge pile of them. We then started four small campfires, in a circle around our group.

"We will have to keep them burning through the night." said Bob.

"There are nine of us," said John, "let's split into two groups. One group will sleep for what looked like four hours then will replace the one that stood guard. I believe the night is about 16 hours long so we will all have two sleeping periods."

"I will do the first watch." I said.

"Then if no one objects," said John, "I will also take first watch and you Tom will be on the second group with the reverend Father. I believe there should be two grown up males on each group; it will increase our chances in case of an attack."

"All right for me," said Tom, "with the reverend I feel like I am in God's protection. If we have to fight; I will be comforted to fight alongside the only one who has ever defeated me."

"Well said my son." said the reverend. "It is always a pleasure for me to walk in your company."

"I will take first watch." Said Joan
"And so will I." said Garry.

Nancy went to sleep beside the reverend and Bob quickly took place on Nancy's open side. Then there was Sandra and Tom. They chat a little but in a few minutes only they were sound asleep.

"I am still very surprised by your fighting ability Joan; yours and Nancy." I said after a while. We had been sitting and looking at the stars while John was patrolling inside of the campfires ring.

"It is so strange," replied Joan, "both times as we fought the giant bear like beast and the Rat Faces, I was caught in excitement. I saw in my mind flashes of what seems like a previous life and in those flashes; I was fighting with a sword in my hand. It seemed to me that I was important; like a Queen or a commander.

When we fought the Rat Faces, I felt invincible, totally confident in my reflexes, my speed and my strength."

"I saw that," I said, "at one point, two of the Rat Faces attacked you at the same time and you killed them both with your sword, Joan; you didn't look nervous; I caught a glimpse of your face and I saw courage and confidence; certainly no fear and you moved so fast; it was incredible."

"The most incredible were Garry and Nancy," commented Joan, "they were much smaller than the aliens and they both kill at least one of them."

"Yes," I approved, "Garry, you are my hero! You have been so far the most important member of the group. You saved my sweetheart life, your mother's life, when a very large wolf-like beast attacked her. You did it with a spear and a spear thrower that you had designed yourself. You did it while we were having our orgy; this is how you spent your time; making it and then practicing with it. And when your mother needed help you were there at the right place and at the right time.

Then you ran straight at a giant humanoid rat and killed it with your spear! Then ignoring the presence of those monsters, you ran to Sandra and Bob and cut them loose. You are just amazing Garry."

"Thank you Richard," said Garry, "I am very proud of having proven useful despite my size. I wasn't a hero on Earth, just an ordinary guy; and when I woke up here in that nine years old body I felt that I would be less than ordinary; maybe just a burden for the group. But thinking about it now, I understand why the Guardians did it; they knew I wouldn't make love to mom and Nancy and therefore, I would be under constant sexual urge. So they did it by compassion and also as a safety for when you are having fun, I can patrol the camping perimeter and stand watch for the rest of the group."

"They thought about all kind of things," said Joan, "the Guardians studied us, our motivations, urges and our customs and they tried to give us everything we needed to increase to the maximum our chances for a successful mission. Those sexual urges we experience also have a purpose. I thought about it and I came to the conclusion that the Guardians wanted us to have children. Nancy and I are probably pregnant already."

"If it is so," I commented, "we will never know who the fathers are. Those children will have one mother and four fathers to cherish them."

"I guess it will be cool to have a little brother or sister." said Garry happily.

"You got that John?" I asked as he was standing a few feet from us watching the woods.

"Yes Richard and it will be wonderful." John replied. "I never had any children and I felt that something had been missing in my life. If that happens, it will be great."

"I guess that those babies will grow up much faster than the ones on Earth." said Joan. "And I won't be surprised if you Garry start growing very fast once you fall for a woman here."

"Otherwise, the babies would impair our mission success!" I replied. "Good thinking Joan, those babies will turn up into teenagers in no time at all."

"I was thinking about our new bodies Joan and I have many reasons to thank the Guardians for it. I just love my new body." I said. "I don't know if it is the hormones flowing in it or if it is the hypnotism of the Reverend Father but I too am now totally fearless. Moreover I feel so strong, so healthy that I feel more optimistic than ever. The other chosen must feel just the same way.

I wonder how they are doing and I wonder who took the leadership, George W Wood the United States president or Donald Rump the billionaire."

"Wouldn't it be nice to be with them?" replied Joan.

"I bet it is George." intervened Garry, who was listening to our conversation.

"Yes, you might be right Garry." I replied. "But he will be much influenced by Bill who will probably find the

242

solutions to get them out of trouble if they meet with difficulties."

"Krishna will be a leader too." said Joan. "He is the most experienced fighter in that group and possibly the most spiritually oriented."

"Look at the sky!" said Garry urgently. "There! It could be a spaceship and its descent is too steep, it is enveloped by a ball of fire."

The spaceship was slowing down though and it became visible for a moment before it disappeared at the horizon.

"It had the shape of a bat." said Garry all excited. "Maybe it carried a load of humanoid vampires."

"Maybe you are right Garry." I said. "John did you see it?"

"Yes I did." answered John keeping his eyes on the forest outside our camping perimeter.

We were looking too for the coming of a predator as we were chatting but John felt responsible for the group safety and preferred to walk around instead of sitting down with us for a while and I admired him for that.

The night went event-less with the exception of angry roars; some of them close by, and came first light, we didn't waste time. We had run out of fire wood so we picked some fruits and left in the direction of the city.

We picked some more of the most nourishing fruits and ate them as we walked down the riverside. There were birds of all kind singing their repertoire and many small animals were crossing in front of us.

Some would stop by and looked us over with much interest and some of them were very cute. Nancy had to restrain herself from stopping and petting them. They were just too cute she thought.

We were enjoying our odors differentiating new acute sense and it was most pleasuring.

In the river we saw some kind of otters playing and
catching fishes and making a show of their abilities.
They seemed unafraid of the sea monsters that could swim
underneath and they kept pace with us for hours down
river.
"I guess these otters have a sixth sense telling them of
the coming of a predator." commented Nancy.

Sandra and Bob were telling us about New Alexandria as
we walked in its direction. They told us about the
everyday life of its inhabitants and their customs.

I was amazed that they had a way of spreading the news
even faster than we could on Earth with the help of
telephone and television. For here there was only the
word of mouth and you had to walk to your friends and
neighbors and tell them the news but in New Alexandria,
the people were not hiding from each other in their
fenced backyards as most Americans were doing in my
time. Here, they enjoyed having neighbors to talk to and
the Birdies were spreading the news telepathically
amongst themselves and then communicating it to the
humans around.

"I remember the almost dead neighborhoods in Florida
with all the people inside or hiding in their backyards
behind closed fences." I said.

"We would have been in a fix trying to spread the news
there when we could not even talk to people with the
exception of a quick and uninviting Howdy and See-you-
later."

"Our way of life had taken a wrong turn." John answered.
"We had really lost it and we were heading towards
isolationism. I believe the television was responsible.
It may have given us some pleasant evenings but it took
away from us the time we would have use to go outside
and chat with the neighbors or do sports or play games."

"You are right John, "I replied, "I remember the time
when we would play cards and chat; taking our time and
enjoying the moment; knowing there was nothing else to
do and no television programs to miss."

"And it was taking an even worse turn," Joan commented,
"with our advances in full body stimulation movies,

people were just about starting on a new artificial source of entertainment. They were fixing a device on their head and electrical contacts on their body and were able to feel the action of the movies. Many had stop living their own lives for the artificial pleasure of sharing the adventures of a few."

"Yes, said John, "earth civilization was heading for its destruction. People had lost their values; they had limited their relationship to a bare minimum with their families, neighbors and colleagues, sending short e-mails as the ultimate friendly gestures."

"We could not expect much of a future for mankind when I passed away," I said, "unless something drastic happened and changed it all."

"But here," said Joan, "people live a much more pleasurable life and they have the help of the Birdies to spread the news. There is apparently nothing more pleasuring to these Birdies than to communicate what they know or what they learn to people around. I can't wait to meet one of those dignified birds."

"We are not too far from the city now." said Bob. "A few more hours of walking according and we will reach the river crossing the valley."

The alien odor alerted us.

"There are a large number of Rat Faces close by." said John.

We looked around worriedly and couldn't see any of them. Suddenly, we heard their growls and calls.

"The Rat Faces must be attacking some people," said Sandra, "maybe my father and uncles and the rest of the Boy Scouts."

John didn't ask if we should or not try to rescue our brothers from another world, he just ran towards the melee and we did not hesitate either, we just ran behind him and came into a large clearing covered by short grass and bordered on the other side by large oak like trees.

The Boy Scouts had backed against the tree and three men were trying to protect them. The men were fighting with clubs against their attackers armed with razor like claws and formidable jaws. All three of them were bleeding but they were defending themselves with courage and great fighting abilities. A few of the beasts were lying on the ground motionless but there were at least twenty more assailants surrounding the three men and they were just about to overcome them in a concerted assault from all directions.

John pulled his bow and set an arrow; we did the same. At a sign from him we let it go and felled five of the backward attackers. Some of the rat faces turned around and at our sight they shouted a warning and the whole lot of them turned around and charged us ignoring the presence of the three men on whom they had just turned their backs.

"Use your javelins to impale an attacker, "shouted John, "and don't try to pull them out of their bodies, let it go and use your sword."

As I levered my javelin, I felt a rush of adrenaline and my fear left place to an implacable determination to fight those brutes. Facing coming death, I felt stronger and more alive than I had ever felt. I experienced a savage pleasure as I impaled one of them right through its chest. I quickly look around calling for a new acute awareness, trying to see everything at once, and saw in a fraction of a second that my friends had done well. Many of the brutes lay on the ground but some of the beasts were rushing gleefully for our weakest members, Garry, Bob, Sandra, Nancy and Joan. I ran to their help and swung the sword sideways, parallel to the ground and connected with one of the brutes' legs, slicing one clean. In a jump I was right behind the next brute. I swung at its neck and cut its head clean and it rolled on the ground and I saw its snarl; it did not know yet that it had been severed from its body but in an instant its eyes became cloudy and turned up under.

One of the Rat Faces was out of my range and it was already leaping at Joan. She waited the onslaught with set feet and determination and I had never seen her yet with such a grim face. She was holding her sword in an iron grip, facing the charging monster motionless but the beast never caught her for at the very last instant, she moved at an incredible speed, she jumped sideways, swung at the beast neck, and cut its head off.

I turned around to face incoming assailants, one was leaping at me and I felt the impact of his heavy body as I fell on my back. The beast clawed at my chest and its jaws were closing on my arm as its neck was severed by Nancy's sword. I jumped back on my feet just in time to watch Garry throwing his spear and killing one of the beasts.

Nancy, Joan and I formed a defensive triangle around Garry, Sandra and Bob. We fought and killed many of the beasts. We were bleeding, we had been clawed and bitten by the brutes but we were still standing up without severe injuries. No more of the aliens were coming for John, Bill and Father O'Leary were incredible fighting machines; in a few seconds, they had knock down or killed all the rest of them.

Nancy, Joan and Garry had shown remarkable composure and ability fighting those giant aliens and there were no more of them coming for us. We looked at the center of the clearing where close to twenty of the beasts were trying to kill some of our friends. Before we could go to their rescue, the action was over; for in a span of no more than three seconds, we saw John fighting and we had never seen such swordplay. He beheaded or seriously injured seven or eight of the attackers. Tom also gave an incredible show of speed and agility. Like John, he could feel what was happening all around him. He had killed or injured five of the assailants while Father O'Leary, very calm as usual had back up to give the two of them enough space of maneuvering. Father had taken a position half way between the center of the action and the rest of our group. At one point, four of the Rat Faces rushed towards us and the Father killed two of them with powerful blows to the chest, one passed by and came to my range. I was waiting for it; I swung at its neck and beheaded it as the last one jumped on Joan. She was quick that Joan; I saw her crouching under the beast put one knee on the ground and lift her sword right through the beast belly. It caught one of her shoulder in an iron grip, its claws piercing the soft flesh but Nancy plunged her sword in its neck and took its life away before it could do further damage to her mother.

Johnny, Paul and Victor Rodriguez had stood between the boy scouts and the beasts and fought some of the brutes who had turned back to get the children. They swung at the beasts with their quarterstaffs and none of the beasts went past them. In moments only all the aliens were either dead or dying.

I look around and smelled the odor of a great number of the wicked beasts; hundreds of them and they were almost on top of us.

"Others are coming," John shouted, "one of you citizen, take the lead, the women and kids will follow and the rest of the men will constitute the rearguard. Let's run for our life, go, go."

Paul Rodriguez took the lead, followed by the boy scouts, Sandra, Nancy and Joan. Victor Rodriguez grabbed Garry and put him on his shoulders and followed behind; then there was Johnny Rodriguez, Father, Tom, John and I.

We ran for half an hour and the Rodriguez were getting winded. Father and Tom had taken their turn at carrying Garry. Now we were not running as fast anymore, and Garry insisted in running too.

"Let me down," Garry said, "I can keep pace with the group."

Tom put him down and we went on at reduced speed for an hour but the boy scouts just couldn't run anymore.

"Let's slow down to a fast walk." John shouted

The alien odor did not reach us anymore.

"We must have outdistanced them appreciably." I told John.

"Yes Richard," John replied, "but it would be best to alternate fast walk and jogging."

That's what we did for the last two hours it took us to reach the river. But the aliens were not far behind; they had gain back some distance and their odor was coming strong now.

There were three empty rowboats on the riverbank, not enough for everyone.

"Is it safe to swim across?" asked John nervously.

"There are some saurian beast swimming on the surface or lying underneath and some of them can reach thirty foot length." answered Paul. "If we swim in close ranks we have a chance to get to the other bank alive but some of us will not make it."

The rowboats could carry four or five at the most. John ordered the twelve boy scouts plus Nancy and Garry to get inside.

At John's order, we took our backpacks off and threw them in the boats amid the boy scouts. We also gave them the swords, the scabbards, the lances, the bows and arrows. Our weapons and precious equipment filled whatever remaining space in the boats. We only kept our belt and long knives secured in the holsters. We pushed the boats in the water and the boy scouts started to paddle their way across the river.

We went in the water right behind the boats and started to swim in a close pack. The aliens were right behind us but did not try to follow us in the water. Some people across the river had watched the events and were quickly putting boats afloat to come to our rescue.

"I have the gut feeling of impending danger." Shouted John. "Watch out for the seawater monsters."

Some of the big saurian beasts swimming nearby had noticed our presence and were charging towards us, attracted by the prospect of an easy catch. One of the beasts came closer and suddenly charged and caught the Father, its formidable jaws closing on his right leg. At that moment, Tom and John who were the closest to the father surged on the beast and knifed it repeatedly.

It opened its mouth to belly a roar of pain and anger and released the father who caught the rear of one of the boats. Blood was running along its injured leg and he could hardly swim with it; he just hung at the boat with both hands and let it pull him.

More of the saurian beasts were getting closer but they viciously attacked the bleeding and dying saurian, feasted on it, giving our rescuers enough time to reach us.

We were pulled aboard the rescuers' boats. Joan and Nancy had stayed by the Father and were pulled alongside him. Joan looked around, quickly and found nothing she could use to stop the Father's bleeding and he had already lost a lot of blood; his face was turning white. She pulled his boots and pants out and took a look at the injury. Even though the pant material had remained intact, the material had not been thick enough to prevent the saurian teeth damage. There was a long and deep cut and some blood was running out.

Joan took off her shirt and used it as a tourniquet to close the wound and keep the blood from flowing out.

The men caught a glimpse of her beautiful breast and kept politely their eyes away. One of them pulled his sweater over his head and handed it to her, Joan took it gratefully and covered herself.

We reached the shore and were brought to the City's Grand House, the very first house ever built on Ghama-2, hundreds of years ago by half of the Odyssey's spaceship crew.
Four men were quickly walking alongside carrying the father on a stretcher.

The Grand House served as the official residence for the City mayor counselors and as a guesthouse for the Birdies' and Teddies' leaders. There were plenty of rooms for every one of us. We got inside and followed the group carrying the father to his room and once there, Nancy took over. She had studied medicine and performed many surgeries on Earth. She asked the majordomo in charge of accommodating the visitors to bring her whatever they had to sew the flesh of the bleeding wound.

250

The father was lying down on a large size bed, he was very pale and his eyes were close. A doctor came running in the bedroom.

"I have a potion here to give him back some strength," she said, "then I will proceed to sew his wound."

Nancy told her that she was a doctor too and she meant no offense but she would do the sewing herself. The women helped the Father with the potion and Nancy started to work on the wounds. The good doctor helped Nancy as much as she could without interfering with Nancy's work and proved herself very useful.

Nancy took her time with the sewing so that the Father would not be left with permanent scars or damages. She could sense the pain she was inflicting on him, he was awake, she noticed, but he was keeping his eyes close and didn't complain.

"I know how much it hurts," Nancy said softly, "I am so sorry for you but it won't be too long before I finish."

"Go ahead, hurt me bad," he said, "I have sins to be pardoned for."

"What sins, you are a great saint." Nancy said. "I hope you are not referring to our little sex orgies because all the ancient rules are worthless here. Rome will not decide on the celibacy of its priests, their sex or the limitation of birth. Rome has no way of contacting us here. You will be the new pope. You will be the one who set the rules and I am sure you won't make them too painful for your followers."

There were many wounds on that leg but at least she didn't have to worry about bacteria or viruses. They weren't allowed to live on this world; something was killing the small life.

We had scratches, all of us; for while we had drawn blood fighting the Rat faces, we had been clawed by the beasts but no infection would ever developed.

The doctor's potion contained a substance that acted as an analgesic and a sleeping drug and drowsiness took over the Father who slept through the rest of the surgery.

Two hours later, Nancy looked at the leg with a critical eye and was satisfied with her work. The Father's leg would not be impaired and would function properly in a few days.

The doctor had watched Nancy's work with much interest.

"My name is Christina," she said, "may I know your name?"

"I am Nancy and I don't know how to express my appreciation for your help. We made a good team."

"I watched you perform the sewing and I am amazed at your technique." said Christina. "I don't know what to think; you have just shown incredible mastery of plastic surgery. Even with all my experience, I would not have done it as well and this is impossible since you are only 12 or 13 years old. Who are you? I never heard of you. You are not from here, I can tell and I thought the City was the only human settlement on this world..."

"I understand your puzzlement, "said Nancy, "I am older than you think. I come from another world, your ancestor's world, Earth! I was sent here on a most vital mission for mankind and I am thirty years old. I mean that I was thirty when I passed away. I learned medicine there, a crash course that included many surgeries. The very best doctors trained me."

"When you passed away??…" blurted Christina.

Nancy did not reply for at that moment, the majordomo came and knocked at the door.

"I am here to take you to your room," said the majordomo, "where you will be able to take a shower and rest prior to the dinner with the city mayor."

"I need to look after the other members of my group before." said Nancy. "We were all clawed and bitten and some might have open wounds."

The majordomo led her to each of her friends' room but to her surprise, none of us needed medical attention. We bore scratches on our hands, faces and necks but the rest of our bodies had been spared. The clawing over our clothes hadn't opened the flesh. The clothes and the boots had protected us…

The majordomo led Nancy to her room.

"Please leave your clothes in a basket outside of the shower," said the majordomo, "somebody will come to pick them. They will be cleaned and ironed and brought back in time for dinner. Oh yes, I left a bathrobe in the shower room."

"Thanks, that's very kind of you." Said Nancy.

Nancy had left Christina to follow the majordomo just before she would ask her what she meant by "before I passed away".

There will be a lot of questions to answer, Nancy thought, better let John answer them at dinner time.

I had a shower, my first shower on this world and when I came out of the bathroom somebody had left a steaming coffee cup and a full plate of cookies on the table.

I sat comfortably in a well-cushioned wood and leather chair. The chair was a work of art; it had been tastefully carved and the carvings represented flowers and birds. The wood was of an unknown essence, it was multicolored and the dominant hues were in the blue, red and green. The leather was made out of the skin of the saurian beast.

Coffee at last, will it taste like Earth coffee? Yes, delicious. I thought.

I used to drink a lot of coffee on Earth, five to six cups a day. I was addicted I supposed but it was one of my rare weaknesses. I went through hard times in my first life but I always scratched enough money here and there to have my daily coffees. I could live out of peanut butter and toasts for a while and it didn't matter much; as long as I had my steaming cup in the

morning to take away my brain cobwebs and face the
miseries of a new day.

Yes I lived through real tough times; I have been sick
most of my life and suffered the presence of loneliness.
But what really hurt me most was the injustice of our
legal system, which allowed the college of physicians to
bully me out of my physio-magnetic clinic with one
hundred and sixty-nine charges of illegal medicine.

There had been the injustice of bank managers too, the
loss of dear ones... Life had been at times an unfair
deal but looking backwards, each of those misfortunes
had contributed to the building of a strong soul.

I would not have been able to make those beautiful
paintings had I not live them and my books would be
empty of emotional content. Beside, the Guardians would
not have wanted me for without the hard times; I would
probably have turned into a proud and imbued man; one
that wants to show everyone how great he is while being
quite empty inside. But all those slaps in the face, all
those unfortunate events had humbled me. I had come to
think that I was just an insignificant man, not worthy
of people's sincere admiration and that made me quite
grateful towards those who gave me some affection. I
also decided that at least I would do my best to turn
into the best possible person and this way, I would be
acceptable to myself.

The bed was of a large size, four-posters with a
beautifully carved head. The carving showed a Birdie
talking to a group of people holding Teddy Bears. There
was a magnificent painting on one of the walls, the
painting was four by five feet in size, I estimated. I
went closer and no it couldn't be, that style… that
style was the style of my old friend Ron Davies.

I had recruited him the first year I went into art. I
had bought my first art gallery and had been looking for
better artists than those showing their work in that
gallery. At that time, I wasn't an artist myself; I had
been a chemist and a businessman. I had started a
specialty coatings company with an Indian (India). We
had made a quick success with a novel line of water-
based coatings for the pre-finishing of cheap plywood.

Seven years later, I became allergic to chemicals; I sold my shares to my partner and bought that art gallery in a big mall. There were piles of 24″ x 48″ original oil paintings being sold for $350.00 framed. Those paintings were coming from Taiwan or from commercial artists able to produce loads of them each month.

I wanted better art; and each Sunday I was traveling to visit artists' studio. I had been introduced to Ron Davies and he turned into my bestseller artist for years.

He was coming every Friday night with his work of the week, usually five or six small size paintings. We smiled and clasped hands and sat together and chatted about nothing and everything. After a while I asked him to show me his paintings one at a time and I was marveling at the atmosphere and the subtle beauty of each one, and praised him for his wonderful talent.

That moment was the reward for his weekly efforts and I expressed my admiration and approval sincerely with much enthusiasm.

He usually did landscapes but sometimes he would do wolves or a howl on a snow covered tree limb. Whatever the subject, the colors were soothing and there was an element of grace in them.

His paintings were an act of praising God for the beauty of the world he had given us.

One day he moved to a new home, he had loaded the truck with the few belongings he had kept over the years but before departing, he went back up the stairs for a final inspection; a last look to his apartment, a fatal look for he died coming down the stairs. It was on April fool day 1982.

I had accumulated one hundred and sixty eight of his paintings. I had bought everything he brought over a number of years even when the business was slow and I had a hard time to meet with months' ends for I knew that he depended on me and not only for the income but mostly for my encouragement and friendship. In the following twelve months, I sold all of the paintings.

That was impossible I knew it for the business wasn't that good and I had tripled the retail prices but it seemed to me that he was still around and helping me in my selling efforts.

There was another artist, Landry Le Chardon, from whom I was buying all the production but he wasn't as prolific as Ron. Nevertheless, listen to this; one year later on April fool day 1983, Jean-Paul Landry brought me the last six paintings for his coming show. It was Saturday morning; he had come with his wife all the way from the south shore of Montreal to my art gallery in Laval. They were going to the sugar barn, he said, for feasting and dancing the whole afternoon.

In Quebec people do that once a year.

That day, for the very first time, Jean-Paul opened up to me and we had an hearty exchange of ideas. He gave me some sound advice and I was surprised because he wasn't much of a talker. They left smiling and drove to the sugar barn. Two hours later he died on the dancing floor and he was still smiling. It was April fool's day, one year after Ron Davies fatal April fool's day.

Two days later, I drove to Drummondville and passed by the South Shore not very far from Jean-Paul Landry and suddenly he was there sitting by me looking straight ahead.

"Jean-Paul, you are dead?" I cried. He didn't answer and didn't turn around and I was grateful for I would have been scared to look at his dead eyes.

I stop the car at the next telephone booth and called his wife. She was crying and had a hard time to tell me what happened.

"He died happy," she said, "and kept his smile frozen on his lips. He has found peace at last for my husband was a tormented man."

I made the show of his recent work on Wednesday night of the same week for I had sent two thousand invitations. I tripled the retail prices since these would be the last paintings I would ever get from him. I wasn't too sure I would be able to sell them at the new prices though.

The morning of the show, there was half a page in the newspaper talking about him and announcing the night show in my gallery. I would have never spent two thousand dollars for half a page of the main town newspaper. But there it was, half a page on my show of his latest works and it was an incredible publicity for it wasn't a pub but an editorial article.

I questioned his wife that day and she told me she had no idea who called the newspaper and who decided to put that article that very same day.

There was a crowd that night and I sold everything, a sold out show at three times the usual prices.

I lost my two and only friends on April fool's day with one year in between and both of them helped me to make a lot of money with the work I had bought from them. Incredible? Yes, but true.

Those years were the best in the art market. People attached more importance in the artworks on their walls than the rich look of their furniture. The social life was also more active and less television oriented.

I was selling an average of twenty paintings a week and getting the custom framing business from another twenty-five customers.

I was running all day long, assembling the frames with mats and glass, or touching up a painting or replacing the sold ones, filling up the empty walls, packaging the sold ones or doing the paperwork but nobody knew how much work it was to run an art gallery. For when a customer walked in, I would stop at once, take a long breath and walk leisurely in the gallery like somebody that had nothing to do. The visitors thought I had it easy, how could they know I was working at full speed, all day long, six days a week and buying art on Sundays.

Nevertheless it was good time those years and I made many friends. I would often go to my customers' homes to deliver their paintings and help them in setting them up on the walls. Then they would open a good bottle of wine and we would talk. They would treat me like a precious guest giving me a value well over what I deserved.

Looking at that painting brought it all up.

How could Ron Davies be here? Will I meet with him? Will he remember his past life and me? I can't wait to go in search of him. I will search everywhere; I will ask questions and find him. But thinking about it, if Ron is here; who else might be here too? Will I also find my father? I still miss him so much; I don't think I told him enough of my love and appreciation for him and I wish we could have spent more time together before he got so sick. Everything is becoming more and more mysterious...I thought.

After the coffee and cookies I lied down in my new bed, my first real bed in a long time and it was so comfortable that a moment later I was sound asleep.

The majordomo woke me up as he brought me back my clothes. I took a second shower and put them on. There was a reflecting surface in the room; a mirror it was, and I took a good look at myself.

I looked great, I thought, I must be taller and stronger than I was on earth, since I am about Tom and John size now.

I look like D'Artagnan in the Three Musketeers movie with my cape, my big hat, my long boots and the sword dangling on my side. The blue and gray pants go well with the red and gold cape, the blue and gold hat and the red feather; I am magnificent, thank you Guardians.

The clothes were of the finest material I had ever seen and they were extremely resistant. I had walked through bushes; I had slept with them for days; the Rat Faces had clawed me and there was no sign of damage, no bloodstains, no nothing. I looked for my scratches and bruises and they were gone too. The fabric had kept its luster and looked brand new, and my body had repaired itself inside of a few hours. The guardians had been kind and careful, providing us with the best bodies and clothes we could dream of ever having; thank you again Guardians.

I went out of the room and trailed down the staircase, which led me to the dinning room. What a staircase it was, all precious wood, carved, sanded smooth and varnished. There were paintings on the walls depicting life scenes of this new world. I could see people battling against monsters, tragic scenes and yet exciting, showing the courage of the people who had founded a new civilization against all kind of mortal dangers.

The fresh scent of autumn, of falling leaves, had been most soothing in my bedroom with the window wide open. Now, as I came down the stairs, a great variety of odors came to my attention. There was the smell of cooking food, the odor of hundred years old wood and more fragrances, all kind of them.

One scent was so alien that it had to come from some other world. *It must be the Birdies body odor*, I thought and I was anxious to meet with one of them.

Chapter Eleven - The reception

The majordomo assistant was waiting at the dinning room
door and directed me to my place at the long table.
There were 15 chairs on each side. Facing me were the
mayor with the chief recorder on his left and the
Sheriff and master security officer on his right.

The Teddies' highest official was right beside the chief
recorder on a high stool and the Birdies' highest
official was sitting beside the Sheriff.

The ten city councilors occupied the rest of the chairs
on the City officials' side of the table.

John was sitting in front of the mayor with Joan on his
right and I on his left. On each side were divided the
rest of our group along with Johnny, Paul and Victor
Rodriguez, the boy scouts leader and the two boy scouts
Sandra and Bob.

"We will now proceed with the introduction" Said the
majordomo as he came to the end of the table.

"Mayor Ed Kimpley."

The mayor stood up and bowed his head in a gentle salute
then sat back.

"Senior Recorder Jerry Green! - Sheriff Paul Stuart! -
Birdies' leader Krzzzurr! - Teddies' leader Vrroosh! -
Councilor Ted Roosevelt! ..."

Once the city officials had been all introduced, the
majordomo asked us to introduce ourselves starting with
the right end side.

"Father O'Leary, Earth religious emissary," said the
Father without standing up, "please excuse me from not
getting up but my leg won't allow me."

"Nancy Mathers, Earth Emissary!"- "Garry Mathers, Earth
emissary!"- "Bob Rodriguez!"- "Sandra Rodriguez!"- "Joan
Brunet, Earth emissary!"- "John Foster, Earth
emissary!"- "Richard Riverin, Earth emissary!"- "Tom

Hardings, Earth emissary!"- "Johnny Rodriguez!"- "Paul Rodriguez!"- "Victor Rodriguez!"- "Christina Davidson!"

Mayor Ed Kimpley looked at us, one after the other and said:

"There are a lot of questions coming to my mind, but first of all I would like to know what happened on the other side of the river."

"We were looking for the leather bark trees when I realized that Sandra and Bob were missing." said Johnny Rodriguez.

"We were kidnapped by monsters," said Sandra, "ten foot tall humanoid monsters with a rat face. They tied us up to a tree and they would have devoured us if it were not for these Earthmen who came to our rescue."

Sandra went on with more details about the kidnapping and the rescue. She depicted us as the most fantastic fighters with unlimited courage and ability.

"Yes," approved Bob, "these people are true heroes!"

"They saved my children, they saved us all..." completed Johnny Rodriguez, "we were overwhelmed by the numbers and the ferocity of the beasts but these people were incredible; they killed dozens of those monsters in seconds only. I have never seen anybody moving as fast."

"We thank you all for your heroic actions." said mayor Kimpley. "We realized that you are taller than us by a foot with the exception of Nancy and Garry and this might indicate that you are the result of a longer evolution. Are you coming from the future? Who are you? Where do you come from? What are your intentions?"

There was a moment of silence; we had accepted John's leadership without ever discussing the matter with him. The person that would answer would be looked at as our group leader. For all of us, I guessed, John was the leader and this is why we didn't answer. John realized the reason for our silence; we would let our leader answer; we had accepted him as our leader. He looked quickly around to make sure about it and then answered heartily.

"We come from your ancestors' world; from your past and not your future." John said. "We were chosen by immaterial beings that call themselves the Guardians to come here for a mission most vital to mankind."

"From our past?" interjected Mayor Kimpley. "That's strange; I read all the books our ancestors brought with them in the landing shuttle; books that relate the history of starship travel and starship Endeavor was the first starship ever to come to Ghama."

"We didn't come in a starship," replied John, "we come from an era where there wasn't any starship yet. At that time, New York, Chicago, Washington and Los Angeles were thriving cities with populations numbering millions of people."

"That would be seven or eight centuries ago," commented mayor Kimpley, "for those cities were utterly destroyed by nuclear bombs; terrorists' bombs."

"I personally died just before their destruction," said John, "some of my companions survived the plague and died a few years later."

"What!? You died, you said!?..." blurted Mayor Kimpley. "Does Heaven exist? Are you coming from Heaven?"

"We are not coming from heaven and I am not sure if it exist. One of my companions Father O'Leary is a preacher and he will be pleased to enlighten you all on spiritual matters if you express the desire to learn about it but no, we came here as spirits and the Guardians gave us a new body. We were awoken on a plateau that you call sky-wall no more than a few days ago."

John told them about the Guardians and our contacts with them.

"They tried to communicate with you," John said, "They approved of you as a species, they liked your compassion and they didn't want you to become enslaved, tortured and destroyed by your enemies. They tried to warn you of great coming dangers to no avail; telepathic communication was impossible. So they traveled to your past and then to Earth and went on searching through the centuries for someone that could hear their message.

Richard was the first one; the first human that could hear them. He wrote a book to recruit some people to come him to your help and I was one of the few who believed in his story. Later on, I could hear the Guardians too; they communicated with me because like Richard, I had an unusually high level of magnetism and iron in my blood.

So we recruited fourteen people, maybe more but I know of only fourteen of them. We were split in two groups of seven and awoken thousands of miles apart.

Our group was awoken close to your city so that we could come here and raise a little army if needs be. The second group was to be awoken near the second human settlement on this world, a city sitting at the canopy of a jungle of giant trees, a city called Jungletown."

"Amazing," said mayor Kimpley, "we thought that the crew of the second landing shuttle had perished since we never heard of them until now.

But tell me who those enemies are? And how come are they our enemies? To my knowledge we have done no harm to anyone."

John told them about the lost cities and the demons that are helping some wicked species to get there first and enhance themselves to such powerful beings that all other species in the galaxy would fall under their reign.

"We have already met people of a sentient species who live on the plateau and we have seen the Old ones, the gigantic trees that may be this planet protectors." said John.

John told them about our encounter with the Centaurs before we came down the cliff and their decision to try coming down too, in a makeshift balloon and help us in our mission.

"As soon as we reached the valley floor," said John, "we smelled the evil Rat faces and heard the cries of the children and we went to their rescue."

The majordomo's staff served us a salad of leaves, unidentifiable fruits and vegetables along with a small loaf of crusty and fresh warm bread and a bowl of soup.

The mayor interrupted the questioning at that moment and proposed to eat and relax for a while. The soup was delicious, I was hungry and I had to restrain myself not to gulp it in. We ate the soup and the bread in silence and we started on the salad and soon we were chatting with our companions and hosts.

More plates were borne to the table, three kind of meat with cooked fruits and vegetables. It was exquisite. I don't remember such a feast in both worlds. We had roasted boar and fowl's meat two nights ago in the company of the centaurs and it had been great but not quite as well seasoned and tasty.

Nancy and the Teddies' leader were laughing together while Joan was engaged in a serious conversation with the Birdies' most noble and worthy leader.

Like mother like daughter, I told myself.

The evening meal had finally ended. We couldn't eat anymore even though there was still a lot of food on the table. The mayor was appalled at the news that we had climb down what they called the wall to heaven.

"But that is impossible," he said, "the wall is miles high and in some part so smooth that it would not offer any grip."

John explained how we did it. We showed them our boots and gloves and Garry went to the wall and climb it like a fly.

"You see," said Garry, "there is nothing there; it's very easy except for the icy spots."

"There were icy spots," interjected John, "and we had to use the ropes to get down in some places."

"So it is a plateau with a forest of gigantic trees and plains." said the mayor interrogatively.

"Yes and with a lot of leather bark trees and all kind of life including the Centaurs' tribes, a sentient specie with whom we have developed instant kinship. They are telepath too." John said, looking at Krzzzurr the Birdie leader.

"I am not surprised," said Krzzzurr, "we sensed something coming from up there; evanescent thoughts, murmurs of emotion; it is fuzzy, the plateau is probably too far to catch a meaning to their flitting mind exchanges but you see, most sentient species communicate telepathically; you humans are the only species ever met by my ancestors who achieved a high level of technology without the capacity of telepathic exchanges.

What I don't understand," said Krzzzurr "is why the Guardians did not contact us. We are strong telepaths and we could have conveyed their messages to our human friends."

"There are other forces," said Father O'Leary, "who prevented them to contact you. The Guardians said that they were limited in their actions by some unimaginable power. They were surprised and puzzled by our concept of God and said that if God exist, He might very well be dwelling on this world.

I can assure you that God does exist and He sent His Son to Earth, almost three millenniums ago, to teach us how we could mature into a worthy species. I will be please to tell you all about his teachings, later on."

As the Reverend Father spoke those words, I saw a change in Krzzzurr expression, the Birdies leader almost drop from his chair, he seemed to be under shock.

"We will be honored to serve you Oh Father in the spreading of those teachings." said Krzzzurr. "My ancestors and I are in a way, no offense intended, surprised by God's interest in humans since they are telepathically deficient.

Usually this disability leads species to self-exterminating wars and nuclear holocausts. You had some

265

of that too as we were told but what might have save mankind is that rare compassion quality that John mentioned earlier.

We, Birdies, don't have that and we are amazed at your sorrow, bitterness, grief, self pity, bereavement, tenderness, upwelling sense of love, self inflicted pain and despair, hope, anger, suspicion, uncontrollable expression of merriment giving birth to guffaws, body shaking and eventually ground rolling and paws tapping."

By that time, we had all burst in laugh, overwhelmed by the very merriment he had just mentioned and we came very close to the ground rolling and paws tapping.

"See, "Krzzzurr said, "you are a most amazing and interesting creature. You are laughing at yourselves. The thoughts of your shortcomings do not drive you into despair and self-annihilation. Unexpected reactions are your lot and make your kind irresistible to us. We Birdies live for knowledge, acquiring it and passing it along is our duty. We thought we would know mankind after a few weeks of living with you but we haven't yet achieve total knowledge of even one unit of mankind and all units differs in many ways; that may explain why we became addicted to your presence."

Hector, the majordomo invited us to come to the main living room for a concert.

"Music at last!" said Nancy joyfully.

"What a wonderful evening," said Joan softly in John's ear.

I noticed that exchange and felt a little pang of jealousy. Obviously Joan was in love again with John and I felt that I should not be in their way.

They deserve each other, I thought, *they are both true heroes and I am just an ordinary guy with a lot of shortcomings. I will look for a woman whose presence will heal the pain with time… Boy it hurts; just the thought of letting her go is breaking my heart but I have to. I promised remember? And I always keep my promises. But I promised to no one just to me…*

266

There were more people anxious to meet with us in the large room. There were six tables, each sitting eight. There was a dancing floor and a small platform for the musicians. John and Joan were sat with Mayor Ed Kimpley and his wife Laura, Jerry Green senior recorder and his wife Claudette. Sheriff Paul Stuart and his wife Maria completed the table.

Tom and I were introduced to two very beautiful young women, Annie Fowler and Patricia Laure and we sat with them. The alien's leaders joined us trailed by Nancy who wouldn't leave Teddies leader Vrrossh and Father O'Leary who was overwhelmed by his desire to communicate with the most dignified birdie leader Krzzzurr.

There is my chance to enrich my mind with alien philosophy, the Reverend Father told himself happily. Bob wanted to sit by Nancy but there were no empty chair left. He went to another table seemingly dejected by this turn of event.

A string orchestra quartet of musicians started with chamber music. It was very soft and soothing at the beginning but it turned into dramatics and became heartbreaking with sorrowful parts and stimulating with bursts of glory. The rhapsody lasted half an hour and underlined the importance for the City of this first and incredible meeting with their ancestors, us, the Earth emissaries.

The musicians were very talented and when the music stopped, everyone was standing up, applauding them warmly. The musicians stood up in turn and one of them made a short speech.

"Thank you, thank you all. We are celebrating tonight the rescue of our boy scouts and Boy Scout leaders by a group of visitors from far away. On this special occasion, it would be great if Patricia Laure, our most beloved singer would entertain us with one of her wonderful songs. Bob, our young virtuoso will accompany her at the piano."

Like Nancy, I love music with a passion and when I heard Patricia singing, I felt very attracted to her. I always loved the company of artists. The night had started well in her company and we had warmed up towards each other just by sitting side by side and listening to the rhapsody. Now, I caught the powerful emotional content beyond her beautiful voice and my warmth for her turned into a flame.

That Patricia, I thought, is just the kind of woman with whom I could fall in love again. She is my type of woman, and I am a free man now that John is back to care for Joan. If there is anyway to win her heart, Patricia will be mine to love and cherish.

In the mean time, Nancy was thinking that even if Bob was too young for her, he deserved her gratitude for that heavenly music. So, if he wanted her tonight...

While Tom was entertaining Annie Fowler and Nancy and I were entranced by the musical performance, Father O'Leary had a most interesting conversation with Krzzzurr.

"My species, "Krzzzurr was saying, "evolved on the third planet gravitating around the star called Rigel in the Orionis constellation; and that is 900 light years from this world. We, Birdies, are a very old civilization and our history goes as far back as one million years ago.

We are telepathic and able to communicate over long distances. Since we can read each other's mind, we have serious, sincere and truthful interrelationship.

We eliminated the most dangerous predators roaming our world very long ago and have live in peace for hundreds of thousands of years wondering about the stars and the existence of other worlds and other sentient species.

The desire to fly to the stars and learn about the universe became overwhelming and the legend said that a long time ago, at the beginning of our history, we built a tower to reach the stars. That was impossible for the higher we built, the farther the stars seemed to go.

Once we realized the impossibility of such a task, we

started to investigate other ways. On our world there were plants growing pods that exploded at maturity and flew quite a distance from the mother plant. There was a flame underneath the flying pod; the result of a swift chemical reaction; it lasted a very short time but long enough to propel the pod a good distance away.

We observed that phenomenon and got some ideas. We developed our sciences and eventually came to build rockets and spaceships. We colonized a number of planets as we went through with the exploration of the galaxy.

A few hundred years ago, one of our ships came in the vicinity of Ghama-2 and a force of some kind crashed our starship. We survived our forced landing and like the humans we built a settlement, which became a small city.

Again we were overwhelmed by our thirst for knowledge and many of us left in small groups to explore this most puzzling world.

Predators and wicked sentient species decimated some of those groups. One of those species, the harpies have a bird like body with a wing span of sixteen feet and talons armed with six inches long claws. Their heads is somewhat similar to humans' females but larger with the vampire's fang of your legends. A short arm sprouts from the side of each wing, halfway upon its length and terminates with fingerlike tentacles ending into claws.

They stand 12 feet high on their long knurly legs and can outrun us. They were no way we could escape should they decide to catch us. We tried to communicate with them, sensing intelligence in their brainwaves.

We told them we meant them no harm, we were just travelers on a learning epic but when we quested delicately their intentions, moving just a little inside their mind to read their thoughts, we gagged at the filth we found there in their brain.

Their rotten and evil thoughts were unbearable and there was a vicious glee at the prospect of what they were about to do. They attacked our party and ate them a little piece at a time keeping them alive as long as they could, rejoicing in their pain.

Another wicked specie, the Greees, decimated one of our groups. They have a feline body and their front paws end in clawed fingers. They are ferocious and often fight each other. They are brutal killers and big, ten feet long, they weight a thousand pounds and can outrun a harpy. They can swim and climb too; there are no ways to escape them. Our group flew away from them but we can't fly over long distance and they followed us and caught us in the trees where we had branched.

Some of our people are still roaming the planet in search for knowledge and sometimes we catch their messages but it is not always possible to have clear communications; there are interferences and sometimes their messages can't go through. It all depends on their location.

One group has crossed the sea and they are now exploring a fairyland. They said they saw dragons flying in the sky and trolls guarding ancient bridges and there are castles with drawbridges inhabited by humanlike giants called Ogres."

"Pardon me to interrupt," said the father, "but I need to know if you believe in God and the possibility of an afterlife. Your philosophy is of great importance to me and surpasses the interesting epic of your voyagers."

"For us Birdies, the presence of God doesn't have much importance." Krzzzurr answered seriously. "When a Birdie die, his immaterial part or spirit is attracted to the closest living relative and flee instantaneously over long distances and wedge its way inside the host's brain to share and communicate.

We talk together all the time and sometimes one of the spirits who dwell inside takes over for a short while. It is not ethical to take over for long and the spirit eventually give back the control to the undead. Some of us are so strong mentally that a takeover is impossible.

But we are immortals and when the host dies, all the spirits who had found a home inside the undead including the host spirit scatter away, each one going to his next closest living relative.

We can stand, a thousand of us, over the surface of the point of a needle if I may say so to illustrate the fact that the brain of one live individual can shelter hundreds of thousand of his deceased ancestors and relatives.

We are quite happy with the way we are so we never pondered about the existence of God. In fact, God seemed to be a human concept since my ancestors tell me right now that they have never met another sentient species sharing that concept but now, everything has changed; now that we have met you, we believe that there is more than what appears to be in our universe."

"I am just a preacher," said the reverend, "but if my presence is motivating you to learn more about the spiritual elements of our universe, I will be happy to share my knowledge and beliefs with you.

Tell me, why did you personally come to the human settlement?" Asked the Father. "Were you driven by one of your spirits or did you decide to come on your own?"

"I came because I am puzzled by the human units. Each of you is so lonely that a human unit's desire to live and do things without the comforting presence and experience of thousands of elders and relatives is incomprehensible.

Humans are of great interest to us. Leaving the Birdies' settlement to come here was not difficult since I didn't come alone. I came with thousands of ancestors inhabiting inside of me with whom I communicate all the time. We watch the humans units participating in projects with other very lonely units or doing sports with them and we are fascinated.

Humans have that incomprehensible concept they call competition. We don't understand, we never had any motivation to compete between ourselves because we are not individuals or single units as you are. Each Birdies is an entity composed of many thousands units, some of them have lived as far back as the earliest time of our evolution."

"How many of you came here? How and when did you come?

How far is your city from here? I have many questions
for you." Said the Father eagerly interested by the
beautiful birdie.

Krzzzurr was taller than the father.

It looks like we were given tall bodies, thought the
reverend, *we are taller than the New Alexandrians, we
are close to eight foot tall but Krzzzurr is taller than
me, the Birdies are about ten foot tall.*

The Birdie had feathers of all possible and impossible
colors. Its arms were covered with dark blue and green
and red soft, short and very dense hair. Its hands had
four fingers terminated by short claws.

*Those fingers were flexible and it could move them in
amazing ways. Those are builders' fingers, they built
starships while we were still monkeys*, the father
thought.

The Birdie had two huge wings in its back like the
angels of the bible. The wings were of pale hues, blue
and silver hues. They were closed on its back right now
but when it opened them, it was a sight. From tip to
tip, they spanned twelve feet.

The Birdies could fly short distances only. They were
walkers and fast runners. Krzzzurr had long legs, maybe
five feet long. It had a shorter body about three feet,
a very short neck hidden by the feathers and its
head was almost as big as a human head with two owl
eyes, large, round and green, with a catlike vertical
slits, and it had a short and sturdy beak. It had on the
top of its head long and firm hairs that were moving
according to its emotions as it talked.

Sometimes they would go straight up. Sitting in front of
the father, Krzzzurr didn't look so tall. Its body
seemed very light, made of empty bones, ropes and
feathers.

"Delightful, delightful," said Krzzzurr, "we Birdies
love to talk and teach but we have nothing to talk or
teach to other Birdies since we all know the same
things.

Our City is at forty running days from here, on the same continent and right on the coast. We can cross the whole City here in one hour without getting winded and we can run eight hours in one day... There are very high mountains between our city and yours, impossible to cross over.

The air becomes very thin at such height and would not support our wings. We would have never known about your existence if it weren't for some of your courageous explorers who came by sailboats.

We met with them and learn their language very quickly since we are telepaths. They told us about their City and a group of us decided to follow them if they would allow us. They waited for us while we built a few sailboats for a great number of us wanted to come. We received a warm welcome from the humans and we decided to stay and we have been living here for a little more than one hundred years."

"Very interesting," said the reverend Father, "and you get along well, you are happy, contented with your life?"

"Yes and no, you see, we Birdies like to talk and teach but we like to learn, we love to learn, it is the most important activity for us. Some birdies are thinking about leaving this City and try to find other species. There might be some interesting ones. We like the Teddies, they are cute and funny but they are not interested in learning and they don't talk much. We made contact with the Rat Faces but they are evil, wicked and most disgusting.

There might be other interesting species though on this world. If you agree, I would like to go with you when you leave the City for your most important mission."

"We will be honored and most comforted to have your help and company," said the Father.

"What do you intend to do in the next few days?" asked Krzzzurr. "Could I be of assistance?"

"Maybe you can. I am a religious preacher and I would like to invite the people here in a place where I could

273

talk to them about the world they come from and about
Jesus and his teachings, about God and his commandments
and the churches. I wish to transmit the words
of God to my brothers."

"Would you mind if I asked you a question, Reverend
Father?" asked the birdie. "Have you met with God? What
does he look like? When did He become God? Did He create
the whole universe? What is the purpose of His
creation..."

"Wait please," said the Father. "You are asking too many
questions at once. First, I don't recall having ever met
with God. So I can only speak of what was written in the
Holy bible."

"But then, how can you be certain that you are telling
the words of God?"

"One must have faith in the writings of the bible for it
was written by some of the disciples of Jesus who came
upon Earth to teach the people of his time how to get
salvation. He became very famous once he started making
miracles."

"My ancestors tell me that making miracles is a
dangerous practice for it usually brings misfortune.
Tell me what happened to Jesus after he did the
miracles."

"He was tortured and killed but only because he wanted
to. He accepted this most horrible fate to get God's
pardon for our great sins".

"My ancestors said it figures, they were expecting that
answer. But we would be pleased to see how you are going
to manage in bringing the words of God to the people
here and we wish to help you. There the concert hall
that you can use; it is big enough for one thousand
people and the sound carry very well in it. Except for
the concerts, it is always empty."

"I would also need an altar and a tabernacle, many bread
loafs, a cup of wine and a priestly costume for the
ceremony. Also, people must have a good time and a
pianist and some excellent singers would do well for
that first ceremony. You are a telepath! Would it be

possible for you to read from my mind some of my favorite religious musical compositions and transfer them into the mind of our young pianist prodigy? I would write the songs, which I know by heart and then the singers and the pianist could practice them for the next few days. I would like my first grand mass to be an important event; one that people will remember with pleasure. It must be memorable, that's very important."

"Yes Reverend Father I can help you and I am grateful that you asked. You see, being useful is very important to us Birdies, and I feel a closeness to you that I have never experienced before--with anyone else. I sense a comforting approval by a presence, a greater entity that surrounds you. Could it be the presence of those guardians that took you here or even more exciting, could it be the presence of the greatest of all beings, the creator, God Himself!? My ancestors and I don't know about God and His will but if indeed He exists, perhaps can we be of assistance in the realization of that will. Would my presence to the mass be acceptable? My ancestors and I wish to come and learn from you!"

"You sure can Krzzzurr," said the Father, "and from now on let us be brothers. Later on, if you wish, once you have learned of the word of God, I will baptize you, take your oath and ordain you as my first Abbott and you will help me spread the word around."

Patricia came back to the table; I got up and helped her to her chair. As I sat down I looked at her and met with her gaze. We might not be telepaths we humans but there are some exchanges going on at a subconscious level. She knew then that I was hers for the taking, she was troubled by it and felt the need to know more, much more about me. She asked me about my life on Earth and my wife and kids, my interests and so on.

"I was married once to a beautiful woman," I said. "She was a kind and very serious lady with limited interest for adventures and changes. Marrying me gave her the torments and worries of constant changes and a most uncertain future. I moved a lot, from one city to another and then to a foreign country where we couldn't even speak the language. She wasn't made for constant adaptation to new ways of life and new surroundings. She

275

wanted to live a discreet life in her small town with the same neighbors. She needed her routine; so one day we talked about going our own way apart. She would return to that small town she grew up in, where our only daughter was living with our three grand children, and I would go on living my adventurous life in different places. She left me to possibly find answers to questions she had not yet been able to formulate."

"Have you seen her after you parted?" Patricia asked.
"Yes many times. I visited her and my daughter and spoiled my grand children every time, as much as I could, until the nuclear bombs started to explode everywhere and the plague started to kill almost all the survivors.

"At that time I met Joan, John's girlfriend and only love and when John died, we started a relationship. I fell in love with her and married her. We lived many adventures together over a period of ten years, until we both died together in a car accident.

I had promised myself to give her back to John when we wake up on this world. Since our awakening, John, Tom the Reverend Father and I have all been her lovers for we were under constant sexual urges and there were only two women with us. But now, I am willing to find the right woman for me and I am very pleased to be in your company.

"Would you talk about your life on Earth with Joan Richard?" asked the lovely Patricia.

"These events, the nuclear bombs and the plague, changed life on Earth forever. The plague took my wife away, and my daughter and grand children and the rest of my family and acquaintances too. I had no one left and felt very lonely. I started to play golf with Joan; she had lost her boyfriend, John, our group leader and we were both quite miserable. We fell in love and we shared eight years of our life.

At first, the reverend father came to live with us in our refuge at Everglades City along with Nancy and Garry who are Joan's children. They left after a while; the father to help the survivors and the children to work at

276

Silicon Valley. Joan and I took on farming in a region called West Virginia. We had horses, cows, pigs, chicken, dogs and cats and farming was a lot of fun. We went almost every day in the wild country for fishing, picnics and horse riding. These were wonderful years; it was quiet and relaxing. Joan and I used to talked about all kind of things as we rocked on the balcony at sunset. One day we got the bad news; Garry and Nancy had died in an explosion at the Silicon Valley research center. We were going to their funeral when we had that car accident. We held hands in our last moments and wished each other our farewells. Joan died first and I felt very lonely and so sad as I waited alone my final moment.

We were transported here by the guardians and woke up in those new bodies they made for us. The Guardians also gave us our outfit, our weapons and clothes. We found them nearby as we woke up. Look at that fabric Patricia, it is incredibly resistant. Even the rat faces clawing didn't affect it. We are here on a mission to save mankind. We have to find a lost city and use its enhancing devices to transform ourselves into Godlike beings. Then, we, humans will become masters of this galaxy. We might even be able to build a heaven for those who deserve salvation and we would be able to prevent the wicked species, the Bullies of this galaxy to enslave and destroy the good ones. We would build a galactic federation in which all species live together in harmony."

I told her the rest of it, the part that mentioned the presence of demons on this world and their servant species.

Patricia was entranced; she had forgotten all around us. We were enclosed in our own little world, the two of us, our souls embracing.

"That's the strangest story," she said, "I have ever heard. It is fascinating. But what about Joan, she looks happy with John but surely you are still loving each other--."

"I promised to myself that if we ever get reunited with John, I would interrupt our affair for I felt guilty about it. He gave me his trust and when he died, I started to invite her to play golf and eventually we fell for each other."

"And now, you are willing to let her go, have you already lost your feelings for her?"

"No, I still love her. When we woke up, she kissed us on the mouth lustily, the four men in our group, one after the other and she declared herself a free woman. We had sex orgies and she made love repeatedly with all of us, including the father who had sworn celibacy and abstinence on Earth.
But now, we have found civilization and everything will change, I think... Each one will find his mate and our life will return to normalcy--would you like to dance Patricia?"

We joined other couples on the dancing floor for a slow moving dance. The music was very soft and romantic; she let go and huddled in tight. At one point, I lifted her head and kissed her on the lips.

In that new body, I was very handsome and I had more wit than I used to have on Earth. I believed I could charm a serpent if I wished to.

"On my world," I said, "this is when I would invite you to come to my bedroom to look at my family pictures but I don't have any. I could show you the armament I was given by the Guardians though. The carvings on my sword and knife would amaze you. But really, I don't know if I should, I don't know anything about your rules of decency here."

"Tom has already left with Annie Fowler," she said as she pressed her body tighter in a most arousing way. "And she didn't find anything indecent at the same proposal. Let's go, the musicians are just about to call it a night."

So we left holding hands under the gaze of Joan who could not refrain a pang of jealousy. She thought she was loosing her ten years long companion and lover and it hurt her. John didn't miss her gaze as we were leaving neither did he miss her emotions of the moment.

He understood Joan's feelings and he promised himself to do everything he could to make her happy and compensate her for the loss.

Tonight I will have her for myself, John thought, *and I love her more than ever before.*

John felt grateful for my decision to give her back to him and get myself another woman.

If Richard ever needs me, John thought, *I will be there.*

"I will always love you," said John, "as he took Joan's hand, "and Richard will always love you too. He will remain our closest friend."

"Come John, let's go back to my room." Said Joan softly.

Bob played for an hour and left the piano under loud applause and went directly to Nancy's table.

"Did you like it?" Asked Bob with adoration in his eyes.

"Oh yes, it was incredible, the coolest music I have ever heard." Nancy answered warmly.

"But it was not supposed to be cool; I played it to be as warm as my feeling for you."

"Whatever! It is just an expression. Your music was just heavenly beautiful." Nancy said smiling. "I supposed you want me to hold my part of the bargain now. It will be only for one night but if you want me, let's go to my room before I change my mind."

Bob couldn't believe that he was going to get more than a few kisses but he went with her all excited inside.

What if-! He told himself.

They entered the room and Nancy closed the door. There was the flickering light of a large oil lamp, and the four posters looked very comfortable, very inviting. A soft breeze came through the open bay window facing the sea and the view was breathtaking.

The water was quiet, unmoving and its dark blue surface was sparkled by the reflection of the stars. Suddenly the emerging head of a dinosaur broke the water.

It looked quietly around and after a while it disappeared silently under the water. The birds had interrupted their songs and Nancy could only hear the distant romantic music coming from the main living room.

Ghama-2 was even more mysterious at night and she would have stayed there by the open window, looking at the sea for hours, dreaming of the coming adventures and possibly her eventual meeting with God.

The Guardians said, she recalled, *that He might be here for they sensed the presence on this world of a being far greater than anything they had ever met. What does He look like? Will He approve of me?*

She turned around and looked at the expectant and silent young musical prodigy. She went closer and kissed him on the mouth then backed up to undress under his gaze.

That is not happening, Bob thought, *but she removed everything and she is so beautiful. She might look twelve but her small firm breasts are most arousing.*

He undressed quickly and she pulled him to the bed…

Father O'Leary was back to his room. He knelt on the floor beside his bed and started his prayers. He thanked God for the wonderful and unforgettable evening with his new friend Krzzzurr; and asked Him to protect the members of his group and the city people. Then he went to bed but didn't sleep immediately. He wanted to think it over; to remember everything he learned from Krzzzurr and his ancestors. For he had realized one of those ancestors was taking over from time to time to talk about those other worlds it had visited. He/they had told him about the strangest life forms they had met.

He/They had talked about the sentient species inhabiting some of the worlds they had visited, and Krzzzurr had described in details their ways of living. There was so much more to learn from Krzzzurr.

We will meet everyday from now on, thought the reverend
Father, *and we will talk endlessly as we prepare
ourselves and set everything up for the coming grand
mass.*

I walked inside my room with the very beautiful and
incredibly feminine Patricia.

I took her to the large bedroom window and we just held
each other looking at the stars and the sea. We saw a
large dinosaur merging for a moment and sinking silently
under the water.

"Are they dangerous?" I asked Patricia.

"Sometimes, if they are hungry or protective of their
territory but they rarely attack a sailboat. We can't
swim in deep seawater though for there are other
predators, even more dangerous ones."

We stood by the window for a while and then I kissed he
on the lips, took her in my arms and carried her to the
large bed.

I must be stronger than the strongest men on Earth, I
thought, *for carrying her is quite effortless. I will
have to be careful not to hurt her; she is certainly
more delicate than Joan.*

I help her undress and started to kiss her everywhere;
from knees and up, there wasn't a spot that I didn't
lick. I loved her scent, the taste of her skin and I
finally went in and we made love, slowly tasting and
sensing our charnel contacts.

"Let's have a walk outside in that starry and most
mysterious night." I proposed as we were resting after
our sexual climax. She was huddling into my arms but not
in the least ready to sleep. She was thinking about us,
our future together if there was going to be anyone at
all.

I felt I could almost read her mind. For her it was a
very serious situation; she had fallen in love with me

and now she was wondering where it would lead her life to.

We walked to the beach, which was only five minutes walking from the grand house and then we went on silently, side by side for an hour. I held her hand and I too was thinking about what the future was going to be for me and for mankind.

I didn't know if any dinosaur or sea creatures would come out of the water to catch us; the thought of the dangers awaiting beach walkers at night had not been a deterrent for an optimistic like me but I had my sword, my long knife and even my bow and a quiver of arrows.

John had made us promise that we would be armed and ready for a fight at all time and after Joan close call with the wolf like beast we had learn our lesson.

The nights on this strange world were even more mysterious than the ones I spent on Earth, walking on a country trail, watching the stars. It was not very dark, that night as I walked on the beach, side by side, with Patricia. There were no clouds and three moons were shedding light; moreover, the sky was packed with stars and many were so close that they looked ten times as big as the brightest stars visible from Earth. As I walked silently beside the most beautiful woman I had ever met or seen, I had that feeling that important events were about to take place, events that will alter mankind destiny.

What am I to think that my role here is of outmost importance for the whole of mankind, I thought, and yet, I have that gut feeling, I have the intuition that my future actions will be decisive for its destiny!

Already I have played an important role since I was the first one ever contacted by the Guardians. I am the one that recruited that group of heroes and important people and even if they are much finer people than I ever was; I am the one who recruited them.

And now, what will I do with Patricia? She wasn't gifted with that kind of superhuman bodies the Guardians gave us; she is delicate and fragile compared to us; she is

*vulnerable. Will it impair the success of our mission
here he I take her along for the ride?*

*Somehow, I feel that she is important for the success of
that mission. The very fact that we were sat side by
side at this table tonight, two strangers from different
worlds and yet absolute soul mates is more than a fluke.
Someone wanted us to meet tonight and that someone
provided that special occurrence. It might be God
Himself that wanted us to meet here on our first night
and if it is so, I am not going to let her go.*

"I took my decision Patricia." I said. "I have been
thinking about us for the last hour."

"So did I Richard." Patricia answered softly.

"I believe that God or one of his angels made us meet
tonight. It is not a lucky encounter for I am in a
mission that will ultimately decides the fate of
mankind. I am totally sure of that.

The chances that I would meet my soul mate on my first
night here in New Alexandria are slim at best for I was
very much in love with Joan and any other woman than you
would have look quite insignificant compared to her.

It is totally crazy but I fell in love with you as you
sang your first song at our dinner party and when you
came back at the table, I look at you in the eyes and I
felt a stirring deep inside; I had been waiting for you,
all my life, you are the one I was destined to live
with."

"I love you Richard." Patricia answered calmly.

"We might not be here for long. John wants to recruit a
small army here and build some boats to cross the ocean
but we might not have the time to do that. The city
might be attacked at any time and we may have to flee
this city tomorrow on some of your small boats. So there
is no time to lose and in our case, I feel that
decisions concerning our future have to be taken now.

This is how gallant men do it on Earth." I said as I put
one knee on the sand.

283

"Patricia, will you be my companion of fortune or misfortune in the coming odyssey? Will you be my partner in life to share my joys and sorrows, to care for me as I will care for you, for better or worst? Will you leave your city and your friends to embark with me on a boat that will cross the ocean and will possibly never come back?" I asked.

Patricia looked at me kneeling in front of her, expectant and wishful. She felt my powerful emotions for her.

"Yes Richard," she answered, "I will be your companion, your life partner and I will leave my quiet and comfortable life here to share your adventures and fight on your side."

I took her in my arms and we hugged for a long time and then I got aroused.

"We are alone on a soft sand beach." I said as I kissed her.

We made love again, on that beach, under the stars with my weapons and clothes at easy reach. I had all my senses wide open and I was ready to jump, sword in hand to face any monster that would dare come close to my sweetheart.

Next morning Joan, John, Mayor Ed Kimpley and Sheriff Paul Stuart were having breakfast together.

"Do you have any idea where that billion years old city might be located?" asked Mayor Ed Kimpley.

"The Guardians showed it to me." said John. "I saw the emplacement relative to the two human settlements and Richard was given the finder gift by the Guardians. He can sense its location but not its distance. It is on another continent. We will have to cross the sea and go inland and walk thousands of miles to reach it. We might have to fight other sentient species to get there, some of them far more dangerous than the Rat Faces. We need help to augment our chances for we must not fail.

If you don't mind, I will recruit a small army of volunteers, maybe 60 men and women for the mission, a few Teddies and two dozen Birdies. We might also get the help of a few centaurs if they find their way down the cliff before we finish the boats.

We must build two boats with a capacity of 100 passengers each and load them to only half their capacity. If one sink or get into trouble, the second one would come to the rescue."

"We have many small boats," said the Mayor, "but none capable of carrying fifty or more people across the sea. We have built a few larger ones but they are not available right now. They are gone with their load of courageous explorers. Some of those might never come back.

So far, none of our ships have ever crossed the sea. The seawater is drinkable and there are fishes aplenty. The problem is the distance and the probability of never finding our way back. Once you leave for your mission, we might never see you again. There are other risks too, the sea monsters and the occasional but very violent storms."

"Can we be lodged in the city for the time it will take to build the boats?" asked John. "We wouldn't mind to do additional work to cover up for the roof and food."

"You will keep the rooms you slept in last night," said the mayor, "the grand house is yours for as long as you need it. We will be honored to serve you, the people will help you in the building of the ships, and there will be plenty of volunteers once they know about the mission.

Recruiting your small army will not be a problem. It will take time though to build the ships, maybe a year, and we will need to go on the other side of the river to get the wood for the boats and the material for the sails.

The problem is the Rat Faces; they will kill every one that crosses the river and we don't have much of an army right now; we had it easy for over a century."

"That period of peace and easy life is over." said John. "The demons will probably influence many species to come over here and destroy you all. They know about our mission. What you need is a well-trained army and all the help you can get. The Birdies must contact their city and call for help. There are a few sentient species with which you have established trade and good relationship; they must be contacted too and it is in their interest to come and help us since the failure of our mission means the end for all the species of the galaxy.

I can recruit and train the army if you allow me." "You will have my backing," said mayor Kimpley. "We didn't have the need for an army until now and we only have a few security people working under Sheriff Paul Stuart. The City is crimeless since the Birdies came to live with us."

"What do they have to do with crime?" asked Joan with much interest.

"The Birdies are telepaths and suspected criminals can't deny their actions in front of them. The Birdies read their minds and they are convicted and deported far away. Sometimes, potential criminals are even stopped before they commit their crimes when their intentions become clear to the Birdies."

"Remarkable friends you got with those birdies." said Joan.

"Tom and I have substantial combat experience," said John coming back to the city defense subject. "And we were given excellent training at Camp David. I suggest the immediate opening of an army recruitment office. The word should be spread around and the volunteers should start coming right away. Tom and I will devote our time to their training since we can't start on the boats before we can travel freely to the other shore.

Once we have a small army of well-trained soldiers, I would like to take them inland and exterminate the Rat Faces before they become too much of a menace."

"Excellent proposition," said Mayor Ed Kimpley. "Under those demons' influence, other wicked species might already be on their way you said, but they live much further than the Rat Faces. The city needs to be fortified; it is too vulnerable. You see, our ancestors built the communal grand house and then other ones, much smaller but quite spacious for each of the Shuttle-2 crewmembers. We built them with plenty of land in between for the fruit trees and the gardens.

We wanted our village to be comfortable and pleasant but it grew to a large and very poorly defended city for we felt safe here and we tried to make a little heaven of the city.

We have parks and golf courses, baseball and football fields, three concert halls, marinas and beaches all along the seacoast. We don't need much; there is plenty of food and clothes for everyone. Nobody is forced to work and in fact there is not much work to do here. We have plenty of people eager to help when there is something to build or repair.

The trees supply everything we need. We found a kind of flame resistant ironwood and our stoves are built with it. The wood can be cut and carved when fresh but harden over a period of one month to become as hard as a stone.

We cover the inside and the top with flat stones and we can cook our meals or warm up the houses in the wintertime. We didn't find much open-air ore deposits and we are not equipped to dig deep into the ground but we found enough ore for our construction tools and nails.

We have a monetary system based on unit of labor. We will supply each of you with plenty of units so you can buy anything of interest in the little shops. We have bicycles for you and here we used them all the time. They are made of wood and leather and perform well on our packed ground streets. The streets are sprayed against plant growth once a year. In wintertime we travel on skis."

"That will be a welcome change from our Earth cities with their car infested streets." Said John happily.

I was having breakfast with Patricia a few tables away. So I heard much of John's conversation with Ed Kimpley. Tom and Annie Fowler came to our table and asked if they could join us. We were happy to see them.

"You look like a cat that has just caught a cute little mouse." I said looking at Tom.

"And you look just the same," he answered as he pulled the chair for Annie.

Tom had a most relaxing presence on me; I just felt very comfortable with him. He never seemed to be in a hurry and would take his time in sitting, eating and speaking--the world would rush by and he wouldn't bulge unless urgent action was needed. Then he would surge at incredible speed... I wouldn't be surprised to find some alligator's blood cells in his body... We became excellent friends and we knew we could count on each other.

On Earth I didn't have any friends except for Ron Davies and Landry Le Chardon but they died a few years only after I met them but now I had the rest of our group to share with and a new girlfriend.

Life can't be better, I thought, this is heaven, *I wouldn't be happier anywhere else.*

Sitting at another table were Nancy and Garry along with Bob and Sandra Rodriguez. Sandra had great admiration for Garry's courage and in addition she found him most interesting. He seemed to understand her as well or better than her own long time female friends.

This boy, she thought, *will have all the women after him when he grows up. He is presently of no threat to anyone though for his body doesn't have the hormones yet and he doesn't have any sexual drive but what great company, I just love his presence.*

Further away, I saw Father O'Leary who seemed to be preparing something most private with Krzzzurr. They sat at the farthest table and were engaged in intense low voice conversation.

"Would you like to visit the town?" Said Ed Kimpley in a voice that carried through the dinning hall. Everyone raises his hands.

Chapter Twelve - The visit of the town.

"OK then, let's meet in front of the city hall in half
an hour." said the mayor. "There will be bicycles for
everyone. The visit will take the whole day since we
will stop at many of the most interesting places.

We will lunch on a beach at the far end of the city and
will then come back. Tonight, I would like to introduce
you all to our people. Krzzzurr spread the word
telepathically to the other Birdies and everyone is
telling the news to their neighbors.

We will sell admission tickets at ten labor units each
and I believe it will be a sold out. You will all become
rich overnight. There are enough places for 100,000
people standing up in the baseball field and 50,000
sitting places in the baseball stadium. The stadium is
located in the heart of the city.

It will be packed solid you will see, people will
be coming from the four corners of the town to see you.

One of you will tell them the story of your mission. You
choose which one is best for it.

You need one gifted with a powerful voice and an
excellent pronunciation and with our sound-expanding
gadget; the words will be carried to everyone.

We will erect a platform in the center of the field and
you will be sitting at a long table. I will introduce
you individually first and then the one you chose will
tell your story."

"That one should be the Reverend Father," said John, "he
has a booming voice that carries and he excels in
telling stories. Will you do it please?" John asked as
he looked at the Father with his most engaging smile.

Everyone had guessed the answer--.

We were enjoying our bike ride. There were children
playing in the streets, chasing or being chased by the
funny gamboling Teddies. Little girls were playing

289

mothers with them under the gaze of their parents and the most imposing Birdies. There were beautiful trees Everywhere and each house was different; the wood doors and window openings had been carved and multicolor curtains were flapping in the wind.

There was no glass in the windows but they had shutters.

Peddlers and shopkeepers were offering all kind of things in the commercial sectors; clothes, materials, food, seashells, and even live pets.

The temperature had reached the high seventies and there was a soft breeze coming from the sea. The sunrays were playing with the leaves in the colorful trees and we could hear the rumbling sound of the waves hitting the sandy shore.

The birds were singing their heart out at our passage and fragrances of all kind were flirting with me.

What a pleasure to be gifted with a keen sense of smell, I thought.

We went to the beach and sat on very fine pearly sand. Joan sat in the sand alongside Patricia.

I bet she wants to know about last night, I thought.

"This is Paradise." Said Joan; all honey, to Patricia.

It was evident to me that Joan wanted to know more about the woman that had caught my interest. She was wary of her, considering her as a rival and the way she hide her resentment was most commendable.

"I never heard of Paradise before." Answered Patricia with a most charming and friendly smile.

Just before we all met in front of the grand house, I went to Joan's room and John was there…

"Would you mind John if I could talk for a moment with Joan?" I asked.

"No problem Richard, I will be waiting downstairs." He replied.

"Joan, I love you, I will always love you but I have to tell you that for now on, I will consider you as John's girlfriend." I said.

Joan waited calmly for the rest of it.

"Patricia and I spent the night together as you surely have guessed when you saw us leaving the dancing room together. It became more than a simple sexual encounter; I felt something powerful for her and it was mutual. Last night after we made love, we went to walk on the beach and I thought about it and I asked her to become my girlfriend! I intend to take her along when we leave this city. I am sure that you will become the best friends. I know that you never agreed with my decision to give you back to John but I would feel like a traitor otherwise and Patricia is a true lady, you will enjoy her company."

"I understand how you feel Richard and I know that one can love two persons at the same time for that's what is happening to me. I hope you will still love me as much as before in the future. I don't know if I like that woman though and your decision seemed a little hasty…"

"Please Joan, my lovely sweetheart; try to be nice with her. She is not taking me away from you, it's me; I am the one that wanted to find me another woman and I used all my tricks to charm her out of her clothes."

I knew there might be some sparks between them and I had warned Patricia already about possible hard feelings from the woman who had shared my life for almost ten years. And Patricia had promised me to do her best to gain Joan's approval and friendship.

"Paradise is where you may go when you die according to religious beliefs." said Joan.

"You lost me there again, I never heard of religious beliefs either." answered Patricia.

"Well, you are going to hear about it soon. I expect Father O'Leary to tell everyone about it in the coming weeks. But Paradise means a place of happiness and contentment where we can live forever."

"I like it here, everyone is happy except for a few, the adventurers, that can't stay in place and prefer to go exploring the world." Patricia said.

"I have a few questions impatient for answers," said Joan. "Tell me Patricia, how come I didn't see old people here?"

"There are none to be seen for on this world, there are no virus nor bacteria." answered Patricia. "We do grow old but it doesn't show and one day, we die of a devastating and sudden breakdown of our vital organs."

"What is your life expectancy?" asked Joan.

"About one hundred years even though some have lived up to one hundred and twenty years."

"What about the wild life here? We didn't see any corpse or dead trees..."

"The trees probably live forever and the ones we cut to build our houses grow back." answered Patricia. "You didn't see the corpses because they are eaten by the worms at nighttime. There are worms everywhere on this world and they have teeth but they never attack a live animal or plant. They eat the fallen fruits and this prevents the formation or spreading of forests; they also eat the dung and they fertilize the soil.

The whole planet is a park with well-planned forest and plains; even the grass grows in rectangle and squares to add to its incredible beauty. We never met the builders or the keepers of the world but we believe they are nature artists and architects."

"How often do women have children here? Can they get pregnant every year if they have sexual activity?" asked Joan.

"We are fertile for a period of twenty five years," replied Patricia, "from thirteen up to the late thirties. We loose our fertility for a period of two years after giving birth. Our fertility diminishes with each new born. No woman ever had more than ten children to my knowledge.

Nowadays, most married women are contented with four or five children. For those who are not ready yet to raise children, we have a fruit that prevent fertility. Fortunately that fruit tree doesn't grow close to the sea; otherwise there would have been no city. We were lucky to find it.

We test unknown fruits by feeding them to a fast breeding species of little runners for a period of time before we start eating them and grow the trees on our land. If we eat one infertility fruit per month, we don't get pregnant. These fruits are available to everyone but I guess it is too late for you."

"Why did you say that?" asked Joan showing surprise.

"Because you are pregnant," replied Patricia, "it is easy to guess looking at your eyes."

"What!? Are you sure!?" blurted Joan.

"Yes dear I am and I guess the baby will be very beautiful."

I had missed that conversation having gone to test the water. This beach was the safest one nearby New Alexandria. A few miles long and half a mile wide coral belt was protecting its shallow water from deep-sea predators. The water was crystal clear and we could see a myriad of small colorful fishes chasing or frolicking each other.

It was my first chance to swim with my new body and it was performing much better than my first one. I swam effortlessly the whole length of the protected stretch of shallow water and came back. I would bet that it took me less time than what it would have taken to the best sprinters on Earth.

I wasn't alone for John was with me and we raced all the way back. John easily won the race and ran up the beach full speed and I followed closely, he grabbed Joan and lifted her in the air while I dropped by Patricia's side breathing heavily.

"The seawater is crystal clear Patricia and smell real good." I said. "Swimming here is a rare pleasure; it is very refreshing, let's go back together."

John was swinging Joan in his arms.

"Be careful," said Joan. "Our baby might not like being shaken like that."

"What did you say!?" Said John; stopping at once. And that stop me dead in my track too as I was about to run to the water.

"Patricia just told me that I am pregnant!" Said Joan.

"That is just too wonderful," John said shakily. "We are going to have a baby; I love children and never had any; that's terrific, it's a most wondrous news."

John was very excited; I had never seen him like that.

"You are pregnant Joan? How do you feel?" I asked.

"What's the commotion here?" asked Nancy.

"I am pregnant." said Joan.

"Oh my God!" blurted Nancy.

"And you too Nancy." added Patricia.

"What? Are you sure?" asked Nancy.

"Looking at your eyes, there is no doubt in my mind." replied Patricia. "Congratulation to both of you."

By that time the reverend father, Tom and Garry plus a few of the local people had come around to find out about what was happening and everyone congratulated the two women.

"To answer your question John," said Joan, "I don't feel bad at all; I got no symptoms; I feel great actually and I guess it won't change our mission, my darlings. I will probably be the first pregnant Earth woman going across this world great sea to the far and fairy lands but just to cross the ocean might take us more than a year and

294

when we finally reach the other side, it might still take many more years to find the abandoned city. I believe that is what the Guardians wanted; when we finally reach the old city, we will have our children with us."

"Good thinking but it will take a while to build the ships and we have to war against the Rat Faces. When we finally leave the City, our child might be born already." Said John.

Joan then told us what she had just learned from Patricia.

"All right, I also have a question for you Patricia." Said John. "Where do the Birdies live here?"

"They live in the Baama trees." answered Patricia. "There is at least one of those big trees for every dozen houses in the city. The Birdies nourish themselves almost exclusively with the Baama fruits. Each Birdie has a nest at the tree canopy and a news stand at its base. There are benches in front of the stand for the people of the nearby houses and every morning the people come to sit on those benches and ask their local Birdie about the latest news.

The Birdies never get tired of talking to the people; they love to spread the news. Then they spend the rest of the days flying over the city or running through it and they watch the people playing games or they chat with them."

"Do they live in bunch together in those nests?" I asked.

"No each Birdie nest alone, they don't need the company of other Birdies for each one is a crowd of relatives and ancestors. Thousands of them inhabit the body of a live one and they talk together. If something important happens, they broadcast it to the other Birdies all across the city; they can communicate telepathically over a distance of hundreds of miles.

Nesting alone is probably a defense mechanism, this way, most of them can escape if attacked by overwhelming forces."

"Very interesting, and talking of defense mechanism, and your pregnancy, I am inclined to believe that it won't take nine months for the baby to come out of that wonderful body of yours, Joan." I commented. "For we have been built to be as much functional in an hostile environment as possible."

"Actually, I didn't want to tell you for it seem crazy but I can feel a bulge inside already." said Joan; as she pressed questioningly on her belly. "It's incredible for we were awoken less than ten days ago…"

I pressed or her belly delicately and yes I could feel there was something there.

"I can feel it too, John, try it." I said.

"My God, it's true," said John, "there is a bulge."

"All right men, stop touching me, I am getting aroused and mentioning it just aroused you too; so let's go to the water and cool it off a bit." Said Joan as she got up gracefully; felinely I should say.

We all went to the sea then and swam for a while before we resumed with our trek across the town. We stopped at the Teddies' sector. Even though most of the Teddies were sharing people's house, they had a little sector of their own in New Alexandria.

Nancy and Garry were looking at young Teddies and they both picked one in their arms to pet it.

"Those little ones are so cute." said Nancy; as she caressed her little Teddy lovingly.

But when they tried to put them back on the ground and get on their bikes the small Teddies clung at them and just wouldn't let go.

"Once a Teddy had been held and caressed," said Mayor Ed Kimpley; "it becomes bound to you for the rest of its life. It is too late now; I should have told you before it happened. It would be most cruel to abandon them now for they would die in sorrow."

"So the Teddy is mine?!" cried Nancy happily.

"It sure is if you want it." said the mayor heartily.

"Mine is cutter than yours." said Garry teasingly.

"No way hosay." replied Nancy joyfully.

Garry and Nancy set their Teddies on their shoulders and picked up their bikes. The young Teddies were very agile and looked like little monkeys. They were about sixteen inches long and weighted about three pounds. They had long fingers and their feet had prehensile toes. They could walk or run erect or on all fours.

They purred with pleasure and hugged their new masters.

"Teddies are intelligent and playful." said Patricia. "They came on this world very long ago; they were taken along by a species which did not survive the crash of their spaceship or could not reproduce themselves on this world.

The Teddies survived their masters but missed their presence and caring. The humans provided what they long for. There was immediate bonding between us."

Joan spent most of the day asking Patricia all kind of questions about the city's everyday life. She found her most gracious and discovered in her an excellent sense of humor. She liked her tight lips false and humorist statements and found her very funny and profoundly understanding of the human unconscious behavior and motivation.

Most of the times, Joan could easily differentiate when Patricia was serious or joking. Sometimes though she had to think a little bit about what she had been told when Patricia's statements were right between serious truthful and tight lips joke.

Joan liked the guessing game and at the end of the visit, the two women had set the foundations of a great friendship. They really liked each other's company.

We were back to our rooms by the end of the afternoon and I felt a tad tired. A good refreshing shower was too much of a temptation and I came out of it ages younger.

Patricia who had stayed with me took her turn at the shower while I lay down for a moment. She came out in her bare splendor and I pulled her to me. We made love and we slept an hour or so.

It was time to get up now, there was a crowd anxious to meet with us and we went on our bikes to the baseball stadium where we joined with our friends at the long table set upon the platform right in the center of the field.

The stadium was packed solid. Mayor Ed Kimpley introduced each one of us telling our name and our profession on Earth. Some of these professions were unknown by the city people. They had no idea what was a preacher or a CIA agent or Navy officer or computer specialist. Each one of us went to the microphone like gadget to salute the crowd as we were introduced and we all thanked them for coming and we praised the city officials for their warm welcome.

Father O'Leary then took the stand and captured the audience with his booming and most eloquent voice.

"Daughters and sons, Teddies and Birdies," started the reverend father, "we came from the human original home world, Earth. We lived there at troubled times, just before the partial destruction of our species by terrorists' nuclear and biological weapons.

It was unsure if man had evolved in vain or if we could hope for a better destiny than total annihilation. God, the creator of the universe had foreseen the difficulties we would be facing in our evolution and had once sent his son to Earth to teach us how we could one day reach wisdom and salvation. That was a great help and after Jesus, God's Son departed, religion bloomed up setting for the millenniums to come the rules we would have to respect if we were to be saved.

We have since slowly lost our ways and when we died the future of mankind looked bleak at best.

Not only should we feared self destruction or the
possibility of cataclysmic events that would wipe us all
but we had learned about the possibility for a wicked
species to enhance them to Godlike beings with some
devices left on this world by Les Semeurs, one billion
years ago. Les Semeurs were living once on this world,
they reach the ultimate technological level and built
those devices that they left in their cities. Their
cities were left protected by unbreakable energy fields
but for one that is now accessible.

Many species heard about it and came to this world to
find it and fortunately are still searching for it for
if one of those wicked species finds it they will become
invincible; they will destroy all sentient life in this
galaxy.

We must get there first.

The Guardians, immaterial beings of great power, angels
perhaps, came to this world and found the two humans
settlement. They watched you, daughters and sons and
approved your qualities of heart, your compassion and
friendship for your brothers and your allies. They
decided to help you in getting to that city; they tried
to contact you but they couldn't. They were also very
limited in their actions here by an unknown and
incomprehensible force.

This is why they traveled in time to your home world
and eventually found a man with whom they could
communicate. This man, Richard, then proceed to recruit
all of us, Earth Emissaries. As we died, each one of us
was carried to this world; our essence or soul was
carried here and the Guardians were allowed by that
strange and incomprehensible force to create our new
bodies. We woke up on a plateau at the top of what you
call the sky wall less than ten days ago.

Jesus once said, help yourself and perhaps God will help
you. We are determined to fight our way to the lost city
but many dangers await us. Evil forces might destroy
this city anytime now that they heard about our mission
here for powerful spirits called Demons have sworn our
destruction.

We must pray God to help us for we are in great need of His help. Jesus showed us how to do it through a ceremony called a mass and I intend to celebrate the first grand mass on this world next week. During that ceremony, I will tell you more about Jesus revelations and teachings. I hope that you will all come to receive God's benediction.

There are also positive actions to be taken to face the coming troubles and we will need your help to build the boats that will carry us to the other side of the sea where the lost city still stand in an unknown and well protected location; on a land of magic we were told by the Guardians; a land where dwells Trolls and Dragons, fairies and witches and all kind of predators.

The mission is dangerous and we may need your help; will some of you dare join us in our odyssey? The perils are great but the rewards surpass anything you ever dreamed of. God bless you all."

As the reverend father ended his speech, tremendous applauds erupted all across the stadium.

We all stood up and applauded too.

Then a group of musicians took over and we left to come back to the Grand house.

On our way back, Nancy took the Father's hands for a moment and told him she had been awed by his performance.

"I will come to your room tonight and show you my appreciation". She whispered. She had made it clear to Bob on their way back from the city visit that she had been serious when she told him he was too young for her and she didn't want to start any serious relationship with him. He had given her a musical treat and she had given him something to remember and fantasize about; they were quits.

Tonight she had found out that she was in love with Father O'Leary and she would be his if he wanted her.

On Earth, she thought, *catholic priest can't marry but this is another world and this is afterlife, the rules don't apply here. The Father will set his own rules. He will be the pope for his followers and I will be his wife.*

Nancy remembered how thrilled the reverend father had been when he had made love with her. There had been for him that tremendously erotic feeling of committing what was once a sinful thing with a matured woman and even more sinful to a woman that look like a young girl.

Chapter Thirteen - The first mass.

The morning after, Father O'Leary met with his friend Krzzzurr, Bob the prodigy and Patricia Laure the singer for the teaching of his favorite religious songs and a practice session.

They had agreed to do it for a few hours everyday until they were good enough at it to give a great show at the mass.

Mayor Kimpley gave the Father the daytime use of the concert hall for his masses and practices.

"I have to warn you reverend father," said mayor Kimpley, "you can't invite the whole population of five hundred thousand people for your first mass. The concert hall capacity is less than ten thousand and they will all want to come. You must proceed to a ticket sale; the first ten thousand buyers go to the first mass, the second lot to the second mass and so on. The dates and hours and the seat number should be written on the tickets.

"Do not worry about the tickets oh father," said Krzzzurr, "I will take care of the tickets and their distribution."

"Since there so many," said the father, "I will celebrate two masses per day, every morning, one at 8:00 AM and the other at 11:00 AM. The masses will last one hour. Will you sing at those masses Patricia and you Bob will you play the piano along with the other singers and musicians?"

"It will be a pleasure to assist you reverend." They said enthusiastically.

In the mean time, Johnny Rodriguez and his brother Paul had arrived to the Grand house to meet with us.

When they arrived, I was in the dinning room chatting with Joan. The other ones had left already. John and Tom to the recruiting office and defense quarters, Father

O'Leary had left with Krzzzurr, Bob and Patricia; and Nancy and Garry were gone fishing with the young Rodriguez.

We went to the living room and talked about all kind of things.

"That day, when you fought the rat faces," Johnny said, "Paul and I were holding back the few beasts that turned back on the boy Scouts. We had time to watch your performance and I just couldn't believe it. You and Joan cut the heads off many of the beasts slicing their necks clean."

"You are unbelievably strong and quick." said Paul. "I am sure that Johnny or I can't cut the neck of the giant beasts with one swing of your swords, they are all bones, hard muscles and thick hide and their necks must be sixteen inches wide."

"You know," I said, "I was surprised myself by our performances and I remember when we crossed the forest of gigantic trees, we jogged for half the night and a full day without getting exhausted."

"And our scratches and bite wounds disappeared inside of a few hours." said Joan. "Even the Reverend Father terrible wound was completely cured in twenty-four hours."

"Yes," I added, "the guardians gave us unbreakable swords and knives, indestructible clothes and self regenerating bodies. We are stronger and more resistant than we could have thought in our wildest dreams.

Who knows; we might not even be submitted to the normal aging process! It seems that whatever the Guardians build, it is built to last forever.

They gave us a body that looks fragile compared to the dangerous beasts roaming this world but with our uncanny speed, resistance and strength, we have a fair chance to come out alive of any encounter."

"So you think we are kind of immortals, Richard?" asked Joan.

303

"Yes I do." I answered. "Moreover, I think that in addition to our augmented body performances, we have been gifted with all kind of yet undiscovered powers.

My sense of direction for example or John's intuition of coming dangers and our acute sense of smell to notice anything coming our way..."

We talked about Ghama-2 for a while and then Johnny hit us with his mention of Golf.

"We played golf for years on Earth Joan and me." I said excitedly.
"Then would you like to play a game with us?" asked Johnny.
"Sure! Right away if that is possible." answered Joan joyfully. For it was still morning, we were full of energy and we couldn't feel better or happier.

"Then let's go." said Paul. "We will make a good foursome and you will tell us some more about Earth in between plays."

We went to the closest of the City's dozen golf courses. There was a clubhouse and a pro-shop, a restaurant.

Very earthlike, Joan thought.

We rented our equipment and asked our friends if we could go to the practice range first. We didn't know yet how our new body would perform and we surely needed some practice.

After fifteen minutes of practice we could hit the ball accurately and longer than ever before. John and Paul were amazed by our performances.

"Practicing and playing the real game are two different things," I said. "I remember some games when the practice had gone real well and the game turned out into a fiasco and the reverse happened too."

Walking on the first tee off I gazed at the view and I couldn't remember having seen such a beautiful alley.

There was wildlife on the course; a fox-like predator was running after a flock of partridges under the

304

watchful eyes of a pair of gazelles and a wild female
boar was nursing a dozen offspring.

There were fruit trees, squares of different color of
grass, sand traps, a beautiful lake with aquatic plants
and birds and two Birdies flying lazily overhead.

I set my ball on the tee, made a practice swing and then
I hit it; vlam… the ball flew five hundred yards and hit
the middle of the seven hundred yards par five alley.

The game went very well for Joan and I and after the
first nine holes Johnny and I were leading at five over
par, Joan followed closely with six over par and Paul
was nine over.

"OK, now let's make a friendly bet," I said to Johnny.
"What about one labor unit per hole; birdies pay
double."

"All right Richard, let's do it." answered Johnny.

We played with even more concentration and I played two
over par on the back nine. Johnny beat me by one stroke.

After the game, we went for a shower and we met at the
bar for a chat over a few bottles of excellent ale.

Paul drank a little too much and started to mess with a
big guy sitting next table. Johnny told us that he had
been forced into quite a number of fistfights in
rescuing his brother who had the talent to put
himself in trouble and then call for help.

The big guy got fed up of Paul and pushed him so hard
that he fell over the table. Then he hit Paul on the
nose and knocked him out. He was just about to hit him
again but this time Johnny grabbed his wrist and said
in a calm voice "OK that's enough."

"I know you Johnny Rodriguez; you may be the light heavy
weight champion but you wouldn't stand a chance against
me, I can beat you easily and it has been a long time
since I have been looking for the chance of smashing
your face."

The big guy swung his left fist at Johnny who moved instantly escaping the blow and swung in turn two very quick and solid uppercuts. The big guy was just about to fall; he was already unconscious. Johnny held him and sat him on his chair and placed his head delicately on the table.

"He will be all right," he said to the big guy's friends. Then he went to pick Paul.

"Let me do it." I said as I picked up Paul unconscious body and carried him outside. As we got outside, Paul woke up and I set him up on his feet.

"I am sorry for Paul's behavior, he is a good fellow but after a few drinks he turns on into a kid." Johnny said.

"We had a great game, you played an excellent game Johnny and I hope we will play again, soon. You owe me a revenge." I said. "By the way, you got quite an uppercut, would you mind to train me? I have watched boxing for years on Earth; it was my favorite sport and now that I am young again and have the height and the muscles I would love to learn the art."

"We can start the training tomorrow, I will come right after breakfast and take you to the gymnasium." Johnny said.

We parted and Joan and I talked about our day as we went biking back to the grand house.

"You know Joan," I said, "there is something peculiar, deja vu, that I have witnessed today. That fight, happened before on Earth and I was there. Johnny is so similar to my long dead uncle that I wonder how such similarities could be possible. My uncle was also a boxing champion and his brother used to behave just like Paul."

"Tomorrow, after your boxing practice," said Joan, "ask him if he remembers anything of an anterior life. Who knows what we might learn."

"Yes, I will;" I said, "but there is more; there are paintings here that could not have been made by anyone

306

else than my old friend Ron Davies. His style was too unique; it just can't be another artist.

So I come to the conclusion that there is a play master in action and we are probably the peons in a cosmic chess game. The Guardians might have been influenced to help us and some of the people I once knew might have been brought here, seven hundred years in the future, to become part of this incredible odyssey."

"Very strange and most interesting;" said Joan, "I love mysteries and I love that afterlife and I love you and your mystical wanderings."

At that, she kissed me on the lips and I forgot everything for a moment, overwhelmed with emotions. As we parted, I looked worriedly around but neither Patricia nor John had been witnessing our kiss.

"I got to go my little darling;" I said, "Patricia and John might be awaiting us…"

"I had a real good time today;" said Joan, "see you later."

Patricia was waiting for me in the living room and came a few minutes later to the bedroom. I was already in the shower and was happily surprised to see her by the window when I came out.

"So what did you do today?" She said with a smile as she came into my arms.

"I played golf with Joan and the two boy scouts leaders. What a great day it was. Something happened there, something very strange--"

"Before you tell me about it, let's have a drink. I brought a bottle of excellent wine and two cups, they are filled already. Here you are "a votre santée!".

My mother taught me a little bit of French. She said my ancestor came directly from France and I was told that you came from Canada and you grew up in that language."

We sat down on the luxurious armchairs and I took the most comfortable position. I drank some wine and called the yellow and blue bird that had just flown inside looking for a good spot to perch on. It came to me and set down on my extended finger. I petted it for a moment and let it go. He flew to one of the bed poster and perched there to observe us.

"You see Patricia, we have a soul, it is immaterial, made up of wavelengths, knots of them and they stick together somehow to make an entity. And the soul is the true self, the part of us that think and love and remember. It uses the material body and partially controls it.

When the body die, the souls may function for a while before disintegrating into nothingness or it may survive forever; nobody knows. Some people hope to go to heaven when they die but they don't know what heaven might be. They hope it is the place where God dwells and where they will be given everlasting happiness.

The guardians took our souls at the moment of our death and transported it here and gave it a new body. This is true for the seven of us, Earth emissaries, but what about the others, where do they scatter to?

That painting on the wall can't have been done by anyone else than my old friend Ron Davies. His style is unique and I can't conceive of two different persons having the exact same style and colors unless one is copying the other. But here on Ghama-2 nobody knows about Ron Davies.
I pondered about it and came to the conclusion that some of the Earth people souls, maybe the finest of the souls, the more compassionate and mature ones can somehow resist the final disintegration that awaits them on Earth and fly far away and scatter across the galaxy until they find a suitable embryo in which they can set in.
If such is the case; Ron Davies is here and maybe some others of my friends since I choose them carefully after evaluating their value as human beings. My own beloved father might be here too.

Today, Johnny and Paul did things and it was the exact repetition of an event that happened before on Earth and it make me believe that these two are my mother's brothers and they were given the same name. It is too much of a coincidence and you Patricia, you are just too beautiful and wonderful and I wonder if I am not presently in heaven."

"You are not dreaming, I can assure you of that." Said Patricia. "People die here. This is not heaven; it doesn't have enough population for that. Surely there would be more than a few hundred thousand people here out of the billions of people that lived on Earth."

"But it is probable that some of the Earth people are here." I said. "Some might have gone to other worlds and find a suitable embryo there awaiting them. Beside, I can hardly conceive of a place where everyone would be given everlasting happiness. God may be moving all the time across the universe and He would surely get fed up of having billions of followers bothering Him with their endless asking and incessant adoration.

You must be right, Patricia, this is not heaven but to me it is and yet, I feel very much alive. So, I am sure I am not dreaming but how can you be so beautiful, desirable and yet show such acute intelligence and maturity? Only in Heaven I would think could we find such incredible combination of qualities in one person."

That did it; Garry is not the only one; I know what women want too and the last thing they want is to feel belittled by macho men.

Praising their intelligence and maturity is the best way to get them in your bed. But you have to really think what you tell them. Threading with women, you got to be careful for in some ways, they are more intelligent than men. Psychology is their point fort. They look into your eyes and they can read you just like an open book. They know when you are buttering it up, when it is false and then it just doesn't work.

Fortunately, I was sincere and she felt it; there was no mistaking. I had learned long ago that when a person deserves praise you give it without hesitation.

So the first thing I knew, she was in my arms, kissing me, willing to give me heaven on (earth) Ghama-2.

That night we had dinner with the mayor and the city officials, all of us Earth emissaries, along with Patricia Laure and Annie Fowler.

"We had so many recruits today," John said, "that I don't know how we would have done without the help of the Birdies. They were of invaluable help. The training will start tomorrow."

"I can help with the training if you need me." I said. "Johnny Rodriguez will give me some boxing training and I intend to do a lot of work out. We might as well do that at the defense training field and work out a battalion of your recruits."

"Why don't you do that," said John, "we will split the recruits in three groups. Tom and I will train one group each and you and Johnny will train the third one. We will teach them the tactics of war once they are done with the physical work out. In addition, they will need to be taught swordsmanship and they should practice shooting with bows."

"I will put all our manpower in the making of bows, arrows, javelins and swords." said Mayor Ed Kimpley.

"How long before we have enough weapons for every one of the ten thousand soldiers of our first regiment?" asked Tom.

"One month maybe less; we will do everything possible to accelerate their making." Ed Kimpley said.

We started to talk about other subjects of less importance. At one point I asked the mayor:
"Do you have books, novels, here?"
"We have one book which relates the story of our city since its founding. It is in the main living room and it is a rule to keep it there at all time. But anyone can read it."
"I wrote a book on Earth," I said, "a novel relating the adventures of a group of earth emissaries to Ghama-2. The personages were fictitious. I would like to rewrite it and relates what happened until now. The personages would be real this time and the fiction would start when I finish the true part. I can write a saga of three

310

books inside of twelve months if you supply me with the pen, ink and paper.
I would have time to finish them before we depart to cross the sea."

That caught the attention of everyone. They were all excited. Reading had been one of our most cherished customs on earth but here it would be treasured. For there were no writers in the city; none ever thought of writing tales. People had taught their children how to read using the two books on Earth Biology and Plant life and the one on Medicine that were found aboard the shuttle.

Everyone in the city would eventually read the books I was intent on writing and on our long trek across the sea, it would fill the time and give everyone something to dream about.

"What we will do," said the mayor, "we will put a few dozen birdies on the project. They will rewrite a number of times each of the pages as they come out. They will do it with great care using all of their skill and their infinite patience and will reproduce the book in a few hundreds copies and scatter them in every part of the city. You will have some of the copies to take along with you and I am sure everyone will read them a number of times as the days pass and grow longer on the sea."

"All right, I will write them and I will start as soon as you provide me with the paper, pen and ink." I concluded.

The City was bursting with excitement, everyone was at work or getting worked out into a fighting machine and my days were now completely filled from sunrise to sunset.

Johnny was a born leader and respected by all and John was very pleased with him and told the mayor about it.

"He should be promoted," John said to the mayor. "And if it is acceptable to you, I would have him take over the defense as soon as we get rid of the Rat faces and I could get on with the boats' construction."

"I got no objection," said the mayor, "let's do tonight, right after dinner, we will do a city officials meeting. You will present a motion to have Johnny nominated as army commander and we will vote on it."

I was at the defense-training center all mornings and then I was spending my afternoons at the grand house writing my book.

Some of the Birdies had already left the city on an errand to the nearest friendly aliens' settlements. They were charged to convince them to come in large numbers to help us in the defense of our city.

Other Birdies were constantly patrolling the country looking out for the coming of new foes. Some were spying on the come and go of the Rat Faces; they were flying across the river and were perching on the tallest limbs at the treetops.

In the mean time, the reverend father and his assistants had finished their preparation; the reverend father was ready for his first grand-mass. Tickets for the ten first grand-masses had been put on for sale at the Four Corners of the City and none were left unsold.

It was 10:00 AM, the six of us Earth emissaries had been given seats on one side of the altar and the musicians and singers were sitting on the other side.

The musicians started their play and Patricia Laure her first song. The music was tragic and catching us deep inside. The choral made out of a dozen of the finest city voices marveled everyone. They did two songs and when they stop, there was silence and expectation. Nobody was moving as we heard the footsteps of the Reverend father coming up to the pulpit with his eyes cast down all the way. The reverend father was showing profound meditation and humility. He reached the pulpit and said in a powerful voice "Daughters and Sons, Sisters and Brothers!"

At that moment, he lifted his eyes and looked up at the people massed before him and I saw in his face an expression of surprise and incredulity. The expression lasted a moment only but for the first time I had seen the Reverend father taken abashed; he was dismayed,

312

troubled but that didn't last; he recovered so quickly that nobody that didn't know him as well as we did, would have notice it.

For in front of him there were a solidly packed crowd of Birdies, some of them with Teddies sitting on their laps and not a human face.

There were some of the city people behind, hidden by the tall aliens who had taken the first rows. It was a sight though worthy of the best funny movie scenarios.

The preacher faced the tall and serious aliens.

These will be the ones, thought the reverend father, *which will take over and spread the words of God after I leave. New Rome will be built on their devoted and unfailing support, their inexhaustible devotion, and their infallible need to be useful.*

Religion and preachers will be approved by all here for there isn't a soul who wouldn't trust these noble and worthy Birdies.

The father started on the story of Adam and Eve living in the heavenly garden of Earth free to do anything they wanted. There was one exception; they shouldn't eat the fruits hanging in the knowledge tree...and it went on to the coming of Jesus, his teachings, his death for our salvation and the building of our civilization.

The story ended with the partial destruction of the world by the Arabs terrorists. The father mentioned the bible, its writings and its teachings.

"I intend to write a version of the Bible which I will leave behind when the time comes for our group to depart and go on with our mission. We will try to find God as we proceed towards the lost city for we have reasons to believe that He might dwell on this very world. We will give our life if needs be for the salvation of us all, brothers and sisters of the galaxy.

Our success may very well open the way to Heaven for all deserving souls."

The Reverend Father finally left the pulpit and went on with the mass and the prayers. At one point he took a piece of bread and lifted it up over his head and said:

This is the body of Christ for it now attracts a parcel of his godly presence.

Then he lifted up a cup of wine up over his head and said:

This is the blood of Christ that was spent for our salvation.

He then ate the bread and drank the wine.

"Please now, everyone should come to me, starting from the first row. I will ask God to forgive you for your sins, will baptize you, will bless you and give you a chunk of Holy Bread. As you return to your place, you will eat it and for a moment, a tiny link between you and God will be created.

That's when you have the greatest chance to be heard by God. Take advantage of that moment to ask God for his approval and protection."

Everyone started to come forward in a line to be baptized and given a first communion. They came one by one to kneel before the father; they were sprinkled with a trickle of holy water and given a prayer and then a chunk of bread.

"The Body of Christ" the reverend father said as he gave each one the little chunk of bread. "Eat it in his memory and pray for our redemption."

Putting the chunk of bread in the birdies' beaks, had a considerable psychological effect on the noble aliens. I could see it and sense it. They were awed by the ceremony.

Once everyone had come, the reverend father came to our little group and did the same to us.

I must admit that I was touched by the ceremony; I had stop going to church for many years now having lost all

314

faith in man made religions. But that day, on this world, it seemed to me that everything the reverend said and did was for real.

I ate the chunk of bread, closed my eyes and talked to God.

"Please God forgive me for my sins and my irreverence. I thank you for my life and my afterlife, for Joan and Patricia, for my friends, for everything. I promise to become a better man. Please God bless me and my friends and all those nice people and their allies with your protection. Help us in our mission and give us the strength to fight victoriously against evil temptations. I hope that we will prove by our actions that we Humans are worthy of your approval and deserve access to the lost city and its enhancing devices."

The music and the singers made the event memorable. The mass ended and everyone stood up and left with their heart and mind filled with wonder and comfort.

That night, we were talking about the event at the long table of the grand house dinning room. It had become a custom for the city officials and the two alien leaders to have dinner with us and enjoy our unusual turn of conversation.

"We sensed a powerful presence all over you at the grand mass this morning," said Krzzurr to Father O'Leary. "It has been the subject of much talking between the Birdies. We have been pondering about it all day long and we have come to a decision. We will be your followers and we will serve your God, for he must also be our own creator and our God to serve.

The most skillful to oration amongst us will become preachers and good news tellers and comfort givers. We will become your abbots if you would have us. If we ever find our way out of this world and resume our exploration of the galaxy, we will spread the words to all the sentient species we will encounter.

We will tell them all about Jesus, faith, charity, love, compassion, forgiveness, piety, godly music and we will perform the chunk of bread feeding. Will you take us?"

"Certainly," said the Father seriously. "Your offer is most commendable."

I had a hard time holding myself, and almost surrendered to ground rolling and paws' tapping. The situation was most funny and made funnier by the very fact that these birdies were humorless. I could see them preaching people on Earth. I could imagine a noble Birdie surrounded by Arab's Muslims explaining to them that they had got it all wrong.

"You have got it all wrong." Would a Birdie tell them. "You should forget about going to heaven by self-bombing and kids' slaying, you will just end up in body cells dispersion and soul evaporation.

There are better ways, with increased chances at salvation. You must think about forgiveness, charity, and compassion--."

Hum, I thought, they don't know yet that preaching is risky business but since they are kind of immortals they will not be scared to serve anywhere. They will be perfect at it.

"I believe," said Mayor Ed Kimpley that John has a proposal in regards to the city defense."

"Mayor, honorable Krzzzurr, gentlemen," said John, "I have served my country in the armed forces almost all of my life on Earth. I was trained in all aspects of warfare and I have learned to evaluate the leadership potential and ability of potential candidates to lead a battalion or an army.

Some people can show great leadership potential and yet fail miserably in urgent and stressful situations. This is why a defense leader has to be very well chosen. The army combatants must trust him; they should be willing to obey his orders without questions at all time.

I can help with my expertise in the set up of the city defense but we need a local person to take over the defense; one that people know and have learn to respect. This man is Johnny Rodriguez and I propose to give him

316

the city defense responsibility and name him General of the Army."

"Any comments or question?" asked the mayor.

"I wish to mention," said Krzzzurr the Birdies leader, "that we Birdies approved John choice. We read Johnny's mind and we don't see anything objectionable in his personality for the command post. Moreover, we find this human unit most resourceful and creative."

"All right, I second this proposal." said the mayor. "Everybody for it please raise your hands."

All the officials raised their hands.

"All right from now on, Johnny you are the army general but you will function under our supervision. You will have to ask for our approval in important decisions." said the mayor.

"Thank you for your trust." said Johnny. "I will do my best."

We congratulated him and made some jokes that had been quite popular in the defense forces on Earth. Then I told them about my discovery.

"With the help of the birdies, I found Ron Davies," I said loud enough for everyone.

They all looked at me puzzled by that introduction and with no clue to its meaning. I told them about the painting in my room and my conclusion that it had been made by my old friend Ron Davies.

"I met with him today," I added, "and he didn't look the same; he was quite different physically but there was not a doubt that he was the same man. I sensed it. We talked for some time about his art and he told me that he was sure we had met before but just couldn't figure where.

Would you like to know about your past life? I asked him and Ron would for he was curious and liked to ponder about the meaning of life and most of all, he loved to talk at length about anything with a philosophical edge to it. He was like that on Earth, we had been best friends for a few years prior his death.

So his past life was just the kind of things he wished to know about. I told him that when we met for the first time, he was selling his artworks in Montreal and was living alone in the Eastern Township. He was divorced and his wife and two sons were living in Toronto. Ron had traveled a lot and lived a few years in the USA and much of it at Old Orchard. He was always penniless, for he kept just enough to pay the food, the rent and the bare minimum necessities and was mailing to his wife the rest of the money he received for his art.

He was using the free municipal library services in every little town he had been living in and had read extensively History, politics, philosophy, Yoga, religions, art, zoology, botanic and more, he was a highly cultured man and I loved his presence.

We played boggle every Friday night when he came to deliver his weekly work. We also had dinner and chat for an hour or two and look at his paintings.

At that time I was running an encounter service business "Le Club Des Amis Des Arts "in addition to my three Art galleries and a biotherapy clinic.

"I can find you a woman," I once told him, "I have hundreds of them amongst the club members and they are hoping to find a man just like you."

Ron was fifty years old and quite lonely. So he met one that suited him just fine and she was about the same age as Ron. She didn't impress me a bit though and I was quite surprised by his choice. He borrowed $1,000.00 from me to buy a $4,000.00 country house. He could get a $3,000.00 mortgage and needed to pay the cash down. Needless to say that it was a country house in his artist mind only. For in all truth, it was a shack in a swamp. But he could see it when he would have finish working on it.

He bought the shack and died as he was moving his few belongings in it.

The hospital people called me for they had found my business card in his pocket and the girlfriend was nowhere to be seen. I went to the hospital to verify the identity of the corpse and it was he to my great sadness.

I called in Toronto and spoke to his son and when I told him that his father was at the hospital, he started to cry, he asked me to wait for him; he told me that he would jump in his car and come right away. That was a four hours drive from Toronto to Montreal at speed exceeding the limit all the way. But he was there, four hours later and I had to take him in the room and he saw his father and shouted his despair.

I had never seen such sadness in all my life.

There was the hospital window right beside us and we were at the fourth or fifth floor and suddenly a white dove came flying towards us and perched on the window edge. I was sure the dove carried Ron's soul and Ron somehow had taken over the control of the bird mind. He had come back to offer comfort and give us the message that one day we would meet again.

That's what I said to his son and it seemed to reduce his sorrow somehow for it was quite evident that the dove was trying to tell us something.

But now I wonder since he is here and 700 years in the future. The dove might have been an angel.

The guardians didn't know if there was a God but they knew the existence of Demons. I should have questioned them about angels. They might have known…

My conclusion to all of this is that some people's souls survive after death and fly far away in distance and time! And eventually they find them somewhere, some when, a waiting embryo suitable for them."

Everyone was silent for a while, assimilating the story. The New Alexandrians had never driven a car; they had never experienced most of what I had been talking about. Krzzzurr was probably talking it over with the thousands

319

relatives and ancestors living inside his brain. My friends and companions were thinking about the possibility of meeting here some of their dear ones and also the possibility that God was behind everything that had happened so far or was He? Could there be another great and very powerful spirit playing with us like a puppet master? Watching their faces, I could almost guess what they were thinking.

"That story," said Krzzzurr, "was totally fascinating. As you were telling it, we read your mind; we saw images of what you were talking about. We shared your emotions, the memory of your sorrow and your warm feelings, your compassion for a total stranger who happened to be your friend son. We noticed some of your home world people customs and we conclude that you Richard unit offer a most unusual and enriching presence. We hope to learn from you the ability of telling stories and we will have much to think about the spiritual and mystical implications of what you told us."

"I loved it," said the mayor, "what a fascinating story; I could visualize what kind of life our ancestors were living on Earth. Their technology made it so different from our simple way of living here."

And then everyone was talking about the mystery of life and the possibility that they too would meet some of their loved ones.

"If Ron Davies is here," said Joan, "maybe some more of our acquaintances or family relatives are here too. That is just awesome."

The reverend father remained silent and thoughtful; I could see that he had been shaken by that this new turn of event. Krzzzurr was now in deep meditation or interior conversation.

Nancy with her Teddie on her shoulder went to sit by the reverend father and Garry left the table running after his own Teddie who had just stolen his knife.

"See you later." I said as I left with Patricia for a walk in the garden.

320

The night had come with her accompaniment of flickering stars to envelop us in mystery.

I took Patricia's hand in mine and went for the beach. I was fully armed and felt confident that nothing wicked our way would come.

We walked in silence, perhaps trying to catch a sense to the whispering of the sea. The western moonlight was comforting us, bringing romance to our solitary walk and the belief that all will go well; that many wonderful events would be awaiting us.

"You know Richard," said Patricia, "your story was a delightful treat to everyone at the long table. You have no idea how much that kind of story could be appreciated by people who have been living our simple way for so long. I loved to hear about the events happening on another world in a totally different civilization and I had not realized how much I could appreciate mystery. As I get to know you better, the more mysterious and fascinating you turn out to be. I love you; I find your presence comforting and reassuring and yet there is that feeling that keeping close to you is going to be very risky.

If I wanted to live a quiet life, I would start running away and try to put just as much distance between you and me as I could but I will take the risk anytime to live excitingly; to share with you the incredible adventures that are yet to come."

"You are right Patricia; I always thought that a few exciting years are better than a long life of boredom." I replied. "But I will do everything I can to offer you protection at all time. As you see, I am fully armed even for a short walk at the beach. If something tries to kill me, I won't go without a fight and I am more resourceful than many would guess.

I have an excellent intuition and I know that great danger are looming just a short time ahead. There will be war and destruction, many of your friends will die but somehow I got the feeling that we will come out of it; you and me, we will survive for at least a few more years and maybe we will reach the lost city and turn ourselves into some kind of Gods. The seventh level of heaven is awaiting us, I feel it; maybe it is again my foolish optimism but I am almost sure that one day we will get there."

Days and weeks went by and now we were ready to attack the Rat Faces. Their number was estimated to one hundred thousands and according to Johnny; the battle would be a bloody one.

The mayor and the city officials had finally convinced John to let Johnny Rodriguez leads the attack. Our group, the mayor said, was to remain in the city and stay alive for they were convinced that we were the best fitted to accomplish the ultimate mission. A few hours after sunset, the first and second battalions would move up the river in hundreds of small boats, pass the Rat Faces army and land a few miles away behind them. Once there, one of the two battalions would stand its ground and prevent any incoming group of Rat Faces to reinforce their army that had pack the river shore in front of the city. The second battalion would move closer to the alien's army and wait for the coming battle.

The ten cohorts of the third battalion would swim across the river in the middle of the night, when the saurian beasts are asleep. The soldiers were to use floating boards and swim slowly without splashing. They would carry their swords, bows and arrows and lances on their back and the Birdies would just fly over.

Once they get ashore, they were to make a formation and wait. At first light, the Rat faces would spot the humans of the third battalion and attack them and that's when the second battalion would move to their rescue and they would crush the enemy caught in between.

Each cohort was made of 200 birdies and eight hundred men. The two battalions numbered twenty thousands soldiers and they would try to destroy the one hundred thousands giant aliens.

"It will not be easy," said John, "but if we use the strategy we have devised, we should win. The forest where the aliens are standing is two thousand foot away from the river. We should make formation half way to the forest, onto the grassland in open terrain.

The Birdies will form a protective shield; they will carry two long spears each and will squat to let the archers shoot as many attackers as they could before they would be forced into close combat. Some of the men will wander around to attract the rat faces while the cohorts remain still, crouching in the grass and shrubbery, the men baits will then run to their cohort with the rat faces in close pursuit and pass the Birdies' ranks. The shield of spears will then be raised to protect the archers as they shoot the enemy.

The fourth battalion will cross the river on boats as the battle goes on and reinforce the third battalion.

The rat faces army will be encircled and our soldiers will control the fight. Thirty thousand well trained soldiers will be enough to war against one hundred thousand Rat Faces.

It was time now and the battalions started towards the river. They went in silence and the sight of all those men walking silently with a grim face towards battle was breathtaking.

The crossing of the river had gone well; the saurians did not wake up. The third battalion made formation on the grassland and the soldiers just sat or laid down awaiting the sunrise. In the mean time the first two battalions reached their position. One stood ground a few miles away from what was going to be battle ground while the second battalion moved closer to the aliens.

Once they got close enough, they sat down and waited for sunrise.

At sunrise, Bob, Sandra and two dozens boy scouts left the second battalion and moved a few hundred foot towards the woods speaking and laughing loudly. They were spotted by the aliens and they ran back towards the hidden formation.

The plan worked much better than expected. We had prepare for cunning and strategy on the part of the enemy but our army was met with ranks upon ranks of stupid beasts charging and being brought down by the archers or getting impaled on the birdies' spears. It was a slaughter. We suffered very few casualties only.

As soon as the battle ended on the riverside, the battalions moved to help the one that had stood ground and cut enemy reinforcement. In two days of battle, we exterminated them all.

There was celebration in the city streets and a level of joy, contentment and excitement never experienced before.

The soldiers had brought back the bodies of their comrades that had been mortally wounded by the aliens during the battle; there were three hundred and sixty one of them. Their covered bodies had been placed in front of the grand house; their names had been taken to be written on a board of heroes in the grand house family room.

The reverend father did a grand mass and blessed them before we carried their bodies into a large communal grave.

"So what will happen with all those alien corpses?" I asked the mayor the day after the group funeral for our victims.

"The worms will eat the one hundred thousand of them," said the mayor, "in less than two weeks. There are some huge ones laying dormant deep underground and when there are enough cadavers to attract them, they wake up and move to the surface. I once saw one that was thirty foot long."

We now had access to all the wood needed for the construction of the boats. In the following weeks, trees were cut and pruned, brought to the river and carried to the sawmill. The sails were made out of the silky fibers covering what they called the fabric fruits.

As the months went by, I kept writing the new version of my book Ghama-2, An Afterlife story and wondered what might have happen to the second group of emissaries.

These people, I thought, were a bunch of decision-makers and filthy rich people. How will they manage to develop a team spirit? And what happened to my daughter? How is she coping with them? Are they having sex orgies like we had before we came to New Alexandria? I guess that Nicole Teaseman must have been kept quite busy but who knows, in their new bodies she might not be the most beautiful one.

I read once that it would be more difficult for a rich person to get to heaven than for a camel to go through the eye of a needle.

The day after, I found on my desk a pile of paper sheets. They were the next chapters relating the adventures of the second group of Earth emissaries. It was of my handwriting!

My God, I can't believe it, I thought, these must have come from the future carried by the Guardians probably and that meant the Guardians are still around waiting to see the outcome of our mission.

Chapter Fourteen -The awakening of George's group.

George W Woods woke up and realized that he was lying on the ground. He looked at the sky and saw three beautiful moons. He could see that these moons were in fact real live worlds with an atmosphere, blue oceans and green continents. It was daytime and the weather was just perfect.

George got up in a surge and looked around. He was pleasantly assaulted by a variety of fragrances. He was now standing in a clearing surrounded by a forest of unidentifiable trees, quite tall and massive and the clearing was covered by short grass. There were bushes in full bloom and sparsely distributed over the large clearing were smaller trees offering a variety of fruits to the park visitors.

At least there are none yet, thought George, *there are none in sight but I would better find something to cover me before they come for I am bare to the bones.*

George found the clothes; they had been placed a few feet away from where he woke up. There was a complete musketeer outfit from boots to the feather hat, along with a real sword in its scabbard, a knife in its leather sheathe, a quiver of arrows, a beautiful bow and a backpack.

A musketeer outfit! I will be damned... thought George; *I will be the laugh of the town when they see me clothed like that.*

He put on the clothes and everything fitted perfectly; even the boots, to his greatest relief. He pulled the sword out in a quick movement and took a look at the blade, it was silver like and reflecting like a mirror, he looked at the flat side and saw a stranger face reflecting in it.

George instantly plunged forward, hit the ground, rolled on his back, got up and swirled, extending his sword in defense and was immediately hit with a pang of shame. For there was no one facing him; he had acted on impulse; he had reacted swiftly to the unexpected. But now come to think of it, he should have known better.

There had been no warning odor and his sense of smell was extraordinary keen; there had been no hunch of imminent danger and the angle of reflection was such that the face he saw on the sword blade had to be his.

I acted stupidly, thought George; *I could even have broken a shoulder.*

He looked again at the blade reflection.

This is my face, he thought, *how come then that I don't remember it. Could I be amnesic? Where am I?*

He went to the nearest tree and picked a fruit, it looked like an apple and the odor was inviting. He took a bite and it didn't taste like an apple, the taste was impossible. For it tasted like strawberry and there was cheese in the center, creamy and tasty, like the very best Brie.

I will be damned, thought George, *this is the most impossible fruit, I never heard of a fruit with cheese in the center. But it is very delicious.*

George felt hungry and he ate it all and it filled him nicely.

What am I doing here, George asked himself, *I don't know that place; I don't recognize anything, not even my own face. I feel stronger and better though than I ever remember. I had an appointment with --there was a tremendous explosion- -God I must be dead... I remember now, I was the president of the United States of America and this world must be Ghama-2. It worked! I had a hunch that the whole story, crazy as it sounded was true and now here I am; I wonder where the others are?*

That John saved my life before and then brought that incredible story to my attention and by doing so; he gave me a second life to live and a mission that may result in giving mankind immortality and the control of the stars. I hope I will meet with that remarkable man again.

George felt excitement and wonder, he was exulting and he danced a gig or two. He would have dance like an

Amerindian whooping his war cries to the sky but he restrained himself.

What if somebody sees me, he thought, *let's find my companions.*

George went to find the others. He tried to get a hunch as to the direction that he should go but there was none so he tried to walk in a straight line. He kept walking along an imaginary line keeping the sun on his left and the biggest tree of the clearing's bordering forest on its right and tried to remember special landmarks on the way.

Bill Rates woke up, took a look around and immediately came to the conclusion that he was waking up on another world. The sun was different; he had a new extremely keen sense of smell and his body felt different, he had never experienced in his life such a feeling of extreme power and inexhaustible energy.

The story was true, he thought, *I had a hunch it was true and I gave a sizable sum of money for the painting.*

The money spending was irrelevant to Bill, he never had much appreciation for material belongings and even less for money. He just didn't like to be conned into a scheme.

If you are intelligent and creative, Bill thought, *you can always find a way to make a living. Being filthy rich never brought me happiness; in fact it brought me a sense of responsibility and obligations. The celebrity was the worse; it limited my freedom and forced me to hire bodyguards. I would have like to live another kind of life but it was too late, it was already too late at the age of twenty.*

I will live this new life I have been granted quite, differently. I will enjoy every moment of it.

This world is strange and full of surprises; some of them might not be enjoyable, fatal perhaps. Even though I have now the body of a superman, and this is just fantastic, great, cool; I can't see how I can fight a tiger or worse with fingers and toes.

328

I better find my weapons and outfit for surely, the Guardians did not bring me here to become an easy prey to the nearest predator. If they were able to create my new body they were surely able to create some clothes and weapons.

Bill looked around, found his outfit and put it on.

Remarkable, the fabric is shiny and complex. Let's see, it might be waterproof.

Bill look around and spotted a creek, he walked to it crouch took a handful of the crystalline water, sniffed it and tasted it.

It smelled good and taste just as good.

Bill poured a handful of water on his sleeve and the water just drip off; none was left on the fabric and the fabric was totally dry.

Interesting.

Bill put his arm under the water for a moment that seemed long enough for the fabric to become real wet and pull his arm out and the water drip off just like it would over silicone.

Well, well, we will never get wet on rainy days; not that we would catch a cold though, that would be doubtful. They said, they would improve our bodies and I wake up in a body of superhuman strength; I would not think that they would build such a magnificent body and leave it vulnerable to virus or bacteria.

Beside, if the small life was allowed on this world, there would not have been two human settlements. The crew would have been decimated in no time having no built in defense against alien virus.

By the same line of reasoning, it is easy to conclude that on this world I will never get sick. Now let's see if that fabric is resistant to cuts. The map that appeared in Joan's condo could resist to scissors and

could not be burned; in fact it was probably
indestructible.

Bill use his knife on the fabric and could not cut it.
He then tried to cut a tiny piece of one of his boots
with no success.

Wonderful, if the clothes are indestructible, the
weapons must be too. But what about my body...

Bill tried to cut a tiny part of his left arm with his
knife and it started to bleed.

That figures, there must be some rules and one of those
rules is that we could not be created invulnerable. We
will have to take risks and fight for our lives as we
get to the city. The Guardians are powerful beings but
their action was limited by a greater force on this
world, they said, God Himself perhaps.

So I got excellent weapons and clothes, let's have a
look at those boots again.

Bill pulled them out and looked at the sole. It was
covered with some kind of extrusions. He applied his
hand on it and when he pressed with a downward movement,
it stuck. He just could not move it downward any
further. He could unglue his hand with a sideway
movement.

These were probably made to help us to climb a rocky
cliff.

Bill looked in his backpack and found a pair of gloves
with the same kind of extrusions on the interior side.
He put them on and went to the nearest tree and climbed
it just like a lizard.

Better and better, now what else? I got an incredible
sense of smell, a superhuman strength, climbing boots
and gloves and that cut is almost gone already. Oh yes,
there is something else, there is that damnedest sexual
urge. Oh boy! I better move on, I can't masturbate, with
the Murphy's law, the worst always happen and that means
being caught in the action by Queen Elisabeth or Donald

Rump or the president of the United States. Let's find them.

Bill got on his way.

I will walk on a straight line for five minutes then at ninety degree angle for another five minute and walk back; one five minute side square at a time until I find them. If it doesn't work, I will have to shout but that is not safe, who knows what kind of wicked thing my way will come.

Nicole woke up and immediately saw the three blue and green moons and the unfamiliar sun. She could smell an incredible variety of fragrances and she felt great. She realized that she was bare and she looked around and saw no one, just the silky grass, a giant blueberry bush nearby, an orchard of fruit trees and farther away, a forest of very tall trees.

That's not possible, who ever heard of three moons. I must be dreaming.

She stood up, pinched her arm, felt the pain and realized that she was awake.

My God, I am on another world, I remember now, I had a car accident followed by a brief period of fuzziness and now I am here, bare, standing on the grass.

I must have died in the car accident and I am in heaven or what will one day be heaven. The grass is blue and soft with a silky texture and there is a special feel to it and what I smell is out worldly.

Nicole was tasting the different fragrances, differentiating them like someone would be doing tasting new flavors.

That new sense is awesome.

Nicole was once the sexiest female actor of the year. She had heard about the book and decided to send her attorney to the auction to buy one of the paintings in her name but at the last moment she decided to come with him.

She remembered now her meeting at Joan's condo and her visit to Camp David.

There will be two more women here and four men. At the thought of the men, Nicole felt an extremely powerful sex urge. She looked at her body and her nipples were in erection.

I had a beautiful body before but that one is just as beautiful and much , very much more solid and powerful. I never felt so energetic.

Nicole looked around and saw her outfit and realized even more that she was now on a new world, a world where everything might happen.

This is Ghama-2 and they said that this gigantic world was home to all kind of predators and aliens.

How could they leave me alone and defenseless in the woods? Beside, this is no heaven for who would need an outfit in heaven?

Nicole Teaseman regretted her death.

It was unfair to die so soon, after I finally reached celebrity. Without even the time to live the wonders that celebrity had brought me. There were so many things I wanted to buy starting with that sixty million dollars house in San Reno; and now here I am, penniless on a world roamed by aliens and predators and a silly mission to save mankind. Who cares about mankind?

Nicole put the "stupid" outfit on.

Now I look like a musketeer, people will laugh at me. That outfit is ridiculous and those guardians have a very poor idea of what should be a lady's costume.

She loaded herself with the weapons and backpack and went on to find the others.

Elisabeth woke up and looked suspiciously around and called for the servants but none would come.

They left me alone and unconscious on the grass. Wait till I find out the responsible, Queen Elisabeth told herself. *The robbers took everything, even my underwear. They must have knocked me down and they drop me here. They did that to me, Elisabeth the third, Queen of the United Islands and there is nobody about to help me.*

My God, I have the damnedest sense of smell; an army of odors is assaulting me and I feel great, more lively than ever before.

Queen Elisabeth the Fifth looked at her legs and her disgust changed into wonder.

Those legs can't be mine.

And now she looked everywhere and realized that she had the body of a goddess. The breasts were pushing their way up in a most erotic way. She loved them and touched them.

I am beautiful.

Elisabeth felt a tremendous sex urge.

I better stop touching myself at once; what if somebody is watching me.

Elisabeth had always felt like an outcast for in women lay her phantasms. Nobody had ever found out about her sexual orientation and her private maid had kept her mouth shut about what happened behind close doors.

With a body like that, I will now get any disoriented woman of my choice.

She looked around and saw the outfit. She began to tremble and sat down for her legs wouldn't carry her anymore.

What is this? The grass, the trees, the sun, the keen sense of smell and that new body, all of this is impossible. Could it be that I am dead, or dreaming.

333

She pinched herself but she felt the pain and there was no waking up. Suddenly she remembered.

I had been sick for a few days, the plague took my life away and the painting I acquired in that auction in Florida did its magic and now, here I am, on that new world Ghama-2.

There must be others around; I better get dressed right away. So here there will no servants, no royal obligations either. Here, I will not be queen, and I am free at last. I would have never been queen had it been my choosing; but I was born in that damned royal family and was forced into a life of misery. That's what it was, misery, absence of freedom, forced official meetings, day after day, keeping at all time a poker face of happiness and satisfaction and showing a warm and friendly behavior to everyone. For the queen had to be noble and I had to project to the whole world the image of a worthy nation.

She pulled the sword from its scabbard and looked at her reflection in the mirror like side of the blade. She had a beautiful face.

All right, she thought happily, *let's live that new life and enjoy it to its fullest.*

She got dressed, found out how to use all the straps and got on her way to find the others.

Donald Rump opened his eyes and found the sun rather different from the usual. He got up and looked at the grass.

Amazing! Donald thought, for he knew about grass, he was a golfer and owned a golf course in Palm Beach, Florida and a villa, a castle really, built upon it. He also had many other castles, hotels and casinos for Donald was a rich and powerful man. He was cunning and manipulative and many said that like a cat he had seven lives. He had waddle his way into the tortuous currents of finance getting away with his life from the attack of the most dangerous and filthy sharks that have ever roamed the world, the Bankers!

But Donald Rump had feasted on them and built up a financial empire. He would have gone into politics but he had been just too successful to get the votes of millions of ordinary people. They wouldn't trust him, he was too different and they wouldn't know what to expect of him. So, Donald turned into show business with his own television series. In it he was the one to be admired, the successful billionaire and he loved to be admired. He was the boss and loved it.

The grass is blue and silky; the sun is different, and those trees are quite amazing. The painting did it! I knew I should buy one just in case. So here I am on Ghama and it's cool. Earth was getting boring anyway, I had everything I wanted and I had difficulties in finding anything pleasurable. Those damned Muslims must have killed everyone. I tried to escape the plague, got the vaccines and went to live on my ranch away from the rest of the world but the wind must have carried the bacteria.

Donald found his outfit, got dressed immediately pulled out the sword from its scabbard a few times, as quickly as he could, did a few movements with it and found out how incredibly strong he was.

Either the sword is weightless or I am as strong as a gorilla. God I feel great; these Guardians gave me the body of a superman. Let's see what they put in the backpack.

Donald found a pair of gloves with the palm covered with extrusions. He put them on and pulled his sword out with the gloved hand and when he put it back, he realized that it was solidly glued to the glove.

There got to be a trick. Donald thought.

After a few seconds of fuddling with it, Donald found out that moving the glove sidewise he could easily unglue it.

These must be climbers gloves and the boots too.

Donald went to the nearest tree and tried to climb it using the sole of his boots and his gloves and realized that he could climb it just as easily as a lizard.

Wonderful, thought Donald, *now I can climb a cliff as well as a tree, I have superman body and I would bet that as the maps, everything the Guardians gave me is indestructible. What about me? Am I indestructible too?*

Donald used his knife to cut the top of his hand and he started to bleed.

That would have been too good to be true. Thought Donald as he pressed his thumb on the cut to stop the bleeding.

The bleeding stop very quickly.

All right what else? I have the damnedest sense of smell; I feel hungry and oh boy I got the urge. That urge is maddening; I hope the women will have it too. Let's find one of them; I am even better looking than I ever was; hopefully I can seduce one before the rest of the men find her. But first I need to eat something.

Donald picked a big blue fruit from a huge gnarled tree, cut a piece of it and smelled it. It smelled good and Donald had a cautious bite in it.

Wow! Delicious! I never tasted anything like that.

The fruit tasted like a mix of cheese, chocolate and Grand Marnier and there were little bubbles of fruity liquid that burst in his mouth as he chewed on the fruit flesh.

It is extremely nourishing, I don't feel hunger anymore but I am high and a little drunk. Thought Donald, once he finished the fruit.

Now let's find a woman and quick.

At that, Donald went to find the others.

Helen Riverin extended her arm to touch her husband and he wasn't there. She opened her eyes and jumped on her feet looking around wildly.

336

What's that, the sun, the grass, those trees, everything is so strange, out worldly I should even say. How did I get here?

She was close to panic for Helen didn't like the extraordinary; she had avoided stress and always preferred security to adventures. She had kept an average salary job for years while she had the talent, the ability to start her own business but she was a worrisome individual.

Helen was not like her father at all; always looking for new projects and moving every few years from one place to another.

Suddenly she remembered, she was sick, the plague was killing everyone and must have killed her too. So this is heaven, she thought, but there is nobody around.

She found a musketeer outfit, complete with the sword and the knife plus a bow and a quiver of arrows.

That can't be heaven. Don't even think about it, she told herself as she remembered the painting and her father's book, Ghama-2. *That story was preposterous; it came from the unbridled imagination of no one else than the craziest of the daydreamers. Dad sent me that painting with a note that I should keep it at all time, promising me an afterlife if I did so. I kept it and here I am, on a new world. Dad got me here, on this fantastic world of his daydreaming fantasy and according to the story, it is a most dangerous world roamed by predators and aliens.*

I better find the others before one of those predators find me.

Helen dressed up quickly and got on her way to find other people.

The last member of the group to wake up was the first to die. He was the one and only, Prince Mohamed, the best middleweight boxer of all time. He had turned into Muslim religion and became a preacher; making it a moral obligation to spread the word of Muhammad who according to the legend and the Koran was one with the Son of God.

337

Lately, he had questioned the Islam religion realizing that its followers were creating havoc all across the world, slaying innocent people, making additions into the book of writings to denounce the Americans as the Evil and to encourage their followers to destroyed them by all means.

The Iranian leaders considered themselves the best Muslims, the true ones and to solidify their seat of power they had not hesitated in killing thousands of their own brothers. Khomeini had nothing to envy from Hitler, having personally signed the death warrant of thousands of his fellows Iranians.

So the one and only started to study other religions and found himself a kinship towards Hinduism. He discovered that the Hindu teachings found in the Vedic book were written about one thousand years before Christ and Gautama Buddha the founder of Buddhism lived five hundred years before Jesus. Buddhism was a variant of Hinduism and both describe the reincarnation and the laws of karma.

But Buddha set a way to bypass the reincarnation and move to a higher level of life, possibly to heaven through mental and moral self-purification.

The adepts practicing a certain form of yoga and meditation could achieve an incredible control of their mind and bodies.

Prince Mohamed decided to switch religions and changed his name at the same time. His new name was Krishna in memory of a deified hero of later Hinduism. He was just about to open a temple where he would teach Boxing and Hinduism when he got sick. Then he received the Ghama-2 books with an invitation to an auction, bought one of the access key paintings, went to Camp David where cancer took him away just before he could achieve full control of his body.

Krishna opened his eyes to a different world and wondered if in fact he had succeeded to bypass reincarnation.

The grass is blue, the sun is bigger and its color is half way between yellow and orange but it is just as bright as the sun I was used to. There is that acute sense of smell and my body feels different.

That might be Ghama-2, Krishna thought, *and if it so, there will be others and they may very well need my help. Who knows if one or more of my companions isn't being attacked right now by some beasts or aliens.*

He found his outfit and marveled at his sword; its heft and balance gave him a comforting feel.

I love that musketeer outfit; what a sense of humor from these old star voyagers. But there is nothing humoristic in those weapons; they are just what we need.

That body seemed highly functional; I feel more energetic than I ever was; better even than when I was the undefeated ultimate fighter for three years in a row.

Krishna dressed up and looked around for the others. He walked for half an hour and started to shout "Anybody here?" repeatedly.

Someone shout back from his left and quite a distance away and Krishna changed direction shouting every minute or so. They came in sight of each other and by that time others were shouting too.

The first person Krishna met was very handsome and looked like a body builder with the face of an actor.

My God this guy look like Mel Gibson with a much stronger body. The way he walks shows extreme agility and confidence.

"Hi, how are you doing? My name is Krishna and I come from Earth. I come in peace." said Krishna; extending his arm to shake hand with the stranger.

"Hi Krishna, I am doing just fine, thank you and I too come from Earth, I met you at Camp David and I was sitting at the end of the long table." said George W. Woods; the ex-president of the United States of America.

"Mister President, it is a pleasure to meet you again." said Krishna.

"Please call me George from now on; I had enough of those civilities." Answered George.

They shook hands and resumed their shouting and the others came one by one and a few minutes later they were together, the seven of them, all dressed alike and carrying swords, knives and bows. They were four men and three women. Every one of the men had a handsome face, a thin waist and a solidly built body. The women were gorgeous and solidly built too.

They looked at each other waiting for someone to start the introduction.

"My name is Krishna and you might have known me under another name for I was a famous athlete but I would rather not talk about it for the time being."

"I am George and as Krishna I would rather not wake the bygone but for your interest I was an expert in politics."

"I am Donald and used to consecrate my time to the building of a financial empire."

"I am Bill and I used to work in the software business."

"I am Nicole and I was a famous actor."

"I am Elisabeth and I used to work in relationship."

"I am Helen and worked in the software business."

"As I can see," said Krishna, "I am not the only one who wish to start anew and would rather not elaborate on his Earth identity. It might be best since we will probably find ourselves in situations where our past experiences would be irrelevant. We all know why we are here and now that we have told our names, we know who was each one of us."

We are here," interrupted Donald, who didn't want Krishna to establish any kind of leadership, "to find a lost city abandoned a billion years ago by a very old specie that had achieved the utmost level of science and technology."

"They left gadgets in that city," interrupted George, who didn't wish to see Donald take the pole or any leadership, "that could enhance our latent powers a million times over, bringing us right away at the very top of our potential evolution."

"These gadgets," said Bill Rates, "would make us able to transform our body cells at will and the surrounding matters as well."

"And once we reach the top level of our evolution we would become powerful wizards." said Krishna, "At that stage, we could be killed if taken by surprise and attacked by powerful beings or highly destructive forces but otherwise we would be immortals, able to fly and travel at the speed of thought from one world to another and possibly even through time like the Guardians."

"Our mission," completed George, "is to find and enter that city before the other species which are already looking for it, and find a way of using those gadgets to enhance ourselves."

"That's the mission," said Bill Rates, "and apparently it won't be easy for the writer said that the demons know about the mission and will try to stop us."

"But the demons could not act directly," interjected Donald, "there is on this world a power even greater than the demons that won't allow them that. The maximum they could do is to influence the wicked species to come after us. In the city itself, the writer didn't know what they could do."

It was evident to the women that a power game was going on between the four men and it could easily turn sour. Each of the men looks just as powerful as the others and they were parading like peacocks to get the women.

The poor guys must be under powerful sexual urge." thought Nicole Teaseman. "We better do something about it."

"Do you believe all that?" asked Helen. "On my part I don't know what to believe. The writer is my father and he was the strangest man I ever met. I never came to know him well enough to be sure that this preposterous story could be true."

"We are here now, on this world." said Elisabeth. "And so far what he said was true. So I am inclined to believe all the rest of the story. The book itself was fiction up to a point, the personages were different and we died before we could read the final book of the saga. It might be better that way, for we don't know our future.

We now have the possibility to make happen a successful end to the story."

"So what's next?" asked Donald, hopeful that someone would take the lead.

It's better to learn more about the new world before I take over the leadership and its load of responsibilities. Thought Donald. *The leader is bound to make mistakes and those mistakes may very well cost the lives of some of us. It will be difficult for the leader, after that fatal mistake, to seduce one of the women or to get friendly companionship from the other guys.*

I will rather bid my time, wait and see what he will decide and oppose to his decisions if it comes to that. George is the former president, he should be doing the leading, he is an expert in that field but I bet he is too much a politician to risk it at the beginning. That leaves Bill or Krishna; it will be interesting to see which one.

"I believe that we would have not been dumped on a gigantic world with the mission to find an abandoned city without the ability to find it." said Bill genially. "I propose that we sit for five minutes, close our eyes and try to sense its emplacement. Then each one tells what he sensed and we take the direction sensed by the majority."

"That is a remarkable proposition," said Krishna who had done a lot of meditative sitting lately and took a liking at it."

They sat and did it and after a few minutes, some of them, Helen and Donald, were getting impatient.

"Are we done with it yet?" asked Helen rebelliously.

Everyone stood up and told what they sensed.

"I sensed nothing." said Nicole. "And I neither." said Helen and Donald simultaneously.

"I believe it to be somewhere that way." said Bill.

Krishna approved; he had come to sense it there too, but George and Elisabeth thought it to be at just the exact opposite direction.

"We might as well take a vote on that." said George; who had somehow kept the skin of a good politician.

They voted and Helen and Donald voted for Bill's direction mostly because he was the one to propose the idea of sensing the direction. So there were four votes for Bill's direction since Nicole had sided with the ex-president of the United States and the ex-queen of the United Islands.

"We are not really in disagreement," said Bill brightly, "since the exact opposite direction is certainly leading us at the same place. What's important; the major question now is: which way is the shortest? Or which way would allow us to get there? Since one of the two directions might end up into impassable mountains. Let's go my way since it won the majority and see."

That guy, thought Donald, *is just a little too bright to my taste. I have to admit though that what he said made sense.*

They walked for a few miles stopping here and there to pick a fruit and taste it.

"We will not die of hunger," said Helen contentedly, for she was vegetarian on her past life; not fanatic about it though. The strawberry and cheese fruits and the coconut and whipped cream ones were the most exquisite.

There were birds singing their joy to the sunrise and flying nowhere at full speed and their songs were very much appreciated by the little group.

"It seems to me that we are being welcome here." Said Krishna. "I think I will like it here."

"I was thinking the same thing," said Nicole, "and look at all those wild flowers; there is such a variety of them."

"It looks like a well tended park," added Donald, "there is a great variety of berry bushes and fruit trees and they grow in a kind of artistic harmony."

"Yes Donald," said Elisabeth, "it looks like they were planted according to an artist design. Even the grass grows in areas of different colors to add to the serenity of the landscape."

"This world was once home to a highly advanced civilization." commented Helen. "They probably transformed the whole surface to their artistic taste."

"What is a little puzzling though," said George, "is that there are no dead trees and it looks like this park has been made a few years ago; it looks new."

"There must be someone tending it." said Nicole.

"Or something has been put in the soil to prevent undesirable vegetation growth and these trees and bushes, even the grass never grow old and never die." said Krishna.

"Then, everything we see must be one billion years old; would that be possible?" asked Nicole.

"I have the feeling," said Krishna, "that on this world anything is possible."

"But there are predators on this world according to my father; the vegetal life might be immortal but surely not the animals." said Helen.

"Then my question is where are the corpses, the bones?" asked Elisabeth.

"I believe that the builders of such a beautiful park have thought about it." said Krishna. "My conclusion is that they left an immortal waste disposal device."

"What do you mean? What kind of waste disposal device?" asked Nicole.

"It would have to be organic," said Bill, "they might have put some kind of underground life that comes to the surface to clean it up when there is something to clean."

Bill would have been surprised to find out how accurate his theory was.

The clearing pinched in and led them to woodland and after an hour or so; they came out of the woods to face the sea or the bay of a large size lake.

They were on a plateau that rose from the water at ninety degrees for two hundreds feet. The face of the cliff offered no grip. There was no way to get down. On the other side of the lake, on their right and half a mile away, they could see a sandy beach pinched between the sea and a jungle of incredibly tall trees.

On their left and also straight ahead was open water for as far as they could see.

They walked for many hours on the side of the cliff towards their right, hoping to find a way down, to no avail. They were on a circular island that jutted up from the water for two hundred feet offering a smooth un-climbable face.

"It figures," said Bill, "this is why there are only birds here. The Guardians brought us to life on a safe plateau, away from the predators and most probably close to a human settlement. We will have to climb down and swim to the shore."

"I am afraid of heights," said Nicole, "I just can't do that."

"We can make a long rope with those creepers," said Bill looking back at the forest, "we will then tie it to a tree bole and use it to climb down."

"I won't do it, "Nicole repeated." There are no ways to convince me."

"We got climbers boots and gloves." Donald said beamingly. It was evident looking at his smile that for once he was the one that could take them out of a fix.

"I noticed them too," said George, "and I tried them to climb a tree bole and they work very well."

"I know they can be very useful," said Bill, "but we might hit an area where they won't stick and the rope will be a safety."

"Let's splice the rope anyway and we will think of a solution later." said George hoping to calm down the lovely Nicole.

He knew already what he would do about her.

When the rope is ready to be thrown over the cliff, he thought, *I will knock her unconscious. We will fix the rope to her belts and get her down slowly. She will wake up when she get into the water and cut herself free.*

They made the rope and checked its length from time to time and finally it was long enough.

"There is another problem, "said Bill softly in George's ear, "I didn't want to talk about it before but the sea might hide monsters ready to devour us. Moreover, if you look well at the shore, you will notice those rocks lying on the sand. Well, I saw one of the rocks move; these rocks are in fact some kind of crocodiles."

"What will we do then?" asked Helen who was standing close enough to hear Bill's comments.

"We have a mission," said George, "we can't give up at the first difficulty."

"I got an idea," said Bill. "Do you remember those thorn-bushes growing sparsely on the grassland? They grow high enough to serve our purpose. We will cut one for each one of us and remove the inner branches, thorns and twigs. We will carve a space free of branches big enough to slide in and we will keep enough pointed branches to surround us. The bush will act as a shield and will also hide us from the crocodiles.

That's the first part.

Once we are ready and each one of us has his bush shield, we will fix one of them to the rope and bring it down. Then the one for whom the bush was carved, will climb down and get inside his shield and wait for the others. Once we are all in the water, we start paddling our way to the shore as silently as possible. If some of us reach the shore, we will try to get on the beach as far away from the crocodiles as possible. If one attacks us, we have our swords and we will try to protect each other, working as a team. What do you think George?"

"I think that plan might just be the best one we could devise." replied George. "I can't think of anything else that would be safer with the exception of quitting on the most important mission for mankind and spend the rest of our lives on this small island."

"And you Helen? What do you think about it?" asked George courteously.

"I believe it to be the best plan but," said Helen, "I must admit that I am scared stiff about going down the cliff to reach the sea. The rest of the plan is going to be even scarier and much more dangerous; we might perish without even having a chance at enjoying our afterlife."

"Let's talk about it to our companions." said George.

That's what George did.

"I saw the two of you talking secretly about it," mentioned Donald, "I would appreciate being part of your next discussion. That plan might work though. What do you think about it Krishna?"

"It might work and I don't have anything better to offer." replied Krishna.

"I won't do it." said Nicole. "I can't even come close to the cliff."

Nobody had a better idea; so they went back to the grassland to get their thorn bush and walked back to the cliff. Everyone then carved it into a shield and then they started to work altogether at the making of the rope.

They were working in silence most of the time thinking about what was going to happen, wondering how they could come out alive past the beach and into the jungle.

A few hours later, they were ready; they had a solid rope tied to a tree bole and ready to be thrown over the edge.

Nicole was desperate, she didn't want to be left alone but she couldn't do it.

George went to Nicole, took her shield and fixed it to the rope. Then he came back to her.

"I don't have any other choice," George said, "once you touch the water, you will wake up and get into your shield and cut the rope loose."

And before she could register his intentions, he hit her on the neck, with the side of his hand, cutting briefly the blood circulation and Nicole fell unconscious.

Krishna came quickly to check if she was breathing well.

"She is just unconscious; there is nothing to worry about but we better hurry up before she wake up."

They moved her limp body to the cliff and fix the rope to her belts three feet up from her bush shield, then

all of the others gripped the thick rope and they
started to get Nicole down.

Unfortunately for her, she woke up almost immediately
and looked down. She was already fifty feet from the top
of the plateau but at least two hundred feet over
the water; she couldn't do a thing, and her life
depended on the rope solidity and the good will of her
companions. Horror crept in her face; unbearable terror
gripped her soul; there was still one way out perhaps,
and she fainted!

But intentional fainting doesn't last very long and she
woke up shortly after. She was still half way into her
descent; there was a period of body shaking and legs
jerking but terror has its limits and tends to fade
after a while. She grew more and more quiet and
eventually looked down at the water, steadily.

She wasn't terrorized by the heights anymore, but now
she was scared to death by the so far invisible sea
monsters. She couldn't see any of the beasts yet but she
was sure they were there waiting for her. The fainting
trick wouldn't work anymore so she gathered the traces
of courage that had disperse through her body as terror
took over and somehow armed herself with some energy;
the energy of despair in front of the inevitable.

The shield touched the water and then she too was now
floating in the nicely refreshing element. She took her
knife and cut the ropes, grabbed the bush and slid
herself in the body size cavity, hugging to the rough
bole. She could float and she moved herself a short way
aside and held herself against the rocks waiting for
the others.

The rest of the group pulled up the heavy rope and then
took the bush shield from Helen who was to be next. She
had never been so frighten in her entire life for she
too couldn't stand the heights.

"You won't have to knock me down." She said accusingly,
staring at George and meeting his eyes with much
defiance. "I will do it by myself."

Sometimes getting angry has a limiting effect on surging
fear keeping it in check before it transformed itself

into shear incapacitating terror. So Helen made herself angry at George who would have surely knocked her down just like he did to Nicole. She gathered whatever she had of pride and bravery and walked quickly to the side of the cliff, grabbed the rope and tested it. It was thick enough to offer a good grip; she held the rope and backed into the abyss keeping her feet in contact with the cliff walls and she walked down supporting herself through the raw strength of her legs, hands and arms, never looking down.

For she thought that if she did look down, she would let herself fall to her death.

Soon she reached the water level, cut the bush loosed and slipped into her shield. Then she paddled it towards Nicole waiting for the others alongside her.

They all came down without incident.

"All right," said George, "let's swim as silently as we can towards the beach. Good luck everyone."

They started to paddle their way to the shore, keeping close ranks. From time to time, a sea beast would come to investigate what was floating, brushing against the pointed thorn-bushes' branches.

Some of the beasts were so big that they propelled the bush and its occupant a few feet clear of the water. Everyone held their bush with an iron grip, sticking firmly to it.

They were close to the shore now but one of the biggest crocodilians noticed them and came over to investigate.

Bill was the closest to the predator, he pulled his sword out of the scabbard and waited, the crocodilian surge to him at tremendous speed and bite the pointed branches that were keeping its prey away from its gaping mouth. Bill extended his arm and slipped his sword through the monster chest then moved the point sideways, slicing what ever came in contact. The crocodilian let go and turned belly up floating limply in the water.

"The blood is going to attract the sea beasts," said
Bill all excited by his close brush with death. "let's
get ashore quickly and run to the jungle."

They paddled energetically, no more concerned about the
noise. They had to rush now, they could see the sea
beasts very close, tearing at the crocodilian, getting a
big bite and moving quickly away fearing an encounter
with other sea monsters.

Suddenly the water seems to explode as a giant squid
came to the surface. One of the crocodilians on its way
to the feast was seized by tremendous tentacles and was
pulled under.
There was still great depth under the horrified group
and anything could seize them at any moment. Nicole and
Donald were the most frantic but everyone was in near
panic. They reached the shore gasping for their breath
to find themselves surrounded by the crocodilians.

They couldn't back up into the sea, the water was
churned by the swimming of hundreds of sea beasts and
some of them were coming ashore.

"Let's move together, pull your swords and try to walk
holding your shield with one hand. Let's go right ahead
and attack the ones blocking our way." said George.

The bush shields were very heavy and the women just
couldn't do it.

"Bill come on beside me; Donald and Krishna back up and
let the women walk in between." ordered George in a
domineering voice. "Women get rid of your shields and
jump in between, now!"

The women let go of the shields and jumped in between;
the whole group moved forward and the women tried not to
brush against the pointed branches and thorns of the two
men ahead. They were afraid of being squeezed in between
the two groups and were looking behind.

"Make sure you don't rush on us for we might be speared
by the pointed branches of your shields." shouted Helen
to Donald and Krishna.

All of this happened in a matter of less than a minute
while George and Bill were busy keeping the crocodilians
at bay, thrusting their swords at them and scoring a few
blows at the ones in front.

Suddenly, George move out of his shield to get more
freedom of movement; he jumped forward and thrust his
sword into one of the eyes of the beasts blocking them.
He quickly backed up and picked up his shield as the
beast started to roll over in a death swirl agonizing
before their eyes and leaving just enough space to surge
forward.

George and Bill rushed forward and the women kept pace,
running right behind them. There were no more beasts
ahead when George dropped his shield and Bill copied
him. The two men and the three women were now able to
run at full speed and they would reach the jungle well
ahead of Donald and Krishna who couldn't keep up
encumbered as they were. For the two men had to keep
going, holding their shields to keep the crocodilians at
bay. They were afraid to drop it for the crocodilians
were in close pursuit and seemed to be able to outrun
them.

George looked backward as he was rushing forward and saw
no beast on their heels but realized that the last two
men were just about to be caught. He stopped and turned
around, easing his bow out of the quiver; he set an
arrow and let it fly at the closest of the crocodilians.

He scored right in the side of the beast. Bill and the
women stopped too; they all winged an arrow and released
it and more of the beasts were hit.

The grunting and moaning of the injured beasts and their
convulsive agonizing soon stopped the rest of the beasts
that turned on the bleeding ones, attacking them and
eating them while they were still alive.

Donald and Krishna let go of their shields and ran
towards the others. They were all in total elation for
having survived what now looked like an impossible feat
but the pain roars of the victims were now attracting
even bigger predators.

The bellows of gigantic animals and the sound of their

approaching strides, the ground vibration under their heavy mass were enough warnings to get the group away from there and to cut short their effusions. They ran through the jungle, away from the coming monsters. The ground was firm and empty of bushes but there were creepers hanging from the branches and some of them were coming all the way to the ground.

In some areas, the creepers grew so dense that they had to waddle their way through. The light was dim at best and there were dark areas where the multicolor foliage of the massive trees obscured the daylight.

Predators could be hiding in there, thought George, *and we might be running straight to them.*

"We have to climb our way to safety and get some rest." said George. "We are gasping for breath and we might just run into some jungle predators. The huge monsters are some way back; we can't hear them now and their fetid odor doesn't reach us anymore. But who knows, they might be sniffing our trace. Let's try to climb up a tree making good use of those creepers."

They tried to grip their way up without much hope but their new body was much more powerful and resistant than the ones they were used too and they made it up to the lowest branch.

"We are probably one hundred feet from the ground and safe from the giant beasts." said George; sitting on the branch still gripping the creeper and looking down.

"I can't believe we all escaped with our skin." said Krishna to no one in particular. "For a moment, in the sea, I had my doubts about the outcome."

"I have never been so scared." said Helen. "I believe we owe our lives to these two men; Bill for the good idea of the shields and George for his courage and leadership."

I have to admit that the smart one and the president have done pretty well, thought Donald, *let's see how they will take a little bit of praising.*

353

The others approved her and praised the two men joyfully.

George and Bill didn't show any pride for their exploits and cleverness. They were very happy of the outcome though and joked about the recent events; teasing Nicole for her tendency to terror and pessimism while forgetting that man had proved over and over again to be the ultimate predator.

They looked around and saw some tempting fruits higher up.

"Why don't we get to the top?" asked Elisabeth. "We could feed upon those fruits and at the same time have a look at what is happening on the seashore."

They climbed to the top, unafraid of the heights. They couldn't see the ground underneath, hidden by the foliage and there were creepers everywhere to hang on but that wasn't the sole reason for the absence of fear. They had been so horrified and terrorized lately that fear had no more grip on them.

The fruits were exquisite and sustaining and they felt much energy flowing inside. They were bursting with it. They could see the shore and there were two tyrannosaurs feasting on the dead crocodilians.

"We will have to be careful and keep away from those brutes." said Donald appraisingly. "Also, I believe we should have a leader and keep close ranks behind him or her. Somebody has to decide what to do next."

"Yes Donald, I believe you are right." Agreed George; the ex-president of the United States. "If an urgent situation happens one should give an order and the others should follow it or we won't be able to work as a team and we will become much more vulnerable.

I will add that with leadership comes responsibility. Whoever is voted as our group leader, will also risk losing the affection and the comradeship of a few if not all of the members of our group.

If an order is given in an extreme situation, and result into the death of some of us, the leader will be afflicted by unbearable guilt.

To take leadership might very well be a duty to the one that think that he or she is the best fitted for the job."

"I propose we vote on that," said Bill, "a secret vote perhaps using those multicolored leaves. Our hat feathers differ in color and they identify each of us with one color; mine is green, George is blue... There are more than seven colors of leaves around. Let's pick one leaf which color identifies the one we choose as our leader and put it into my hat.

The chosen one will then have to decide if he or she accepts the job and in case of refusal, we will proceed to a second vote."

They did it and seven leaves, all of the same color, were found in the hat.

"Seven leaves of the same color." said Bill. "That means that one of us voted for oneself and we won't have to proceed to a second vote, whoever has been voted unanimously has already accepted the job."

Yes, and that one thinks he is the best for the job. Thought Donald. *George is that smart-ass for I voted for him. Why not, I didn't want it for the time being and George has already proven his value.*

"George is our leader," said Donald joyously and there was not a doubt in anyone but Donald's mind at that moment that he was the best for the role.

We should have voted for Bill, thought Donald, *he wouldn't have been such a smart-ass voting for himself and his bright ideas may well prove to be more precious than George's natural leadership...*

On sunrise side was the sea or the large lake and the Island they had come from. In the opposite direction was a wide clearing with a river in its center.

"The river seemed to take its source in that large lake or sea and is heading towards the lost city." said Bill. "There is no visible end to the clearing and apart from fruit trees and bushes here and there, it is mostly grassland."

"I know what you have in mind, Bill." said George. "We would travel faster walking on grass than jumping from one branch to another.

I believe it would be safer to travel on the canopy towards the clearing; we will not risk getting lost in that maze of giant trees and the biggest predators are probably living on the ground.

So, let's get to the jungle edge and then will climb down and walk on the grassland staying close to the jungle. If we get charged by a tyrannosaur, we will climb again to the safety of the canopy."

"Once we are down onto the grassland," commented Bill, "I suggest that we follow the jungle edge keeping at all time a safe distance from it. The reason is that the jungle edge is probably a good place for predators to wait their prey."

"Good point Bill." said George; who had already thought the same way.

They could see slowly moving spots in the distance but they were too far away to be identified as prey or predators.

They started to move in the direction of the clearing and they walked for hours. They were getting closer but the sun was sinking and the land ahead was beginning to acquire a shimmer under a sky gradually covered with vibrant hues dominated by reds and yellows.

"The night will fall shortly," said George, "and we should look for a shelter."

They went on, away from the lake, walking on wide branches and sometimes stepping or jumping from one to another. The sun had sunk for a while now and it was getting dimmer when they found a large cavity at the juncture of a huge branch and the bole of one of the immense trees.

The cavity was deep enough and wide enough to hold them all securely and they would be able to sleep without the fear of falling.

"The temperature was nice and warm today," said George, "and I don't think it will get too cold during the night. Let's pass the night here; we might not find anything better. We will huddle together if needs be."

"Good idea, "said Krishna; as he laid down ready to fall asleep. "We are very tired now."

"I will stand guard for the first two hours and wake one of you for replacement." added George. "Who knows what wicked things may roam the branches at night. There will be about twelve hours of darkness according to my estimate. Next watch will be Krishna; who will be the first asleep; then Donald, Bill, Helen, Elisabeth and Nicole.
The first few hours of the night will be the most dangerous for that would be the most active hunting time for ravenous predators. This is why I choose the men first."

They all lay down close to each other and in moments only everyone was sound asleep.

George had a hard time staying awake but there were some mewling, not too far away, and some slithering even closer. Occasional growls, howling and hooting had replaced the daytime birds' songs and in the background, little gusts of wind were murmuring in the foliage. The night was soft, comfortably and warm and looking upwards, George could see innumerable stars scintillating on the bluish blackness of the sky. It wasn't very dark with the light shed by three blue and green moons and George's vision seemed to have adapted to the night; he could see quite clearly.

Many of these stars are circled by life sustaining worlds, thought George, *and I am now standing watch on one of the strangest of them. We made it through our first day, barely! -- But the night is not over*

357

yet. How vulnerable we are compared to many of those predators and yet in that vulnerability lays our force. For we have no choice; we have to be more cunning and resourceful; and that has brought us to the very top of the food chain on Earth and may now possibly give us the control of the galaxy.

Two hours had gone by; George estimated, as he shook Krishna to wake him up silently. Everyone was sound asleep.

"Anything special?" murmured Krishna, to George's ear.

"There are movements in the canopy and I heard the mewling of something but nothing came close." answered George in a low voice.

Soon after George fell asleep leaving Krishna to his meditations. They all stood guard for a few hours except Nicole for when her time came, the first light of dawn had woken up the birds and their joyful chirps had woken up everyone.

They were ravenous and they went to pick their breakfast fruits and the most popular fruit that morning was the one tasting strawberry with a cream cheese center.

"We should get to that endless clearing and follow it to what I will call the south." said George. "I still think that if we climb down to walk on firm ground, we will get lost in that jungle maze. Let's walk at the canopy, making use of the branches and the creepers until we reach the clearing. Once we get there, we will climb down and carry on the grassland for as long as it leads us towards the city."

"Last night," said Krishna, "I looked at the stars and found out a constellation in the shape of a pyramid and one of the tips is very bright. We can even see it in the early morning light; it gives us the way for it is in its direction that we have sensed the emplacement of the lost city."

"Very good, we will do that. Let's go my friends and may our good fortune stay with us." said George.

Chapter Fifteen - George's group trek.

When the group finally reached the end of the jungle, the entire stretch of grassland was laid out before them. It was full daylight and they could see very far, for the horizon on this huge world was much farther than the one on Earth. Half a mile away on their right, herds of longneck deers and unicorns-like grazers were watched by a horde of wolf-like predators as they came by the river to quench their thirst.

Further up North they could see a variety of dinosaurs leisurely walking by the jungle. Everywhere they set their eyes and gaze steadily for a while, something would move, there were all possible and impossible variety of animals and birds walking, running, jumping, skittering, pursuing, swimming or flying, grazing or resting, roaring, bellowing, chirping, singing and what else.

"What a fascinating world!" exclaimed Krishna.

"Only in a few African reserves could we still see a fraction of this wild life." replied Donald.

"The grass, to sustain all these grazers, must be growing quickly," Helen commented, "I wonder how tall it could grow to."

Patches of long grass wavering with the breeze alternated with areas where it had been grazed close to the ground. There were fruit trees, growing in group or alone, everywhere they look, and they too provided nourishment to a variety of wildlife.

A pack of feline predators, tiger like, with color stripes all over their rust brown fur were silently and carefully edging closer towards a herd of grazers. As they got closer, they split and surrounded the herd. The way they moved indicated some kind of communication.

"These tiger-like predators have developed a hunting tactic," said George, watching them.

"These predators are probably sentient," replied Helen, "they may be the result of a long evolution."

Upon a silent signal the tiger-like felines surged at the herd all at the same time. The massive buffalo like grazer herd exploded in action, running at a tremendous speed for their mass, but two of them were caught and in moments only they had suffocated to the strangling fangs. Vultures were flying in from all direction waiting for their turn.

"You have seen that," said George, "these tigers are quite intelligent and the same could be said for the wolves and the crocodilians. To survive on this world, we will have to travel in pack too, keeping close to each other."

"Our new acute sense of smell and possibly an improved intuition for incoming danger will warn us in time." said Krishna. "But we must try to develop our awareness and listen to our slightest brain signals. If we do so, we will in time learn to decipher those feeble signals and give them a sense.

We should put ourselves in a state of relaxed alertness and walk in silence, avoiding ambush sites."

"I think," said George, "that Krishna's words indicate a knowledge that could be very useful. If there is any training that would improve our chances for survival, Krishna, I am sure that we would all be very much willing to get it."

"Let's find first a suitable shelter where we could spend a few days, and then I will tell you what kind of training I can provide you all." answered Krishna.

They climbed down and set foot on firm ground with evident pleasure. Patches of gold and grain tipped grass grew up to their shoulders all about them but they could walk through and waddle around the more dense patches.

The air was fresh and cool and the grass smelled like late summer wheat fields. There were the fragrances of wild bush flowers in full bloom and the sunlight was flickering on the undulating grass. To add to the fairy Ambiance, small birds were twittering about.

"That's Paradise," Elisabeth said happily, "it's just like a Sunday morning of leisure in the country with a group of friends. And this had been denied to me on Earth. I am so happy to be with all of you here that I wonder how I could express it properly."

"You are right Elisabeth," replied Nicole warmly, "I too feel the same way."

"And me too Elisabeth," said Helen, "you were denied the pleasure and comfort of week-end trek with a group of friends but on this world, I will be your friend and I am sure it is the same for all of us. We will be a group of friends."

The men approved warmly maybe a tad too warmly for Nicole could easily sense the sexual urge they were secretly trying to hide and control.

These two women are absolutely gorgeous, thought Elisabeth, *even those young men present an interest. God, I don't know what's happening to me but I feel like a cat in heat. It may be that new body, my blood must be filled to capacity with progesterone hormone. I hope we find that suitable shelter today. There should be a pond of clear water to bathe and get rid of our sweat, then maybe I can comb the hair of those two beautiful women and give them a massage....*

They walked silently in groups of two behind George, careful not to sprain an ankle in a dinosaur footprint or get caught in the occasional thorn bushes.

Sometimes they could smell the presence of predators and they would stop and wait or walk away. The men had their swords in hand and it was getting heavy.

"Why don't we cut ourselves some quarterstaffs," said Bill in a low voice, "it would help the walking and serve in case of attack. We could have one side pointed so we could use it as a spear and we could carve two hand width grips for such usage."

"Good idea," said George, "we can cut them off the fruit trees and pick some fruits at the same time; I am getting hungry."

They came by a pond of crystal clear water surrounded by a variety of fruit trees. The stream coming from the

361

jungle was further up resuming its course towards the river. A few rabbits scampered away at their coming and there was an explosion of beating wings as a flock of pheasant-like birds flew in panic. Yellow and blue birds perching in the trees went on with their songs after a short period of watchful silence.

It was quiet, the breeze was gone, the sun had reached the zenith and it was getting hot. The predators were probably going to sleep through the hottest part of the day and they felt safe in that little corner of paradise.

"I really appreciate the total absence of critters, flies and other bothersome insects," said Helen happily. "Let's see if the pond doesn't hide anything harmful or lethal, I would very much like to bathe and wash my clothes."

There was nothing else than a few fat trout-like fishes swimming lazily at the sandy bottom.

"I will climb to that treetop and stand watch while you do that." said George. "Later on one of you guys come over and replace me."

"I am going to take off my clothes if you don't have an objection." Said Nicole; in a most sexy way.

Elisabeth and the men looked at her as she took them off exposing perfect breast and an exquisite body.

Then Elisabeth and Helen took off their clothes too as the men stood watching in full erection and unbearable urge.

The men followed the women example, took off their clothes not looking at each other and conscious that they just couldn't hide the way they felt.

They went into the water, it was cold to get in but after a while the temperature was bearable and refreshing.

They started to splash each other, like kids, enjoying themselves, laughing and joking at low voice. The men

were still in erection when they came out of the water
and the women were unusually aroused.

*Something is definitively wrong or right with my new
body but whatever it is, it is turning me into a nymph,*
Elisabeth thought, *I am not only aroused by these two
gorgeous women but I need to get laid by one of those
machos.*

Krishna took Helen's hand and pulled her close, they
looked at each other and kissed, Bill went to Nicole who
embraced him, hugging him close, wishful to properly
thank him for saving their lives with his brilliant
ideas. Donald and Elisabeth didn't wait; they came at
each other hungrily and made love right away.

George was watching the orgy from his perch, wishful to
be replaced and share some of the fun. After a while,
Krishna got up and came to replace him. George rushed to
the pond, got bare and dived in the refreshing water.
Soon after, Elisabeth joined him; they played for
a while and made love on the sand.

Krishna came down his perch, there was nothing scary
roaming about and he joined with his new friends.

They just relaxed all afternoon by the pond, swimming,
playing and making love. Elisabeth, who had already made
love with each of the men, asked Nicole if she would
like to have her hair combed. Nicole knew about her sex
appeal, she was used to catch the attention of many
women and she could tell when somebody look at her with
lust. She looked at Elisabeth in the eyes and said
"Elisabeth dear, you are still aroused and I have been
with women before. Come here in my arms."

Elisabeth hugged her and kissed her passionately on the
mouth and then everywhere on her beautiful body and they
made love, the men, watching, got aroused again.

After a while, Krishna and Donald joined Elisabeth and
Nicole and made love to the two women as they went on
kissing and caressing each other.

Finally, the orgy was over and there was no more
hormones roaming their arteries. There were still many
hours of daylight and they weren't tired anymore.

"Let's shoot a few arrows," said George, "our mastery of the bows might save our life or our friends' lives. Perhaps we can make a friendly competition! The first one to score ten points will be the winner and will not have to stand guard coming night while the worst shooter will have first watch; the second worst will have second watch and so on."

"Good idea," said Krishna, "but since we never know in advance when predators will be jumping us we must add a time factor. The shooter will face the target, someone will say go; at that moment, the shooter will pick his bow from his back, wing an arrow and let it fly. We start counting at go and stop at the thump of the arrow on the target. Any impact over ten seconds doesn't count."

They started the competition and the results were surprising for the women scored very well. The winner was Krishna and the second best was Helen who beat George by one point. The worst shooter was Nicole and second worst was Donald.

It had been a good practice and they had improved their marksmanship and speed remarkably.

"We should also have another kind of training," said Krishna,
"and I believe it is as vital or more than the shooting. We will be attacked sooner or later by packs of predators or even worse by a group of sentient aliens. We have a mission to accomplish and we must put all the odds on our side. I noticed that our clothes resist tearing. I stumbled on a thorn bush today and my pant got stuck. I pull energetically without thinking at protecting the only pair of pants I have. The pointed branch broke and the pant didn't have a scratch.

This afternoon, I tried to cut a little piece of it with my knife and couldn't. Then I tried with my shirt to no avail.
The guardians gave us clothes that will resist the raking of claws and the piercing by fangs. The clothes are indestructible but they don't cover our neck, hands or head and we may suffer broken ribs or bones. It will help and give us a chance to survive an attack by a tiger pack if we close ranks and fight as a team and if we are trained fighters with extremely quick reflexes.

We have swords and knives and we should practice with
them, get the feel of it, and learn to swing or thrust
hard and fast. We must be able to severe a paw or a neck
or crack a head open in a swift movement.

I suggest we use the creepers. We can hang some of those
large size and thick shell fruits to a dozen creepers
cut in different heights, from head to feet level. Then
one of us gets in the center while the others
pull at the creepers and propel the fruits at him or her
with a warning shout. The one in the center must not
only escape their impacts but also crack them open as
they are swung at him or her.

That kind of training can be harmful so I suggest that
we set up to make a head and body protector to prevent
injuries."

"The best ideas must be put at use as we get them and
without delay." commented George. "Bill, you show us how
to do the body shields."

They took their time and found everything they needed
from the trees; bark strips, fast setting resin glue,
strips of fabric like twisted palm leaves and they made
two lightweight shields of different sizes, one
for the men and one for the women.

The sun was a hand width from the horizon when they
finished them. It was time to get a shelter for the
night. They climbed the creepers up to the jungle canopy
and looked for another cavity at the intersection of a
huge branch and the bole of a tree. They found two
of them not too far away, one was big enough to shelter
four of them and the other one offered enough space for
the remainder of the group.

Before splitting, they sat together on a high branch,
looking at the grassland and the sunset.

"It is such a lovely world," said Helen, looking at the
long neck dinosaurs immersing their head in the river
and coming out with a mouthful of aquatic plants.

At that moment, a white dove came to perch right beside
her. She extended her finger close to the bird's foot

and it walked on it emitting a joyful twitter. She patted it for a while and put it on her shoulder where it stayed twitching its head to look at everyone.

"You know," said Donald, "we have just lived the two most vibrant days of our lives. In my case, there is not a doubt about it. Yesterday, we woke up in a new body, a bunch of strangers, on a new world. We found out that we were in fact prisoners on a high plateau with no way out; an island in a sea populated by beasts and monsters.

If we found a way to get down, we still had to escape the monsters to get to a shore pack solid with crocodiles. But we did it, thanks to the inventiveness of Bill, the courage and quick thinking of George and the determination and bravery of the rest of the group. Now we are starting to develop into soldiers and I have no doubt that with Krishna's experience in training we will achieve a high degree of fitness in no time at all.

We have a leader whose leadership is to be praised for he listens with interest to everyone's' good ideas and I could observe that he is comforted by our contribution.

I pondered about it and came to the conclusion that George is used to operate at the top, working with a team of advisers and letting them find the solutions to different situations. Working more like an arbiter, a chairman, and using his power of decision with parsimony.

Was it like that George when you were the president of The United States of America? "

"Yes it was." answered George; imperturbably.

"And you Bill," added Donald, "I met you at Joan's condo and then at Camp David. I never had the occasion to ask you about it and anyhow I wouldn't ask you for I respected your need for privacy. But here, on this world, I don't think you will mind my curiosity. You remember me of a genius who built a software empire before the age of twenty-five. You are that one, aren't you?"
"Yes, I am."

"Since we are now a band of brothers, we might as well know each other a little more. Who are you really Elisabeth? Your language is showing great culture." asked Donald; who was set to find out everything about everyone.

"I am Elisabeth, ex Queen of England and the United Islands." said Elisabeth with just a trace of pride.

"And you Krishna," said Donald, "you have to be the one and only; the best pound for pound boxer of the history. Aren't you?"
"Yes I am." said Krishna; without any trace of arrogance.

"And you Nicole, we know that you were a cinema star and the sexiest one. I am Donald Rump, ex businessman and owner of a chain of Casino, Hotels, golf clubs and what else." said Donald. "And apart from Helen, the writer's daughter, we are a bunch of decision makers and filthy rich people with very little hope of ever going to Heaven, according to the legend. I would say we didn't do badly so far. What do you think?"

"Do you think we are in Heaven, Donald?" asked Elisabeth sweetly.

"I don't know for sure," answered Donald, "but I sometimes wondered what kind of heaven I would like to go to when I pass away and it wasn't the kind of heaven that was described in the scriptures. I would have been bored to death in an eternity of praising God. It would have turned into Hell after twenty minutes only. So I was hoping that there wouldn't be either Hell or Heaven, just nothing. But to me, this, what we are living now, is the best kind of Heaven I could have wish for.

I wasn't very open to sentimental confidences in my first life but not knowing what is going to happen in the next hour, day or week, changed me. Maybe that new body changed me too, somewhat. Or maybe it is the experiences we have lived through but I feel different. I want to thank you Nicole, Helen and you dear Elisabeth for making love with me today and I want to tell you George, Bill and Krishna that I really appreciate your company."

"I feel different too." said Elisabeth. "I remember everything of my past life; I remember that I felt old; I remember that I had lost my zest for life and nothing seemed to interest me anymore. And now, I feel like a young girl. I was a lesbian in my first life and I had no attraction for men and tonight, I enjoyed making love with all four of you guys and I had incredible orgasms. But making love with you Nicole was for me the ultimate moment; all those phantasms, a lifetime of them were finally fulfilled."

"If you wish to make love to me too," said Helen, "I will. I like you very much and you are the most beautiful woman I have ever seen."

"Can I kiss you?" asked Elisabeth.

"Yes." answered Helen.

 Elisabeth moved closer and took Helen in her arms and kissed her passionately.

"Let's go to our shelter Helen." said Elisabeth.

"I am going with you." said Donald before any of the other guys and the three of them walked to the smaller shelter.

"Wow!" said Krishna.

"Let's go to our shelter," proposed Nicole, "and if you wish to, I can take you all."

Later on, George went out of the shelter and sat near its entrance. The birds had gone to sleep and the mystery of the night had landed a muffling hand on his companions' chatting which had turned into whispering and finally long silences.

They laid down and soon found sleep.

Two hours later, George woke up Nicole. She went out and sat nearby and stood her period of watch wondering what to fear most and finding nothing too scary.

I am getting quite brave after all the past events, she thought, *nothing seems to scare me anymore. God it was fun today, I never enjoyed myself that much; thank you Guardians, thank you Richard for sending me that invitation. One day I hope, I will meet you again and I will show you my gratitude.*

They were up at first light, picking some fruits and chatting about the new ones they had just found and tasted. They went down for a training practice with the swords under the coaching of Krishna.

None of them could be as good as Krishna though and some of them were wondering how he could know when something was coming silently and fast at his back. Krishna would swirl and cut the fruit in halves swinging his sword with a double-handed grip and instantly moving sideways to escape more fruits coming at him from all directions and slicing them almost at the same time.

"It is a matter of sensing," Krishna said, "you must chase any thought from your mind and keep it empty and sense. You soon develop your awareness and your reactions become swifter if you don't think. Your reflexes will improve with each practice as well as your sensing."

And they went on practicing for hours before they went to bathe in the nearby pond and make love. They stayed by the pond for six days before George decided that they were now able to face whatever would come their way.

Their new bodies were incredibly resistant; they were not getting tired easily and their recuperation was swift. They were also much stronger than ever before.

On the morning of the seventh day of camping by the pond, they left and headed "South" again. For a time they walked in silence, unwilling to attract the attention of some of the dangerous beasts roaming the grassland but after a while they chatted at low voice; commenting on the sight. They were all kind of animals and birds about them and some of the plant life was absolutely amazing. So, they took their time, stopping here and there to observe the whereabouts and the behavior of the animals.

At one point they came upon a group of long neck
dinosaurs. They had seen them from a distance, perched
at the canopy and their behavior appeared to be
peaceful. Now seen from a few feet away, they looked
formidable. One of them spotted the group and emitted a
low tone grunt. The dinosaurs looked at the group of
humans with curiosity, their heads towering fifty to
sixty feet from the ground.

One brought its head down for a much closer look and the
massive head came to a few feet from Elisabeth who
reached out her hand in a royal manner to the beast
muzzle and patted it.

"Good Dino, you are a nice looking Dino." Elisabeth
said; closing on a head bigger than twice her body to
pet it with both hands under the stricken gaze of her
companions.

By now the dinosaurs had them surrounded.

"I don't think they will eat us," said George, "we have
plenty of space to walk between the beasts, let's move
on slowly."

And they moved on, restraining themselves from looking
backwards. Elisabeth was the last one to leave.

"Farewell grand ladies, we got to move on now." said
Elisabeth and the beasts let them walk away.

The wooden cross had been crudely made. It was standing
at the head of a heap of small rocks; the size of which
just big enough to cover a man's body. There was a
stream close by, gurgling its way through the clearing
and heading towards heavily forested hills. All around
them, fruit trees were growing in rows and George had
the eerie feeling of intruding on a private property and
standing in a well maintained orchard.

On their right, the riverbanks were getting steeper as
the river cut its way into the hills. They had reached
the end of the grassland and the jungle was giving way
to a forest of oaks, maples and birches like trees.
Further away they could see some high mountains covered
with coniferous trees.

Krishna crouched by the cross to read the few lines that had been carved into the wood.

Bob Dawson, 2252-2386. Here lay in peace First lieutenant Bob Dawson, the last of the five faithful companions who sided with me when the Spaceship Crew went into mutiny. Signed: Jack Duncan, Earth ship Endeavour Commander.

They looked around and found the log cabin. It had narrow slits in lieu of windows and the door was closed.

They went inside and found the skeleton of Jack Duncan laid on a wooden bed covered by dry leaves. On a crudely made desk were neatly stacked sheets made of thin birch peels. Jack Duncan had written the story relating the crash event and the mutiny. It was a sad story showing rage and despair.

According to the story, Jack and his followers had built a raft to cross the river and a sea beast had capsized the raft. They were very close to the other shore when it happened. Jack Duncan and Bob Dawson were able to reach the shore while the beasts killed all the others.

They had traveled up to the end of the clearing and found the orchard and a more familiar forest. They built the log cabin and lived in loneliness and regrets wishing secretly for the companionship of the crew and the company of women. One day, they were attacked by a grizzly bear like beast. They had killed it but had been inflicted terrible wounds. Bob died in the following hour. Jack put him into ground, erected the cross and carved the text. He then lived alone for a while before he apparently took his own life away.

"Why did they try to cross the river?" asked Helen.

"Because Jack Duncan was afraid to loose the few that had sided with him." said Donald. "By crossing the river, he was making it impossible for the women to get back with the rest of the crew. I am sure he would have either destroyed the raft or just push it back into the river after they reached the other shore."

"So we are on the wrong side of the river," said Helen, "that's why we didn't see any trace of the human settlement; that Jungletown my father described in his book."

"Yes," said George, "and it means for us to take the same kind of risk and possibly face the same fate if we decide to go for the human settlement."

"Not mentioning the risk of crossing the clearing on its whole width with the tigers and wolves packs, the tyrannosaurs and other wicked things." said Bill.

"Anybody thinks that we need to build an army of men to find the lost city and get inside?" asked George.

They talked at length about it.

"You know," Krishna said, "there was a time when I would have wanted to get with them, our descendants at the human settlement and start a new religion based on the teachings of Hinduism, Confucianism, Christianity and Islam. For all of them have their good sides; but I believe there is no point in trying to save the souls of our descendants and let them perish in the claws of a wicked specie that would find the city before us and enhanced themselves to super beings' powers.

No, we have to find the city without delay and move on as quickly as we can in its direction."

"Beside, a small party may have better chances to go through alien territory unnoticed if it means doing it to get to the lost city." said Bill.

"So what about you, women?" asked George with much interest.

The women concurred, they agreed to move forward, even Nicole, to George's surprise, for she would have been the one, not a long time ago, who would have opted for the security of the settlement and the fame of coming from their ancestors world. But Nicole was another person already and they were a band of brothers rejoicing in each other's presence.

The three women, George thought, have shown exceptional courage and Elisabeth's royal petting of the long neck dinosaur was appalling. We could have been stepped over or gulped in one mouthful by the gigantic beasts; we were defenseless for swords or arrows could not have pierced the dinosaur tough hide but Elisabeth, Queen of the Islands, had deigned to pet the beast and treat it like a fine lady of the highest circles and the beasts let us through--.

"The sun is way passed the zenith," said George, "I believe we should relax for the rest of the day, bathe in the stream and pass the night in the log cabin."

"Not with the remains of a dead man." said Nicole. "Let's dispose of him first and do some cleaning, it's quite dusty inside and I prefer not to think about the dust or where it came from--."

They put Jack Duncan skeleton over the ground right beside Bob Dawson's tomb and fetched some rocks from the stream shore to cover it. They made a rudimental cross, and carved the name of the defunct and planted it at the head of the tomb.

Krishna said a short prayer and everyone showed respect and kept silent meditating about the strangeness of the situation.

"For more than a hundred years," said Donald, "this man commanding one of the first spaceships ever made by mankind, had been sleeping in hibernation. He had been selected amongst many other applicants for his great qualities of leadership. He woke up at the last moment, a few weeks only before the ship arrived to that very strange world. He lost his ship upon arrival but escaped with half of the crew. Then he lost the rest of the crew or most of it through a mutiny the next day. Soon after, all but one of the few faithful were dead.

One year later, he lost his last companion and finally took his own life. What a fate--."

Everyone kept silent. They had been saddened by that terrible story and they thought that they could very well be killed too before they even get acquainted with the new world.

They cleaned the cabin and prepared their beds of dry leaves and grass for the night and then they bathed in the stream. They were hungry and very curious about the fruits of the orchard.

Helen picked the first one and tasted it. It had the taste of a baba-o-rhum, one of the most delectable French pastry. It was sustaining but it contained alcohol and soon the party was going on. They needed to forget about the sad story and they were all drunk after a while and nobody would care about the necessity for one of them of standing watch. They party went on for the evening and they finally fell asleep on their bunks in the log cabin, the door wide open.

Krishna was dreaming. Confucius was telling him he should be ashamed of his sins and for punishment he was to be hung by the feet over a cliff for twelve hours.

They took him to the cliff and they showed him the rope he would be hanging from and the rope was rotten. No he said, I won't let you and he woke up gasping in fright. At that moment, Krishna remembered where he was; the log cabin and the door was open and he could see the beast shadow coming through the door. It was bear-like and huge.
Krishna looked for his sword and it was there on the floor right beside him. He grasped it and eased it out of the scabbard, very slowly, for the beast was hesitant. Krishna leaped on his feet and thrust his sword in the beast heart as it was jumping for his throat.

The beast fell with Krishna caught underneath but it had died already. Everyone woke up and tried to see what was going on.

"Can you pull me out, I am caught under and it is very heavy." asked Krishna; suffocating.

Their eyes could now distinguish the shape of the beast and they pulled it out grasping it by the fur and it took all their combined strength to get it out of the cabin.

"I am ashamed," said George, "for what happened. I should have kept sober but I forgot my responsibilities. Are you hurt Krishna?"

"No, just bruised." he answered. "It raked at my chest with its paw but it was dying already and the clothes protected me."

"You saved some of us this night," said George, "and shown again a high degree of awareness and extremely fast reaction. For you had eaten as many fruits as the rest of us.

I woke up as the beast was jumping at your throat and it all happened so fast that I could do nothing."

"Nothing there to boast about, "Krishna said, "for I trained my body and my mind for combat ever since I was a teenager. I was known as the best pound for pound boxer of all time, remember? Beside, we should thank God for his help for Confucius sent me a message as I was dreaming and it woke me up."

They went out sword in hand and looked around the cabin for more of the beasts but there were none. They went back inside and closed the door before they lay down. Krishna stood watch for he was too unnerved to sleep.

The rest of the night went on without any more incidents. At first morning light they were on their way across the drunks' paradise leaving the tempting fruits untouched.

"That orchard," said Elisabeth "has apparently been very well kept. Nothing but the grass would grow between the trees. I wonder if gardeners of some kind do not tend it."

"The whole planet might have been tended for the last billion years." answered Bill. "There are no insects, the trees grow well apart and we didn't see one dead jungle tree yet. All the trees bear edible fruits of some kind and we always find new ones with different taste."

"I wonder what they look like." said Krishna. "The gardeners I mean."

"They probably look like flying saucers with all kind of gadgets including weed killers and cutters." said Nicole; half jokingly.

They were now walking in the woods having left the orchard a few hours ago. There were no trails but walking was easy for there were very few shade-loving bushes. The ground was made of patches of short grass or just bare and there were short ferns and giant mushrooms; some of them up to ten feet high. The trees were of all kind of essence; they grew tall but not quite as tall as the jungle trees and there were no creepers but very much Earth like foliage. The lowest branches were in easy reach but usually overhead; for the first ten feet of the boles were free of limbs.

The sun reached through the multicolored foliage and the air was fresh and cool. Fragrances of all kind were playing with their new keen sense of smell and a new variety of birds were singing their best welcome to the travelers.

They were now walking in silence for there was majesty there in that old forest and some kind of welcome home feeling.

"That forest is a glory to its creator." said Krishna.

They all commented about it and after a while they were whispering their comments to each other, like if they were walking through an ancient cathedral.

Here, thought Krishna, *is a place where the saints amongst the monks would go. It would be paradise to them.*

Chapter Sixteen - The Bugs.

They camped on a sand bar in the middle of a stream.

"It would be great," Bill said, "if we could make a fire. We could catch some trout and cooked them over the fire."

Bill walked around, investigating the plant life that grew by the stream. There were some very dry bushes with yellow sulfurous crystals exuding at the junctures of the twigs to the branches. Bill played with them, rubbing them together to create heat and a flame burst and caught the twig swiftly. He threw the flaming twig in the water then picked a handful of the twigs and some dead wood and returned to the sand bar.

Nobody had noticed anything.

"Would you mind to have a real dinner tonight?" said Bill to his friends. "Roasted trout and partridges along with mash potatoes? Do you miss looking at the flames of a campfire? That would change from the fruits diet."

"Oh come on now," said Donald, "don't talk about that. Feasting was my greatest pleasure and sin for I had a hard time keeping from becoming fat and ugly."

"I am not joking," said Bill, "I can make fire and I noticed the presence of vegetables in this clearing. The roots might taste like potatoes when properly cooked.

We scared a flock of partridges as we came to this clearing and they didn't fly far, they must be close by."

"All-right," said George all excited, "why don't you women pick the vegetables while Krishna and I hunt the partridges. In the mean time, Bill and Donald, why don't you try to find a way of catching a few fishes?"

That night was memorable; they were sitting by the campfire, listening to its crackling and watching the flames. The wind was playing a soft background music in the nearby foliage and the stream was gurgling its way by the sand bar.

The partridges were properly roasted and they had made some crude wooden plates. Now they were filled with cooked vegetables, partridge pieces and trout.

They took their time savoring every bite and chatting between bites. A large predator came walking by, attracted by the odor but it kept its distance wary of the group and the fire. At time they could see it partially hidden by the bushes and it looked to be of the same specie as the one killed by Krishna at the log cabin and they had smelled it coming before they could hear its footsteps.

Dusk had laid its mystery coat over their head and it was sprinkled with stars. It was one of those nights when you don't want to fall asleep. There was an ambiance of magic leading to dreaming of far lands and worlds, and mystery.

"Let's say we find the city," said Donald, "and use the gadgets to enhance ourselves into super-beings able to transform our bodies into flying saucers and travel at the speed of thought. What would you like to do?"

"I would like to visit this world," said Krishna, "and meet with our descendants and all the other species scattered on its surface. I would talk with them and later on go visiting the home world of the most interesting species."

"I would like to go back to Earth and live there hiding my powers and helping the people in their efforts to expand peacefully across the galaxy." said Helen.

"I would like to travel from world to world with all of you, stopping by Earth for a while." said Nicole.

"I would like to meet with the Guardians and find out how they travel in time and how they snatched our souls and gave us a new body." said Bill. "For I believe that we could build something that would do that soul-snatching. We could bring it back to prehistory time and set it up to snatch the souls of dying people as time goes by, bring them here, and give them a new body."

"We could set it up to snatch only the souls that have reach a certain degree of compassion and qualities letting the others go to chaos." said George.

"Or we can snatch everyone but wake up the nasty people on less interesting worlds and snatch their souls there again and again as they die on those worlds and return them right back for another life of misery until they learn and change for the better." said Donald. "These worlds would be forever hell for those who would never learn and purgatory worlds for those who are not so bad but not good enough for Ghama-2."

"And those few," said Elisabeth, "who were really great individuals, could be awoken close to the lost city and have the opportunity to enhance themselves and become super beings. So there would be many levels of heaven and who knows, the super beings souls might be snatched by God himself if they are killed by powerful aliens and given an even greater state of life in which they would be able to live in a multi-dimensional universe. There could be no end…"

"I believe that everything that comes to our thinking was thought before by other older species, said Bill, "and I am inclined to think that mankind will go to heaven if we give ourselves a heaven."

"It's a deal for me; if we become super beings," said Helen, "I will contribute to the building of a soul-snatching device and try to set it back into prehistoric times. The guardians are surely watching us right now and they are listening; so shall we succeed with our mission, I am asking you dearest Guardians to help us in getting the soul snatching device way back in time. This way, we will meet again with all the people that we loved or the great ones we admired; and maybe we could settle an account or two with some of the nasty ones for whose behinds our foot had wished contact; those guys for example: Khomeini, Hussein, Hitler, Bin Laden and his big mouth acolyte Mohamed Omar.

Wouldn't it be great to pay them a visit on a hellish world and boot them so hard they would clear the ground by a few feet and not be able to sit for a week or two?"

"My God Helen," said George, "you are surprising me; you, the serious lady, with those thoughts."

They were all laughing at the thought of booting the ass of a few of the nasty ones and they went out chatting until they finally got tired enough to sleep the rest of the Ghama-2 long night.

Days went by and the group went on their way enjoying themselves, stopping here and there for lunch or to play with each other. They left the thickly wooded forest for sparsely forested hills. The climbing was not difficult even though there were some steep areas where their quarterstaffs were quite handy. They topped the highest hill and went to a rocky outcrop to take a look at what was lying ahead and there were more hills, some valleys, a few lakes and very far away the hills were giving way to high mountains with white peaks.

"It will take us a few weeks to get to those mountains," said George, "then, I hope we will find a way of crossing them."

"We will find a way," said Krishna, "or maybe I should say Bill will get us through with one of his brilliant ideas."

"Let's take it one day at a time," said Elisabeth, "there is no point in getting discouraged. Who knows how many years it will take us to get to the city. We just have to do an honest day of walking and rest in the most attractive areas and take a few hours each day to enjoy ourselves. I am done with deadlines and I am very happy to just walk through that wonderful country."

Two weeks later they were getting close to the mountains when an odor hit them and it was alien to all the thousands of fragrances this world had brought to their keen sense of smell.

They went ahead silently to investigate its source and came to a very strange city. The streets were busy with the coming and going of man size beetles carrying fruits from the nearby orchard on their left and vegetables from a plantation on their right. The city had been built on the shore of a great lake. On the other side of

the lake were the mountains they needed to cross to keep going "south".
The buildings or houses bordering the streets were made of hardened clay or cement and were two to three stories high. Round holes, five to six feet in diameter were regularly spaced on the side of the buildings and were giving access inside.

The beetles were armed with pincers. Under the pincers they had two chitin arms terminated by four tentacles, which served presently to carry the baskets filled with fruits and vegetables. They were moving on six legs, they had two antennas terminated by a faceted eye. Vestigial wings were tucked neatly on their back.

The bugs were looking straight ahead and seemed to be unaware of the human presence. The ones coming in the city were moving on the left side of the streets to give way to the ones going out. Like the ants, the beetles would stop for one very quick face to face contact with the other beetles going in the opposite direction.

"It's probably their way to communicate with each other and transmit their queen's orders." said Helen. "For they don't seem to have an individual consciousness."

"They may have notice us and called for their soldiers already." said George. "Let's cross the city quickly and let's not get in their way. These giant critters could outrun us and they could cut our head off with those pincers."

So they went across the streets of the city, moving aside to give way to the bugs coming their way. A massive spaceship partially dug in the ground occupied the heart of the city. Some of the bugs went inside the ship while others exited and there were bigger bugs guarding the entrance.

"We better move away from here," said George, "these bigger ones are probably the soldiers and our presence might be discovered at any time now. Let's rush to the lake."

It was too late already for the big ones were moving quickly in their direction, their pincers clicking, and the smaller bugs were moving aside to let them pass.

They ran full speed across the streets, between the critters, but the soldiers were gaining on them. They rounded a corner and saw on their right an entrance to one of the clay buildings.

"Let's run inside and hide while we are out of sight," said George.

They moved inside and ran along corridors and entered one of the rooms. There were bugs handling the fruits and vegetables, exuding a waxy substance from their mouths on them and placing them in alcoves. The beetles looked at the intruders and emitted a piercing buzz sound of alarm.

They rushed back to the corridor and ran to another room. Here there was only one bug and it was placing vegetables in wooden basins filled with moving larva.

They went to hide behind the basins. The bug hadn't noticed them. They stayed there for an hour or so and nothing happened. They went back to the corridor and moved quickly out of the building and ran to the lake, using the more quiet streets. There were soldiers roaming the city streets and one of the big critters saw them and moved quickly to block the way.

"Let's cut its antennas, or its pincers" shouted Bill."

"Let's charge it from all direction," Ordered George.

They attacked the bug and before it could do harm to anyone it had already lost its antennas and its pincers under the quick swords' blows, but other critters were coming now in great number. George's group had reached the shore and the lake was free of bugs, its water looked calm and safe.

"Let's plunge in and swim across the lake." said George.

They dived in the water hoping for the best but some of the bugs' soldiers entered the water and went after them. The bugs were rapidly gaining distance on the humans who were swimming clumsily, encumbered with their swords and backpacks.

"There are a dozen of the bugs soldiers coming after us, we should split, and if one of the critters comes too close, dive under the water," said Bill. "I am sure they can't do that with their shell. When you surface, get behind the attacker and grab it by the shell and move up their back. Cut their pincers with your sword and try to ride them to the other side of the lake. They will swim where they look, grasp their antennas and drive them by orienting their eyes antennas in the right direction."

They split and one after the others dived under at last moment and emerged behind the attacking critter. Holding tight to their chitin, they slid their way up the bugs' back, hacking the pincers off with powerful blows of their swords.

George was the first to gain control of one of the critters. Its back was wide enough to sit comfortably on it with his legs encircling its short neck. He seized its antennas and forced it to turn around and move towards the struggling members of his group. But there was no need to do so, they were all in good shape and had made it up their attackers' backs.

The bugs could swim faster than the humans but had not been able to cope quickly enough with that new situation. Seeing no more humans in the water, the rest of the bugs retreated towards the city.

"All right, Bill's genius saved us again," said George, "let's uses our bug-horses to move to the other shore."

As he said that he oriented his bug's antennas in the right direction and the bug swam in full panic towards the far shore.

When they reached the shore, the bugs went on at full speed. Bill tried to slow down his bug by pulling on the antennas and shouting slow down to it and somehow the bug understood and reduced its speed. They all did the same with similar success.

George was hesitant, *should we stop the bugs and get down their back*, he thought.

"Let's keep moving on the bugs," said George, "the hills are steep and we will save a lot of energy using them as our horses. Also, there will be less risk to be attacked by them if we wait until they are exhausted to get down."

They went up the hills and rode the bugs all day long. The bugs had been running at a speed exceeding that of a galloping horse when they got on the beach but now the ride was comfortable and yet they were probably doing twenty miles an hour. The sun was now a hand breath from the horizon and they had covered in one day what would have taken a full week in walking.

They were close to the mountains now; the hills had been sparsely forested making it easy to drive the bugs. Now they had to do something about them.

"What do you think Bill?" asked George, "should we kill them with our sword before we get off their back or should we try to stop them, disembark and see what happens?"

"Let's try to stop them close to a tree and tie them up to it before we get down." answered Bill. "I got an idea that might work, let's see."

We could kill them driving our swords through their short necks but what if we could go on using them, thought Bill.

They came upon a clearing with a stream running across. There were fruit trees all around and they had a good view on the valley. Bill stopped his bug by pulling hard on the antennas. The bug stopped just under a tree's limb. He took the rope from his backpack and he tied it up to the limb and attached the other end to the bugs' antennas giving it some leeway but not enough for the bug to catch the rope in its snout and chew it for freedom.

The others had stopped too and were looking at Bill's actions. When the bug was secured to the limb, Bill jumped down from it and smiled to his friends.

384

"You can do the same," said Bill, "we will feed them with fruits from those trees and have them handy to ride by morning."

They camped there amongst the trees, enjoying the comfort of a campfire. George had spotted something moving into the bushes at the far end of the clearing. He went silently towards it, easing out his bow from his quiver loop and winged an arrow. What looked like a small boar erupted behind the bush at his approach and George let the arrow fly into its side. The boar rolled over kicking in agony and George put an end to it with a swift blow of his sword on its head. He opened its belly and emptied it; then he brought the boar back to their camping area.

"Dinner," he said as he dropped the boar to the ground. The women went bathing and washed their clothes then shook them dry. The fabric would not stay wet. The water was just dripping out of it as if it had been waxed. The men had kept watch.

When George returned with the boar, Krishna and Donald went to fetch some dry wood and Bill started the campfire and proceeded to get the boar roasting. The women came back and the men went to the stream to get clean for the coming night. They came back ravenous and the boar smelled good. The women had found some vegetable and cooked them along.

They ate their fill then George and Krishna went to the bugs and threw them more fruits. The critters had squatted on the short grass and looked calm and resigned. They were as big as a horse but looked like elongated giant turtles. There was a spot of tender skin at the base of their neck and on an impulse; Krishna started to massage it talking softly to the bug and it started to do a low buzz similar to the purr of a cat.

"It loves it." said Krishna, "Why don't you do the same to the others?"

Everyone came at once to watch what was happening.

"See," said Krishna, "it has a calming effect on the bug."

385

Everyone went to their bugs to do the same and soon, all the bugs were buzzing contentedly.

"They probably never experienced tenderness and the soothing of caresses," said Krishna. "They may become addicted to our presence and become bounded to us."

After a while, the bugs seemed to be asleep and they returned to the campfire. They were relaxing now, looking at the flames.

"How did you know what to do when we were swimming for our life?" asked George to Bill admiringly.

"I noticed a few things that gave me the idea." Bill answered. "I had noticed that the bugs were always looking straight ahead as they walked the streets. So I thought we could ride them and drive them by the proper orientation of their antennas. The next thing was they seem to have a chemical exchange language; they were communicating by short face to face contacts and it looked like they were transmitting orders and information.

I thought they were behaving like ants and they probably had a queen and mass consciousness. That meant to me that they would have a slow response to unusual situations. They would have to ask the queen how to cope with it. A group of them would ponder it over and find the solution eventually. The bugs are well protected by their carapace and chitin's legs and arms. They probably feel safe from predators and their pincers and fanged snout are formidable armament. They wouldn't expect us to climb on their back and hack off their pincers. They couldn't dive under the water or they would have done it already beside I thought that a lot of air was trapped under the carapace and would keep them afloat; so all of that gave me the solution to the situation. We did the unexpected and we won our freedom."

"It looks like our small group of frail humans, can survived through a lot of desperate situations." commented Elisabeth. "The guardians chose us well."

George was sitting beside Helen whom he had come to like more than Nicole or Elisabeth. She wouldn't take the pole in a conversation neither create a polemic and she was always respectful of others' opinions. She was intelligent and very subtle, serious and careful in anything she did and she remembered him of his wife, a highly devoted and charitable person. George thought that she had the most beautiful eyes he had ever seen.

Elisabeth and Donald were often sitting together and enjoyed each other's company. They had been kings, he of the casinos and nightlife and she of the United Islands. They both had royal manners and were highly cultured.

Krishna and Nicole had found an unusual kinship and George wouldn't be surprised that love was already budding in their heart.

Bill was the most solitary person of the group. He was way more intelligent than any of them and had already saved their skin a few times. He was indispensable and George was more and more convinced that he should be the leader of the group.

The only thing that still stopped me to transfer him the leadership, thought George, *is that I don't know him yet enough. How will he react to emotionally stressing situations? Until then, I am going to lend a good ear to any of his suggestions.*

They chatted for hours as they used to do every night, feeding the fire from time to time, looking at the stars and the immensity of the universe and huddling close to each other. Sometimes they would think about their loved ones they had left on Earth but they were too happy and serene to let those thoughts affect them. It would have been quite impossible for them to describe to anyone of their lost ones how wonderfully good they felt. There was just no place for sorrow.

Bill and Donald had studied the religions but had loss their faith. George, Helen and Nicole had never paid much attention to that matter. Elisabeth and Krishna believed in God but thought that the Almighty had nothing to do with them.

He couldn't care less, they thought, *for there are billions of inhabited worlds in the universe and He is creating new ones all the time.*

"I was thinking about the people I loved and lost." said
Elisabeth. "What a tragedy for mankind to live such a
short life span with sicknesses afflicting them all the
way to the end. When we finally achieve maturity, it was
too late; we were already done with. This is what
I reproach to God if our creation was intentional but
that would be surprising for I believe that mankind is
the result of the natural laws of evolution."

"Thanks to the guardians, we will not experience early
aging again. This time we are starting at maturity and
we have endless years ahead." Bill replied.

"What do you mean?" asked Krishna.

"I mean that we have been given a self regenerating
body." answered Bill. "We will not grow old or
experience sicknesses. We might be killed but otherwise
we can live forever."

"And how did you come to that conclusion?" asked George.

"There are a few clues. First our clothes can resist
wear and tear and our swords are unbreakable. The
Guardians are immortal and can't conceive of doing
something that wouldn't last forever. I guess it would
be unethical and shameful to them. You have all realized
that we can do wonders with our new bodies, like
climbing two hundred feet of creepers without a sweat.
We have an amazing endurance and we are incredibly
strong.

When we get a scratch or a cut, it cures without a trace
in hours. We never get up with painful muscles, we never
get sprain and we have an acute sense of smell and
probably other powers as well that we are yet unaware
of. If you wish for immortality, you got it now, it's a
done deal."

"Do you think that we will have children? Will they be
immortals too?" asked Helen.

"I can't conceive it to be otherwise. We have strong
sexual urge and that wouldn't happen if our bodies would
not be made for procreation. Beside, you are probably
pregnant by now, all three of you. I saw a change in
your eyes and your breasts."

That shook them all. They started to talk excitingly about the presence of toddlers in their group.

"I believe you are right," said Helen, "I felt changes in my body but it didn't come to my mind that I could be pregnant, it won't be a first time for me; I was devastated by the loss of my two children when the plague took them away so the appeal of motherhood is even greater than ever before."

"And me too." Said the once sexiest star and the ex-queen simultaneously.

"I would very much like to have children again," commented George, "I had two beautiful and lovable daughters…"

The conversation went on and everyone of them were very happy at the thought of the coming babies.

At first morning light, they got up and went to the stream to refresh with always one standing guard and their swords at easy reach. That was unknown territory and as for the saying, any wicked thing might come their way.

They picked some fruits for breakfast and fed the critters still squatting on the ground and looking calm. Once the bugs had finish eating the fruits they had been given, they mounted them by the back, careful not to be caught by surprise in the bugs' snouts. They removed the ropes from the limbs and the antennas and tucked it in their backpacks.

Once everyone was ready, George took the lead, pulling upwards on the bug's antennas to signify getting up and depart and the bugs understood the meaning.

"They are intelligent," said George, "enough to build starships and roam the stars but their intelligence is of a different kind than ours. They have no individuality and now these ones are away from their city and their queen; they don't seem to resent us and they are probably ready to serve their new masters."

The group went up the mountain and the bugs could grip
their way up the steepest areas on their six legs ending
with small pincers.

"They seemed to be able to make their paws sticky at
will." commented Bill.

The people had used their ropes to secure themselves to
the bug with one end of the rope noosed around their
short chitin's necks and the other end around their
waist. They were sometimes edging deep ravines, making
their way up cliffs jutting up at almost ninety degrees.

Everyone was scared but Nicole and Helen were terrified
at times when the heights gave vertiginous sights.
George was trying to find a pass but there were none,
they would have to go over the mountain and travel on
the snow which started half way up the mountain. They
had reached the snow level and George was hesitant to go
any further.

"The bugs are perfectly fit to walk on the snow, "said
Bill, "the pincers ending their legs will perform as
snow shoes. We have to cross those mountains; there is
no way around them for their chain might go on for
thousands of miles. We will have to do it and hope for
the best. But first, we need to make some warm and
long coats for we might be caught on the snow banks for
days. We also need to build a sleigh and filled it with
fruits and meat and take along some reserve.

"I noticed on a plateau," said George, "the presence of
trees with leathery bark. I cut a piece of it and played
with it for a while, let me show you."

George took the piece out from his backpack and showed
them. It was still flexible and smooth.

"I also noticed the presence of goat like grazers." said
Bill. "They are covered with long wool like fur. With
our fast running critters, we can outrun them and catch
them with lassos and cut their fur out.
Then we can find some sticky and hard setting resin and
stuck the wool to the leather strips and sew the strips
to make the fur coats."

They went back to the hills and made some suitable lassos out of their ropes. Once that was done, they went on in search of the goats and they spotted them.

Krishna tried to talk to his critter of the idea of running after the goats and urged it to full speed. The critter seemed to catch the idea that it should run after the goats and it started to chase one on its own and Krishna could now use both hands to throw his lasso at the goat. But there was no need for it, the critter caught the goat while running at full speed with its chitin paws, stopped quickly and went over it, immobilizing it under with its pincers ending legs.

Krishna made signs and talked the critter into releasing the goat and somehow it understood and complied with his demand but the goat went under shock and died.

They caught seven of the goats that way and the critters seemed to enjoy the experience. They let the people cut the fur out, then the legs and started to feed on the remains of the goats.

Krishna and George made a fire, roasted and smoked strips of meat while the others went in search of the leathery bark, the glue resin and suitable wood for the makeshift sleigh. They found all they needed and came back, the bugs pulling the small trees, the bark and the resin.

"The bugs seem to have bonded with us," said Bill joyfully, "they may even be catching our intentions for they do exactly what we wish them to do and they are making themselves very useful."

"That must be some kind of one way telepathic communication." Commented Donald "For we don't catch anything from them; we don't know what they want."

"They just want to be loved and caressed, just like you men." said Nicole. She was trying to be nice and jovial but it was evident that she was quite worried.

"They often buzz something incomprehensible to us," said Krishna, "but I don't sense any anger or menace in that buzzing. They like our company."

"Their pincers are growing back and they will soon be the most formidable predators we could face." said George. "I hope they are not bidding their time for proper revenge.

"No, I don't think so." answered Bill. "They don't think like us; revenge is probably meaningless to them. They were made to protect the Queen and now we are the ones they will protect. I have a strong intuition that we have nothing to fear from them."

They made the fur coats and the sleigh, packed the meat in the leathery bark, found plenty of fruits and they were now ready to face the snow covered mountain.

"You know George," said Nicole, "I am not sure it is the proper thing to do; we might fall from a cliff and that will be the end of our mission."

"Or we might freeze to death," added Helen, "We might be caught in a snow storm or maybe victim of an avalanche or just slide into an abysm."

"Who knows how long it will take to cross those mountains." added Elisabeth. "We might run out of food and die of hunger. To cross those mountains seemed to me extremely dangerous."

"And I am scared to death of heights." added Nicole.

"And me too." said Helen.

"You know," said Krishna; looking at the women, "fear can be controlled; I learned it with the Buddhists monks. It just doesn't last very long if you don't let yourself drop into a state of panic. Self-suggestion can help and I wouldn't be surprised if after the first few hours of moving beside chasm, you will experience a total absence of fear."

"What we can do," said George; "is move towards the summit, looking for a pass and come back if we realize that the mountains are impossible to cross over."

"We might be forced to move on anyhow." said Donald. "I have been looking downward and I believe that there are aliens following us; a whole army of them."

They all looked down and they could see little dots moving up in their direction.

"There may be thousands of them." said Krishna.

"And they seem to be bigger than us." commented Bill.

"It looks that we are now forced to move across those mountains," said George, "but those Bugs will prove to be very useful. Our climber boots would not be of great help in contact with loose and powdery snow but our Bugs have those glue producing pincers, six legs to hold on to and two arms ending with small but still growing pincers. Put on your climber gloves and hold yourself tight to their shell. We will move in a chain formation and in the most dangerous areas, we will ask the bugs to hold on to each other."

It was sunset when they found a cave spacious enough for all of them. It had been a long day and they slept well without anyone standing guard for the campfire in front of the cave would keep the predators away.

The next morning they were back at the snow line.

"Wait!" said Bill. "Let's fix a rope between the bugs; if one slide down, the other bugs will hold it and bring it back to safety."

Krishna jumped down from his bug-horse and took care of that as George was holding his bug. But it wasn't necessary; it was not trying to go away.

What a group, thought Krishna, *looking at his friends in their musketeer outfit riding scary giant bugs.*

They were ready now and they moved on towards the mountain peak. They went as high as they could and then sideways for miles, looking for a pass. The bugs had no problems moving on the snow and they did not get tired; they went on and on at same speed.

They found a pass by the end of the afternoon after a dozen hours of travel. They had saved days of hardship getting there riding the bugs instead of moving on rudimentary ski or snow shoes. The pass was miles long and led them to the other side of the first high mountain. They went all the way down into the forested valley where they found refuge for the night.

Twelve days had passed since they started across the mountain chain. They sometimes had to ride the bugs up vertical icy cliffs and the bugs seemed to glue themselves tightly to the icy walls. It was the most frightening experience for all of them. They were sometimes hanging on, hoping that the bugs would keep moving on and keep a tight grip to the wall, hundreds of feet high but finally they were on the top of the last mountain, gazing down at a wide valley carved between them. It was possibly fifty miles wide and seventy miles long and ended at a seemingly endless sea.

"There is no city in the valley," said Helen looking at Bill, "what is your sense of direction telling you?"

"The lost city is straight ahead," answered Bill, "and that means that we will have to cross the sea."

"We may enjoy it dear, said George, "we can relax there for a while and build ourselves a nice house."

"We will build a boat," said Bill, "and take our time to do a very good job of it. If it takes one year to build it, so be it, but we will build a good solid sailboat that we can move by the power of our hands, if need be. I mean with openings on the sides for oars like the ancient Viking sailboats."

"We will have to build it as light as possible," said George. "We may find some bamboo like trees to build the boat like the Chinese did on Earth. I saw some kind of bamboo in the forested hills two weeks ago. If we can find something like that in the valley ahead, it would be great."

"Let's keep a sharp look for anything that could be useful as we get across this valley." said Bill.

"It was a long trek across the mountains," commented Krishna; as they got halfway down to the valley floor. "Why don't we camp here, by that pond; the water is crystal clear; we can bathe and tonight we will look at the sunset over the sea and the valley down below."

"Yes," said Elisabeth, "and we will talk by the campfire and enjoy the night."

They were huddling together, all seven of them, close to the fire and looking towards the horizon. Dusk had covered the valley and it was getting dark. Helen kissed George and grasped his hand.

"How long do you think it will take to build the boat?" She asked.

"Maybe a year, maybe less, all depends how close to the water we will find the building materials." answered George. "But the boat has to be roomy enough for that sea might be very wide and it may take a year or two to cross it."

"You know what I would like," said Helen, "I would like us to build a log cabin with a few rooms and a fire place with a view on the sea. Once we are comfortable, we can start working on the boat. I would like to enjoy a quieter life for a while; take it easy, do some fishing and hunting, play games and give birth to my baby. We can resume our trek once our babies are born."

"Yes, we could build some chess and checkers' games." said Bill and Donald simultaneously.

"And cards, I like to play cards." said Elisabeth. "Bridge, Five Hundreds and Queen of Spade."

They held their hands and kissed and laugh--.

Chapter Seventeen. -Satan and God encounter.

So my daughter is here and I am just about to become a grandfather, I thought happily; as I finished reading the notes I had found on my desk.

That's wonderful, I told myself, *they have made it up to the sea and they are probably on the other side of these impassable mountains, Krzzzurr told us about; a few thousands miles from here along the coast, and our two groups might very well meet on the other side of the sea.*

I went downstairs hoping that I wasn't too late and there would still be some of my friends to have breakfast with. I was anxious to share the news I received about the second group of Earth Emissaries. To my relief, everyone was still there even the Father who was sitting with Krzzzurr talking about clerical matters.

"Hi everybody," I said; with the papers in my hand. "I got news about the second group of people that were transported on Ghama-2. I found those sheets on my desk this morning and it tells us about their adventures."

"How the hell did you get those sheets?" asked Joan wonderingly.

"Please don't mention hell here, who knows what it might attract." I answered.

"Well said my son." approved the reverend father.

"Thanks, but to come back to the question," I said, "it has to be the guardians. Those sheets relate their adventures, from the moment they woke up on Ghama-2 up to now. The notes have my handwriting and that puzzles me. I read the story and there is a ring of truth about it. I am sure of its veracity."

"Are they the same ones we met at my condo and later on at Camp David?" asked Joan.

"Yes they are George W Wood, Bill Rates and Prince Mohamed (Krishna), Nicole Teaseman, the Hollywood star,

Queen Elisabeth the Fifth, Donald Rump, the Casinos'
king and Helen my own daughter.

They became a band of brothers and lovers and they carry
on real well. They survived all sorts of dangers;
predators, crocodilians, sea monsters, and bears.

Aliens with the look of giant beetles attacked them but
they survived without a scratch. They traveled hundreds
of miles across the jungle, the woods and the mountains
and went up upon their snow peaks and crossed a mountain
chain to get to a valley bordering the sea. Now they are
building a log cabin on its shore where they will live
while they build a sailboat. The three women are
pregnant and they will have their babies before they
sail to the other side of the sea. Oh yes, they use
the giant bugs as horses now, they tamed them and rode
them all through the mountains."

"So we might meet with them on that strange land
awaiting us across the sea." said Father O'Leary; who
seemed to anticipate that moment excitingly.

He would rejoice in it, I thought, *as much as I will
rejoice in getting my daughter back with me and moreover
a grandchild to spoil.*

"You can read the sheets at your leisure; I will leave
them in the living room on the book shelves." I said.

They had some news for me too. Some of the Birdies'
scouts had spied the coming of thousands of harpies in
our direction. Other scouts had reported the coming of
tiger like aliens, maybe as many as one hundred
thousands of them. They were coming toward our city
and they were killing everything on their passage. They
were still a few thousand miles away but the news was
disquieting. Yet some more scouts reported that a new
army of rat faces were coming our way. They had just
left their city located two thousand miles north.

"It looks like a concerted attack from all directions."
said John.

"The demons might be behind the whole scheme." commented
the reverend father. "They want our destruction and it

would be a good thing to accelerate the city's defense and our sailboats' construction."

"How long until they get here?" I asked.

"Three to four months at the most." said Krzzzurr.

We went our different ways. Tom and John to the construction site; the Father with Krzzzurr, Nancy and Garry left on some errands, and Patricia was already working at the construction site on the making of the sail; I was left with Joan.

"What do you plan to do today? I asked her.

"I don't know," she said. "John doesn't want to see me on the construction site. He said he already has too many people working on the boats and the whole town wants to participate to the project. There is nothing to do; what about you Richard?."

"I have to finish my book but right now, I am too excited about the news from the second group. What about a golf game? Maybe we can fetch my old friend Ron Davies and the Rodriguez" I offered.

"That would be wonderful, I need to walk and do some exercise."

"All right let's go sweetheart."

"Am I still your sweetheart, Richard? I thought Patricia had taken hold of all your thoughts?"

"You know Joan that you will always have an important place in my heart. We have lived almost ten years together and shared so much; surviving the plague and starting farming and then dying together and all the adventures we have lived on this world. How can I ever stop loving you? Yes, you are still my sweetheart and will always be."

She came to my arms and we hugged.

"Take me to your room--." She said. "We have plenty of time before golf."

I did it and we made love passionately. It had been a few months already since we had come to the city and we hadn't had a private moment together. It was great and I didn't feel guilty since after all she was my wife and I didn't think that Patricia would have objected. But Patricia came back unexpectedly and surprised us in the bed.

"Come here Patricia," I said before she had any time to react to the situation. "Please sit here between Joan and me; I want to talk to you."

She came and sat.

"I don't know what your customs here are on Ghama-2, but on Earth, it is quite customary to have sex as an expression of friendship and companionship." I lied. "It would in no way be considered an offense to the woman with whom we are in love. Moreover; it is considered a mark of intellectual maturity to love more than one person and Joan didn't object to my affair with you and I hope you won't find objectionable that once upon a time, I express my comradeship to Joan whose pregnant state renders emotionally weak and sometimes quite sad--."

"Please Richard, stop the flow of explanations and excuses." said Patricia with a smile." The very fact that you are using so much of your imagination to make me believe that there is nothing wrong with it, shows that you care about me. Were you done with the companionship or just at the beginning of your expression?"

"We were quite done with it." I said. "And were about to go golfing. Would you like to join us? You played a few times but never with us."

"Sure I will." said Patricia graciously.

We went to the clubhouse to get the clubs and then to the practice range to get some practice. Johnny Rodriguez, my defunct uncle and recent war hero was already there practicing. He gladly accepted my invitation to complete a foursome with us.

We played a good first nine holes; Patricia and I were ahead in the bet. We stopped after nine holes for a cup of coffee, some fruits and cookies.

"So Johnny, how is it going on with the war training of our new army." I asked.

"Quite well," he said, "we now have a team of a dozen highly qualified trainers and we have started to train the whole population. Everyone has a sword, a knife, a bow, a quiver of arrows, and a javelin. The whole population is armed and resigned to the coming war. They have made a game of their training and everywhere we see the people practicing with wood swords. We are also erecting walls and digging trench on the West side of the town. We will connect the trench with the river so that the crocodilians will have access to it and protect the City on all sides against the attackers."

"Excellent, these are good news." I said

"Your sailboats will be ready in three months, if the war hasn't yet started; the city officials want you out and away. You must be spared at all cost." said Johnny.

"Will you come with us?" I asked.

"If the war is over, I would love to and thanks for asking, Richard."

"I have something to tell you Johnny." I said. "You had a past life on Earth and I met you there. Do you recall anything, anything at all? Things that couldn't have possibly happen on this world but are there to remember?"

"Well Richard, I knew we had met somewhere and felt a kinship for you. A kinship I didn't feel for the other members of your group. I fuzzily remember boxing in an arena with strange lights, artificial light, which is impossible for sure."

"On Earth there is electricity and artificial light." I said. "And I have identified you as my defunct uncle."

There was emotion in the air; he looked at me and stood up. I stood up too and he hugged me. I had water in my eyes for I had loved my uncle very much and it was so strange to be with him again.

We played the last nine holes and I must admit that I didn't try very hard to win the game and was most happy to praise him for his victory and great golf. But he knew I had wanted him to win, I had offered a decent competition but my heart wasn't for victory and there were no ways to hide anything from him. We left shaking hands.

I went back to the Grand house with the two women, we went to the living room for a drink and Joan left soon after. That night, as we were sitting together for dinner, the city officials and the whole group, a Birdie came rushing in.

"The centaurs have made it down the sky wall." he said. "I am in communication with them and they are coming to the city."

"How many of them and when will they be here?" John asked.

"They say, they are a dozen of them coming over. But more will join later on for the entire population is coming down by balloon, four at a time. The first group will be here by the river any moment now."

"Let's get some boats on the other side." said Ed Kimpley, the city mayor. "We will encircle them to prevent them to be seen by the crocodilians, shall they decide to swim across the river."

We all went outside and down to the river. Already boats were set upon the river and people were paddling them across. I was on the first boat that reached the other shore and the centaurs were there already and they seem to be very excited.

I walked to them thinking clearly my welcome speech for I knew they were reading my thoughts.

"Hello Richard, I am Genamel, the first of our tribes to meet with you a few months ago and here is our leader

Benamel." answered Genamel silently but very clearly for at close distance we can easily catch their telepathic communications.

"Hi Genamel, Hi Benamel, it is a pleasure to meet with you again and exchange some thoughts." I thought.

"Hi Richard, Hi Joan--, it is a great moment for us. We wished to join you in your mission and we hastened the making of balloons but we also had another reason to contact you as quickly as possible." Benamel communicated. "We have caught fleeting thoughts, aliens thoughts, from the valley on the other side of the plateau.

We couldn't read them clearly for these thoughts had such nastiness and spitefulness that we couldn't linger long enough into their brainwaves to comprehend them.

The slightest contact smeared unclean able filth over our souls. But what we gathered is that they are coming to destroy the biped aliens."

"Yes we knew about their coming and we are preparing ourselves to defend the city." I said/thought. "But thanks for your friendship and kindness.

Let me introduce you to Mayor Ed Kimpley and Krzzzurr the Birdies' leader. "

They gave a warm welcome to the centaurs and express their gratitude for having taken the risk to come down the sky wall-plateau to warn us.

"We are all coming down, and wish to help in the city's defense." said Benamel. "Every three hours, four more of the centaurs touch ground in the valley. It means that forty-eight of us touch ground each day. But we are building more balloons now that we found how to do it. In two to three months, all ten thousands of us will have joined you."

"How do you make the balloons work?" asked Joan.

"Thanks to you for the idea," said Benamel, "we are

manufacturing a lighter than air gas. We use our own dung and some natural fertilizer and we found a way of getting the gas into the balloon."

"Wonderful," said Joan. "Would you like to come on the other side and visit the city? It will be risky for there are crocodilians in the river but we can surround you with boats and have our archers ready to shoot anyone coming too close."

"Thanks; but it is preferable that we stay on this side of the river until all the members of the tribes are down. We must build our number close to the touch down site and protect it against the coming aliens. Once all of us are down in the valley, we will come to the city and cross the river all at the same time.

We will join minds and emit scary feelings to all life around. The crocodilians will stay clear. Now we must go back to the drop zone to help our brothers, see you later and farewell."

The centaurs left and we returned to the grand house. There were still a few hours left before sunset and we went to the beach for our usual nighttime plays and games and fussing around.

I like to wrestle and now that I was almost as tall and certainly as strong as John, I was teasing him into a grappling and tripping game.

"Try the father," John said, knowing that I usually got the upper hand in wrestling with everyone except Tom who was strong like an ox and had practiced Judo just as much as I did on Earth. With him it was usually ending without a winner. But I had never tried wrestling with the reverend father.

I was doing an hour and a half of intense work out everyday to make sure I would stick amongst the very best in any kind of competition. That's one aspect of my personality I should be shameful about. For to be competitive and excel in games is a way to prove your value to the rest of the world and one shouldn't have to prove anything to anyone. But I am not a perfect philosopher and I love to compete.

I could take defeats fairly well when I know that I have
done my best but have faced a better opponent. I would
praise the winner sincerely, hiding or pushing away the
surging bitter shame of loosing. But how gracious
can I be when I win; praising the opponent for the good
fight and seemingly ignoring my own prowess.

Nobody was really fooled by it, though, I suppose, and
they probably had an additional motivation to beat me
the next time. True competitors are like that and it is
all right, it's the man way and we have fun that way, as
long as we don't get into hard feelings.

So I went teasing the good father who looked at me with
his kind eyes and his most engaging smile. Nancy was on
his back, partly encircling his large shoulders with her
arms. They were in love and they had been sharing the
same room for months now. She couldn't care less for the
fact that one should be respectful to a pope.

"All right my son," said the father suddenly standing up
in front of me. It had been so quick and smooth; he was
sitting and then he was standing and there had been no
time in between. How quickly could he move this large
body was just incredible but I had seen him in action;
fighting the rat faces, and he had been glorious with
his quarterstaff.

We grappled and I simulated a push hoping for an
opposite reaction. I was ready to pull and move sideways
extending my foot to trip him but he didn't fall for it
and instead he pulled at me. I was prepared for that too
and as he pulled I pushed, quickly moving around; and I
tried to trip him but he had read my mind somehow and
I went nowhere with my plan. We struggled for a while
but he was much stronger and possibly even faster than I
and I found myself on the ground.

I looked for some figments of shame, ready to repress
them, but there was none coming for thinking about it, I
realized that it would have been a shame to throw the
reverend father to the ground. It was good that he won
for whom would trip a pope except the most unrespectful
sun of a ditch.

I still have a lot to learn, I thought, if I ever want to become a great guy. I congratulated his excellence and he hugged me warmly.

"Never go against the clergy," he said laughing and we all laughed and teased each other and ran after each other like happy kids ignoring for a while the coming war.

The weeks passed as I wrote my book and the father wrote his bible in the presence of many Birdies who were reading our thoughts and were writing them at the same speed we were writing our books. We were doing it in the large family room of the grand house in which we had rows of little handmade desks and chairs.

The whole population wanted to read them and we didn't have a press or a printer; it was all hand writing.

I took breaks everyday, riding my bike through town in the company of Patricia. Joan, Nancy and Garry were often joining us. John didn't want the women to do physical work at the boats' construction site for their bellies were already bulging and we could expect the babies at anytime now.

Nancy and Garry usually had their Teddy on their shoulders and they loved it.

One day I went with Patricia to a reception at her parents' house. I met them and they look just as young as my sweetheart. It was strange to share the table with her three brothers and one sister and her parents for we all look the same age, we all look in our early twenties. I was taller than the other men by almost a foot but otherwise, it would have been hard to tell which one was an Earth emissary.

These people are the descendants of the Endeavour starship crew, I thought, *and their ancestors had been selected amongst billions of people; they were the fittest and the healthiest so no wonder we look alike, these people are the end result of an accelerated evolution and the absence of sickness has certainly help.*

"Do you have a cemetery here?" I asked Patricia's father.

"Yes, we do," he replied, "it is not too far from here, passed the municipal beach just by the jungle."

"I would like to visit it." I said.

"I will take you there after this afternoon." said Patricia.

"So, Richard, you are taking our Patricia with you across the sea on your search for the lost city?" asked Patricia's father.

"Yes," I said, "but I promise to come back with her one day if we survive the many dangers awaiting us."

"We might not be here," said her father, "the city might be destroyed by the coming army of bloodthirsty beasts."

"I know, I understand how you feel about it and you might be thinking that it will be our fault." I replied.

"That will be the Guardians' fault, not yours for you came here to help us against a looming danger that we didn't know about." Patricia's father replied.

"Nevertheless, I thought about it," I said, "and I came to the conclusion that there were good chances that no one would enter the lost city in possibly millenniums from now and without our coming you would have been left alone here, leaving peacefully."

There was a moment of silence following that statement.

"We can't change the past," said Patricia's father, "we can only face the future. I like to think that at least one of my children will escape the coming war."

"That's if we leave before the attack as the mayor wishes." I said. "But I don't think that will happen. I have the gut feeling that we will be here fighting those demons and beasts alongside you. I can't see us as worthy of the lost city treasures if we flee before the fight and let you alone to face the enemy."

"Thank you Richard," said Patricia's father, "I understand why Patricia fell in love with you; we will pray at the reverend father mass and hope for God's help."

"And help may come." I replied. "I believe that a superior being, maybe God Himself is testing us right now. I received divine help on Earth in the past; I saw miracles happen, and I often got away without a scratch from deadly situations. So I firmly believe that help will come again if we pray God for it."

We went on chatting for a few hours and then we left for the cemetery.

The cemetery was beautiful; it was set in an oak tree-like preserve with flower and fruit bearing bushes growing by the little white stones.

We went to the crew leaders' graves, Bryan Dempsey, ship astronavigator 2250 - 2488 and Helena Dempsey, ship medical officer 2253 - 2489.

"They lived a long life," I commented, "even if we don't consider the ninety years in hibernation in the starship."

"The two people were responsible for the successful human settlement here." commented Patricia. "They are much revered by everyone in the city."

"What an exciting time it must have been for them" I said, thinking about it. "Their odyssey surpassed Christopher Columbus discover of America."

After an hour of meditation and daydreaming in the cemetery, we returned to the Grand House.

The boats' construction was going well. A few weeks more and we would be ready. Johnny Rodriguez and the City mayor Ed Kimpley were busy preparing the army and the city for a standoff against the coming enemies.

My book was written but left unfinished. I had decided to wait after the battle and finish it just prior to our departure across the sea. Having nothing else to do, I had taken the habit to paint everyday for a few hours

with my old friend Ron Davies. We usually met at the
beach behind the grand house and chat as we worked our
art. Ron had a style that needed infinite patience; he
would spend a long time trying to paint the very air in
a realistic landscape. You could tell the time of the
day and the humidity or even the temperature by looking
at his finished artworks.
I was all impulses and my landscapes were more neo-
impressionistic but people loved the heavy strokes and
the creativity in the special effects and the style. We
were both excellent in our own style but I thought Ron
to be a more complete artist than I.

We also played golf Joan, Patricia and I with Johnny
Rodriguez a few times each week. The Rat Faces had been
spotted close to the river and nobody would go to the
other shore anymore. They were massing up on the other
side and the birdies' scouts who flew across the river
to perch on the highest limbs of nearby trees estimated
their number over four hundred thousand. In the
following days, an army of harpies had joined them and a
few days later, arrived the tiger like aliens. There
was now an incredible mass of snarling and howling
aliens by the river.

"What do you think?" asked John to Johnny Rodriguez.
"What are they waiting for? They are everywhere on the
north side of the river and the West side trench."

"I think they might attack us at any time now." said
Johnny but we are well prepared to push them back. The
crocodilians are pacing the river nervously,
anticipating them to cross over."

As Johnny finished his sentence, the army of beasts
suddenly charged. We were massing along the two sides;
half of the city people were guarding the shore in dense
ranks as the beasts surged to the water. The harpies
attacked the crocodilians as they swam to catch the rat
faces and the tigers. The tigers attacked the
crocodilians too and in no time there were none left in
sight and the aliens were swimming across the river and
the trench in all impunity. They surged out of the water
to be impaled by the javelins of the first rows of our
defenders. The archers were standing on higher ground
and a cloud of arrows was flying to the attackers

falling to the ground in agony with the arrows sticking
out of their flesh.

It went on and on and the aliens were unable to cause us
serious damage. We had a few casualties only when they
stop crossing the river and the ones on our shore
finally retreated to the other side.

I felt something way wrong in the air and I looked
around nervously. There was that sense of impending
danger and I saw in the faces of my friends that they
sensed it too. We looked everywhere.

"There is something wrong, way wrong." said John. "We
should be happy at the wicked aliens retreat but I feel
that I am just about to die or worse. I have never been
so scared; my body is trembling with foreboding. I think
we are foredoomed."

And I felt it too. Even the reverend father looked
worried. The birdies spread the news. There were
monsters coming out of the sea on the other side of the
city and we had left the seashore unprotected. Johnny
ordered three battalions to move to the seaside and try
to push them back. One hundred thousand of our soldiers
left on the run. Now that our ranks had thinned down
appreciably, the wicked aliens started across the river
for a second assault.

The mayor asked us to stay back and protect our life at
all cost. Why don't you move on top of the grand house
with Krzzzurr and watch what is happening. Krzzzurr
could pass the information along and you can guide the
action of our battalions.

We did it reluctantly for we had a mission and the fate
of mankind was at sake. We were not cowards and would
have preferred to fight along with our friends but we
got on top of the grand house. We had a good view and
saw that the sea monsters were in great number and
the three battalions would not be able to push them
back. They looked like small tyrannosaurs and walked on
two massive legs. They were about twelve feet from head
to toe claws and had a long powerful tail.

Krzzzurr requested the addition of two more battalions
and this cut in half our defense power by the river.

The fight was going on and it was becoming bloody on both side of the city. A lot of people were falling under the fangs and claws of the wicked species.

"Look at the sky," Garry shouted. We looked and there was a dark mist coming from nowhere right over the city and as it became darker we saw in the center of the dark mass some kind of pulsating red and yellow light. It was tiny at first but growing rapidly in size and it was coming straight towards us. We could see it better as it came closer; it was a castle with high towers and monstrous carvings of snarling demons. Now the castle was gigantic and somehow immaterial for it was engulfing the whole city plunging it in semi-darkness. There was a throne room and sitting on the throne was a giant demon, as big as one third of the sky. Its eyes were looking at us in malevolence and I felt the infinite spitefulness and filthiness of the damned soul.

I had a hard time to breathe; I felt dirty and sinking inside. At that moment, giant monsters surfaced at the sea. Each of the monsters was a hundred feet tall. They had a frog head with a fork tongue lacing out and they were coming to shore; nothing would resist them.

"I am Satan, Lord of Chaos," said the demon in a booming voice that could shake mountains. "I was there before time, even before God and I will turn down the universe into the chaos it was before.

Give me your souls and I will spare your lives. You will be my servants and the masters of this world."

I felt puny, insignificant and saddened at my puniness. I felt hate surging in my soul and I started to despise my friends for having forced me into these crazy sentiments of comradeship and friendship which are no more than expressions of weakness. I wanted to kill them and smash their faces, spit at them.

The whole world stinks, I thought, *and God is the king of the stinkers.*

"Get away Satan," said the reverend father in a booming voice of his own. "Your words are lies and your presence on this world is forbidden."

410

Satan was now laughing with malice and I couldn't agree more.
What does he think he is that fool of a reverend scum, I thought.

"How will you make me go away, insect?" asked Satan, "I will get the frog servants smash you into nothingness. It is your last chance; which one of you wants to live and give me his soul?"

The monsters were already smashing the first battalion. People were dying everywhere, shouting in pain and crying in despair for the end was unavoidable now.

I fought against the desire of giving my soul away and felt shame at my thoughts, at my hate for the very ones that had share so much with me.

Satan is manipulating my thoughts, I thought with despair.

"Father, don't abandon me." boomed the voice of Father O'Leary and suddenly he grew bigger and there was a great brightness chasing the dark mist away. From the brightness came a lightning flash that hit the father and he grew in size ten times and an oriole of sanctity was now encircling his head. We had jumped aside as the father expanded to a sixty feet high giant.

The father extended his arms and lightening bolts came out of his fingers and each of the bolts went to a frog head monster destroying it utterly. The monsters seem to disintegrate into nothingness as the bolts hit them. Now the father hands were giving life to thousands of angels of death and they flew towards the attackers and in no time there weren't any left.

We could ear the crying of the afflicted and the moans of the injured people lying everywhere around and suffering the torments of open flesh wounds and torn limbs. But that stopped as a soft luminescence enveloped everything in the city. The wounded were cured and the dead people were getting up smiling.

The father turned his eyes towards Satan and a powerful wind came from his open mouth and blew the castle with his howling master into another dimension. The black

411

miss was gone and the sun seemed to shine brighter and softer at the same time.

The father shrunk back in size but still towered us and he was enveloped by a soft radiance that hid his face.

"My children," The Father said in a booming voice that could be heard all over the city, "I have been with you for millenniums and helped you in your evolution. You have known me under many names for I was once Confucius or K'ung Fu-Tzu, Gautama Buddha, Abraham, Jesus, Muhammad and now your friend Father O'Leary.
When I take a persona, I forget who I am and this is a welcome change for a deity.

Mankind is a surprising streak of evolution. My father had never been prayed with such fervor and He decided exceptionally to give a little help. We don't like to interfere in the evolution of intelligent species and that is the last time we do it for you. You want to go to heaven but there is no such thing yet. We wouldn't know what to do with the multitude of souls adoring us.

If you want a heaven, you will have to build it yourselves. If you succeed in your mission and access the treasures of the lost city, you will be able to do that. The Guardians might help you in the building of a soul transference device. This world is a multi-level one. There are one thousand worlds brimming with life beneath your feet. These worlds will be accessible if you succeed with your mission; some of them are sad ones and others almost as interesting as this one at the surface.

On the other side of the ocean you will walk a land we have impregnated with magic. You have hidden powers in you and will be able to cope with any situation if you use them. The demons will not interfere anymore on this world. Farewell my children; see you later little Nancy."

And the son of God disappeared in a flash of brilliance.

We came down the roof to meet people in awe and wonders. Everyone had heard Him.

"I don't believe it," said Nancy to Garry. "You thought you had been cheated waking up in a young boy body but what about me? Falling in love with God? Could you believe the heck of it? Now I am going to miss Him. I will never find somebody like Him. If I had known He was God, I would have tried to love him a little less."

"And I tried to wrestle with Him!" I said. "What do you think of that?"

"We lost a very dear friend," said Krzzzurr, "but I/we will follow his example and spread the words for we know now that God is our friend."

Everyone went on with their own comments.

"So God told us what to do if we want a heaven; we must succeed with our mission and we have a real chance to succeed. And if we do succeed, we will have the powers to open the way to heaven for mankind and the friendly species." said Joan.

Nancy was crying, overcome suddenly by a flow of emotions.

"There are plenty of men to love, Darling." said Joan. "You won't forget the reverend Father but I am sure He wants you to go on and live happily. Apparently that genius Bill Rates is quite lonely in the second group. He is just the type of guy for you."

"I don't know if he will be willing to mess up with God's girlfriend though." answered Nancy, in good humor, for there was something to be proud of, here. She would be missing Him but she wasn't angry with him for he had saved mankind quite a few times.

After all, he was kind of amnesic and didn't realize he was the Son of God until he had to save us all, she thought. *But now he is gone, probably on another mission, trying to help another specie somewhere in the universe.*

That night we had celebration all over the city. People were dancing in the street, singing, playing with the Teddies and laughing under the amused eyes of the Birdies and the Centaurs. The Centaurs had fought

413

valiantly the wicked aliens, attacking them on their
rear. They had come to the City rescue as they had
promised and many had died. But now the rest of them had
cross the river and were milling in the crowd careful
not to step over people's feet and the City was bursting
with joy.
The night had brought the twinkling stars over the sea
and we were walking on the beach, Patricia and I, with
Ed Kimpley, Johnny and Paul Rodriguez, Ron Davies,
Krzzzurr and a few others.

We were thinking about that land of magic awaiting us on
the other side of the great sea. What kind of adventures
would we live there? Would we find the lost city? If so,
what kind of super beings would we become? Will we make
the dream of heaven come through?

The Centaurs and the Birdies and possibly other kind
species would share the glory with us if we succeed.

*There is so much to think about. That land of magic
might have the green giant, fairies, trolls and dragons,
sorcerers. And my daughter, it will be great*, I thought,
*to find her again and her companions as well. Will they
take their bugs with them across the sea?*

We went to bed late that night for we were under shock.
Who would have thought that Father O'Leary was Jesus,
the very one for whom he was carrying the word for.

Patricia shared my dreams that night; as most of the
city people. We had met with God and He had wished us
well. He had approved of us and treated us as a worthy
specie and He had lived as one of us. But He would
interfere no more, He said. We would have to deserve our
fate.

Next morning, we had breakfast, all the six remaining
members of our group along with our girlfriends and the
city officials. Nancy and Joan were more silent than
usual. They had waited until we finished but now a
delegation of Birdies came in with armful of flowers.
They put the flowers at Nancy and Joan's feet.

"Your holiness, Saint Nancy, would you bless us please!"
asked Krzzzurr along with eleven more of the Birdies.
And they knelt down and bowed to Nancy who was struck

cold and stiff not believing what was happening. Finally she found her voice.

"What is that silliness? Have you been infected by the human sense of humor?" asked Nancy; under the puzzled gaze of everyone around.

"No," said Krzzzurr, "you are the greatest of the saints, even greater than Holy Mary and we wish to become the twelve disciples of Jesus and carry the faith and his words. Would you bless us please?"

"I am no saint, far from it; I am a sinner, a rebel, a slut and what else..."

"On the contrary, you are the mother of the Son of the Son of God for we sense the presence of a baby in your womb and that baby is the son of Father O'Leary, the Son of God. There are no doubts, we can almost catch his thoughts and for a few months old fetus that is as impossible as the aura of power we sense in the reverend father. Moreover, you were God's girlfriend and mistress so there can't be any greater saint." said Krzzzurr.

"I will be damned, you are serious! Whatever! You got my blessing and thanks for the good news; it's cool. Hey guys you heard that? I'm going to have the Reverend Father's baby; great!" said Nancy; happy again.

They went to Joan and kneeled in front of her.

"You are the greatest Saint on same level as Nancy for you too will be the mother of the Son of Father O'Leary, the Son of God and you have been God's mistress. Please give us your blessing."

"You got my blessing but from now on, I don't want anyone to treat us, Nancy and I, as Saints for we aren't and we know it." said Joan with a smile.

The Birdies went to take care of their new clerical responsibilities. They had to prepare the next masses and they were very excited at the thought that they would now do the chunk of bread feeding.

The boats' construction was finished and John had made the final selection. Genamel, along with nineteen more centaurs would come across the sea. Twenty Birdies would also join our group. Sixty humans along with their Teddies had been selected. The Rodriguez were coming with their wives and Ron Davies too. Nancy and Joan had not given birth yet but there was no reason why they should not have their babies on the boat. We were ready to depart and Patricia was standing with me on the boat deck and we were waiting for Paul Rodriguez.

I was thrilled like all of my friends but there was something missing for me to be really happy. A person was missing, a person that I wished so much to have with me, and that person was my father whom I had lost too early.

I would give so much to have him with me, to share with him those coming adventures. For my father was one of those rare men that would spend years in studying the history of mankind. He knew about Alexander the Great and Napoleon Bonaparte and their war strategies. He knew the story of the Count of Montechristo, of D'Artagnan and the three musketeers, of King Arthur and the Knights of the Round Table. My father was a reader and he knew much about history but these things interested no one else amongst his tavern friends. He was a welder and the people with whom he worked were not the kind of people interested in cultural matters.

My father had live a life of loneliness and I knew how much he would have loved to be with us on that greatest of all adventures.

Paul Rodriguez, trailed by another man, came running to the boat all excited.

"I found Charles-Armand, your father!" He said.

"What!? Where?" I replied.

"Here he is!" Paul said; giving way to a middle-aged handsome man. I looked in his eyes and they were the same color, hazelnut; and there was that kindness and hint of knowledge that I had remembered all my life. I felt an intense kinship, there was no doubt, he was my father.

"Father," I said as I hugged him.

"My little boy!" he said. "When Father O'Leary left, I was stroke by a lightening bolt and I recovered all of my memory including the games of Cribbage we played together."

"So, like Ron Davies, Johnny and Paul Rodriguez, you found your way here, by yourself, through the shear power of your soul. That's incredible. I am so happy to have you with me for great adventures are awaiting us."

John gave the order and the men pulled the sails up and the boats left the shore packed solid with all of the city people. "Farewell," they were shouting, "and come back". I took my father and Patricia in my arms and met Joan's gaze and her eyes were wet.

I was suddenly overwhelmed with love for Joan; I was taken by an intense desire to hug her lovingly in my arms and I told her through my eyes, silently, that I knew that she was there for me, sharing my emotions as I would always be there for her, sharing hers.

Our time will come again, I said silently, forgetting for a moment that here in my arms was the one I had chosen to share my life with.

I am totally in love with the two of them, I thought, and we are living our afterlife; should we not create new rules? At any time, anyone of us might lose his or her life; doesn't it give us the freedom of being together sometimes? Without hurting John or Patricia? There will be a way; I will find it.

We left Alexandria hoping to reach one day the land of magic...

That's the end of the first book of the trilogy; I hope that the Guardians will bring it back through the time line to my publisher to replace the initial and fictive version. If you read it, we might meet on Ghama-2 one day for I asked the Guardians to fetch the souls of all the ones that read my book and bought one of my paintings. See you then, later on, on the wonderful world of Ghama-2.

About The Author

Richard Riverin was born in Quebec City in 1942. He graduated from Sherbrooke University with a BSc in Chemistry. He worked as a paint and coatings chemist for six years and then started his own business Encoat Chemicals Ltd.

The venture was an immediate success. A few years later, Richard sold his shares to his Indian partner and left the world of research and development for the world of Arts. Since then, he always managed at least one art gallery. He recently became an artist and a writer after a week of very strange dreams...

His paintings are just as unique as this book is; the style, the heavy and rich texture, the harmony of colors and the unusual expression turn each one of them into a real masterpiece.

"I don't deserve much admiration, even though a little bit of it is quite soothing, for after all the Guardians are helping me. I am the hand mainly for much of my mind is absent when I paint; it is lost on a far away world which may well become my heaven, one day."

CPSIA information can be obtained at www.ICGtesting.com
Printed in the USA
LVOW10s2335080715

445496LV00001B/88/P